Our Reunion

Our Reunion

Jenah Watson

P.D. Publishing, Inc.
Clayton, North Carolina

ISBN-13: 978-0-9754366-1-5
ISBN-10: 0-9754366-1-9

First Printing 2005

9 8 7 6 5 4 3 2 1

Cover art and design by Cal
Edited by Day Petersen/Stacia Seaman

Published by:

P.D. Publishing, Inc.
P.O. Box 70
Clayton, NC 27528

http://www.pdpublishing.com

Acknowledgements:

It's been quite an experience, writing a story and then being fortunate enough to have it published. I'm extremely grateful for the kind feedback and words of encouragement I received during the writing of *Our Reunion*. To those responsible for the outpouring of support, please know that each and every comment was very much appreciated. Special thanks to Mary D. Brooks, Carrie Carr, Jan Carr, Kathy G-G, Missy Good, Stephanie Solomon-Lopez, Gin Stanley, and Wolfie. All references to Florida State University are for Steven L. Sears. Thanks to PD Publishing, Barb and Linda Coles-Daniel, Karen Hamilton, Day Petersen, and Stacia Seamen for their efforts in turning my story into book form. It's been over five years since I began *Our Reunion* and it's a time that I'll remember for the people I've met and how my life has been enriched. Thanks to everyone who has been part of the journey.

For Mom

Chapter 1

Samantha Whitwell turned into the parking lot of the Hyatt Regency and looked for a space as close to the front door as possible. Fortunately, someone in the first row was just leaving. *Must be my lucky night,* she thought as she pulled her Toyota Rav 4 into the prime spot. She went behind the vehicle, opened the tailgate, and removed two instrument cases. Lugging her guitar and saxophone into the lobby, she followed the signs to the ballroom. The place was a madhouse of activity, and Sam moved carefully to the stage, trying not to get in the way of the numerous hotel personnel who were bustling about, making final preparations for the party.

She smiled at the woman standing at the keyboard. "Hi, Lisa."

"Hi, sis." Several phrases of electric piano music filled the room. "How's it sound?"

"Great!" Sam climbed onto the raised platform and exchanged pleasantries with her band mates as she unpacked and tuned her instruments.

"I'll be right back." Lisa stepped down from the stage. "I'm going to get my name tag."

With a leap, Sam landed next to her sister. "I'll go with you."

The women strolled toward the lobby.

"So, how do you feel about playing at your twenty-fifth high school reunion?" Sam asked.

"Old."

"Aw, c'mon." Sam poked her with an elbow. "You're not *that* old."

Lisa returned the jab. "Easy for you to say. I'll always be older than you."

"But wouldn't you rather just be a guest? I mean — it's your reunion."

"I doubt I would've come if it weren't for the fact the band is playing. You're the one who's been to all your reunions. You should feel right at home tonight."

"But this time I get to see *your* classmates. That's even better," Sam teased. "Hey, were you able to talk Mike into coming?"

"Yeah. I promised to point out a few people I've told him stories about from my high school days."

At the registration table, the volunteer had just finished arranging the name tags in alphabetical order. He saw his former classmate and smiled. "Lisa, how are you? I'm glad we were able to get your band tonight."

While Lisa talked with her friend, Sam perused the name tags. As she picked up her sister's, one near it caught her eye. *Christina Mellekas? She's going to be here? I remember—*

"May I *please* have my name tag?"

"Oh. Sure." Sam handed it over. "Guess what?" she whispered as they walked back to the ballroom. "Tina Mellekas is going to be here."

"Really?" Lisa whispered in reply. "Is that a secret?"

"Um...no."

"Why are we whispering, then?"

Sam shrugged and spoke at a more normal volume. "Will you introduce me to her?"

"Me? I hardly know her myself."

"She was on the track team with you, wasn't she?" Sam asked, though she already knew the answer. Tina had been the star of the team.

"We were more like acquaintances than friends." Narrowing her eyes, Lisa looked at her sister suspiciously. "Why this sudden interest in meeting Tina? No one has seen her in years."

"I don't know. But if she does come, will you introduce me?"

"All right," Lisa conceded, knowing Sam wouldn't give up until she agreed.

"Promise?"

Lisa held up her hand with her little finger crooked. "Pinky swear."

Grinning in victory, Sam locked her baby finger around her sister's. They'd never reneged on a pinky swear in their lives.

Returning to the ballroom, they joined Robbie, Kyle, and Bryan for a sound check before they finalized the song list for the sets.

Lisa looked at the wall clock. "We have about half an hour before we start, so let's take a break 'til then."

"I'm going to go outside and get some fresh air," Sam informed her sister. "Want to join me?"

"Nah. I'll stay here and say hi to the early arrivals."

"Okay." Sam wandered back to the lobby. Exiting through a door that led to the rear of the hotel, she was happy to discover a large garden area with benches. She sat down and inhaled the fragrant air. *Whatever kind of flowers those are, they sure smell good.* Tucking one leg beneath her, she thought back to the spring of her freshman year in high school.

Because she had to wait for Lisa to give her a ride home, Sam was at track practice every day. She would go to the top row of the bleachers, sit in the farthest corner, and open her books to study. However, not much studying actually got done. She had good intentions and usually accomplished about ten minutes of work before the boys and girls started coming out of the locker rooms. Then, as the books lay open on her lap, her gaze invariably went to the track. From her vantage point, she had an ideal view of the whole field.

Tina Mellekas was, by far, the best athlete on the team. She was always focused, repeating her events as many times as it took to perfect her form. And some form it was.

Sam smiled at the memory.

Long and lean, with jet-black hair pulled back into a ponytail and her face serious in concentration, Tina practiced diligently.

The only person Sam had ever seen crack Tina's solemn demeanor was her brother, Steven. It was obvious to everyone that the funny, outgoing sophomore idolized his big sister. Steven was on the boys' track team and he was trying hard to be as proficient at it as his sibling. Every now and then he would sneak up behind Tina and say something that made the reserved girl smile brilliantly. Watching from the bleachers, Sam often wondered what he had said that could cause such an amazing transformation.

Sam had always been fascinated with what made people tick, and Tina Mellekas was definitely intriguing. Though as often as she'd seen the track star practice, she'd never learned much about her.

Maybe tonight I'll get a second chance.

Sam glanced at her watch. *Uh-oh, I need to get to work.* Jumping up from the bench, she quickly headed back to the ballroom.

~ * ~ * ~ * ~ * ~

Tina paced around the hotel room for what seemed like the hundredth time.

This wasn't a good idea. I shouldn't be here. Whatever possessed me to think I should come to my high school reunion? I must have been out of my mind. If I stay here arguing with myself much longer, the reunion will be over and I won't have to worry about it.

Just do it, T. Sighing heavily, she left the room and slowly walked to the elevator. Staring at the steel door, she debated whether to press the button or bolt back to her room. At that moment, the door opened and a young couple exited. Tina looked at the empty car. *Well, there's a sign if ever there was one. I guess I'm destined to go to this reunion.* Taking a deep breath, she stepped into the elevator.

Disembarking at the lobby, she heard music coming from her left and followed the sound. At the entrance of the ballroom, she stopped and leaned against the door frame. The familiar feeling of being on the outside looking in settled over her as she surveyed the scene. The party was in full swing. Most of the attendees were dancing to music being played by a band onstage in the front of the room. *What song is that? Something that was a hit on the radio when I was in school...can't think of the name of it.* She recognized many of her old classmates and chuckled to herself as she noticed they were grouped into the same cliques they had belonged to in high school. Seeing a relatively unoccupied space near the back, Tina forced her feet to move. *If I can just get over there and hang around for a little while, I'll consider this a success.*

"Class of '74 *rules!*"

The shout from the crowd made Sam smile as she wiped the sweat from her face. The band was well into their second set. They had begun the night with soft background music during dinner. Now they were providing dance tunes, mostly from the seventies and early eighties. Soon they would be shifting into Sam's favorites — sixties classics. Placing her damp towel next to her sax stand, she reflected on the evening thus far. She had seen quite a few people she remembered from Lisa's class and was astonished at how different some of them looked, most notably the football player, Timmy Grant. He'd been extremely popular in high school and dozens of girls had had crushes on him. And there he was with a pudgy belly and practically bald. *You never can tell how people are going to turn out.*

Tina observed the proceedings from the back of the room. Several people came up and talked briefly with her, but otherwise, she kept to herself. The noise level dropped abruptly as a song ended and the leader of the band made an announcement. Tina's attention drifted to the stage. *Isn't that Lisa from the track team? Yeah. And there...the blonde guitar player...that's her sister. Hmm, she cut her hair.*

"All right, folks," Lisa said into the microphone, "we're going to do one more and then take a short break. However, we'll be back with lots more dance music, so don't go away." A cheer erupted from the audience as the band launched into a golden oldie.

Tina couldn't believe it. "*Wild Thing*"? Memories of her brother playing air guitar to that very song flickered through her mind. *I miss you, Steven. So many things remind me of you. Nothing's been the same...nothing.*

Sam looked out at the throng of partying alumni. Her eyes roamed beyond the dance floor to the clusters of people along the sides of the room. Next, she scanned across the back and caught sight of a tall figure. *Oh my goodness.* She missed the chord change and glanced at her sister. *Geez, only three chords in this one; she's going to ask how I could mess that up.* When the song was over, Sam hastily put her instrument in its stand and rushed to her sister. "Lisa."

"What is it, Sam? You forgetting how to play the guitar tonight?"

"No. She's here."

"Who's here?"

Sam pulled Lisa close and whispered in her ear, "Tina Mellekas."

"What is it about that woman that makes you whisper?"

"You promised you'd introduce me."

"Let me get Mike and I'll introduce him, too, then we're going to get our picture taken. They have a photographer here, just like at a prom. Isn't that great?"

"Yeah, great." Sam nudged her sister forward. "Let's go."

Lisa meandered through the crowd, eventually locating her husband. She hooked her arm through his and kissed him on the cheek. "Hey, handsome, do you think I could get my picture taken with you? I want proof that you actually attended this shindig."

"Sure."

"Are the kids over at Marie's?"

"Yeah, I'm going to pick them up on the way home. As a matter of fact, I need to get going soon," he said.

Sam cleared her throat.

Lisa rolled her eyes. "Okay, but first, let's go say hi to Tina. She was on the track team with me, but she hasn't been around in years."

As the trio moved toward the rear of the room, Mike asked his wife, "Where's she been?"

"Nobody really knows."

They were almost to where Tina was standing, and a fluttering in Sam's stomach surprised her. *Why in the heck am I nervous? She was the big track star in high school, but now we're both adults.*

"Hi, Tina," Lisa said. "I don't know if you remember me..."

"Of course I do. From the track team."

Sam barely heard the rest of their exchange as she concentrated fully on Tina Mellekas. The tall woman was wearing a knee-length, sleeveless black dress that revealed a healthy tan and physically fit body. Dark hair fell naturally over her shoulders and, even though the light was dim, Sam could see a bit of gray over her left temple. *She's going to have a shock of gray hair there soon.* As the conversation continued, she examined Tina's profile. It was exactly as she remembered, except this was *much* better — being this close. *There are probably a thousand words I could use to describe her, but it will only take three to sum it up quite nicely: drop-dead gorgeous.*

"And this is my little sister, Samantha."

The sound of her name drew Sam from her musings.

Tina held out her hand. "Nice to meet you."

Sam found herself looking into the most beautiful blue eyes she'd ever seen. She managed to reach forward, grasp the offered hand, and say, "N-Nice to meet you, too."

"Well," Lisa said, "Mike and I need to go get our picture taken. We're glad you came tonight, Tina."

Sam watched with dismay as the couple walked off. *They're leaving me alone with her? What'll I do now?*

There was an extended silence, during which Sam racked her brain for something, anything, to say. She saw that Tina was holding a hotel key card. *Hmm...no purse...and she's staying here at the hotel? Maybe I can ask her about that.*

Tina was ready to leave. She'd been at the event less than an hour, but it was more than enough for her. *Why is this girl still here? I guess I should say something.* "The band is very good."

Relieved that one of them had finally spoken, Sam responded enthusiastically. "Thanks! We have a strong following locally and a steady amount of work. We do weddings and clubs, really just about anything. My sister started the band years ago and it's kind of evolved..." Her voice trailed off as she realized she was babbling.

Good Lord, she sure can talk. Tina couldn't help but grin at the blonde's exuberance.

As she peeked up to see if the former track star was even listening, Sam's breath caught. The serious look on Tina's face had given way to a small grin. *Wow. She has little wrinkles around her eyes when she smiles. And those eyes.* ... Time seemed to stand still. Sam saw pain, sorrow, guilt, and...a good heart. How she saw all that, sensed all that, she didn't know. It was just very clear. *She's the one.*

Feeling as if the younger woman were looking right inside her, Tina broke the eye contact. "I think you're needed."

"What?"

"The band." Tina pointed to the musicians returning to the stage.

"Oh, yes. I have to get going. Are you staying for a while?"

"No. This isn't my kind of thing."

Sam's mind was racing, trying to think of what to say to give her an opportunity to see Tina again. The sound of the keyboard disrupted her train of thought. She knew her sister was signaling her to return to work. "Um...I've really got to go."

"Well, don't let me keep you."

I'd love for you to keep me. "Bye." Sam gave a little wave and a smile before she turned and jogged to the stage.

Tina made her way to the door. *That one would be trouble. Good thing I'm out of here on Monday.* She stopped to take a final look around. The band had started playing a popular sixties tune, and it seemed like everybody in the room was dancing, singing, or both.

I still don't fit in here. I shouldn't have tried to come home.

~ * ~ * ~ * ~ * ~

Sam was exhausted. As usual, the third set had been the longest, and she felt drained and dehydrated. She was soaked with sweat, her bangs sticking to her forehead and shirt clinging to her chest. The band members were the only ones left in the ballroom. Even the hotel personnel had finished cleaning up and were gone. This was always the most difficult part of the night for Sam. Instruments had to be packed, yards and yards of cords wound, and then everything had to be loaded into Robbie's and Bryan's trucks. It didn't matter how tired they all were, it was part of the job.

Lisa called out, "I'm going to get us some drinks. I'll be right back."

While she was getting the refreshments, the rest of the musicians moved the gear over to a side door where the trucks could pull up. Sitting on the amps and equipment boxes, they chatted as they waited for the bandleader.

Lisa returned carrying a tray full of beverages. "Here we go — a well-deserved drink after a hard night's work."

Sam accepted a bottle of water and took a big gulp. "Thanks, sis, I needed that."

"No problem." Lisa took a swallow of beer. "By the way, guess who I saw in the bar?"

"Who?"

"Tina."

"Really?"

"Really."

"Um...Lisa?"

"Yes?"

"Would you do me a favor and take my guitar and sax home for me?"

"Suddenly feel the need for a drink from the bar, huh?"

Sam felt a blush rise to her cheeks. "Well, maybe just one."

"Be careful, okay?"

"I will."

Lisa smiled as her sister dashed out of the ballroom. *I saw the twinkle in your eye when you looked at her. I just hope you meant it when you said you'd be careful.*

The bar was almost deserted and Sam had no trouble spotting Tina seated at the far end.

The bartender hustled over to his new customer. "Good evening, miss. What can I get for you?"

"I'll have a light beer, and please give the lady," she glanced at Tina, "another of whatever she's drinking."

"She's made it pretty clear she doesn't want company," the bartender said as he served Sam her beer. "You sure?"

"Yeah, I'm sure." Sam saw that Tina had changed into jeans and a white V- neck tee shirt. *Can it be possible that she looks even better now than she did in that black dress? Heck, she'd look good in a burlap sack.* Sam paid for the drinks, took her beer, and headed in Tina's direction. *Okay, you wanted a chance to talk to her again and here it is. Now, what in the world are you going to say?*

Tina was monitoring Sam's approach in her peripheral vision. The blonde had a compact, athletic build and she walked with a spring in her step. Her hair, cut in a short, layered fashion, was still damp with sweat, as was her shirt. She had expressive green eyes and a smile that lit up her face.

Sam sat in the empty chair next to Tina. "Hi."

"So, we meet again."

"Um...yeah."

The bartender put a beer in front of Tina. "Compliments of the little lady."

The dark-haired woman nodded at Sam. "Thanks."

"You're welcome. I...I want you to know, I think it's great that you came to the reunion."

"Why?"

"Well, you're one of the few people from Lisa's class that I distinctly remember. I always got a ride home from school with my sister, so I used to be at track practice every day. I just wondered how you were doing."

Tina stared at the TV above the bar and didn't reply.

She sure isn't making this easy. Sam decided to be more blunt. "I'd...um...like for us to be friends."

"Friends?"

"Why not? Unless you seniors are still worried about being seen hanging around with freshmen."

Tina looked at the rows of liquor bottles, her drink, the bartender, anything but the woman next to her. *She's so wholesome. I'd ruin her life in nothing flat.* "I don't think that would be a good idea. Besides, I'm leaving Monday morning."

"Are you busy tomorrow night?"

"Tomorrow night?" Tina immediately tried to think of a feasible excuse.

"Yeah, it's the big Labor Day celebration. It's fun. All summer there are concerts at the park. On the last weekend, the orchestra performs and there's a fireworks display. It's *really* cool. I'm in the orchestra, but I could pick you up and bring you to the park. You can listen to the concert and then we can watch the fireworks together. I'll even make a picnic dinner. I—"

"Look," Tina cut in harshly, "I'm not sure why you're doing this. We don't even know each other." She instantly regretted the remark when she saw the dejected look on Sam's face. *Lighten up, T. You came to this reunion thinking it might be the first step in getting your life in order. And here is somebody actually making an effort to know you, maybe even become a friend. Don't push her away.*

The air-conditioning in the bar kicked on and Sam shivered.

"Are you cold?"

"It's okay. I'm fine."

Tina regarded Sam's damp shirt and raised an eyebrow at the obvious lie. "Here." She removed her jacket from the back of her chair. "Put this on."

The blonde put her hands up in protest. "Oh, no. I'll get it all sweaty."

Tina stood and held out the brown suede jacket. "C'mon. A little sweat won't hurt it. It's the least I can do for the gracious woman who bought me a drink."

"Well, all right." Sam slipped her arms into the sleeves of the coat. *Oh, my. This is nice.* "Thank you."

"What time is the concert?"

"It starts at seven thirty, but I'd need to be there around six forty-five for the orchestra."

"Okay."

"Okay?"

"Yes. Okay. I'll go."

The smile that brightened Sam's face made Tina glad she'd said yes. *It won't kill me to go, and if it makes her that happy, well, it's worth it.*

"How about if I pick you up here at the hotel at six thirty? What kind of sandwich do you want?"

"Whatever you're having will be fine."

The bartender came over to check on his customers. "Can I get you anything else, ladies? Last call."

"No, thanks," they replied in unison.

"Well, I guess I should get going." Sam began to take off the jacket.

"Leave it on. I'll walk you to your car."

"That's not necessary. I—"

"Are you coming or not?" Tina strode toward the exit.

Hmm. You like to get your own way. Sam had to jog to catch up with the long-legged woman. "Do you always stay up this late?" she asked as they walked through the lobby and out of the hotel.

"A lot of times, yes. I don't sleep very well."

"Oh." *Wonder what that's all about.* Sam stopped next to her Toyota, took off the suede coat and gave it to Tina. "Thanks for letting me wear this. I'll pick you up tomorrow night at six thirty, right?"

"Yes."

"Good night."

"Good night, Samantha."

Tina watched as Sam got in the car and drove away. She waited until the vehicle was out of sight before she returned to the hotel.

Sam looked in the rearview mirror as long as she could. She could see Tina standing there until she made the turn onto the main road. *Samantha...I like the way she says that.*

Chapter 2

The sound of a door closing and voices in the hallway woke Tina. She rolled over and looked at the bedside clock. The large red numbers proclaimed it was 7:14. As she lay back, she threw her arm over her eyes to block the sun that was sneaking in around the edges of the drapes. She listened to the sounds of other hotel guests leaving their rooms, excitedly yakking about their upcoming day.

Well, I'm in no rush to get where I'm going this morning. Tina thought about her plans for the day, plans that up until last night hadn't included a concert and fireworks. *How did I let myself get talked into that?* An image of sparkling green eyes flashed across her mind. *You know damn well how you got talked into that. She didn't exactly have to twist your arm, did she? At least the day might end better than it's going to start.*

Tina groaned as she pulled herself into a sitting position. She paused, then slowly stood and performed several stretching exercises, and felt the tightness in her back loosen a bit. Ready for breakfast, she picked up the room service menu. Frowning, she straightened her arm, trying in vain to find the distance necessary to see the small print.

Aggravated, Tina slammed the menu down on the table and grabbed her backpack off the chair. Rummaging through it, she found a small case and pulled it out. After putting on her glasses, she checked the choices again. *Breakfast of Champions...I may need that today...a banana, and some coffee.* Her decision made, Tina called in the order, put her glasses away, and went into the bathroom. *I can probably take a quick shower before the food is delivered.* Looking into the mirror above the sink, she inspected the crop of gray just above her temple. *I can't believe it — more gray hairs. Maybe I should color it. Geez...glasses and gray hair. Like it or not, you're getting old, T.* Scowling, she undressed and stepped into the shower. It was going to be a long day.

~ * ~ * ~ * ~ * ~

Sam put her pillow over her head. *Who in the heck is making all that noise down there?* Even with the pillow muffling the sound, she heard the automatic garage door opening and someone moving around below her apartment. Finally, the door closed and it was quiet again. She tossed and turned, trying to fall back to sleep, but it was impossible. Her mind was too busy reviewing the events of the night before. *I need to talk to Lisa.*

She heaved herself out of bed and went to the front window to see if her sister's car was parked in the driveway. *Yes! She's home.* Barefoot, and still in the tee shirt and shorts she had worn to bed, Sam went down the stairs and across the walkway to Lisa's house. She tapped on the door and entered the kitchen. "Good morning."

"Well, if it isn't Ms. Sleepyhead," Lisa remarked. "You ready for a cup of coffee?"

"Absolutely."

"So," Lisa got two large mugs from the cupboard and filled them with piping hot brew from the coffeemaker, "how'd it go with Tina last night?"

"She's...um...very interesting."

"She is?" Lisa grinned as she handed Sam her coffee. "Do tell."

The sisters took their drinks and sat at the kitchen table.

"It's hard to explain, but the main thing is — I definitely want to get to know her better."

"Uh-huh. And it doesn't hurt that she's beautiful, either."

"She's gorgeous! Her eyes are *so* blue and she has this little patch of gray...and..." Sam stopped in mid-sentence as Lisa started laughing.

"What?"

"You, Samantha Whitwell, have it bad. I've seen that look before."

"I don't have any lo—"

"Ah, ah, ah," Lisa interrupted Sam's objection. "Don't try to tell me differently. I thought you were going to faint when she shook your hand last night."

Sam felt the heat creeping up into her face. "All right, I'm busted. But Lisa, she's the one."

"What do you mean?"

"Remember you told me about when you first met Michael? And how you knew he was the one you wanted to marry? You said somewhere inside it just felt...right."

"Yes, that's true. From the very beginning, I knew he was the man for me."

"I got that same feeling last night. I looked into Tina's eyes and saw...I don't know how to say it...so much pain and conflict. But I think I'm the one who's meant to reach out to her. It was very strange. I felt it way inside of me, deep in my heart. I've never felt like that about anybody." Sam stared down at her coffee cup. "I guess it sounds crazy, huh?"

"No, it doesn't sound crazy. But what are you going to do about it? Have you told her you're gay? Is *she* gay?"

"No, I didn't tell her. And I have no idea if she is or not. We didn't get much of a chance to talk."

"Are you going to see her again?"

A big smile spread across Sam's face. "Yes. She's going to the concert and fireworks with me tonight."

"My goodness, you must have really turned on the Whitwell charm."

"Hey, if it worked for you with Michael, it can work for me, too."

They both laughed.

"Lisa?"

"Yeah?"

"What do you know about her? Will you please tell me?"

"Well, let me think. After graduation, she went to Florida State University on a track scholarship. She came home and was working for some corporation. I'm not sure what kind of job it was. I heard she was engaged—"

"Engaged?"

"Yes. To some guy she worked with, I believe."

"What happened?" Sam was leaning forward now, as if she could hear the words sooner that way.

"Give me a second here; I wasn't even friends with her. Most of this is gossip from other people, so I don't even know if it's all true."

"Just tell me the rest," Sam urged.

"Around ten years ago, she was involved in a terrible automobile accident and her brother was killed. Tina was driving the car they were in, and word had it that she felt responsible for his death."

"I heard about the accident, but I didn't know she thought it was her fault."

"Well, after that, she left town. I don't think anyone has seen her since."

"Tina must've been devastated when Steven died. I used to watch them goofing around at track practice. He could make her smile like nobody else could."

"You had your eye on her back in high school, did you?"

"I just thought she was cool. I didn't even know I liked women then, so stop that." Sam swatted at her sister's arm.

Lisa grabbed Sam's hand. "Please be careful. Tina has a lot of guilt, problems...whatever. Who knows?"

"I can handle it."

"Uh-huh. Like you did with Sally?"

"Sally? What does she have to do with this?"

"Well, I recall being concerned about my sister dating this tattooed drummer chick. But I was told not to worry because all Sally needed was love, and understanding, and—"

"That was *years* ago! Will I *ever* live that down?"

Lisa laughed. "I doubt it."

"This is not the same as Sally, or anybody else you plan on dredging up from my past."

"Even Kim? Are you sure that's over?"

"I'm sorry it didn't work out, Lisa. I know she's your friend and you think she's perfect for me. I really do care about Kim; she's a terrific person. I'm just not in love with her."

"She's still in love with you."

"I know. There's nothing I can do to change that. I'm hoping, in time, we'll be friends."

Lisa took the mugs to refill them. "All right, then. You're sure Tina is the one, huh?"

"Yes. I'm telling you, this is something special. I swear it."

"Pinky swear?"

"Yeah, pinky swear."

The sisters joined pinkies.

"I hope for your sake you're right," Lisa commented. "Otherwise you're headed for a whole lot of hurt."

"I'm sure about this," Sam replied, remembering those troubled blue eyes. "She needs somebody, Lisa. She needs *me*."

~ * ~ * ~ * ~ * ~

Tina pulled out of the hotel parking lot and drove through the familiar streets of her hometown. Becoming more and more anxious as she got closer to her destination, she made the final turn and saw the high school directly ahead. In the parking area, she stopped the car and looked at the three-story, red brick building. *I can do this.* Her hands, resting on the steering wheel, were shaking and Tina took a couple of deep breaths, trying to prepare for the flood of memories she knew would be coming.

Pressing down on the gas pedal, the panic-stricken woman accelerated quickly around the school and parked at the track. She stared out the windshield at the place she had avoided for ten years. *It looks the same, but things have changed so much.* She picked up her backpack from the passenger seat, got out of the car, and slung the bag over her shoulder. Hesitantly, Tina took the few steps necessary to get to the fence surrounding the track, then grasped the chain link with her hands. Tears filled her eyes and she struggled to keep them from falling. This was the last place she and Steven had been before the accident, and she could still picture the two of them happily running around the track on that fateful day. Tina was unable to hold back the tears any longer, and they trickled down her cheeks.

Composing herself as best she could, Tina pushed away from the fence and went through the gate. Several people were there already, either walking or jogging around the track. She ambled onto the grassy infield and sat down.

Okay. I'm here, and the world didn't end. I'll be all right.

She did some stretching exercises before jogging onto the track. Starting out slowly to warm up her muscles, she made her first lap around. Then, increasing her pace, she continued to run, lap after lap, and found that it was helping to calm her. Finally, beginning to feel the fatigue in her legs, Tina picked up the pace to push herself for the last lap. Faster and faster she went, feeling her body hold the form imprinted by years of practice.

The other people had stopped their exercising to watch as Tina sailed around the track again and again. Her long, dark hair was pulled back into a ponytail that trailed behind her. Her tank top and gym shorts revealed a well-toned body working in perfect synchronization. She was a sight to behold.

Tina was oblivious to everything around her. Her legs were aching, but she pressed on, wanting to end at the spot where the finish line had been when she was in high school. She lunged across the imaginary line, reduced her pace to an easy jog and, eventually, a walk. Back in the infield, she drank liberally from her water bottle before doing her post-workout stretches.

She stayed for another half hour, contemplating the direction her life had taken after that horrible day so long ago. There was the Tina from before the accident, and the Tina from after the accident. She tried to reconcile in her mind that she was, indeed, both of them. *I feel better now that I've been here, though. I'm glad I came.* She collected her things and walked toward her car. *Just one more stop.*

~ * ~ * ~ * ~ * ~

Tina drove slowly through the wrought-iron gates of the cemetery. The tires made a crunching noise on the gravel road as she guided the car along the path she knew so well. After a succession of turns, she pulled over and parked. She was the only person in that section of the cemetery. *Good. I like it that way.*

It was a beautiful Florida day. The sun was shining but it was early enough that it wasn't too hot yet. Puffy white clouds dotted the bright blue sky, and a slight breeze rustled the tree branches. In the shade of a large oak tree, Tina knelt down at her brother's grave. "Hi, Stevie." She kissed her fingertips and touched his name engraved in the granite

Steven Mellekas
1959-1989
Beloved Son and Brother

Tina had often thought if she looked at the inscription long enough, maybe she could convince herself that it was really true. He was gone...forever. In one split second on a rain-slicked street, Steven's life was taken and hers irrevocably changed. It was an instant that she'd replayed over and over in her mind. She would have given anything to be able to go back and alter what had happened that day. Many times she'd wished that it was she, not Steven, who had been killed. He hadn't deserved to die. And she was to blame.

Shifting into a sitting position, Tina leaned against the headstone.

Can you believe it? I went to the high school reunion, Stevie. I bet that surprised a few people. I was going to come to visit you anyway, so I figured — what the heck, I'll go to the reunion, too. It was hard to be there without you. But that's the point, I guess — to start trying to live my life again. And to realize that what happened can't be changed: you're not ever coming back.

Tears filled Tina's eyes. *I have you in my heart, though. I carry you everywhere with me, and I always will. I know that you'd have wanted me to go on and be happy. Well, it's taken me a while, but I'm finally trying to pull my life together. So, I made myself go to the track this morning. It wasn't easy. When I saw the school, I almost turned around and left, but I knew I had to do it. I had to face that place...and the memories.*

She sniffled and brushed away her tears.

Lisa Whitwell was at the reunion. You remember her, don't you? She ran sprints and the hurdles. Her sister was there, too. I know you remember her. A smile appeared on Tina's face. *Her name is Samantha and she asked me to go to a concert and fireworks display tonight. I'm not sure how it happened, but I'm going. I bet you're finding that amusing and you're laughing at me right now. She reminds me of you, Stevie. She's one of those people who are full of life, always with a twinkle in her eye. When she looks at me, though, I feel so...exposed. It's as if she can read everything going on inside me. Honestly, that scares the hell out of me. At the same time, there's something about her; I can't really explain it, but I like her. She said she wants to be my friend. I haven't had a friend in a long time. I'm not sure I remember how.*

A flock of sparrows flew from the tree above and landed in the sun-drenched grass a short distance from Tina. She remained still, resting against the headstone, feeling the sense of peace that always came over her when she sat there. She knew it was Steven. It was as if he were covering her with a blanket of love and acceptance, despite what she had done. She watched the birds, felt the breeze, and breathed in the smells of the grass, trees and flowers.

It was extraordinary that there, in the cemetery, was where she felt the most alive.

Chapter 3

"What kind of sandwich did Tina say she wanted?" Lisa inquired as the sisters pushed their carts up the aisle of the supermarket.

"She said she'd have whatever I'm having."

"Evidently she isn't aware that your basic food groups are drive-through, Ring Dings, and diet soda."

"C'mon, help me out here." Sam peered into the deli case. "How about turkey? Everybody likes turkey, don't they?"

"Why don't you make a couple of different kinds?" Lisa looked at the variety of breads on the counter. "You could put some on wheat, too. That way you cover all the bases."

"Good idea."

They made their selections and continued through the store, filling their carts with groceries.

"Lisa?"

"Yeah?"

"If everything goes well tonight, I was thinking of asking Tina to visit again next weekend."

"Moving a little fast, aren't you?"

Sam shrugged. "I want to spend time with her and get to know her better."

"You have a tendency to rush into things," Lisa cautioned. "*Please* be careful. Keep in mind there's a lot you don't know about her. For instance, did you find out where she's been for the last few years?"

"No."

"So, she could be living in California, Alaska...anywhere."

"But she came to the reunion. I thought maybe I could give her another reason to come back."

"What are you planning to do if she says yes?"

"We could have a cookout. I was hoping you'd make your famous barbecue chicken."

"You're kidding, right?"

Sam smiled at her sister optimistically.

Lisa sighed. *She's not kidding.* "You would owe me big time."

"Is that a yes?"

"Yeeees."

"Thanks!" The blonde gave Lisa a lengthy hug.

"Um...Sam?"

"Yeah?"

"People are staring. Would you let go of me now?"

~ * ~ * ~ * ~ * ~

Tina slept for several hours that afternoon. *It seems that's all I can do anymore — get a few hours here and there. It's been a long time since I got a full night's sleep.* She looked through the contents of her suitcase for something to wear to the concert and fireworks display. It had become quite hot during the day and it would still be very warm in the evening. After dressing in a pair of khaki walking shorts and a sleeveless denim shirt, Tina ran a brush through her hair. She grabbed her backpack and went down to the lobby. Force of habit made her glance at her wrist to check the time. *Damn!* No longer able to see the details on the small dial, she had stopped wearing her watch months earlier. Now, whenever she looked at her bare wrist, it was a reminder that her eyesight wasn't what it used to be.

Squinting when she stepped from the hotel into the bright sunlight, Tina decided to get her sunglasses from the car. She fished the keys from her backpack and used the remote to deactivate the alarm as she neared the vehicle. She got the glasses and reset the alarm before retreating to the shade of a palm tree to wait. *I don't know how I get myself into these things. What am I doing hanging around with Samantha Whitwell? And what's she doing hanging around with me? I'm nothing but trouble. Maybe she* likes *trouble. Hmm...Don't go there, T. A few minutes with her and anybody could see that Samantha is kind and open and...everything I'm not. Well, I'll try not to be a bad influence. I ought to be able to handle that for one night.*

When the Toyota entered the parking lot, Tina waved to get Sam's attention and the musician pulled up beside her. Tina got into the car and fastened her seat belt. "Hi."

"Hi." Sam maneuvered the SUV smoothly onto Tamiami Trail.

"Where's the concert going to be?"

"Phillippi Estate Park."

"That's a nice place." Tina looked out the passenger window and added softly, "I haven't been there in years."

Sam didn't know how, or if, she should respond, so the radio playing was the only sound for a while. She was glad when Tina spoke again.

"Is being in the orchestra your profession?"

"Yeah. Lisa's band is an extra part-time job." Sam turned into the park entrance. "What do you do?"

"I work for a travel agency."

"You're a travel agent?"

"Not exactly."

Not exactly? Sam found a parking space and turned off the engine. "Would you help me carry the stuff?"

"Sure."

The women went around to the back of the SUV and Sam opened the hatch.

Seeing the compartment full of paraphernalia, Tina exclaimed incredulously, "We need all that?"

"Well, it's best to be prepared. I didn't know if you'd want to sit in chairs or use a blanket. And we need the cooler. And those are my clothes to change into after the concert. And—"

Tina put up her hand to cut off the protracted explanation. "Let's just use the blanket."

Sam reached for the red plaid cloth and a small instrument case.

As she grasped the handles of the cooler, Tina nodded at the case. "What's that?"

"It's my clarinet. That's what I play in the orchestra."

Tina pulled the ice chest out of the car and practically dropped it on the ground. "Argh! What in the world do you have in there?"

"Um...sandwiches and soda and—"

"Never mind. Put the other things on top and we'll both carry it."

Sam locked the Toyota's hatch and laid the blanket and the clarinet on the cooler.

They each gripped a handle and walked into the grassy spectator area. Tina was having difficulty carrying the heavy container with the shorter woman, having to bend her knees to try and keep the surface level so the objects on top wouldn't slide off. Then, because of her awkward position, her backpack kept falling from her shoulder. *Why was it that I agreed to this?* She looked over at the blonde, who gave her a dazzling smile. *Oh, yeah. I remember.*

"Where would you like to sit?" Sam asked.

"Let's put this down." Tina was already lowering her side of the cooler. "How about we stay right here. That way, when the concert is over, we'll be close to the car and you can get your clothes more easily." *And we won't have to lug this damned ice chest all over creation.*

"Sounds good to me." Sam unfolded the blanket.

Tina took the opposite end and helped spread it on the ground.

"I'm sorry to leave you so soon, but I need to get to work." She picked up her clarinet case. "Help yourself to the food and drinks. I'll be back after the concert."

"Okay." Tina made herself comfortable on the blanket and removed her sunglasses. Her eyes tracked every step of Sam's progress to the stage area.

The park filled up rapidly, and by seven thirty there were hundreds of people camped out on the grass. The orchestra tuned up and the conductor announced the beginning of the concert. As the music floated over the crowd, the people quieted down. The melodies were soothing and Tina lay back, closing her eyes and relaxing. *This isn't so bad. In fact, it's kind of nice.* She remained like that, long body stretched across the blanket, for half an hour. Anyone observing her would have thought she was asleep.

A rumbling in her stomach motivated Tina to sit up and investigate the contents of the cooler. *Good...bottles of water...and sandwiches. She labeled them? Let's see: turkey plain, turkey lt/mayo, ham and cheese. There must be six different kinds of sandwiches in here. Soda, chips, and...what's this?* She zeroed in on a small object wrapped in tin foil. *It can't be.* Tina unwrapped it and smiled. *A Ring Ding? When was the last time I had one of these? Back before I had to worry about things like calories and fat grams, that's when. Well, this is a special occasion, and I already unwrapped it.* She enjoyed her water and Ring Ding while the orchestra played a series of patriotic tunes. A rousing version of *Stars and Stripes Forever* ended the concert, and the audience showed its appreciation with extensive applause. The orchestra members stood and bowed, but Tina couldn't see Sam among them. *She's too small.* She looked at the crumpled foil wrapper in her hand. *But good things can come in small packages.*

~ * ~ * ~ * ~ * ~

Tina decided to stand and stretch her back. As she rolled her shoulders and then twisted at the waist, she felt her muscles loosen slightly. Tall enough to see over the crowd, she spotted Sam making her way toward the blanket.

Sam smiled. "It's a good thing you stood up or I might not have found you." *Not that I ever would've quit looking.* "It's warm tonight." She opened the cooler and got a diet soda. "Did you eat yet?"

"Just a snack. I thought I'd wait for you."

"Let me change my clothes and then we can have dinner."

"I'll walk with you. Do you think it's safe to leave the stuff here?"

"Nobody will bother it, and we won't be gone long." Sam took a swallow of her drink and started walking toward the car. "Did you like the concert?"

"Yes, I did. The orchestra is excellent. It must be a great job — playing music for a living."

"Lord knows I'll never be rich, but I love it."

Tina sidestepped a child who was chasing after a ball. "How many instruments do you play?"

"The clarinet is my main instrument. I started playing the saxophone in high school because I wanted to be in the jazz band. Those two are similar, so it's not much of a feat to play both. In college I was a music major, so I had basic instruction in most of the instruments, but I wouldn't say I can actually play them."

"And the guitar?"

"I wanted to be in Lisa's rock band in the worst way. I bought a beat-up old Stratocaster when I was in college and talked a friend into teaching me the chords. Lisa let me sit in with the band when I was on vacations from school, and after I graduated, she asked me to join as a permanent member. I've been in it ever since. I still play using that same Strat, too. I love the sound of old instruments."

The women arrived at the car. "If you'll hold this for me," Sam handed Tina the soda, "I'll just be a minute." She unlocked the tailgate of the SUV and crawled into the storage area. "One of the benefits of being small." She chuckled as she shut the door.

Tina shook her head in amusement and waited. In a short amount of time, Sam reappeared dressed in sneakers, jean shorts, and a tee shirt with Lilith Fair emblazoned across the front. "Let's go." She locked the car. "I'm starved."

Tina handed Sam the can of soda as they headed back to the blanket.

"Thanks." Sam took a sip. "So, you said you work for a travel agency?"

"Yes."

"And where is this travel agency?"

"Tampa."

Sam stopped abruptly and gawked at Tina. "Tampa?"

"Yeah."

"*Tampa?* You've been in *Tampa* for the last ten years?"

"Um...yes. Is there something wrong with that?"

"No. There's nothing wrong with that. It's just that you disappear for ten years and you've been living an hour away?"

"Do we have to discuss this right here?" Tina asked quietly.

They reached the blanket and sat facing each other.

"I'm sorry," the blonde said in a much calmer voice. "I shouldn't have yelled, but everyone has been worried about you."

"I didn't know anyone was worried about me." *Or that anyone cared where I was.*

"I mean..." *What do I mean?* "Um...well, I'm just glad you're here."

Sam opened the cooler. "What would you like?"

Tina chose a plain turkey sandwich and a bottle of water. "Thanks for bringing dinner."

"You're welcome."

Tina ate slowly, watching in astonishment as her companion consumed another soda, a sandwich, a bag of chips and two Ring Dings.

Sam offered a chocolaty dessert to Tina. "Would you like a Ring Ding?"

"No thanks, I had one earlier."

"Only one? How can you have only one?"

"It wasn't easy," Tina grinned, "but I managed."

"The fireworks are about to start." Sam put all their trash in a small plastic bag. "Let's lie down. It's the best way to see them."

They lay next to each other, peacefully gazing at the stars until a high, arcing bolt of light shot through the air, exploding with a loud *BANG*. The crowd cheered; the fireworks display had begun. The women watched the spectacular show, enjoying it immensely.

~ * ~ * ~ * ~ * ~

"That was fantastic!" Sam exclaimed as the final barrage of fireworks finished exploding above them.

"Yes, it was." Tina grimaced as she tried to sit up. "Argh!" Her body refused to cooperate and she had to lie back again.

"What's the matter?" Sam teased. "Too old to get up anymore?"

Tina looked away quickly, but not before Sam saw a pained expression flash across her features. The tall woman rolled over on her stomach and carefully pushed herself into a kneeling position. She stared down at her hands resting on her thighs.

There was an uncomfortable silence.

"I'm sorry. I didn't mean to hurt your feelings." Sam knelt in front of Tina. "Please, talk to me."

Haunted eyes rose to meet Sam's. "I injured my back badly...years ago...in a car accident."

"Oh my God! Why didn't you tell me? I mean — the cooler, and I could have brought you a chair from the car, and—"

"It's all right. It's just something I've learned to live with."

Sam wanted to throw her arms around Tina, but it didn't look as if she would be receptive to physical contact at the moment. *And it wouldn't be good for her back, either.* Standing, Sam held out her hand. "May I at least help you up?"

"Thanks." Tina took the small hand and slowly drew herself to her feet. She did a few tentative stretches and the spasms subsided.

Sam observed the movements closely. *What else have you had to live with since that accident? I can't even imagine. But I want to help you. I've never wanted anything so much in my life.* "Does it feel any better?"

"Yes. How about we take a walk while the traffic clears? That'll get the kinks worked out."

"Okay. Let's put our stuff in the car first." Sam bent to pick up the blanket. "And don't even *think* about touching that cooler." She folded the blanket and tossed it to Tina. "You can carry this."

Tina caught the cloth and smiled wryly. "Should I be trusted with such an important responsibility in my incapacitated condition?"

Sam laughed. "I think you'll do fine." *More than fine.* She drained the melted ice water from the cooler. It would be much lighter without the ice and full drinks inside. She placed the backpack on top and lifted it. "C'mon."

Tina trailed behind her, embarrassed that the small woman had to lug the bulky container. They put their things in the SUV and took a leisurely stroll around the park.

"It's a beautiful night," Sam commented.

"Yes, it is."

"I hope you had a good time. Well, except for your back. I'd hate to think I dragged you out here and you were bored silly."

"No, I wasn't bored," Tina said sincerely. "I enjoyed it very much."

Happy to hear that, Sam said, "So, you're going home tomorrow? To Tampa?"

"Yes."

"Would you like to come to a cookout next Saturday? Lisa makes fabulous barbecue chicken. You do like chicken, don't you?"

Tina considered the request. *I don't think I've met anyone as nice as her in years. And as unbelievable as it seems, she likes me...and wants to be my friend.* "I appreciate the invitation, but I...I'm not a very...pleasant person. I'm moody...and...I'm not good at—"

Sam moved into Tina's path, forcing her to stop. "Please don't talk about yourself like that. I think you're wonderful."

That's the problem, isn't it? You'll find out soon enough that's not true. "I haven't had much practice at being a friend. I may not be a suitable choice."

"You could humor me and give it a chance."

Tina looked at the determined woman and sighed. *I can already see how hard it is to say no to you. This is trouble, trouble, trouble.* "I love chicken."

Sam jumped up and down. "Yes!"

Tina grinned at her enthusiasm. "Okay. Let's get going."

"Okay." Sam ran ahead a few steps, turned, and walked backward.

"I'll have to give you directions...and I need to ask Lisa what time the cookout is...and what else do you want to eat besides chicken?"

"Anything at all. Don't have her make something special on my account."

Sam had to keep from laughing. *If you only knew Lisa was making the whole meal on your account.*

They got in the Toyota and Sam started toward the hotel.

"You and your sister are close?"

"We're best friends. When she and Mike went house hunting, they looked for a place with a garage apartment so we could live next door to each other. It's been great. I fixed it up, and they charge me next to nothing to stay there. And when Lisa had the kids, I helped a lot. I still baby-sit for her quite often."

"You don't have children of your own?"

"Um...no. My mom was thrilled when Lisa had her two boys. Then she started pressuring me to produce a granddaughter."

"You were married?"

"No. But my mother wanted me to be married and get pregnant. I finally had to tell her that I was gay. I'd been putting it off because I knew she wouldn't take it well. As expected, she made it perfectly clear how disappointed in me she was. She tried to convince me it was just a phase and I'd get over it." Sam paused. "It wasn't a phase."

"You could still have a child."

"According to my mother, that would be worse."

They were both quiet for a few minutes.

"I should have told you earlier," Sam said apologetically. "I'll understand if you don't want to come to the cookout."

"Why?" Tina was confused. "Is your mother going to be there?"

"No. Our relationship is strained and we only see each other on the major holidays. I'm saying if it bothers you that I'm gay, I won't hold you to your promise to come to the barbecue. It's hard sometimes to be friends with a gay person. It's guilt by association, if you know what I mean."

"I know what you mean, and I couldn't care less what people think, including your mother."

I can believe that. Putting those two together would generate fireworks that would rival what we saw tonight. Sam pulled into a parking space at the hotel. "Would you mind if I walk with you to the lobby? I need to use the restroom."

"Okay." Tina winced as she turned toward the storage compartment. "My backpack..."

"Let me get it for you." Sam reached between the bucket seats and grabbed the bag.

They went into the hotel and the blonde swiftly located the facilities.

Tina leaned against the lobby wall to wait. *That mother has some nerve. Samantha is terrific, and her mom is disappointed in her? She should thank her lucky stars her daughter turned out so well.*

Sam emerged from the restroom. "I'm sorry I got in such a funk. Discussing my mother does that to me."

"I know how it is. Someday, I'll tell you about *my* mother." Tina was glad to see that got her a grin. *Hey, I said something right.* "I think I owe you a drink...from last night. Will you allow me to repay the favor?"

"That would be nice."

Tina placed a hand lightly on Sam's back and steered her into the bar.

The bartender smiled when he saw them. "Well, it's my lady friends again."

"Hello," Tina said. "Can we have two light beers, please?" She paid, took the drinks, and followed Sam to a secluded booth in the corner. "Here." She set Sam's drink in front of her. "Are you positive you're all right?"

"Yeah."

"Listen, I really want to thank you for asking me to go to the concert and fireworks with you. I haven't been to something like that in ages. It was...fun."

Sam perked up a bit. "Really?"

"Yes, really." *I'm on a roll; she's smiling again.* "You were going to give me directions?"

"Right. Um...I don't have any paper here. Do you have an e-mail address?"

"Yes." Tina searched in her backpack and took out a business card and pen. She wrote on the card and gave it to Sam. "Here's my home e-mail address."

The dark gray card had lighter gray streaks, which gave it a marbled effect. The purple writing was slightly raised.

Tina Mellekas
ExclusiveTravel
Old Hyde Park, Tampa, Florida

The travel agency's phone number and e-mail address were included at the bottom. Sam turned the card over and saw the script on the back. *She has beautiful handwriting.* She looked at Tina. *She has beautiful everything.*

They finished their drinks while they talked amicably about the concert and the fireworks display. Afterward, Tina escorted Sam to her car. "So, I'll see you next weekend."

"I'll be looking forward to it."

"Me, too."

"Thanks for going with me tonight."

"It was my pleasure, Samantha."

Sam backed out of the parking space and headed for the exit. *What is it about the way she says my name?* She looked in the rearview mirror and saw that Tina was still standing there, like the last time.

Tina watched the Toyota until it disappeared from sight, then returned to the lobby and approached the registration desk. "I'll be checking out tonight," she told the young man behind the counter. "Tina Mellekas. Room 510."

"Yes, ma'am." He typed the information into the computer.

Ma'am? Will I ever get used to hearing that? She touched the gray above her temple and pushed her hair behind her ear.

"Oh, you're with Exclusive Travel. It's all been taken care of. Let me get your receipt."

She signed the bill and took her copy. "Thank you."

"You're welcome. Hope you enjoyed your stay in Sarasota."

Tina went to her room and packed her belongings. *My back will appreciate it when I sleep in my own bed tonight.* She left the hotel, put her things in the car, and pulled out of the parking lot. At the stoplight a short distance up the road, she pondered which way to go. As a rule, Tina avoided Fruitville Road, even though it was the fastest way to the interstate. Her typical route went along Tamiami Trail to Longboat Key before turning east to get to the freeway. *Well, it's been a weekend of doing things I don't generally do.* She drove toward Fruitville Road.

~ * ~ * ~ * ~ * ~

Sam parked her SUV under the carport next to the garage. Taking the leftovers from the cooler, she bounded up the stairs to her apartment. *Tina's coming to the cookout. And I told her I'm gay and it doesn't matter. She's wonderful. I know I'm right about that.*

She put the food in the refrigerator and grabbed a beer. Sitting on the couch, she picked up the remote and clicked the television on. Most stations were carrying the news, and there was a blurb about the concert and fireworks on one of them. Sam watched the segment and then shut off the TV. She took a final sip of her beer, then rinsed out the can and put it in the recycle bin. After a quick shower, she was ready for bed. Drawing the covers up under her chin, her last thoughts before drifting off to sleep were of a dark-haired woman with beautiful blue eyes.

~ * ~ * ~ * ~ * ~

Tina set the cruise control for her trip north on I-75. As she handled the car with ease in the light traffic, she contemplated the events of the previous two days. *It's been quite a weekend. I went to the reunion…and the track. Drove on Fruitville Road. Made a new friend. Quite a weekend, indeed.*

The oldies station playing in the background caught her attention as she heard the opening strains of a Rascals song. She cranked up the stereo and tapped her fingers on the steering wheel along with the beat. *They just don't make music like this anymore.*

Tina exited the interstate, drove through the mostly deserted roads of South Tampa, and turned onto Bayshore Boulevard. Old-fashioned streetlamps illuminated the bay to the left and clusters of homes and condominiums to the right. At her building, she pulled into the underground garage and parked in her assigned space. The elevator took her to the fourth floor, where she strode down the hall to her condo, unlocked the door, and went inside. She wasted no time preparing for bed, and within ten minutes was sitting on the edge of her mattress, adjusting the settings on the control panel. *A little heat and massage should be ideal.* She carefully lay back and took deep breaths, concentrating on relaxing her body. The warmth and gentle massage had the desired effect. Her last thoughts before drifting off to sleep were of a fair-haired woman with beautiful green eyes.

Chapter 4

The next morning, Lisa and Mike were sitting at their kitchen table when Sam came in the door. "Happy Labor Day."

"Good morning," the couple replied together.

Sam went directly to the pot of coffee. She poured herself a cup and carried it over to join her sister and brother-in-law at the table. "What's up for today?"

"We were waiting for you because we thought we might have to make preparations for a cookout on Saturday," Lisa answered with a grin.

Sam's face brightened. "Yes, we're having a cookout."

"The Whitwell charm rules again!" Lisa slapped a high five with Sam.

Mike laid down the newspaper section he was reading. "Who's this new person you're interested in? Lisa said it's someone from the reunion?"

"Yes. The woman you met who was on the track team."

"The one you keep whispering about?"

Sam gave her sister a look. "Do you tell him *everything*?"

"He *thinks* I do." Lisa winked and took her mug to the coffeepot for a refill.

"Hey!" Mike folded his arms across his chest, acting disgruntled.

"Honey, you know I tell you all the important things." Lisa kissed her husband's cheek before resuming her seat.

"Uh-huh." Mike turned his attention back to Sam. "You were saying?"

"Her name is Tina. We went out last night and got along great. So, I asked her to come to a cookout next weekend and she said yes."

"You really like her?"

"Yes, I do."

Mike smiled at the assertive tone. "Does she feel the same way?"

"She doesn't know how I feel yet. I think she could use a friend right now, more than anything else."

"Why do you say that?" Lisa asked, curious about her former teammate.

"She seems so...lost," Sam said sadly. "I think it's all connected to that car accident and the death of her brother. Maybe I can help her with that."

"Sam to the rescue," Mike joked, attempting to lighten the mood.

"Sometimes that's all it takes — one person reaching out to another at the right time." Overwhelmed with emotion, Sam stopped talking.

Mike and Lisa looked at each other with concern. Lisa put her hand over her sister's. "Sam? Are you sure you're going to be okay?"

"Yes. It's very hard to explain, but I know I'm doing the right thing."

"If you say so. That's all I need to hear." Mike went to the sink and deposited his empty cup. "I'd better go get the yard in shipshape condition. I'll get the propane tank for the grill filled, too." He squeezed Sam's shoulder as he walked by. "I hope Tina realizes what a special woman you are."

"Thanks, Mike."

"No problem, sis." He grabbed his baseball cap from the hook near the door and went outside.

Lisa watched her sister get up for more coffee. *This time is different. I've never seen her so certain of what she wants. But of all people...Tina Mellekas?* "Tell me what happened last night."

Sam sat down, blowing on the hot liquid in her cup before taking a drink. "It went pretty well. I found out that she hurt her back in the accident. She lives in Tampa—"

"Tampa? That's only an hour away!"

"That's what *I* said. She works for a travel agency. She gave me her business card so I can e-mail her the details about the barbecue."

"So, you did learn a little about her then."

"Yes. I also told her I was gay. She seemed okay with it."

"Really? What did she say? Is she gay, too?"

"She didn't say much, just that it didn't matter to her. She didn't mention what her preference was."

"That's kind of an important thing to know, isn't it?"

"I guess so." Sam pulled the business card from the pocket of her shorts. "But for now, I think she needs a friend. There'll be time for all that other stuff later." *I hope.* "Isn't her card classy?" She handed it over.

"Wow. This must be some fancy outfit she works for. What does she do there?" Lisa looked at both sides of the card before giving it back.

"I'm not sure. We didn't get into that."

"Well, you already know more about her than anybody else. I'm sure you'll find out."

"I'm working on it. Can I use your computer to e-mail her? Are the kids using it?"

"Haven't you noticed how quiet it is? Marie's daughter came over early this morning and invited them to go swimming in their pool. So, the computer is all yours."

"Thanks. What time shall we say for the cookout?"

"How about around four o'clock?"

"Okay." Sam smiled at her sister as they both got up from the table. "Lisa?"

"Yeah?"

"We talked about you last night. How close you and I are. Maybe I don't say it enough, but...I love you." Sam set her cup down and hugged Lisa tightly. "You're the best sister anyone could ever have."

"I love you, too."

Sam took her coffee and walked down the hallway to the study.

Lisa wiped the tears from her eyes. *Tina Mellekas, if you hurt her, I'll find you and give you a piece of my mind the likes of which you have never heard.*

~ * ~ * ~ * ~ * ~

Tina jogged along Bayshore Boulevard, grateful for the breeze blowing in from Tampa Bay. There wasn't much traffic because of the holiday, but the sidewalk was crowded with walkers, joggers, Rollerbladers, and bicyclists. Tina nodded at the people she knew and received smiles, waves, and nods in return. Most of them exercised there often, and it didn't take long to be recognized and acknowledged by the regulars.

As she walked the last half mile or so to cool down her muscles, Tina thought about her day ahead. *I can finish my book while I do the laundry, and then maybe stop by work and the grocery store.* She went into her condo and did her usual stretching exercises. After getting a bottle of water from the refrigerator, she turned on her computer and waited for it to boot up. She picked up the picture of her and Steven that sat next to the monitor. *We look so happy. It seems like a lifetime ago.* The computer beeped, signaling it was ready, and Tina replaced the picture on the desk. She put on the spare pair of glasses she kept next to the keyboard, connected to the Internet, and pulled up her e-mail.

What's this? Oh, it must be Samantha. Tina clicked on the mail from SamIAm and smiled as she read the text.

> *Hi, Tina!*
> *I talked to Lisa and Mike this morning. The cookout is going to*

*be at 4:00. I'm really glad you're going to come. There will be
tons of food, so you'd better be hungry when you get here!*
See you Saturday,
Sam

P.S. Here are the directions...

Tina knew the area of Sarasota described in the directions, but
printed out the e-mail so she could refer to the left- and right-hand
turns once she got in the neighborhood. She quickly looked through the
rest of her mail, then shut down the computer. After filling the washer
with laundry, she started the machine and settled on the couch with a
book. *Only a couple of chapters to go...damn it!*

She got up from the couch and snatched her glasses from next to
the computer. *Next, I'll have to wear one of those little chains around my neck
with my glasses dangling at the end of it.* Tina frowned as she pictured that.
*Never. I'd rather live with forgetting them than wear them around my neck like
that.* Getting comfortable on the couch again, she opened the book.
Now, where was I?

The sound of the phone ringing woke Tina. The book lay on her
stomach and her glasses were in her left hand. She sat up and reached
for the phone on the end table. "Hello?"

"Tina, it's Vivian. How was your trip?"

"Fine."

"I was going to stop by the office in a little while. Would you like
to meet me at the Cactus Club for lunch?"

Tina rubbed the sleep out of her eyes and looked at the clock.
"Sure. What time?"

"Let's say one. Is that good for you?"

"Yes. I'll see you then."

"All right. Can't wait to hear about the reunion."

"I'll bet you can't. See you at one. Bye."

"Bye."

Tina hung up the phone and stretched. *Hmm, my back feels much
improved today.* She transferred her clothes from the washer to the dryer
and went into the bathroom to get ready for her lunch engagement.

~ * ~ * ~ * ~ * ~

Vivian Karanicholas walked into the Cactus Club. Immediately
catching sight of her tall, dark-haired employee in a booth, she joined
her. "Hi. How are you?"

"I'm fine, thanks."

"I booked your hotel reservations through today. You came home early? Did you even go to the reunion?"

Tina looked fondly at the older woman. *She worries about me like I'm her own daughter.* "I returned last night. I needed to sleep in my own bed."

"Oh? Your back was bothering you?"

"It's okay now. It was just spasms. I must've spent too much time on the ground."

"On the ground? You'd better tell me all about this." *Something good happened. I can see it in her eyes.* "Come on, start talking."

While they ate their meal, Tina recounted the events of the weekend. The reticent employee tended to give only the bare facts when telling a story and even more so if it was about herself, but Vivian had learned over the years how to coax more information from her. She was proud that Tina had gone to the track and the reunion. She knew how difficult it must have been. And when Tina spoke of this new friend Samantha, her voice took on a different tone. *She likes this woman. No doubt about it.* "So, you're going to Sarasota again this weekend?"

"Yes, on Saturday."

"Well, this must be important if you're going to miss the Florida State game."

"I can see the first half before I have to leave."

Vivian smiled knowingly. *She hasn't missed seeing one second of those football games since I don't know when.* "I'm happy you're going. You need to spend more time with friends."

"Yeah, well, we'll see."

"Sometimes it's best not to question things so much. Samantha wouldn't have invited you if she didn't want to be friends. Maybe it's finally time for you to start living again, eh?"

Tina listened attentively to Vivian's advice. They had worked together for nearly ten years and her boss knew her better than anyone. "Maybe."

"Good." Vivian grabbed the check. "And don't you dare come to the office today. I don't expect to see you until tomorrow, got it?"

Tina tried to get the bill, but knew it was useless. It had long ago been established that when Mrs. Karanicholas made a decision, nobody could talk her out of it. "All right. No work today."

The waiter collected the payment and the women left, walking to the parking garage together. Their cars were side by side and both vehicles chirped as the alarms were deactivated.

"Tina?"

"Yes?"

"I'm glad you made a new friend. You deserve some happiness in your life."

"Thanks, Viv." Tina watched her boss get in her car and drive off. *Happiness? I don't know if that's possible.*

~ * ~ * ~ * ~ * ~

Vivian pulled into a parking space in front of Exclusive Travel. *So much has changed since I hired Tina, and all for the better, too.* She entered the building, locked the door behind her, and turned on the lights. She went to her office, sank into her chair, and looked at the stack of files she'd planned to tackle. However, her lunch conversation with Tina caused her thoughts to drift back to the first time they'd met.

One Sunday morning in the fall of 1989, Vivian was catching up on some work at the agency when she heard a knock at the door. A young lady was standing there pointing at the Help Wanted sign posted in the window. She gave Vivian a questioning look through the glass. The owner opened the door and let her in. "You're interested in the position?"

"Yes." The woman moved slowly, as if she were injured.

Vivian sat down and indicated that the applicant should sit across from her. "Are you all right?"

"Yes. I'm fine. I hurt my back in a car accident." Tina sat gingerly in the chair. "It's healing steadily, though."

"Have you had any experience in the travel business?"

"No."

"Tell me a little about yourself."

"My name is Tina Mellekas. I graduated from Florida State University with a degree in business. I've been working at a large accounting firm in Sarasota for about eight years. I resigned after the accident. I need a change."

"The opening I have is for an office manager."

"Okay."

Vivian smiled, finding the woman and her brief responses refreshing. The only people who had applied up to that point were underqualified and talked non-stop, trying to convince her that they could do the job. This one was very different. "I think you're overqualified for the position. I couldn't possibly pay you what a person with your degree and experience would warrant." Vivian waved her arm at the office's cramped quarters. "This is a small business."

"If you want me, I'll take the job. Pay me whatever salary you've put aside for it. I have two conditions, though."

"Conditions?"

"I want to travel...a lot. And no power suits. I want to wear casual clothes."

"That's it?"

"Yes."

Vivian was skilled at reading people and she had a good feeling about Tina Mellekas. She decided to follow her intuition. "All right. When can you start?"

"How about tomorrow? I'll bring my résumé so you can make the necessary calls to verify my information."

"Sounds good." Vivian stood and extended her hand. "I'm very happy to have you here at Exclusive Travel."

Tina slowly got up from the chair and shook her new boss's hand. "You won't regret it. I promise."

And I never have. Vivian took the top file off the stack and got to work.

Chapter 5

"You're not going to use paper plates, are you?"

Lisa was losing patience with her younger sister. "It's a cookout. We're *supposed* to use paper plates."

"But we're having company. We should provide real dishes and utensils for our guest."

Lisa put her arm around Sam's shoulders. "Let's sit down for a minute and you can tell me what's wrong."

They sat at the kitchen table.

"I...I'm so nervous about this." Sam spoke softly. "I want Tina to like us, to like me."

"How could anybody *not* like you? I promise we'll be on our best behavior. Let's see." Lisa started counting off on her fingers. "You said no talking about her brother, the accident, her past, anything concerning sexual orientation, nothing about your old girlfriends — especially tattooed drummers. Geez, I don't know what we *will* talk about."

That got a laugh from Sam. "Have I been that bad?"

"Yes. You've been telling us what to say and not say all week. I know this is important to you, but you should just be yourself. I'm sure Tina will have a great time. How can she not, with all the Whitwell charm around here?"

"I'm sorry. I didn't mean to drive you and Mike crazy."

"We'll be fine. It's you who needs to chill out. Okay?"

"Okay, but Lisa?"

"Yes?"

"We can use the real plates, right?"

"Yes." Lisa rolled her eyes. "Far be it from me to ruin the entire evening by using paper plates."

~ * ~ * ~ * ~ * ~

Everything was going according to schedule and Sam was pleased. The table was set and the chicken was ready to put on the grill. The boys were playing in the yard while Lisa, Mike, and Sam were sitting on the screened-in patio waiting for Tina to arrive.

"Auntie Sam!" Aaron yelled. "Your friend is here!" Both children ran toward the driveway.

"Aaron, Josh, wait!" Sam opened the door and hurried after them.

Mike looked at his wife. "This is going to be interesting."

"That's the understatement of the year."

The brothers stopped short when they saw the vehicle that had pulled into the driveway. "What a cool car!" Aaron exclaimed.

"Yes, it is," Sam agreed as she caught up to them. They all stared at the BMW 323 sedan, painted a metallic silver-gray that shimmered in the sunlight.

The door opened and Tina stepped out of the car. She was wearing a white Florida State tee shirt and jean shorts. Her hair hung loosely on her shoulders. She smiled at Sam. "Hi."

"Hi." Sam returned the smile. "These are my nephews, Aaron and Josh."

The boys shook hands with Tina. "Nice to meet you, ma'am," Aaron said.

Here we go again with the ma'am. "It's nice to meet you, too."

Aaron and Joshua ran back into the yard.

"Um...I didn't know what to bring," Tina said as she reached into the car, got a plastic grocery bag, and handed it to Sam. "I figured I couldn't go wrong with these."

Sam looked in the bag. "Ring Dings? No. You can't go wrong with these." *This is going to be all right.* "Thank you."

"You're welcome." Tina shut the BMW's door and set the alarm.

"That's quite a car. The travel business must be doing well."

"It belongs to the company." Tina shrugged. "You have to have a certain image when you're in a business. Vivian, my boss, wanted me to drive a decent car. So, she told me to go out and find one I liked." She glanced at the vehicle with affection. "I liked this one."

It fits you — sleek, classy. "I like it, too. Maybe we can go for a ride later?"

"Sure."

Sam led the way to the patio. "Lisa, Mike, you remember Tina."

"Yes, of course we do," Lisa replied as handshakes were traded.

Tina looked at Mike's University of Florida tee shirt. "A Gator fan?"

"I graduated from there." Mike pointed at Tina's shirt. "You went to FSU?"

"Now, now," Lisa interrupted. "Before you two argue about which school is better, let's get that chicken on the grill."

Mike started the barbecuing chores while Sam and Lisa began putting out the cold foods. They wouldn't let Tina help, so she sat on the patio watching the boys kick a soccer ball back and forth in the yard. The older child, Aaron, had the more outgoing personality. With light hair, lanky body and hazel eyes, he resembled his mom. The younger, quieter boy favored his father, with dark brown hair, a stockier build, and brown eyes.

"Aaron, come here, please," Lisa called to her son.

Aaron ran through the patio to the kitchen. "Yeah?"

"Didn't I ask you to put Beethoven in Sam's yard?"

"Sorry, Mom. I forgot. He's still in my room."

"We can't leave him cooped up in there all night. Take him out the front door and make sure you latch the gate."

"Okay." Aaron ran up the stairs.

Lisa closed her eyes as she heard the thundering footfalls on the steps. "Can't that child ever *walk*?"

Sam laughed. "I don't think so."

Seeing that Joshua had no one to play with, Tina went into the yard and kicked the ball with him. *Hmm...this is what I thought I'd be doing when I reached this age: a house, a husband, a family, some kids. Isn't that what most women imagine is in their future? Somehow, it hasn't turned out that way for me. I tried that route. The high-powered job...fiancé...everything going as it should, except...I felt like a stranger in my own life. I just didn't fit in that mold. Then, the accident, and my life really fell apart. Now, I find myself plunked right in the middle of the all-American family. The only thing we need here is a dog and we could be in a Norman Rockwell print.*

"Beethoven!"

Tina's head whipped around as she looked for the source of the scream. *Whoever that is...needs help.* She ran in the direction of the driveway just as a large golden retriever came charging around the corner of the house. "Oof. " As Tina hit the ground, the air was knocked out of her . *Well, there's the dog.* She shielded her face with her hands as the animal licked her ears and neck. *Egad, that tickles!*

Aaron tried to get hold of the dog's collar. "Help!"

Sam came running from the house and almost crashed into Mike, who was moving across the yard toward the commotion. She saw her friend on the ground with Beethoven standing above her. "Tina! Oh my goodness!" She rushed over and pulled the pet away. "Are you all right?"

Tina was laughing as she sat up. "I'm fine. I'd been wondering if y'all had a dog. I see that indeed you do."

Mike got control of the animal. "Come on, Aaron. Let's get him in the yard."

"Okay, Dad."

Sam reached out her hand to Tina. "I seem to be making a habit of this. May I help you up?"

The woman who never liked to admit she needed or wanted help from anyone looked into sparkling green eyes and found it very easy to say, "Yes."

~ * ~ * ~ * ~ * ~

Shortly thereafter, dinner was ready and everyone took a seat at the patio table.

"Just dig in and take some of whatever you'd like," Lisa told Tina as bowls and platters of food were passed around and everyone filled their plates.

"Samantha was right," Tina said after tasting her chicken. "This is fabulous, Lisa."

"Thanks. It's an old family recipe."

The dinner conversation stayed within Sam's previously set boundaries and Lisa noticed that her sister seemed to be relaxing as the meal progressed.

Mike and Tina talked about college football, and Sam was amazed at how animated the dark-haired woman got during the discussion. *She can talk a lot when it's something she's interested in.*

"Well, FSU is ranked number one in the nation right now. It's just not your year, Mike," Tina ribbed.

"The season's just started. We'll see."

"Aaron, stop it!" Joshua yelled, causing all attention at the table to focus on the two boys. They had been pushing at each other and they stopped suddenly when they realized everyone was watching them.

"Brothers can be such a pain," Aaron said with contempt.

Sam looked at Lisa, hoping she would intervene quickly.

Tina shocked everyone by speaking next. "I know it may be hard to believe right now, but someday you'll be very thankful you have a little brother."

A long moment of silence followed, during which Aaron looked skeptical and Joshua beamed.

Sam cleared her throat. "Perhaps a change of subject is in order?"

"Good idea," Lisa concurred.

"Tina?" Joshua asked.

"Yes?"

"Do you have a tattoo?"

There was a loud *CLANK* as Sam dropped her fork on her plate. That startled Tina and she knocked over her water. Mike choked on the sip of beer he had just taken, and Lisa began slapping him on the back.

Dinner was over.

Chapter 6

Tina rinsed the last dish and gave it to Sam. "Here you go."

Sam placed the plate in the dishwasher, added the detergent, and switched on the machine. "All done." She grinned at Tina. "Would you like some coffee?"

"If you have decaf, sure."

"I think we do." Sam went to the patio doorway. "Sis, do we have decaf for the coffeemaker?"

Lisa came into the kitchen. "Yeah, I'll make some."

"Auntie Sam?" Aaron hollered from upstairs.

Sam walked to the bottom of the stairway so she didn't have to shout. "Yes?"

"Will you show me that new chord on the guitar again? I forget how to do it."

Sam looked down the hallway at her sister and Tina. "Would you excuse me? It'll only take a minute."

"Sure," Tina answered.

"Go ahead," Lisa added. "I'll get the coffee started."

Sam went upstairs.

Lisa filled the pot with water and poured it into the coffeemaker. "I'm sorry about your brother. I know you were very close."

Tina was taken by surprise at the mention of Steven. "Oh...yes, we were. Thanks." *What's this all about?*

"Then you must know how I feel about Sam." Lisa faced Tina, moved a step nearer, and stared into her eyes.

Uh-oh. Protective sister. Well, that's something I understand completely. "Yes, I do."

"Sam likes you. I'm not sure what it is, but she thinks you two are meant to be friends."

Resisting the inclination to break the eye contact and close proximity, Tina stood her ground and waited for Lisa to continue.

"I don't want to see her get hurt."

"I see," Tina said impassively. "And you think I'll hurt her."

"Maybe not intentionally, but Sam wears her heart on her sleeve.

I'm just asking you to be careful." Lisa's voice trembled with emotion. "I love my sister very much." She turned back to the counter to finish preparing the coffee.

Tina took a deep breath while trying to figure out what to say. *Honesty is usually the best policy, T.* "Samantha is fortunate to have a family that cares about her so deeply. Why she wants to be friends with me is beyond my comprehension. I can only promise to try my best to be the kind of person that deserves her friendship."

Lisa was impressed with the truthful nature of the response. "I guess I can't ask for more than that, can I? Why don't you go relax in the family room? I'll bring the coffee when it's ready."

Relieved to escape any further conversation, Tina wandered into the room that Lisa had pointed out. There was a pair of chairs next to a brick fireplace, a large couch, a television set, and against the far wall, an old upright piano. She walked over and sat on the bench. With one finger she struck the keys.

Plink, plink, plink...plink, plink, plink, plink, plink, plink...plink, plink, plink.

As Sam came down the stairs, she heard someone playing the piano. *"Heart and Soul"?* She peeked into the room and saw Tina sitting at the keyboard. "It takes two to play that song. May I join you?"

Tina slid over on the bench.

Sam sat next to her. "I'll play the chords, okay?"

"Okay."

She played the chord sequence once before Tina jumped in with the melody. After they went through the tune several times, Sam sped up the tempo and her guest concentrated on keeping up. Faster and faster they played, until they broke into laughter and collapsed against each other.

Happy that the evening seemed to be going so well, Sam asked, "May I play something for you?"

"If you want to, yes." Tina started to get up.

"No. Please. Stay right here. I'm not much of a singer, so bear with me." Hesitantly, Sam began to sing.

~ * ~ * ~ * ~ * ~

Mike entered the empty the kitchen and wondered where everyone had gone. "Lisa?"

His wife came into view, making a shushing motion at him from the hallway. "Come here," she whispered.

"Now you're whispering, too?" Mike teased. "What is it about Tina that—"

"Hush!" Lisa took him by the hand and pulled him down the hall, stopping near the doorway of the family room. "Listen."

Mike heard his sister-in-law singing softly. He nodded his head in approval. "'You've Got A Friend.' Good choice."

Lisa pointed toward the kitchen and they tiptoed away.

~ * ~ * ~ * ~ * ~

Sam played the final notes of the song and, not sure what to do next, mutely stared down at the keyboard.

Tina couldn't speak.

The ticking of the wall clock was the only audible sound until Lisa strode in with a tray and set it on the table in front of the couch. "How about some coffee?"

"That sounds great." Sam moved over to the sofa. "Thanks for making it." She took a cup and sipped from it.

"No problem." Lisa sat down. She glanced at Tina, then gave her sister a questioning look.

Sam shook her head to indicate they should give their guest some space. "Where's Mike?"

"He took Beethoven for a walk. He should be back in a little while."

Silence settled over the group. Finally, Tina swung her legs around the end of the bench so she was facing the other women.

"Hey," Sam said gently, "would you like a cup of coffee?"

"Thanks." Tina took a cup from the tray and sat in one of the chairs.

Suddenly, an uproar came from upstairs. The boys were arguing about something. A loud crash prompted Lisa to get up. "Excuse me. I'd better go check on what they're doing." She hastily left the room.

"Tina?" Sam's voice was tentative.

"Yeah?"

"Are you okay?" Sam was worried that perhaps she had gone too far by singing the song. *I have to slow down; she wasn't ready for that.* "I'm sorry. I shouldn't have sung to you. Sometimes my emotions get the better of me."

"You didn't do anything wrong. It's just that...no one has ever done that...for me."

"Lots of times a song can say something better than plain words. I just wanted you to know how wonderful I think you are, and how much I want to be your friend."

"Why?"

"Why what?"

"Why me?"

Sam went over and knelt next to Tina's chair. "Because in my heart, I know you're a good person. Maybe, if we're friends, I can get you to believe it, too."

"Samantha, I...I...don't..."

"Shh." She had to use every ounce of her self-control not to reach out and touch Tina's face. "For now, let's just leave it at that. Okay?"

Tina nodded.

Sam stood, removed Tina's cup from her hand, and placed it on the tray. "C'mon. I want to show you my apartment. And then, someone promised me a ride in a snazzy car." She took hold of Tina's hands to help her from the chair. Smiling, she said, "Some habits are nice, aren't they?"

Tina looked at her hands resting in Sam's. "Yes." *Very nice.*

After leading the way up the stairs to her apartment, Sam unlocked the door and flipped the light on. Ambient lighting cast a soft glow around a large room that comprised most of the living area. Several framed prints decorated the pale green walls. There was an overstuffed, very comfortable looking couch and matching chair. Light oak furniture was tastefully arranged throughout the room. Beige carpeting and colorful throw rugs covered the floor. It was a warm, homey kind of place, and Sam was proud of it.

"It was a mess when I first got here; there was so much that had to be done. I fixed it up myself, a little at a time. I did all the painting and picked out the furnishings."

Tina could envision the blonde spending hours and hours getting the place just right. *And she has.* "You did a good job."

"Let me show you the rest." Sam took Tina to the small kitchen. It was a bright, cheery room with a table and chairs tucked in one corner. "I cleaned because you were coming. It normally doesn't look this good," she confessed. "I'm not the best housekeeper that ever lived."

"Well, it looks great."

"Thanks." Sam walked across the hall and turned on the light. "This is my bedroom."

Tina stood in the doorway and looked in. A small lamp on each side of the bed provided the only lighting. The wall behind the headboard was a pale pink, which picked up the same color in the design on the comforter and drapes. There was plenty of space for the typical bedroom furniture, plus an old-fashioned rocking chair and a desk.

"The bathroom is there," Sam said, pointing to a doorway next to the desk. "But my favorite thing about this whole place is the balcony." She pulled the drapes aside to reveal a set of French doors, which she opened. "Come and see it."

Tina crossed the room and joined Sam on the small screened-in balcony. A couple of lounge chairs with thick cushions almost filled the space.

"I sit out here a lot and watch the sunset." Sam gestured in front of them. "You can see the roofs of the houses for a long way, but after that there are groves of trees and the sun sets right behind them. You can't tell now because it's too dark."

"Maybe another time, then."

"I'd really like that." *How about every night for the rest of our lives?* "So, am I going to get a ride in that car of yours?" Sam asked as they went inside. She locked the French doors and closed the drapes. "Are you going to keep your promise?"

"Of course. Where would you like to go?"

"I think it's time for some ice cream. Don't you?"

"Ice cream?" Tina asked. *I can't remember the last time I had ice cream.*

"Yes. We can go to St. Armand's Circle. They have an awesome ice cream shop there."

"All right. Ice cream it is."

"Let me use the bathroom. I'll be ready in a minute. Okay?"

"Sure." Tina strolled into the living room to wait. She went to the large oak bookcase that filled most of one wall. The three lower shelves were full of books, but the upper shelves and the top were taken up by photographs. There were baby pictures, family pictures, pictures of what must have been friends, pictures of Beethoven in all stages of growth, and pictures of a gray striped cat. *Wonder where the cat is?* Next to the bookcase hung a small poster of an acoustic guitar. There was some writing describing the instrument and Tina tried to focus on the small print to see what it said.

Sam came up behind Tina. "Do you like it?"

"What is it?"

"It's my dream guitar. Someday, I hope to have the real thing. Right now, I can only afford the poster." She grabbed her keys from the table by the door. "Are you ready?"

"Yeah. Let's go."

As the women descended the stairs, they saw Mike in the driveway with Beethoven.

"Mike." Sam smiled at her brother-in-law. "How was your walk?"

"Pretty good. He's been doing much better at staying by my side lately."

As if in agreement, Beethoven barked and wagged his tail. Tina bent down and petted the dog.

Lisa, having heard the barking, came outside.

"Guess what?" Sam said enthusiastically. "We're going for ice cream."

"Really?" Lisa smirked at her sister. "What a surprise — ice cream."

Sam smirked back and everyone laughed.

Tina thanked the couple for dinner and they exchanged good-byes.

"Ready?" Sam hurried around to the passenger side of the vehicle.

"Yeah." Tina deactivated the alarm and they got in the car.

"This is awesome," the blonde said as she sank into the leather seat.

"Glad you like it." Tina started the engine and pulled out of the driveway. "You have a nice family."

"Yes. I'm very lucky." Sam half turned in her seat so she could see Tina's profile. "I'm sorry the boys got a little rowdy. They go through times when they get along great and other times when they're at each other's throats."

"Sounds like typical siblings. What was that about a tattoo, anyway? Why would they think I have one?"

"Oh. Um..." Sam was glad Tina had to keep her eyes on the road so she couldn't see her blushing. "I once dated a woman who had a rather prominent tattoo, and I don't think I'll ever hear the end of it."

Tina laughed. *A tattoo?* She glanced at Sam and noted her flushed cheeks. "I'm sorry. It's just kind of hard to imagine you...I mean, not that there's anything wrong with tattoos."

"It was a long time ago." *Let's get off this topic.* "So, when did you get this car?"

That must be a sore subject. "I guess I've had it for about a year now."

"And you could have picked any kind you wanted?"

"Yes."

"That must be a cool boss you have."

"Yes, she is." Tina turned into a parking spot. "Here we are."

They got out of the BMW and mixed with the crowd of people walking along the sidewalks of St. Armand's shopping area.

"This is the place." Sam opened the door to the ice cream shop. "I'm going to get a chocolate fudge brownie cone," she announced as they went over to the service counter. "What do you want?"

"Hmm..." Tina studied the large sign that listed the many flavors available. "I think a cup of vanilla no-fat yogurt."

"You must be kidding."

"What do you mean?"

"You come to a fantastic ice cream store like this and get no-fat yogurt?"

"Well, they sell it here, don't they? I'm sure it's very good." Tina smiled at the clerk who was listening to their conversation, impatiently waiting to take their order. "You get what you want and I'll get what I want. Then, we'll both be happy," Tina reasoned. "Go ahead and order."

They got their confections and went outside to sit at a table, where they enjoyed their dessert in companionable silence as they watched the people walk by.

Sam finished her cone. "Thanks. You really didn't have to pay for mine."

"No problem. After all, you invited me to dinner." Tina got up and threw her cup and napkin away.

And I'm very glad you accepted. Sam added her napkin to the trash.

They went back to the car and Tina drove toward Sam's house. The radio was on and the musician began softly singing along with the song that was playing.

"You really do have a good voice."

"What?" Sam hadn't even realized she'd been singing. "No, not really."

"Well, I think you do."

"Thanks." *She likes my singing!* "I have to sing a couple of songs in the band, but it's not my favorite thing to do."

"Why not?"

"I love being in Lisa's band, but as part of the ensemble creating the overall sound. I don't particularly like being the lead singer, the center of attention."

Tina nodded in understanding. *A bit of shyness. I can see that.*

"Even after all these years, I still get nervous when I have to sing."

"But you sang for me and you didn't have to."

"Sometimes there are reasons to do things that are more important than your own fears. I wanted...needed...to sing that for you." Sam's voice took on a tone of uncertainty. "I'm not sure I'm explaining this very well."

"It's okay. I understand what you're saying." *Your singing that song means even more to me now. What am I going to do with you?* Tina pulled into the driveway. "Well, here you are, home safe and sound."

Sam unfastened her seat belt. "Thanks for the ride. This is an exquisite car."

Tina cleared her throat. "Um...what are you doing next weekend?" She looked out the windshield. "Would you like to go to the Bucs game?"

"I'd love to go, but it's sold out. In fact, the whole season is sold out; we wouldn't be able to get tickets."

"I already have tickets. So, if you want to go—"

"Yes, I want to go!"

"All right, I'll e-mail you the directions to my place and we'll go to the game from there. Okay?"

"Okay." Sam was grinning from ear to ear. *She wants me to come to Tampa. This is real progress.* When she opened the car door, the interior light came on and she looked at Tina one last time before leaving. "Good night."

"Good night, Samantha."

Sam closed the door and watched as Tina backed out onto the street. She walked to the end of the driveway and waved as the car drove away, just in case Tina was looking in the rearview mirror. She was.

Chapter 7

Samantha held the directions against the steering wheel as she slowly made her way down Bayshore Boulevard. On her right were several condominium complexes in a row. *Let's see, I passed Howard Avenue, now I go for a few blocks and I should see a high-rise. There it is. Next should be Tina's building.* Sam saw a small sign at a driveway indicating parking for Bayshore Palms. She turned in and drove to the gate at the entrance of the underground parking garage. There was a metal box with a numbered keypad to her left, and she lowered her window to press in the code Tina had given her. She could hear a phone ringing.

"Hello?"

"Hi. It's Sam."

"Come on up."

The gate lifted and Sam pulled into the garage. She saw Tina's BMW and parked in the empty space next to it. At the elevator, she pressed the button for the fourth floor. *I'm feeling very nervous about this. I wonder if Tina felt the same way when she came to the cookout.* She had no more time to think about it, as the elevator stopped and the doors opened.

Tina was standing there to greet her. "Hi there. Nice shirt."

"You, too."

Both women were wearing white Buccaneer football jerseys. Sam's shirt had a large number 40 on it, and Tina's had the number 28.

Sam followed Tina down the hallway to the condo. A small foyer led to a large room, and Sam looked around at the combined living/dining area. The floor was a deep gray ceramic tile, with area rugs in both the dining and living rooms. Beyond a half counter that separated it from the rest of the space, she could see the kitchen. There was minimal furniture, though what was there appeared to be expensive. A few pictures hung on the walls, one of which was positioned over a gas fireplace. Huge sliding glass doors provided a view of Tampa Bay. The place was open and airy and beautiful. *Wow.* "Are you rich?" Sam wondered aloud.

Tina laughed. "No." *Not in the same ways that you are.*

"Don't tell me," Sam joked. "Your boss told you to find a place —

any place you wanted — and you picked this."

Tina shrugged her shoulders. "Actually, yes."

Sam stared at Tina in disbelief. *I have got to meet this boss.*

"Would you like to see the rest of it?"

"Of course I would." She tagged along behind Tina as she moved into the kitchen.

"This is the kitchen. It has a little laundry room and half bath over there." Tina pointed to the doors at one end of the room. "And..." turning and heading back toward the living room, she continued, "...the dining room and living room. You already saw those."

Sam was trying to keep up with Tina's long strides. *She'd never make it as a real estate agent, that's for sure. This is the fastest tour in the history of the world.*

"There are a couple of bedrooms." Tina went down the hall and into a room to her right. "This one is mine."

Sam walked into the room. The furniture was teak with black accents. There were floor lamps situated in two of the corners and a fan hung from the center of the ceiling. Plush gray carpet covered the floor. There was a door Sam assumed led to the bathroom and another set of sliding glass doors that overlooked Tampa Bay. *I love it.* "The view is fantastic!" Sam said looking out at the water. "And you have a balcony, too."

"Yes. But, sorry to say, no sunsets." Tina came and stood next to her guest. "We get the sunrise view here."

"Really? I don't think I've ever seen a sunrise. You know — musicians; we aren't early risers." Sam turned and saw a remote control on the bedside table, which she picked up. "You have a television in here?"

"No. That's for the bed." Tina took the remote from Sam's hand and pressed a button. The head of the bed inclined.

"That's so cool! Just like the commercials on TV."

"It's for my back. It's really helped."

"Oh." Sam's voice became somber. "Then I'm very glad you have it."

Tina set down the remote and led the way across the hall. "I use this bedroom for a study."

The women entered the room. The entire wall directly in front of Sam was a series of built-in shelves that were full of books. She couldn't begin to guess how many there were. "You really like to read, huh?"

"Yes, but nothing terribly intellectual, I'm afraid. Mostly mysteries — Patricia Cornwell, John Grisham, things like that."

"I like to read, too. I don't think I've read this many books, though." Sam turned and looked at the large computer desk that took up most of another wall. On the desk there was all sorts of computer equipment, a phone, a framed photograph, and a pair of glasses. *Glasses?* She directed her attention to the only family photo she had seen in the condo. It was Tina and Steven. The siblings had their arms around each other and they were smiling broadly for the camera. Sam suddenly found herself speechless as the enormity of Tina's loss hit her. *I'll never really be able to understand what she's been through.*

"He was a good-looking kid, wasn't he?" Tina asked softly.

Sam nodded. *Just like his sister.* She impulsively reached out and hugged Tina.

Unprepared for the contact, Tina stiffened as Sam threw her arms around her. Then, welcoming the genuine compassion, she relaxed into the softness of the younger woman and hugged her back.

Sam sniffled into Tina's shirt. "I'm so sorry he died."

"Me, too."

They remained like that for a moment, until Tina broke the embrace and looked down at Sam. "So, you ready to go root for the home team?"

"Yeah!"

"All right. I'll drive. Okay?"

"Okay."

~ * ~ * ~ * ~ * ~

They had a blast at the football game. Sam had not been to the new stadium, so Tina showed her around and took her for a close-up look at the gigantic pirate ship that rested at one end of the field. During the game, number 28, a graduate of Florida State, made several long runs and Tina cheered wildly. Number 40, a big running back and Sam's favorite player, ran for a touchdown. Bedlam ensued as cannon shots were fired from the pirate ship and train whistles blew to indicate the "A Train" had scored. The Bucs won, and it was a happy crowd that filed out the exits after the game.

Sam smiled up at Tina as they walked toward the car. "That was fun. Thanks so much for inviting me."

"You're welcome. Thanks for coming with me. I had fun, too."

"And *my* guy scored a touchdown," Sam bragged.

"Only 'cause *my* guy ran the ball close enough to the goal line in the first place."

"Uh-huh." Sam strutted ahead of Tina. "And *my* guy is cute."

"Is that so?" *Not as cute as you.*

Sam chuckled. "Well, for a guy, anyway."

"I'll agree with you there." Tina switched off the alarm and the women got in the car. She turned the air conditioner on high as she backed out of the space and became part of the traffic jam trying to leave the parking lot.

"That AC sure feels good," Sam commented. It had been a warm day, and both of them had rosy cheeks from their hours in the sun.

"Yes. It does. Do you want to grab something to eat on the way back to my place? We can go to a drive-through or we can stop somewhere."

"How about just a drive-through? What do you feel like having?"

A prolonged discussion began, during which they tried to think of somewhere that Tina could get a decent salad and Sam could get a burger and fries. Eventually, they decided to stop at two different places so each of them could get what they wanted. They were almost to Tina's place when a Rascals song came on the radio.

"Do you mind if I turn the radio up?" Tina asked.

"Go ahead. I love this song. As a matter of fact, I sing it with the band."

Both women sang along, and by the end of the tune, they were belting out the lyrics.

Tina lowered the radio's volume. "We sound pretty good together."

"I think so, too." *Anything having to do with us together sounds good to me.*

"The Rascals are my favorite sixties group. This station plays their songs all the time. They must have a disc jockey who likes them a lot."

"Really? The Rascals are my favorite, too." Sam smiled. *We may not agree on food selection, but at least we like the same music.* "What Rascals song do you like the best?"

"Hmm. I like most of them. I guess the one we just heard, 'Good Lovin',' might be my favorite. What about you?"

"Mine is one you don't hear very often. 'Mickey's Monkey.'"

Tina turned into the driveway of her condominium complex. "I think I have that on one of my albums." She pressed a remote that was clipped to the visor and the gate of the parking garage opened.

"You have *albums*?"

"Well, yeah." *Why do I suddenly feel like I'm from the Stone Age?* Tina pulled the BMW into her space.

Sam caught the change in the older woman's demeanor. *Got to watch that age thing; she's sensitive about that.* "Cool. Will you show them to me?"

"Sure, if you want."

"I'd love to see them."

They gathered the food bags and took them up to the condo. They ate at the dining-room table, rehashed the game, and razzed each other again about whose player was best.

"Let me see if I have that record," Tina said after they had finished their dinner. She went to the entertainment center and sat on the floor. Opening a set of double doors at the bottom, she searched for the album.

Sam went over and sat next to her. "You have lots of records."

"Well, these are mine...and Steven's." Tina selected one of the albums. "This is it, I think."

The cover showed four long-haired young men in matching blue shirts with large rounded collars and little ties. Sam burst out laughing. "It's hard to believe we thought that was cool, isn't it?"

"Yeah." Tina looked at the back of the cover to see if the song was listed. She was thankful that the titles were in dark print and she could read them by moving her arm slightly. "There it is. 'Mickey's Monkey.' Want to hear it?"

Sam caught herself before she voiced her surprise that Tina had a record player. *She has records; makes sense to have a turntable, too.* "Sure. I haven't heard it in a long time."

Tina opened a glass door in the entertainment center and pulled out a shelf that held a turntable. She put the record on and adjusted the controls, then returned to her spot next to Sam. "I haven't heard it in a long time either."

The song started and both women sat with heads bobbing and their hands tapping their knees. The song had an infectious beat and it was impossible to sit still. It didn't take long for Sam to get up and start dancing.

Tina stood to increase the volume on the stereo. As the pulsating sound filled the room, she leaned against the wall and watched her friend. She was thoroughly amused by Sam's uninhibited joy in the music. *I could never dance around the room like that. And in front of somebody else? Never!*

Sam went over and grabbed Tina's hands. "C'mon, dance with me."

Tina shook her head. "Me? Absolutely not. No...no."

Sam dragged her to the center of the room and Tina grudgingly swayed a little to the music.

"C'mon." *Let yourself go a little bit.* Sam smiled at the woman to encourage her. *You can do it.*

The vocals started again and Sam sang along.

In spite of herself, Tina sang, too.

Sam did the Monkey, the Twist, the Mashed Potato, and the Swim. Tina couldn't restrain herself any longer. She did the Monkey.

The women laughed and danced during the instrumental interlude. Then, the music changed abruptly as the other instruments dropped out and only the drums and bass guitar played for several measures. The pair stopped dancing as they became aware of someone pounding on the door. Tina turned off the stereo and hurried over to answer it. "What?" she practically shouted as she pulled open the door. Tina lowered her voice as she recognized her neighbor. "Mrs. Burns. What is it?"

Mrs. Burns looked at Tina's flushed face. She peered inside the condo and saw a guest standing in the middle of the living room — a guest who seemed to be somewhat short of breath. "Nothing, dear. I was just making sure everything is all right. I heard a lot of noise over here."

"Everything is fine, Mrs. Burns. Thank you for your concern." Tina shut the door and leaned against it.

Both women burst out laughing.

"I'm sorry." Sam tried to compose herself. "I didn't mean for you to get in trouble."

Tina waved off the apology. "No problem." *This ought to be the source of some interesting discussion at the next condo board meeting.*

"Well, I guess I should be going." Sam walked toward the door. She stopped and looked up at Tina, who was still standing against it. *But I don't want to go.*

"Do you need directions?"

"It's all right. I remember how to get back to I-75. After that, it's easy."

"Be careful, okay?"

"I will."

"I'll walk you to your car." Tina opened the door and strolled down the hallway with Sam. "Can't have anything happening to you, now, can we?"

"I appreciate your concern." *I do feel protected when I'm with you. No doubt about that.* "I had a really great time today."

"I did, too." Tina pressed the call button and the elevator arrived quickly.

As they rode to the garage level, the musician said with sincerity, "I truly apologize for causing any trouble with your neighbor."

"Mrs. Burns?" Tina looked at Sam and they both burst out laughing again. "She'll be fine. It's about time we had a little liveliness around this place."

Sam smiled. *I hope that means I'll get invited back.*

The elevator doors opened and they walked to Sam's car.

"Good night, Samantha."

"Good night." Reluctantly, Sam got into her SUV and drove out of the garage.

Tina watched the vehicle leave before returning to the elevator, singing "Mickey's Monkey" softly to herself.

Chapter 8

I can't wear this. Sam put her hands on her hips and glared at her reflection in the full-length mirror affixed to the back of her bedroom door. *Why did I ever suggest going to the beach?* She turned sideways and looked in the mirror again. *My goodness, that's even worse!*

Sam sighed. *Actually, for almost being forty, I still look pretty good — except for the ten...okay, so it's more like fifteen...pounds that have crept on since I turned thirty.* Sam placed her hands on her stomach, which was protruding over the waistband of her favorite two-piece bathing suit. *Well, it's not going to disappear in the next half hour, so I'd better go to plan B.*

She rummaged through her dresser drawer for a few moments before pulling out a garment. It was a colorful one-piece suit that still had the tags attached. Sam read aloud from one of them. "Tummy control. Slims and contours the waist." With the scissors from the desk drawer, she cut off the tags and tossed them in the trash. *I'll bet that's a psychological ploy to con women into buying the damn thing.*

Sam put on the suit and had to admit that it was an improvement over the two-piece she'd had on first. *It'll have to do.* She finished getting dressed and quickly did some last-minute straightening up of the apartment. *Just in case Tina needs to come in for anything.* She picked up her beach blanket and went outside to sit on the steps and wait.

It was only a few minutes before the BMW turned into the driveway. Tina lowered the power window. "Hi. Ready to go?"

"Yeah." Sam jogged down the steps and got in the car. She stared at her friend. Tina was wearing a black tank top and light blue nylon running shorts. She had her hair pulled back into a ponytail, which accentuated the bone structure of her face. *You take my breath away.*

"Are you all right?"

"Hmm?" Sam cleared her throat and looked out the windshield. "Yes. I'm fine. It's a beautiful day, isn't it?"

"It certainly is." As Tina merged with the traffic, she said, "This was a great idea. I haven't been to Lido Beach in years."

"I love the beach. Sorry we're getting such a late start."

"No problem. How were the soccer games?"

"Aaron's team won, so they'll move into the next round of the play-offs. Josh's team played well and the score was tied at the end of the game. They had a shoot-out to decide the winner. The other team scored more goals in the shoot-out, so Josh's team lost."

"That's too bad." Tina thought about the young boy she had met at the barbecue. "Is he upset?"

"Josh? Nah, he handled it very well. Aaron is the competitive one. Lisa says he must have inherited her competitive streak."

"I see." *Goes right along with that protective streak she has.* Tina drove through St. Armand's shopping district and onto the street that permitted parking for the beach. "Here we are." She smoothly guided the BMW into an empty space.

The women got out of the car. Tina opened the rear door and leaned in to get her backpack and sweatshirt.

"Hey, Tina."

Tina stood and looked across the roof of the car at Sam. "Yes?"

"Last one to the water has to buy the ice cream!" She slammed her door and took off.

Tina reached into the car, got her things, then closed the door. She set the alarm and hurried to the beach access. Jogging to the crest of the wooden footbridge that connected the sidewalk to the beach area, she spotted Sam running for all she was worth, about halfway to the shore. *Hmm...not bad form for a musician.* Tina started running, her long legs quickly covering the distance.

Sam stopped, dropped her blanket, pulled off her sneakers and stripped off her tee shirt and shorts. She looked up to see Tina running toward her and bolted across the last few yards of sand to the water. *One more step and I'll be—*

Her forward momentum came to an unexpected halt as a long arm wrapped around her waist and pulled her backward. "Oh no you don't." Tina held Sam tightly against her body. She inclined her head and spoke into Sam's ear. "You don't *really* think you can run from me, do you?"

Sam's heart was beating wildly and the exertion of the sprint wasn't the only reason. "I'll never run so far that you can't catch me...if you want to." She tried to turn, and Tina loosened her grip enough to allow her to do so. Sam gazed up into playful blue eyes. Several seconds passed. *If this were a movie, this is when she'd kiss me.*

Sam broke the eye contact and glanced to her right. "Oh my God!"

Tina relaxed her hold as she turned to see what was wrong.

Sam pushed with all her strength and escaped from Tina's grasp. "Ah ha!" She ran into the water. "You have to buy the ice cream," she said in a singsong voice.

Tina walked over to where she had dropped her backpack and

sweatshirt. She looked at Sam with narrowed eyes. She took off her sneakers, she took off her socks, she took off her tank top — but she never took her eyes off Sam.

Uh-oh. Sam was watching from her place in knee-deep water. *This water is kind of cold.* "Tina? I was only kidding. Really, you don't have to buy the ice cream."

Tina started moving toward her target with purposeful strides. For each step she advanced, Sam took a step backward.

"The water is cold," Sam pleaded. "And I don't wanna get my hair wet." Despite the imminent threat of attack, she noted that her friend was wearing a sports bra with the nylon shorts rather than a bathing suit. *Those have got to be longest legs I've ever seen. And can it be?* She observed a thickness around Tina's midsection. *Nothing on the order of mine, but I feel a little better.* Sam was in waist-deep water now.

Tina reached out and grabbed her. "You said something about wanting to get in the water first?"

"Not *in*. I said *to* the water, not *in*."

PLUNK!

Sam was unceremoniously dumped underwater. She came up sputtering, a furious expression on her face.

Tina looked very pleased with herself. "Oh? I'm sorry. Did I misunderstand?"

"Yes!"

You are way too cute for your own good, Samantha Whitwell. "Would you like to go sit on the blanket and warm up?" She saw that Sam was shivering. *Maybe I shouldn't have done that. She really is cold...and mad.*

"Yes. Promise you won't dunk me again?"

"I promise."

They waded out of the water, spread the blanket and sat down.

"I'm sorry. Sometimes I get carried away—"

"No," Sam interrupted. "I asked for it. There's no need for you to apologize." *And I like when you get carried away, even if it means getting dunked. You drop your guard and I get to see the real you.*

The women enjoyed the sunny afternoon. They lay in the sun, walked along the shore, collected shells, and talked.

Sam learned that Tina had wanted to major in history in college, but her mother insisted she choose business. Tina's father had left when she was young and Steven was only a baby. Her mother had struggled to hold down two jobs and provide for her children. She was rarely home and money was tight. She was determined that her daughter would never find herself in the same situation and stressed the importance of an occupation that would offer financial security.

You had to grow up fast, I bet. "So, you took care of Steven?"

"Yes, he was my responsibility, always."

And you think you failed him. I understand.

Tina learned that Sam had graduated from the University of Central Florida. She had majored in music and worked at several Orlando-area theme parks during college. She told funny stories about things that had happened in school and at the parks. Tina's favorite was when Sam was called into service to be Mickey Mouse for a parade. The employee who normally wore the costume called in sick at the last minute, and Sam was the only one around who was the right size. *That must have been a sight to see.* Tina pictured her friend dressed as Mickey Mouse, standing on a float and waving to the spectators.

~ * ~ * ~ * ~ * ~

It was getting late and there were only a few people left on the beach. Feeling chilled, Sam was wearing Tina's sweatshirt and sitting with her legs pulled up in front of her. *There she is.* She saw a small figure in the distance. *I feel like I'm in high school again — watching her run.*

Tina had been gradually increasing her speed, and she blazed by Sam before slowing down and jogging again. She turned and walked back to the blanket. After opening a bottle of water from her backpack, she took a long swallow. "Would you like some?" She passed the plastic container to Sam.

"Thanks." Sam took a sip and handed it back.

After a few stretching exercises, Tina sat down cross-legged on the blanket.

Sam was watching the sun setting on the horizon. "Beautiful, isn't it?"

"Yes."

"One of the most beautiful sights in the world, and it's free. All we have to do is take the time to stop and look at it."

"People don't do that enough, though — take the time."

"I'm glad we are." Sam continued to observe the colorful sky. "Some things are definitely worth it."

Tina's attention shifted from the sunset to the woman next to her. Sam's hair had dried and was well tousled by the wind. Even though she was wearing the large Florida State sweatshirt, she appeared to be shivering. "Are you cold?"

"A little, but I'd really like to finish watching the sunset. Can we stay for a few more minutes?"

"Sure." Tina straightened her legs and patted the blanket in the space between them. "Sit here."

Sam gave the woman a questioning look. *There?*

"I mean, if you want to." Tina suddenly sounded uncertain.

Sam quickly scrambled over one outstretched leg. *If I want to; are you kidding?*

She settled in front of Tina, pulled her knees up and hugged them. Tina pressed her legs in against Sam and put her arms around her, covering Sam's smaller hands with her own.

Sam leaned back slightly against the other woman's body. *This feels nice.*

Tina rested her chin on Sam's shoulder. *This feels nice.* "Is that better?" she asked softly.

"Yes, *much* better."

"Good."

They sat there, enjoying the closeness of each other and the beauty of the sunset. Neither one spoke. They didn't need to.

And on the way home, Tina bought the ice cream.

Chapter 9

Sam read the e-mail again.

> *Hi, Samantha,*
> *There's going to be an outdoor concert in Old Hyde Park Village on Wednesday night. Do you want to go? It'll be right outside of where I work. You could come a little early and we could eat at the Cactus Club.*
> *They have really good hamburgers<g>.*
> *Tina*

Lisa walked into the study. "Any word from Tina?"

"Yeah. She asked me to a concert Wednesday night."

"Terrific. Things are moving right along, huh?"

Sam swiveled the chair around so she was facing her sister. "Yes."

"Are you going to go?"

"Of course. I wouldn't miss an opportunity to be with her. I find myself constantly daydreaming about her; I can't wait until we spend time together again."

"You're in love."

"Yes, and...um...a little scared."

"Scared?" Lisa's voice took on a tone of concern. "Of her?"

"No, not at all. I'm afraid I'll do something to mess it up. I'm not sure what to say or do; I feel like a damn teenager."

Lisa chuckled. "Sounds like love all right."

"You're a big help." She turned back toward the computer screen.

"Sam." Lisa placed her hand on her sister's shoulder. "Just be yourself and follow your heart. You'll be fine."

"Thanks, sis."

~ * ~ * ~ * ~ * ~

Vivian poked her head into Tina's office. "Hello there." She went in and sat in a chair.

"Hi."

"You look nice and tan. What have you been up to?"

"I went to the beach over the weekend."

"Alone?" Vivian held back a smile as she watched Tina fidget.

Tina sighed. She knew Vivian would get it out of her sooner or later, so it might as well be now. "I went to Lido Beach with Samantha."

"You really like this Samantha, don't you?"

"Yes." Tina dropped her eyes to her desk, unable to hold Vivian's penetrating gaze.

Well, will wonders never cease? She's clearly nervous even talking about her. And that look in her eyes... This new friend has broken through Tina's shell. Samantha must be very special. "Am I going to get to meet her?"

"I asked her to the concert Wednesday night." Tina quickly clicked open her mail program and saw that SamIAm had responded. "Let's see what she said." Smiling, she scanned the letter. "Yes, she's coming."

"Good." Vivian stood up. "I'll be sure to be here."

Tina looked at her boss in alarm. *I know there would be no point in trying to talk you out of it.*

"Don't even ask. There is no way I'm going to miss this," Vivian said as she strolled out of the office.

Putting her head in her hands, Tina groaned. *What am I getting myself into?*

~ * ~ * ~ * ~ * ~

Sam followed the directions that Tina had given her and parked in the Hyde Park garage. She took the elevator to the street level, went out the glass doors that led to the sidewalk, and turned right. *She said go past the Cactus Club, and then it's about a block up the street.* Sam walked past the restaurant and continued until she saw a door with the words Exclusive Travel painted in gold lettering. She took a deep breath and went in.

A woman seated behind a desk just inside the door greeted her. "May I help you?"

"Yes. I'm here to see Tina Mellekas."

"You can sit right there." The receptionist indicated a couch to her left. "And you are?"

"Samantha Whitwell."

"Thank you." The woman headed toward the offices in the back of the room.

Sam hummed along with the background music as she took in her surroundings. The agency was rectangular in shape, with a color scheme of gray, beige, and a deep mauve. There were two desks, one of which belonged to the employee who had greeted Sam. The other one was unoccupied. The small waiting area where Sam was sitting had a couch and a pair of wingback chairs. In front of the couch was a coffee table with a selection of magazines. The walls were decorated with framed travel posters. Silk plants arranged around the room and soft lighting gave the place a relaxed, pleasant feeling. *Very posh.*

The receptionist came out of one of the offices with a petite, older woman dressed in a navy blue tailored skirt, matching blazer, and a white silk blouse. Her gray hair was stylishly fashioned and she carried herself with a stature and grace that suggested class. As they approached the waiting area, she said, "That will be all for today, Brenda."

"I'll see you tomorrow, then." The receptionist went to her desk, gathered her things, and left.

"Hello, Samantha." The older woman extended her hand. "I'm Vivian Karanicholas."

Sam shook Vivian's hand. "It's nice to meet you."

"Tina is finishing up something for me. She'll be here in a few minutes. I'm sorry for the inconvenience."

"That's okay. I don't mind waiting."

Vivian sat in one of the chairs and regarded the woman across from her. The small blonde looked tense, sitting stiffly with her hands folded in her lap. She was wearing a light green sweatshirt that brought out the green in her eyes. She wasn't wearing makeup and didn't appear to be in need of any, with her fresh-faced all-American look. Jeans and sneakers completed her outfit. *Tina said she went to school with her, so she must be around forty, but she looks to be in her early thirties. A very attractive woman.* "So, you've been spending quite a bit of time with Tina."

"Yes, I have."

"She's not an easy person to get to know."

"That's true." Sam smiled. "But very much worth the effort."

"I see. You like her a lot, then."

"Yes."

"I think she likes you, too."

"I...I'm hoping so with all my heart."

Hmm. There's no pretense in this woman. She is open and honest, and probably the best thing to come into Tina's life in a long time. "Be patient with her, Samantha. It takes her a while to trust people."

"I know. She doesn't say much about herself at all. I'm trying to wait and let her talk when she's ready."

Vivian nodded. "She'll appreciate that. And she will open up if you give her time. Meanwhile, I recommend that you pay more attention to what Tina does rather than what she says."

"What do you mean?" Sam asked, thrilled to receive advice from someone who was close to Tina.

"She lets her actions speak for themselves." Vivian leaned forward and lowered her voice. "For instance, in all the years Tina has worked for me, you're the first person she has ever invited here. That speaks volumes, wouldn't you say?"

Stunned, Sam sat silently for a moment. Finally she answered softly, "Yes."

"Let's go see if she's about done." Vivian led Sam to the back of the room. She knocked on the door to her right and opened it.

"Tina? Your friend is here."

Sam followed Vivian into the small office.

Tina was focused on the monitor of her computer, typing rapidly on the keyboard. "I'll be right there."

Vivian cleared her throat and Tina turned toward the sound. "Oh. Hi, Samantha."

"Hi," Sam responded, tilting her head to one side and grinning.

What's she grinning at? Argh! Tina pulled off her glasses and laid them on her desk. "Vivian, I'm sorry. I haven't finished yet."

"That's all right. It can wait until tomorrow."

"Are you positive? I can have it done in a few—"

"Don't worry about it. Tomorrow morning will be sufficient."

"Okay." Tina shut off her computer. She put her glasses in the case, and the case into her backpack.

Sam was watching Tina's every move. *I never thought anybody could look so sexy in a pair of glasses!*

Vivian was observing Sam. *She can't take her eyes off Tina. It's going to be very interesting to see what develops between these two.* "Well, it's time for me to go home; it's been a long day. Tina, will you do me a favor and get my car for me?"

The dark-haired woman immediately stopped packing her things and looked at her boss. "Are you all right?"

"Yes, dear, I'm fine. I'm just a little tired and would appreciate not having to trek through the concert crowd to get to the garage tonight."

Slinging her backpack over one shoulder, Tina came around the desk. "Where are your keys?"

"Let me get them for you." Vivian collected her purse and brief-case from her office. She handed the keys to Tina and the group walked to the front door.

"I'll be right back," Tina said, and hurried outside.

Sam and Vivian stood quietly for a couple of minutes, looking through the window at the people going by.

Vivian, having decided that the couple could use a nudge in the right direction, broke the silence. "Her birthday is this week."

"*What?*"

The older woman laughed. "Well, she certainly won't tell you. She usually gets in a very grumpy mood and stays in all weekend. I thought perhaps you could get her out of the house."

"Thanks for telling me. I'll most definitely give it a try." Sam began formulating a plan.

Vivian glanced at the blonde, who seemed to be lost in thought. *She'll think of something, I bet.* A white Mercedes pulled up in front of the office. "There she is." Vivian opened the door and they went out onto the sidewalk.

"It was wonderful meeting you," Sam said sincerely.

"Likewise." Vivian's hazel eyes twinkled as she smiled at Sam. "I hope to see you again soon."

Sam smiled back at Vivian. "Me, too. Bye."

Tina, who was holding the Mercedes door open for Vivian, watched as the women exchanged good-byes. *They're acting awfully chummy. I wonder how long they chatted before they came into my office.*

Vivian thanked Tina, got in her car, and drove off.

"Ready to get some dinner?" Tina asked Sam.

"Yes." *I hope you put on your glasses to read the menu.*

Tina locked up the office and they began the short walk to the restaurant.

Sam looked at the small park in the center of the bustling shopping district. The sidewalks were red brick and there were benches scattered throughout the nicely landscaped grounds. A three-tiered fountain was positioned in the center of the park. Several large trees formed a canopy above the entire area. "It's so pretty here."

"Yes. It is. The band will be set up right there in the park. The audience will sit around the fountain and on the benches. It's very pleasant." Tina stopped walking. "Here we are." She opened the door of the Cactus Club and they went in.

They enjoyed a leisurely dinner. Sam was disappointed that Tina never even looked at the menu, claiming that she knew it by heart because she ate there so often. Tina had the chicken fajita salad and Sam had a hamburger and fries. They talked about current events, good-naturedly debating things about which they had differing opinions, but finding that they agreed on most issues. Tina insisted on paying the bill and they left the restaurant.

Sam stopped just outside the door, gasping with delight at the scene before her. Darkness had fallen and the park was illuminated by thousands of tiny white lights strung through the trees. "It's beautiful."

Tina looked at Sam and saw the reflection of the lights in her eyes. "Yes, it is."

They meandered through the crowded park listening to the soft sounds of the jazz group that was performing. When they found there was no place available to sit, they wandered along the sidewalks and looked in the windows of the upscale shops. Sam led the way, excitedly exploring the area. She went into some of the stores and Tina trailed behind her. Sam's favorite was the Godiva chocolate store. Tina liked the Sharper Image, where they let the customers try out all the latest gadgets.

Down an alleyway, they came upon a small leather shop. In the display window, Sam saw briefcases, luggage, and backpacks. "Is this where you got your backpack?"

"Yes, a few years ago."

"I like it." Sam reached out and touched the brown leather. "It's very...you."

"Thanks."

"Oh, look." Sam pointed at a store on the corner. "Ice cream."

Tina rolled her eyes. *I knew she'd find that.*

"Let's get some, okay?" Sam was already on her way to the shop. She purchased two cones and handed one to her friend. "It won't kill you to have a little ice cream." Tina grumbled but accepted the chocolate chip cone.

The women ambled across the street. They went up the stairs where they could stand on the second-floor walkway and look down at the park. Leaning against the railing and eating their ice cream, they were quiet as they listened to the music.

This tastes really good, though I shouldn't be eating it. Tina glanced at Sam, who was seemingly engrossed in the music. *She has that effect on me — I do things I might not normally do. But nice things, fun things. She's brought some happiness back into my life. I never expected that would happen to me.*

The concert ended and the crowd began to thin as people headed for home. Tina and Sam had finished their ice cream and were resting their arms on the railing, watching the activity below.

"Can we go see the fountain?" Sam asked.

"Sure."

They went down the steps and over to the fountain. Sam fumbled in her pocket for some change, then placed a coin in Tina's hand. "We should make a wish, don't you think?"

All the times I've been right here in this park and I never thought to do this. "Yes, we should."

Both of them stood silently thinking for a moment before tossing their coins into the water.

"Ready to go?"

Sam nodded, still looking at the fountain.

Tina lightly put her hand on Sam's back as they started moving toward the garage. "Did you find the garage okay? What floor did you park on?"

"Yes, your directions were very good. I parked on the third floor."

They crossed the street and Tina opened the glass door to the elevator vestibule for the garage, where they took the elevator up to the third level and walked to Sam's car.

Sam leaned against the Toyota's door and smiled at Tina. "Are you doing anything this weekend?" *Please don't lie to me.*

Tina suddenly found it difficult to look at Sam and dropped her gaze to her feet. "I...um...I'm not sure yet." *Don't ask me to do anything, not this weekend.*

"I have to work Friday night and during the day on Sunday, but maybe you could come over Saturday night?"

Tina started shuffling her feet and Sam sensed that a negative reply was on the way. She quickly went on. "How about we hang out at my place? We can watch the sunset, rent a video, and order a pizza."

Tina put her hands in her pockets and hunched her shoulders. "I was just going to stay in this weekend. Do some things around the house."

Well, at least she's not lying. "Please?" Sam stepped closer so she could look into Tina's downcast face. She saw eyes full of sorrow. *Vivian wasn't kidding; you really don't like your birthday. And you have no intention of telling me about it either.* Sam regretted having pressured the woman. "I'm sorry. I shouldn't have—"

Her next words were smothered as Tina pulled her into a hug. "It's all right. I'm a little moody this week. If you can put up with that, I'll come over on Saturday. I can't promise to be great company, though."

"It's a deal." *Oh, I like it when you hug me.*

Tina reluctantly let go of Sam. *Just hugging you makes me feel so much better.*

Sam unlocked her car and got in the driver's seat. "How about around six o'clock?"

"Okay."

"I had a really good time tonight. Thank you."

"You're welcome. Good night, Samantha."

Sam closed her door and started the car. As she drove out of the garage, she saw Tina standing, hands in her pockets, watching her leave. *I love you, Tina Mellekas.*

Chapter 10

Sam entered her sister's house through the back door. "Lisa?"

"I'm in the laundry room."

Sam went into the small room off the kitchen. "Can I borrow your electric mixer?"

Lisa stopped sorting the mountain of clothes on the floor. "You want to use a *mixer*? What for?"

"I'm going to make a cake."

"You? Make a cake?"

"Look, if you don't want to help, just say so." *I'm in no mood to get teased about my lack of cooking skill, which will invariably lead to more teasing about my less-than-nutritious fast-food diet.*

She's stressed out about something. "Of course I'll help. But why in the world do you want to make a cake?"

"It's for Tina's birthday. She's coming over tonight."

Well, that explains the stress factor. "Sam, I don't think trying to bake something for her is a good idea. I mean—"

"I *want* to do it. It's the thought, the effort, that's important. I already bought the cake mix and a can of frosting. How difficult can it be?"

"It's not hard. Let me get a load of clothes started. Why don't you bring the stuff over and we'll make it here."

Sam visibly relaxed. "Okay. Thanks, Lisa."

"No problem, sis."

As Sam left to get the ingredients from her apartment, Lisa put the first load of clothes into the washer. *Geez, wanting to bake a cake...this is a first. No doubt about it — she's in love.*

~ * ~ * ~ * ~ * ~

Tina shut off the television. The Florida State football team had won again and remained undefeated. *They'll still be ranked #1 in the country.* She glanced at the clock on the mantel over the fireplace. *I'd better get going. I'll have just enough time to stop and visit Steven before getting to Sam's.*

She picked up her backpack on the way out the door, rode the elevator down to the garage, got in her car, and pulled out onto Bayshore Boulevard. *It's a beautiful day. Funny how I seem to be noticing things like that more lately. Must be the influence of a certain little blonde.* Tina smiled. *It's true. She has me thinking about sunsets and music and...and green eyes.* She sighed. *Admit it. You like those eyes; you like her...but...*

We're friends, nothing more. And that's how it should be.

~ * ~ * ~ * ~ * ~

Sam used a butter knife to make little swirl patterns in the frosting on top of the cake. "It came out really well, didn't it?"

"Yes." Lisa smiled at her. "Are you going to put candles on it?"

"No. Well, maybe one." *Somehow, I don't think Tina would appreciate having the entire cake ablaze with candles.*

"Here." Lisa took a Tupperware cake container out of the cupboard. "Put it on this plate and then the cover snaps on top." She showed Sam how to do it. "And when you want to take the cover off, you pull the small tab on the side to release it."

"Thanks."

"Any time, Sam. What do you want to learn to make next? Spinach casserole?"

"Yuck. No way. This will be quite enough cooking for me for a while."

"I thought you might say that."

"I need to get going." Sam picked up the cake. "Wish me luck."

"Good luck. You'd better be over here tomorrow morning to tell me what happened."

"All right, I will."

Lisa watched her sister carefully climb the stairs to the apartment, holding the cake with both hands. *I don't know how Tina will be able to resist you.*

~ * ~ * ~ * ~ * ~

Tina knelt in front of her brother's headstone and looked at the epitaph with profound sadness. She kissed her fingertips and touched his name.

Hi, Stevie. It's that time again. Another birthday. Hard to believe, isn't it?

She sat down and leaned against the headstone.

I never imagined I'd be this old. Never thought I'd be an only child, either. I guess one never knows where life is going to take them, or when life will be taken from them.

I'm on my way to Samantha's. She's wonderful and we've kind of become friends. I think I'm finally starting to put my life back together; I know you'd be happy about that. It's been...strange, having someone to care about again. It's a little scary, but worth it. Samantha is definitely worth it.

~ * ~ * ~ * ~ * ~

Sam rushed around the apartment one last time, making sure everything was just right. *I'm a nervous wreck about this. How am I going to broach the subject of her birthday without her getting mad? Should I give her the cake or not? Maybe the cake wasn't such a good idea. I have a feeling this is either going to go very well or very badly. I need to be careful tonight. She warned me that she might be in a bad mood.*

She picked up the novel she was currently reading, went outside, and sat on the steps to wait for Tina. Ten minutes later, Sam was so absorbed in the story that she didn't hear the BMW pull into the driveway. The sound of a car door closing caused her to look up from the book. Tina was standing at the bottom of the stairs, dressed in black jeans and a light blue denim shirt with a button-down collar.

Sam's breath caught. *She's so beautiful. I don't know how much longer I can wait before I tell her how I feel.* "Hi."

"Hi." Tina started up the steps.

Sam stood and found herself at eye level with her tall friend who had stopped two stairs below her. *That shirt is the same blue as her eyes...and I love button-down collars. It will be my favorite shirt.*

"What are you reading?"

She managed to stop staring at Tina long enough to note the title, which she suddenly seemed unable to recall. "Oh...um...it's called *Tropical Storm*. A friend of mine got it for me for my birthday. I'm only just now getting around to reading it."

"I think I've heard of it on the Internet. May I see it?"

Sam handed her the novel before turning to open the door of the apartment.

Tina looked at the front and back cover as she followed Sam inside. They both took a seat on the couch.

"Yes." Tina laid the book on the coffee table. "I've heard of this online."

Hmm, that's interesting. "Would you like something to drink?"

"Sure."

"Beer?"

"That sounds good."

Sam went into the kitchen and got two beers from the refrigerator. She went back to the living room holding the bottles. "Would you like a glass?"

"No, the bottle is fine."

Sam handed one of the beers to Tina. "Let's go sit out on the balcony."

"Okay."

They walked through the bedroom and onto the balcony.

Sam pointed at the lounge chair to the right. "There you go."

Sam relaxed into the other chair. *So far, so good. When I look at her from this side, I get to see that gray streak. I love that.*

"You were right." Tina looked out into the distance where the sun was already descending toward the tops of the trees. "The view here is fantastic."

Yes, it is. With considerable effort, Sam directed her attention toward the sunset. "Yes, it is."

They sipped their beers and watched the sunset in silence. As the sun disappeared behind the trees, Sam sat up, preparing to light some candles. She looked over and saw that Tina had her eyes closed and was breathing deeply.

She fell asleep! Sam lay back down, turned on her side, and propped herself up on one elbow. Taking advantage of the opportunity, she gazed intently at the woman next to her. Tina had both hands resting across her stomach. *I love her hands — big...and strong looking.* One leg was stretched out straight but the other one was bent and pointed off to the right. Her head also was tilted slightly to the right. *I want to kiss those gray hairs just above your temple and—*

A dog barked and Tina's eyes fluttered open. Momentarily disoriented, she looked to her right and then her left...and into the very green eyes of a smiling Samantha Whitwell.

"Hi. I think you fell asleep for a few minutes." *And you don't snore. You get bonus points for that.*

Fell asleep? Here? "Oh? I'm sorry."

"It's all right. I've done that more than once." Sam sensed that her friend was slightly embarrassed and decided to change the subject. "How about if I light a few candles and we'll order the pizza?"

"Okay." Tina rubbed her eyes, then watched as Sam lit several candles.

"So, what kind of pizza do you like?" Sam asked.

"Anything will be fine."

"Oh, no. You won't get away with that this time. You like pizza, don't you?"

"Yes."

"What's your favorite kind?"

"Plain."

"Just cheese, you mean?"

"Yes."

"Great, that's my favorite, too." *Hooray, a food item in common!*

As Sam went inside to order the pizza, Tina looked around. The flickering candles and the view of the emerging stars created a nice atmosphere. There was a slight breeze that made being outside quite comfortable. *This is really pleasant. I can see why she likes it so much.*

Sam returned to the balcony and sat down. "The pizza is ordered." She lay on her side again so she could see Tina. "I enjoyed meeting Vivian the other day. She seems like a terrific person."

"Yes, she is."

"How did you end up working for her?"

Tina looked out at the stars as she answered. "Well, after the accident, I had resigned from my job at the accounting firm. I moved to Tampa, in the Hyde Park area, so I would be close to Tampa General Hospital. I had rehab therapy there for my back every day for a few months and then several times a week after that." Tina paused, seemingly mulling over what more she should say. "I tried to walk as much as possible; it was really the only exercise I could do at that time. Anyway, one morning I was walking around Hyde Park Village and I saw a help wanted sign in the window of a travel agency. I guess it must have been on a weekend because the agency was closed, but there was a woman inside, so I knocked on the door and she let me in."

"It was Vivian?"

"Yes." Tina grinned. "She didn't know what to make of me — limping in and asking for the job, but she hired me."

"It seems to have worked out well for both of you."

"Yes, it has."

She seems fairly talkative. Maybe I can get a little more information. "You didn't like the firm you worked for, is that why you resigned?" There was a long silence and Sam was just about to change the subject when Tina answered.

"I didn't feel like I belonged there."

Sam thought carefully before commenting. "Everybody needs to feel like they belong somewhere. You feel that now, don't you? That you belong with Vivian's company."

"Yes."

"Good. I'm glad." *And we belong together. I know that for sure.* Sam plunged ahead. "Vivian and I talked a little when I was there on Wednesday."

Tina turned her head and looked at Sam. "I figured that."

"She cares about you a lot."

"I know."

"She told me..." Sam hesitated, unsure whether to go on.

Tina could see that Sam was worried about whatever it was she wanted to say. *I can't believe Vivian would've told her anything bad.* "What did she tell you?"

The gentle tone of the question convinced Sam it would be all right to finish the sentence, and the words tumbled out in a rush. "She told me your birthday was this week."

Tina sighed. *I'll get you for this, Vivian.* "Yes, that's true."

"She also said you don't like your birthday."

"I don't," came the brusque reply.

"I'm sorry. Maybe I shouldn't have said anything."

"It's just that I...this..." Tina's words became choked with emotion and she stopped speaking.

Sam waited, correct in her assumption that, given time, the woman would continue when she was ready.

"This...is a...difficult time of year for me." *Though it's been easier this year...with you around.* "Steven...died...right before his birthday. Every year, on my birthday, I'm reminded of all the birthdays he never had...he'll never have..."

So, you don't think you should celebrate yours. Sam's eyes filled with tears. *Two lives were lost that day, but maybe we can get yours back.* She slid off the side of her chair, squeezed her small frame into the empty space on Tina's left, and curled up next to her. And then she cried.

What's going on here? Tina wrapped her arms around the sniffling woman. "Why are you crying?"

"The whole thing is such a...tragedy."

"Yes, it is."

"Do you ever cry about it?"

"All the time, Samantha." Tina's voice was barely above a whisper. "On the inside."

They lay there quietly until the sound of the doorbell startled both of them.

"That must be the pizza." Sam didn't want to move. *I like it right where I am.* Loud knocking echoed through the apartment. She sat up and ran her fingers through her hair. "I'll be back in a minute." She rushed to answer the door.

Tina was struggling to process everything that was going on. Her body was warm from having the younger woman lying against her. *But that felt...nice. And her crying like that — for Steven...for me, I've never met anyone like her.*

Sam came to the doorway of the balcony. "Do you want to eat out here or in the house?"

Tina got up from the chair and stretched. "Let's go inside, okay?"

"Okay." Sam led the way to the kitchen. She opened the pizza box and looked inside. "This looks good." She got plates out of a cabinet above the counter and put two slices of pizza on each one. "What would you like to drink?"

"Water will be fine. Let me get it." Tina reached for the handle of the refrigerator.

"No!" Sam quickly grabbed the handle. "I'll get it. Would you take the food into the living room for me?"

"Sure." Tina took the plates into the other room and placed them on the coffee table. *She's rather territorial about that refrigerator. What's that all about?*

Sam opened the refrigerator to get a bottle of water and a diet soda. The cake was on the top shelf in plain view. *Whew, that was close.* She shut off the kitchen light and took the drinks around the corner to the living area. "What kind of movie would you like to see?" She set the water and soda on coasters. "I rented a sci-fi and a comedy."

"Let's go with the comedy."

Sam took the video out of the case and inserted it into the VCR. "Have you ever seen *Sister Act*?"

"It sounds vaguely familiar."

"It's the one where Whoopi Goldberg plays a Las Vegas lounge singer who hides out in a convent. She ends up conducting the choir." Sam joined Tina on the couch. "It's very funny." She took one of the plates, laid it on her lap, slipped off her sneakers and plopped her feet on the coffee table in front of her. She smiled at Tina. "It's okay. Go ahead."

Tina followed her example.

They ate their pizza, laughed at the movie, and sang along with most of the songs.

"Did you like it?" Sam pressed the remote control to rewind the tape.

"Yeah, it was good." Tina began putting her sneakers on.

You can't leave yet! "Um...I kind of made something special for dessert."

"Dessert? I don't usually have dessert."

"Well, this is a special occasion, and I made it myself."

The last words revealed Sam's pride of accomplishment, and Tina couldn't say no to that. "Okay."

"Great! You wait right here." Sam went into the kitchen, took the cake out of the refrigerator, and put it on the counter. She pulled on the tab to release the top. *What the heck?* Sam tried it again. The top refused to budge. She wrestled with the container and almost lost the whole thing off the counter. "Damn!"

"Is everything all right in there?"

"Yes." Sam tried to make her voice sound unconcerned. "I'll be there in a minute." *Relax. Pull on the little tab.* She tried again and the top came off. *Yes!* She stuck one candle in the center of the cake and lit it.

Tina looked up as Sam came into the room. *A birthday cake?*

Sam placed the cake on the table and sat on the couch. She took one of Tina's hands in her own. "Please don't be angry with me."

"I'm certainly surprised, but not angry." *When was the last time I had a birthday cake?* "Thank you."

"You're welcome." *She likes it!* "I'd sing to you, but I thought that might be a bit much."

"I like it when you sing."

My goodness, she's a real softie underneath it all. Sam kept hold of Tina's hand and positioned herself so she could look directly at her. She sang the birthday song all the way through, never breaking eye contact.

At the conclusion of the song, Tina stared down at their linked hands.

"Are you going to blow out the candle?" Sam asked.

"Oh. Yes."

"I'll get the forks and plates." Sam hustled into the kitchen.

Tina wiped her eyes with her shirtsleeve. *Geez, get a grip, T.*

Sam made Tina follow birthday tradition and cut the cake. The women enjoyed their dessert which, Tina assured Sam, was very good...all three times that she asked.

Tina put her empty plate on the table. "Thanks for...everything." She shifted forward as if to stand.

"Wait, please."

Tina sat back on the couch. "Yes?"

"I...I know it wasn't easy for you to come over here tonight. I feel very special that you'd let me share in even a small part of your birthday."

That's because you're very special, don't you know that? "I'm glad I came."

"Me, too." Sam moved closer to Tina. "I want to tell you something before you leave." She looked deep into the eyes of the woman she loved. "I'm so happy that you were born. Whether you believe it or not, the world is a better place with you in it; *my* world is a better place with you in it." She leaned forward and lightly brushed her lips against Tina's. "Happy Birthday."

~ * ~ * ~ * ~ * ~

"You *kissed* her?" Lisa refilled Sam's coffee cup.

"Well, it was only a little kiss." *But she has the softest lips.*

Lisa sat down at the kitchen table across from her sister. "What did Tina do?"

"She didn't do anything. She thanked me for inviting her over and we said good night."

"That's it?"

"Yes. That's it."

"Did she like her present?"

"I forgot to give it to her. I think I'll take it to the travel agency tomorrow."

"You forgot?" Lisa asked, surprised. "You were so excited about that present."

"With everything else happening..."

"Why? What else happened last night?"

Sam shrugged her shoulders. "Nothing, really; we just talked."

This is not like you, Sam. You usually talk nonstop about every detail of the evening. "Getting Tina Mellekas to talk is a major accomplishment."

"She's very nice." *Very nice. And those blue eyes...*

Lisa saw her sister drifting into a daydream. "Ahem."

"Yes?"

"You have to work today?"

"Oh, yeah. I need to get ready!" Sam drank down the rest of her coffee.

"You're playing at the art festival?"

"Yes. A morning and afternoon performance."

"Maybe I'll bring the boys by later. Want me to bring you some lunch?"

"That would be great." Sam got up and put her cup in the sink. "I'm so happy!"

"I can see that." Lisa waved her sibling out of the kitchen. "Go on, get ready for work."

~ * ~ * ~ * ~ * ~

Tina pulled open the door to Exclusive Travel and used her foot to hold it open so she had both hands free to carry a cardboard coffee tray.

"Good morning, Brenda." Tina placed a Styrofoam cup on the receptionist's desk.

"Coffee? For me?"

"Yes." Tina headed back toward her office.

"Thanks," Brenda called out to the retreating form. *She's in a good mood. And on a Monday, no less.*

Shortly thereafter, Vivian arrived. As she entered her office, she saw a cup of coffee and a small white bag on her desk. Inside the bag, she found her favorite pastry from the bakery around the corner.

"Good morning."

Vivian looked up to see Tina standing in her doorway. "Good morning. What's all this?"

"Just thought I'd thank you properly for being so friendly to Samantha when she was here. I understand you two had quite a little chat."

"Oh." Vivian sat down and removed the plastic cover from the coffee. "Now, Tina..."

"Yes?"

"You were finishing that project for me and..."

"Viv, it's okay."

"It is?"

"Yes. I went over to Samantha's Saturday night and it was...nice."

"I'm glad to hear that." Vivian took a bite of her pastry. "Mmm. This is scrumptious."

"Well, I guess I should get back to work."

"Tina?"

"Yes?"

"For what it's worth, I think Samantha is good for you. Give it a chance. Don't run."

She knows me so well. "I...I'll try." *But fighting that instinct won't be easy.*

"Good." Vivian smiled. "And thanks for breakfast."

Tina smiled back. "You're welcome." She returned to her office, the smile lingering on her lips.

Chapter 11

Brenda hung up the phone and jotted down the message. When the front door opened, she looked up to see who it was and recognized the blonde woman who had been in to see Tina the week before. "Hello."

"Hello."

"You're here to see Ms. Mellekas?"

"No. I just wanted to drop something off for her."

"Are you sure you don't want me to tell her you're here?"

"That's not necessary. If you'd give this to her for me, I'd appreciate it." Sam handed Brenda a paper grocery bag.

"No problem. I'll take care of it for you."

"Thanks." Sam turned and slipped out the door.

Brenda carried the package back to her coworker's office. "Tina?"

"Yes?"

"Someone was just here and she asked me to give this to you."

"What?" Tina took the bag and set it on her desk. "Who—"

"It's from that woman who was here last week."

Samantha? "Where is she?"

"She asked me to give this to you, and then she left."

She left? "Thanks."

Brenda returned to the reception area. *That was highly unusual. I wonder what's in the bag.*

Tina immediately went back to work on the report she needed to complete. She typed a few words on the keyboard before stealing a quick glance at the bag. *Just open it, T. You know you can't wait to see what's in there.*

Curious, Tina unfolded the top and peered inside. She pulled out a small gift bag with birthday decorations all over it. Tina dug through the tissue paper and took out a gray plastic box. *Hmm. What's this?* She opened the box and smiled. *It's from Samantha, all right.* She looked into the grocery bag again and saw a card and a large object wrapped in tin foil. Taking out the card, she removed it from the envelope. The front showed two little girls, holding hands, standing on the seashore and looking out at the horizon. Inside, Samantha had written a note.

Tina,
I forgot to give you this the other night. Everybody should get at
least one present for their birthday, don't you think?
Thanks for coming over on Saturday. I really had a good time.
Happy Birthday!
Samantha

P.S. I sent some cake for you.
P.P.S. You'd better eat it, too.

Tina sat there staring at the card. *What am I going to do with you?*

Vivian came into the office and grinned at the sight of the gift bag on the desk. "What's going on?"

"Samantha dropped off a birthday present."

"Where is she?"

"I don't know. She left it with Brenda. I didn't even see her."

"Well, if she was just here, she can't be far, can she?"

"Right." Tina stood and picked up the plastic box. "I'll be back in a few minutes."

Vivian watched Tina practically fly out the door. *That's the spirit. This might work out yet.*

~ * ~ * ~ * ~ * ~

Tina exited Exclusive Travel and looked in both directions before turning left. She continually scanned the busy shopping district as she walked swiftly toward the parking garage. *There she is.* Tina crossed the street and went into the park, where she sat next to Sam on a bench near the fountain. "Hi."

"Hi."

"I got my present." Tina opened the gray box. "How did you know I needed a watch?"

"You kept looking at your wrist. I figured you must have had one and it broke or something."

"And you thought this watch was...me?"

Sam laughed. "Actually, I thought it might remind you of *me.*"

"You're right. It will." Tina took the Mickey Mouse watch out of the box.

"Here, let me help you." Sam took the watch, unhooked the brown leather band, and wrapped it around her friend's left wrist. She buckled it at the appropriate notch so it wasn't too tight or too loose. "How's that?"

Tina extended her arm and looked down at her wrist. Mickey was posed in the center of the watch, waving. The gold hands on the large dial were easily visible. *Hey, I can see what time it is!* "It's perfect."

"I'm glad you like it. I was a little worried that you'd be upset because I got you a present. That's why I just dropped it off."

"I'm not upset, but you shouldn't have bought me anything." *Even though I love it.*

"It's not much, and I really wanted to do it."

"Thank you."

"You're welcome."

They sat in silence for a few minutes.

"Would you like to come over to my place for dinner this week?" Tina asked.

"Yes." *I want to be with you every minute of every day.*

"I can make something. What would you like?"

"You cook?"

"Yes. What would you like?"

She cooks! More bonus points. "There aren't a whole lot of things I like. I have kind of a boring diet. Pizza, chicken, hamburgers and spaghetti — that's about it."

"How about spaghetti and meatballs, then?" Tina suggested.

"That would be wonderful. Um...but..."

"Yes?"

"Are you going to put anything in it? I mean like mushrooms or peppers?"

"I take it you don't like those?"

"No. I'm sorry."

"It's okay. I can make it plain."

Sam's face brightened. "You can?"

Tina chuckled. "Of course I can. How about Wednesday night? Seven o'clock?"

"That sounds great."

Tina stood up. "I have to get back to work. Thank you so much for my present. I really do like it."

"I should be going, too."

"All right then, I'll see you Wednesday."

"Bye." Sam watched her leave the park. *I can't wait to see you again.*

Tina walked back to Exclusive Travel deep in thought. *Wednesday night, we need to talk.*

~ * ~ * ~ * ~ * ~

Sam stepped into Tina's condo and inhaled deeply. "It smells good in here."

"It's Grandma Mellekas' spaghetti sauce."

Sam trailed behind Tina into the kitchen. She watched as the cook checked the contents of a large pot on the stove.

Tina took a spoon out of a drawer. "C'mere." She dipped the spoon into the pot and then held it out to Sam. "Try it."

Sam blew on the steaming sauce before tasting it. "Yum. That's good."

"Would you like something to drink? Beer?" Tina opened the refrigerator. "I have wine, if you prefer that."

"Beer is fine. I've never been into fancy wines and drinks."

"Me neither." Tina handed Sam a bottle of beer and gestured toward a stool at the counter. "Have a seat."

"Thanks." Sam sat down. "Do you actually like cooking?"

"Yes." Tina put a hefty portion of spaghetti into a pot of boiling water.

"How did you learn?" Sam put her elbows on the counter and rested her chin on her hands, thoroughly enjoying watching Tina moving about the kitchen. *And she's wearing the watch I gave her.*

"Well, when I was very young and my mom first had to start working, Grandma Mellekas took care of Steven and me. She would let me 'help' her cook. I can remember being in that kitchen for hours at a time, talking about everything under the sun with Nana — that's what we called her."

Sam smiled at the thought of Tina as a little girl, chattering to her grandmother.

"I'm sure I was underfoot and no real help at all, but she was always kind to me. If we weren't cooking, I constantly asked her to read to me, and she did. Story after story she read, about all sorts of things and places. And then I'd ask her question after question, which she patiently answered. She was a wonderful woman." Tina paused, absently stirring the spaghetti. "I guess she felt terrible that our dad had left and she wanted to try to make it up to us."

"Or maybe she just loved you very, very much," Sam added.

Silence settled over the kitchen as Tina made a large bowl of salad. "I don't imagine you want salad, do you?"

"No, thanks."

Tina took a small bowl out of a cupboard and transferred some salad into it. She placed plastic wrap over the top of the larger bowl and put it in the refrigerator.

"So, you learned most of your recipes from your grandmother?"

"Yes. Later, when I got older, I had to do all the cooking. I would make meals for Steven and me, and I also had to have dinner waiting for my mom when she got home from work. I wasn't too crazy about cooking then."

Sam laughed. "I guess not."

Tina leaned against the counter near the stove where she could keep an eye on the food. "You don't like cooking at all?"

"No. It's too much trouble and mess. If I can't pop it in the microwave or pick it up at a drive through, it's not on my menu."

Tina shook her head. "It's a wonder you're so healthy."

"Well, truthfully, I've been spoiled. Being the youngest, I got away with a bit more than Lisa. She learned all the domestic type things and I guess that pleased my mom enough that she didn't pressure me too much. Lisa makes extra of the foods I like and gives it to me. She's a great sister."

"Yes, she is." Tina poured the spaghetti into a colander. "We're just about ready. Would you carry the bread and salad in?"

"Sure." Sam jumped off the stool and picked up Tina's salad and a large basket of bread. She took them into the dining room, put them on the table, and returned to the kitchen.

Tina was heaping generous amounts of spaghetti on both plates. "You want meatballs, right?"

"Yes."

"Okay." Tina used a ladle to add the sauce and meatballs. "Here." She handed Sam a plate and picked up the other one, then they both walked carefully into the dining room.

After setting her plate down, Tina went over to the wall switch and dimmed the lights on the chandelier that hung above the table. She grabbed their unfinished beers from the kitchen, then sat across from Sam. "Do you have everything you need?"

Sam looked at the woman she was thoroughly in love with. "Yes. Everything I need is right here."

I am not what you need, but we'll discuss that later. "Okay. Well, dig in."

"This is really good," Sam commented after they had eaten quietly for a few minutes.

"I'm glad you like it." Tina was amused at the gusto with which Sam ate her meal. *When she likes something, she really likes it. That's part of the problem, isn't it?*

"Seeing as how you work for a travel agency, have you had the opportunity to travel a lot?"

"Yes. Part of the deal I made when Vivian hired me was that I could travel whenever I wanted."

Sam buttered another piece of bread. "That seems like a pretty good deal."

"It was compensation for what she considered a low salary."

Genuinely interested, Sam asked, "Where have you gone?"

"Oh, lots of places. All over Europe, Australia, New Zealand, South America."

"I've never even been out of the United States."

"It was okay, seeing all those countries, but the U.S. is still the best." *It's home.*

"But it sounds so...romantic, traveling all over the world."

"Nah." Tina shrugged. "At the time, I just wanted to get away."

"Oh." *You must have been so hurt and lost. I wish I'd been there for you.* "What was your favorite place? I mean, of everywhere you visited?"

Tina thought for a moment. "I think I'd have to say New Zealand. It's a beautiful country. It's one of the few places that I would go to again, if the opportunity came up."

Sam was fascinated with the details of Tina's life that she was ferreting out. "Do you still travel a lot?"

"No. I guess I've had enough for a while." *Besides, it never changed anything. When I got back from my trips, my brother was still dead and my life was still in shambles.* "I haven't traveled much in the last couple of years."

"Well, I'm sure glad you're here instead of gallivanting all over the globe."

Tina looked across the table at the smiling blonde. *Guess it's about time we had that talk.* She set her empty salad bowl and utensils on her plate. "I'm stuffed."

"Me, too," Sam agreed, having completely cleaned her plate and finished off most of the bread.

Tina stood up. "Let me rinse these dishes."

"I'll help. It's the least I can do." Sam took her plate and headed for the kitchen.

They took care of the dishes before getting another beer and sitting on the couch in the living room.

"Thanks for dinner. It was very good."

"You're welcome."

Several moments of silence followed and Sam noticed that Tina suddenly seemed nervous, fidgeting with her beer bottle.

"I think we need to talk." Tina took a sip of beer. "I...um..." *Geez, T, what are you going to say?*

"Talk?" *Uh-oh. Something is wrong.* "About what?"

Tina looked all around the room before focusing once again on Sam. "I...I can't...be what you want me to be."

"I don't want you to be anything but yourself." *Well, I wanted to know how she feels and I guess I'm going to find out.*

"You seem to have some vision of me. I'm not sure I understand it." *But I know I can't live up to it.*

Sam took a long swallow of her beer. "I'm not exactly clear on what you're trying to tell me." *Although, so far, I don't like it.*

"At your house, you...kissed me."

"Yes. I'm sorry. Well, I'm not sorry I kissed you." Sam smiled at the memory of that kiss. "I mean, I'm sorry if it made you uncomfortable." *Time to put your cards on the table, Whitwell.* "I can't help how I feel about you."

"I care about you a lot, Samantha. As a matter of fact, you're the first person I've really cared about in a long time." Tina paused to collect her thoughts. "I just don't think we should take this — us — in that direction."

Sam took a deep breath. *Ask her; just ask her.* "Is it because I'm a woman?"

"No."

No? Sam closed her eyes for a few seconds and thought about what that meant, and it wasn't good. "I see. It's okay that I'm a woman, I'm just not the woman you want?" *I didn't expect that.* Sam's eyes filled with tears as she looked at Tina. "I should have known. You're so beautiful, you can probably have anybody you want. Why in the world would you choose—"

"I *have* had anyone I wanted," Tina interrupted. "Is that the kind of woman you want?"

"I want you. That's what I know. And I know it with all my heart."

Tina stood and paced back and forth before moving to the large glass windows and looking out at the water. "I...let's just say, I'm not very good at relationships."

Sam got up and walked over to Tina. "Please, don't shut me out."

Tina turned and looked down at her friend. *I'll hurt you. Don't let me break your heart.*

Sam saw eyes that were so troubled and sad that she started to cry. "Don't do this."

Tina was having a hard time controlling her emotions. *We need to get this over with. I can't stand seeing her upset and knowing I caused it.* "It would be for the best."

"I know you don't really believe that." Sam wiped the tears from her eyes, stood at her full five feet four inches and looked up at Tina defiantly. "Tell me you don't want me."

Confusion clouding her eyes, Tina stared at the feisty little blonde. "What?"

"If you can honestly tell me you don't want me..." Sam saw she had Tina off balance for a moment and took advantage. She stepped forward and grabbed the front of Tina's shirt. Pulling her down, she kissed her, and this time her intent was clear.

Tina could have stopped it, could have easily removed Sam's hand from her shirt, but she didn't. She let Sam kiss her, and she responded.

Sam let go of the shirt and slipped her arms around Tina's neck, never breaking the kiss. *She wants me.*

Tina reluctantly pulled away. *I have to stop, while I still can.* She backed up a step so there would be some distance between them.

Sam was smiling. "I knew that you—"

"It doesn't change anything," Tina said firmly.

Sam's heart was racing with excitement from the kiss. *Doesn't change anything?* "You want me, but you don't think we should be together?"

Tina was trying to get her feelings under control. *My instincts say run; Vivian says don't. My body says ravish her; my heart says she's special.* "I'm not sure what I mean." *How did I ever get myself into this?*

"I think I overwhelmed you with my emotions again," Sam said. "Can we sit down for a minute and talk?"

They went back to the couch and sat silently for a while, each of them reviewing the events of the evening.

I'm the one who recommended we talk, and I haven't said a word yet. Sam snuggled against Tina's side and hugged her. *But what should I say? It should be something simple, so I don't overwhelm her any more than I already have.* "I like being with you."

Tina looked at the small blonde wrapped contentedly around her. *You are so damn cute.* "I like being with you, too."

Sam breathed a sigh of relief. *That's a promising response.*

Tina picked up the remote off the table. "Want to see if there's anything good on TV?"

"Okay." *You're asking me to stay? Absolutely, positively, yes!*

They watched TV and Sam eventually ended up lying on her side with her head on Tina's lap. *I could spend my life like this. It just feels right.*

Tina found herself stroking Sam's hair. *I like this. I never thought I'd want anyone hanging around here. What's wrong with me? Maybe it's some kind of midlife crisis.*

"The band is playing this weekend." Sam turned so she was looking up at Tina. "Will you come?"

"If you want me to, I'll try. Where?"

"Saturday night, at the Beach Bar in Longboat Key. Do you know the place?"

"Yes, I know where it is."

The news came on and Sam realized it had gotten quite late. "I really should be going. You have work early in the morning." She ran her fingers through her hair to bring some order to it. "May I use the bathroom before I leave?"

"Sure." Tina got up and led Sam into the kitchen. She pointed out the bathroom and leaned against the counter to wait. *Oh, yeah, I almost forgot.* She opened one of the cabinets above the sink.

Sam came out of the bathroom. "Hungry already?" she asked teasingly.

"No." Tina held out a foil-wrapped object. "It's for you. A little something for the road."

"A Ring Ding?" Sam grinned and accepted the snack cake. "Thanks."

"You're welcome."

They walked to the door and stood there awkwardly, neither one sure how to end the evening.

"Thank you so much for dinner," Sam finally said. "It was very good."

"I'm glad you came."

"Really?" There was uncertainty in Sam's voice.

"Yes." *I must be losing my mind.* Tina ducked her head and kissed Sam lightly on the lips. *But she's irresistible.* "I'll walk you to your car."

"I'd like that." Sam's eyes were sparkling as she smiled at her friend. *She wants me.*

~ * ~ * ~ * ~ * ~

As Lisa pulled into the driveway, she saw Sam sitting on the steps to the garage apartment. *Something must have happened last night.* "Waiting for me?" she asked as she got out of the car.

"Yeah." Sam jogged down the stairs. "How was work?"

Lisa related the latest job gossip as they walked to the house and went inside. She put her purse and briefcase on the kitchen counter. "Do you want a soda?"

"Yes, thanks." Sam sat at the table.

Lisa got two diet drinks out of the refrigerator and took a seat across from her sister. "So, what's up?"

"Saturday night, I might want to do the new song we've been working on."

"You might, huh? I gather that Tina will be there?"

Sam shrugged and examined the design on her soda can. "She said she'd come."

"But you're not positive?"

"No."

"What's going on, Sam?"

Sam felt the tears starting to form, making it difficult to speak. "I'm not sure. I know she likes me, but she has this idea that she's a bad influence or something. I really love her and I don't want to lose her."

Lisa grabbed the box of tissues off the counter and placed it in front of Sam. "I have to be honest — I've had my doubts about this. However, I trust your judgment. If you love her, then she must be okay. And if Tina is as smart as I think she is, she'll know a good thing when she sees it."

Sam took a tissue and wiped her eyes. "Thanks, sis."

They sat quietly for a few minutes. Lisa surreptitiously kept an eye on Sam until she was satisfied her words had sufficiently calmed her sister. "Hey, I have an idea." She looked furtively around the room as if checking to be sure no one would overhear before she lowered her voice to continue. "Let's break into the ice cream and watch some VH-1 before the kids get home."

Sam's face brightened at the suggestion. "Okay. Do you have any chocolate syrup?"

"Like you even need to ask."

Both women laughed.

~ * ~ * ~ * ~ * ~

Vivian stood in the doorway of Tina's office.

The accountant was sitting at her desk, staring at the computer screen. It was obvious, however, that her mind was elsewhere.

This is the second time today I've seen her like this. "Tina?"

Tina was startled when she heard her name. "Yes?"

"Are you all right?" Vivian entered the office and sat down.

"I'm fine."

Vivian wasn't the least bit convinced and she had no intention of leaving until she found out what was going on. "Is it Samantha?"

Tina took her glasses off and sighed. "Yes."

"Is something wrong?"

How much do I tell her? Tina fidgeted a little before answering. "She wants...a relationship. I don't think I can do...that." *I don't know how to do that.*

"Have you talked to her?"

"I tried, but...it didn't turn out like I thought it would."

"You need to tell her what you're feeling." Vivian's voice was gentle. "I'm sure she'll listen. Samantha seems like a sensitive woman; she'll understand."

"I'm not sure I understand it myself."

Maybe you've never been in love before. "You will." Vivian stood up. "Follow your heart, Tina. You have a good one. It'll tell you what to do."

Tina watched her boss leave the office. *Just follow my heart? Is that supposed to be easy?*

~ * ~ * ~ * ~ * ~

Sam grew increasingly morose as the evening wore on. *She's still not here and it's almost midnight.* The band started the next number and she played mechanically while her eyes searched the audience in hopes of seeing her friend. She beamed when she spotted Tina standing at the bar.

Lisa noticed her sister's sudden cheerfulness. *Tina must be here. Thank goodness!*

Tina ordered a bottle of water. The band was playing a current top-forty hit and she hummed along. She paid for her drink and moved to the back of the room. Between her natural height and the raised stage, she had an unobstructed view of the band. For the next thirty minutes, she enjoyed listening to the music and watching the people dance, but her gaze never strayed too far from the blonde guitar player on the stage.

Sam looked at the song list taped to her amplifier. *We're almost to the end of the set. I need to do this. ... I* can *do this.* She looked across the crowded room and made eye contact with Tina, who smiled. *She has the most beautiful smile.*

Lisa tapped Sam on the shoulder. "Do you want to do the song?"

"Yes."

Lisa went back behind her keyboard and spoke into her microphone. "Sam is going to sing one now. It's for someone special, and you know who you are."

Sam took off her guitar and moved to center stage. She adjusted the height of the microphone stand and nodded at her sister. She was ready.

What's this? Tina's attention was riveted on her friend. *She's going to sing? To someone special?*

The band played the opening strains of the song and Tina recognized it immediately. It was one of her favorites that had been on the radio recently.

Sam started singing so softly, she could hardly be heard above the noise in the bar. It didn't matter. Tina knew the song word for word.

All the other sounds and motion in the room fell away as Tina became totally captivated by Sam's singing. *She looks so small, and not even an instrument to hold on to. She must be scared.* Tina lifted her water bottle to take a sip and noticed her hand was shaking slightly. *So am I.*

Sam had been standing very stiffly and barely managed to sing the first verse. She relaxed a little during the chorus as her bandmates joined in with the vocals. As the second verse started, she placed both hands around the microphone, looked at Tina, and sang the words of love and acceptance with more strength.

The singer dropped her eyes and studied her feet as the band played the short musical interlude between verses. *She seems frozen in place back there. That could be good or bad.* Afraid to see any more of what Tina's reaction might be, Sam sang the final verse continuing to look down.

When the last notes faded, the audience clapped and shouted its approval. Sam immediately looked toward the back of the room for the one person she wanted to see...the one person she had sung for. Tina was gone.

Sam whispered a few quick words to her sister and hurried from the stage. She worked her way through the packed bar and out the front door, then briefly surveyed the vicinity. Seeing no sign of Tina, she walked up and down the aisles of the parking lot and was relieved to discover that the BMW was there. *So, she's here somewhere.* Sam went around to the back of the building. The wind was blowing off the water and she could hear the surf breaking on the shore. There was a low cement wall that ran along the rear of the property and Sam walked beside it. *It's pitch black on the beach. If she's out there, I'll never find her.* She peered into the darkness at the last section of wall before a high fence intersected it. Her heart skipped a beat. Tina was sitting there.

The cement was precisely the right height to put the women at eye level. "Hi." Sam stepped between Tina's legs and moved in close. "I'm glad you didn't leave."

"I needed some air. I was going to come back in a few minutes."

"It's all right. I'm just happy you're here." Sam kissed Tina tenderly.

Tina looked at the woman who had invaded her life in so many ways. *What am I going to do with you?*

Sam caressed the side of Tina's face. "Take me home."

"What?"

"Take me home." She hazarded another kiss. "Please."

Tina's body was responding to the sensations caused by the kisses. She fought to maintain her self-restraint. "But what about the band?"

"There are only two songs left. They won't mind." *And it's not like they don't all know what's going on. They're rooting for me, even though I'll get teased unmercifully at the next gig.* Sam smiled as she took Tina's hands. "May I help you up?"

~ * ~ * ~ * ~ * ~

They were silent during the short ride to Sam's apartment. Tina pulled into the driveway and turned off the car. Neither woman moved as several minutes passed. At last, Sam unfastened her seat belt.

Tina drummed her fingers on the steering wheel and stared out the windshield.

"So," Sam grasped the door handle, "are you coming up, or should I say good night?"

Tina didn't look at her passenger. *We both know what's going to happen if I go in there with you.* An imperceptible shake of her head was her only reply.

"I guess it's good night, then." Sam got out and closed the door. *I'm not going to ask again. The ball is in your court, Mellekas.* She walked to the bottom of the stairs and looked back at Tina, who remained motionless. Sighing, she waved good-bye, then slowly climbed the steps to her apartment. *Maybe she's just not ready. I know she has feelings for me, I can see it in her eyes...and taste it in her kisses.* Sam sighed again. *Women.*

She unlocked the door and went inside. Following her nightly routine, she got ready for bed. When she went into the living area to extinguish the lights, she glanced out the window and saw that the BMW was still parked in the driveway. *What's this?* She opened the apartment door and found Tina sitting on the top step. "Are you all right?"

Tina stood and walked to the doorway. She looked at Sam, who was wearing an oversized Mickey Mouse shirt and gym shorts. "I need...want...you."

Sam moved back so Tina could enter. *Geez, when she does say something, she sure knows what to say.* Sam closed the door and locked it, took Tina's hand, and led her to the bedroom.

They sat on the edge of the bed. Sam turned sideways, tucking one leg under her body. She observed Tina's profile for a moment before reaching up to touch the crop of gray hair she adored. The contact caused Tina to face her.

Sam leaned forward and kissed Tina with every ounce of love she possessed, hoping that she could convey with a kiss what her friend was not yet ready to hear. *I love you.*

Tina responded and eased Sam back onto the bed. By the time the kiss ended, they were both breathless. Tina was resting her weight on her arms, dark hair hanging down and brushing the sides of Sam's face. She gazed into green eyes that were open and honest. *This is the kind of woman who only sleeps with people she's in love with. What am I doing here?*

Sam looked up at Tina's conflicted expression. "I want you. I know you want me. It's really very simple, isn't it?" She started unbuttoning Tina's shirt.

"No. It's not." Tina was fighting the overpowering urge to forget about talking and take the willing woman beneath her. *It would be so easy.*

Sam tilted her head to one side, watching the emotions flicker in

Tina's eyes. "Tell me why it's not."

"You...sang about...love," Tina whispered. "I...can't make any promises." *But you deserve someone who can.*

"I don't need promises. I want you, even if it's only for tonight." *And I believe in us enough to know it'll be much more than that.*

"I'll take you, and use you, for as long as it suits me...and..."

Sam looked deep into the blue eyes that were mere inches above her own. "I accept."

"That wasn't exactly a proposal."

"Close enough." Sam slid one hand behind Tina's neck and pulled her in for another kiss.

The tight rein Tina had been holding on her desire began to slip. She wanted Samantha, and she wanted her badly. *I've been honest. If she gets hurt, it's not my fault.*

Sam saw Tina's eyes fill with passion and the atmosphere became charged with sexual energy. *Her just looking at me like that makes me tingle all over.* "I believe you said something about taking me?"

Tina's voice turned deep and seductive. "Yes."

Chapter 12

Something was tickling Tina's nose. *What the heck is that?* She slowly opened her eyes. She was lying on her side, pressed up tightly against the back of Sam's body. She had her arm around the smaller woman's waist and her head was resting just above the blonde's. Tina's breathing was causing the hair to move, tickling her nose.

She carefully removed her arm from Sam's waist and rolled onto her back. It was dark outside and she looked at her watch to see what time it was. Mickey was waving at her on the luminous watch face. *Four o'clock. Now what? This is when I usually leave. I can't do that to her.* Propping herself up on one elbow, she looked at Sam.

Her friend appeared even more youthful and wholesome in her sleep. *Yeah, but she sure knows how to get what she wants. Who seduced whom last night?* Tina reached over and trailed her fingers along the side of Sam's face. *Something is different with this one.*

Creeping carefully out of the bed, Tina buttoned up her shirt as she went into the living room. *If I have to hang around here, what am I going to do?* She spied the book, *Tropical Storm*, on the coffee table. *There we go — a little reading material. I'll need my glasses.* Tina tiptoed back into the bedroom, retrieved her keys from the nightstand, and went outside to get her backpack from the car. Quietly returning to the living room, she reclined on the comfortable couch and began reading.

~ * ~ * ~ * ~ * ~

Sam felt cold. She turned over and pulled the covers up under her chin. She had just started to fall asleep again when she realized she was naked. *No wonder I'm cold. Wait a minute — naked?* She sat up with a jolt and looked around the room. The shirt and shorts she'd worn to bed were on the floor. *Tina was here. It wasn't a dream.* She got out of bed and put on her shirt. She noted that the keys were gone from the nightstand and, afraid of what she might *not* find, she hesitantly made her way to the living room. *Please let her still be here.* Rounding the corner, Sam smiled when she found Tina sound asleep on the couch, glasses in one hand, *Tropical Storm* in the other.

Sam went over and tried to remove the glasses and book from Tina's hands without waking her. She placed the items on the coffee table and glanced back toward the couch. Tina was watching her with sleepy eyes.

"I'm sorry I woke you," Sam whispered. "Go back to sleep."

"Here." Tina patted the small area next to her. She shifted a little so she was on her side and Sam slipped into the space provided. Tina put an arm around Sam and pulled her close. Their breathing slowed into a similar pattern and they drifted off to sleep.

~ * ~ * ~ * ~ * ~

Tingling in her left arm woke Tina. She blinked her eyes several times to adjust to the bright sunlight streaming in the windows. Sam was still asleep, curled up against her. Somehow, Tina's arm had become Sam's pillow and it was protesting the lack of blood flow with sharp pins and needles. Tina tried to slide her arm out from under the blonde's head without disturbing her.

Sam mumbled several unintelligible words as her pillow disappeared.

"I'm sorry. My arm was asleep."

Sam turned, nestling against the tall woman and listening to her slow, steady heartbeat.

Tina's back felt tight from her cramped sleeping position on the couch. "Samantha, I need to get up."

"Mmm."

Tina tried to stretch a little but found it impossible with Sam clinging to her. "My back—"

"Oh!" Sam's eyes popped open and she scrambled to get up. "I'm *so* sorry."

Tina tried to avoid the sudden flurry of arms and legs, but wasn't entirely successful. "Oof."

"Are you all right?"

"My back is a little stiff." Tina sat up and then slowly stood. "Nothing out of the ordinary."

"I can massage it for you. Come on." Sam took Tina's hand and tugged her toward the bedroom.

"That's not necessary. I'll just stretch a bit and it will be fine."

"It's all right for people to help you. It's all right for *me* to help you, isn't it?"

"I guess so, but—"

"Good," Sam interrupted. "Then let me get cleaned up first." She stepped into the bathroom. "I'll just be a minute. Okay?"

"Okay." Tina sat on the edge of the bed. *How does she do that? When I say no, that should be the end of it, but somehow she turns things around and the next thing I know, I'm agreeing with her.*

A few minutes later, Sam came out of the bathroom with her hair combed and looking much more awake. "Would you like to take a hot shower first? To relax your muscles?"

Tina stared down at her hands. "No, really, I'm fine."

Sam looked at the complex woman seated in front of her. *She wouldn't let me make love to her last night. And now this morning, she balks at a massage.* Moving closer, Sam softly cupped Tina's chin and lifted it so she could look into those beautiful blue eyes. "It's only a massage. I promise." *You can trust me.*

The women held the eye contact for a moment, and then Tina capitulated. "May I use the bathroom first?"

"Of course you can."

Tina went into the bathroom and closed the door. After using the facilities, she washed her hands and splashed some cold water on her face. She smirked at herself in the mirror. *This is what I get for not leaving. I have no clue what to say or do the next morning.* She shook her head at her reflection. *This woman has me all turned around. I don't like this confusion I'm feeling.*

There was a new toothbrush, still in the box, on the counter. Tina opened it and brushed her teeth. As she looked around for the trash can to throw it away, she noticed Sam's lone toothbrush in the holder attached to the wall. Tina put hers in the empty slot next to Sam's. She crossed her arms and regarded the two toothbrushes. *You know you'll be back, T. No point in making her buy another one for you.* She combed her hair and ventured back out into the bedroom.

Sam was sitting on the bed waiting for her. "Everything all right?"

"Yeah. Thanks for the toothbrush."

"No problem." Sam began unbuttoning the other woman's shirt. "Can we take this off?"

Tina started to assist with the buttons.

"Please, let me." Sam gently removed Tina's hands. She finished with the buttons and slid the shirt off. Crawling to the middle of the bed, she smiled encouragingly. "If you'll lie down right here, we'll get started on making that back of yours feel much better."

Tina lay on her stomach in the center of the mattress. Sam knelt with her legs astride Tina's hips and bent down to whisper in her ear. "I keep my promises, okay?"

Tina nodded her head slightly.

"Okay." Sam rubbed her hands together to warm them. Then, taking her time, she worked the tenseness from Tina's shoulders and upper arms. She moved to the midback and considered whether she should undo the bra clasp or not. She touched the material. "May I?"

When she received another nod, Sam released the clasp and pushed the material out of the way. She massaged the area thoroughly, pleased at the results she could feel under her fingertips. Scooting back a little to get at Tina's lower back properly, she felt the extreme tightness there. *My goodness, is it always like this? She hardly ever mentions it.* Having a difficult time getting at the muscles that were directly along the waistband of the jeans, she crawled forward so she could whisper to Tina again. "Can we take off these jeans? I can't really get that tight area just below your waist." *And they're not very comfortable to sit on, either.* Sam looked at her shorts that were still on the floor. *Maybe I should have put those on this morning, too.*

Tina put her hands beneath her and raised her hips enough to unbutton and unzip her pants.

"Thanks." Sam got hold of the waistband. "I'll get it." She pulled the jeans down past Tina's hips, careful not to pull off the underwear. From the end of the bed, she grabbed each leg bottom and pulled until they came free of a pair of very long legs. *Wow! What a body. Well, nobody ever said keeping promises was easy.* Returning to her previous spot, Sam resumed the massage. She worked hard on the section of Tina's lower back that was so incredibly tight. She continued until her hands and arms ached. Finally, exhausted, she lay next to Tina and pulled the sheet up over both of them. "Does that feel better?"

"Yes."

Tina's voice was sleepy and Sam was happy with the results of her diligence.

They remained there, dozing, for a half hour or so. Tina woke up first. "Hmm." She began kissing Sam's neck. *She smells so good.* Her hands began roaming over the smaller woman's body. *And she has the softest skin.*

"Mmm?" Sam was not quite awake.

"Good morning."

There's that deep, sensual voice again. Sam felt her body respond to the exploring hands and the words spoken close to her ear. She opened her eyes. "Good morning." She kissed Tina and smiled. *What a way to wake up.*

Tina rolled Sam onto her back and leaned over her. "You're a special woman, Samantha Whitwell."

Sam chuckled. "You're just figuring that out?" She kissed Tina again.

At the conclusion of the lengthy kiss, both women's faces were flushed, their breathing erratic.

"Listen, if we're going to do...this," Tina said decisively, "it has to be my way."

"I understand." *I won't ask you for more than you're ready to give.*

Tina gently positioned Sam's arms above her head. "Will you keep these here for me?"

Sam gazed into very serious eyes. "Yes." *You can trust me.*

"I..." Tina paused. "I..." She stopped again.

Sam tilted her head to one side, trying to read Tina's expression. "I've been told to follow my heart."

"Really?" Tina looked thoughtful. "Me, too."

"Then I guess that's what we should do, huh?"

Tina slid a hand under Sam's shirt. "Know what my heart's saying right now?"

"Yes." Sam grinned. "I believe I do."

"Good." *'Cause, right now, I'm following my heart.*

~ * ~ * ~ * ~ * ~

"Would you like cream or sugar?" Sam took two steaming mugs of water out of the microwave and put a heaping teaspoon of instant coffee into each cup.

"No, thanks. Black is fine." Tina was looking at the magnetic memo board attached to the side of the refrigerator. *Hmm. Important numbers: Mom, Lisa, aunts and uncles, various women's names. Wonder who they are—friends, ex-lovers?*

"Here." Sam handed Tina her coffee. "Want to sit in the living room?"

"Sure."

The women sat on the couch, sipping their drinks. "So, what are your plans for today?" Sam asked.

"I'll probably do my laundry, run, read a little bit. The usual stuff."

"Ack. Laundry. I need to do that, too." *She looks ready to bolt again. She gets very fidgety when she's nervous or uncomfortable.*

"I...I guess I should be going." Tina got up.

"Okay." *But I wish you'd stay.*

They went into the kitchen and put their cups in the sink. "Hang on just a second." Sam hurried out of the room.

Where's she going? Tina looked at the memo board again. There was a pencil hanging by a string and she picked it up. After a quick peek toward the opening of the kitchen to see if Sam was coming back yet, Tina jotted her name and number at the end of the list. She went into the living room, got her backpack, and stood by the door.

"Tina?" Sam called out as she returned to the front of the apartment. She found her guest at the door, poised to leave. "Oh, good, you're still here." She walked over and took one of Tina's hands. Rotating it so the palm was upward, she placed something there, curled Tina's fingers over it and kissed the closed fist. "Whenever you want me, I'm yours."

Tina stared at the little blonde in front of her for a long moment before shifting her eyes to her fist. Slowly, she uncurled her fingers. There, resting on her palm, was a shiny brass key. *The key to her house.* Tina looked back at Sam's smiling face. "I...I don't...can't..."

Sam threw her arms around Tina and hugged her tight. As she had hoped, two things happened: the tall woman returned the hug, and it quelled any further objections.

"I...I really should go." Tina bent down and kissed Sam good-bye.

"Okay." Sam opened the door and they went out onto the landing. Tina descended the stairs and stopped at the bottom. She looked at the key in her hand again and then up at Sam.

"Bye." Sam waved and went back into the house. She closed the door and leaned against it. *Whew. Wonder what she thinks of that?* Hearing the motor of the BMW start, she went to the window and watched the car pull out of the driveway. *Please come back — tonight, tomorrow night, soon.*

The phone rang and Sam picked it up. "Hello?"

"Well? You'd better get over here and tell us what happened!"

"I'll be right there."

Sam went down the stairs and across the walkway to her sister's house. When she entered the kitchen, Lisa and Mike were sitting at the table looking at her expectantly.

"Well?" Lisa asked.

"Good morning to you, too." Sam chuckled as she sat down. "Can't a person at least get some coffee around here?"

Lisa sighed. "All right." She prepared a cup of coffee and placed it on the table. "Now tell us — how did it go?"

"It went...pretty well." Sam felt the color rise in her cheeks. *They just saw her car leave; they know what happened.*

"Pretty well? Is she your girlfriend now? I mean, are you officially a...couple?"

"This isn't high school, Lisa," Mike interjected. "Next you'll ask if they're going steady."

"She's my little sister and I think—"

"Excuse me!" Sam interrupted.

"Yes?" Mike and Lisa said in unison.

"We're dating. That's it, okay?"

"Okay," Lisa answered contritely. "I can't help it if I worry about you."

"I'm a grown woman, Lisa."

"You're right." *Something is bothering her.* "Really, I'm very glad to hear it's working out."

"Thanks."

They all drank their coffee quietly for a few minutes.

"So," Mike cleared his throat, "does she have a tattoo?"

"Michael!" Lisa scolded her husband and then looked at Sam, interested in hearing the answer herself.

"You two are something else. No, she doesn't." *And there's not a tattoo in this world that would make that body look better than it already does. I like it just the way it is.* "Now that I have answered all the...pertinent questions, I have laundry to do." Sam got up and put her cup in the sink. "Thanks for the coffee."

"Sam." Lisa caught up to the blonde as she reached the door. "I'm sorry. I didn't mean to say the wrong thing. I'm very happy for you."

"Thanks." Sam hugged her. "I know you are." She released her sister from the embrace and walked back toward her apartment.

Lisa watched, concerned. *She should be ecstatic. There's more to this than she's telling us.*

~ * ~ * ~ * ~ * ~

Tina had gone running, done two loads of laundry, and taken a nap. She'd just finished dinner and was stretched out on the couch watching TV when the phone rang.

"Hello?"

"Um...hi. It's Sam."

"Hi, Samantha."

"I was about to put a frozen dinner in my microwave when I saw your phone number here." *And you can't imagine how surprised I was!*

"Yes?"

"Well, I figured you wouldn't have put it here unless it was okay to call."

"It's okay, yes."

Silence ensued as each woman listened to the other breathe for several moments. "You're not one for talking much on the phone, are you?"

Tina laughed. "No, not really."

Several more seconds of breathing followed before Sam spoke again. "I miss you already." Receiving no response, she continued, "I guess I just wanted you to know that, that's all."

"Okay."

"Good night, then."

"Good night." Tina hung up the phone. She went to the table by the front door and picked up the key Sam had given her that morning. She paced back and forth before standing and looking out the window at the bay. The water was barely visible in the darkness, but the streetlights lit up the sidewalk and balustrade that bordered it. Several people were enjoying an evening walk along Bayshore Boulevard. Tina went back to the table and picked up her key ring. She added Sam's key to the others and looked at the shiny piece of metal resting alongside her well-worn keys.

Just follow your heart.

She grabbed her backpack and headed for the door.

~ * ~ * ~ * ~ * ~

Sam hung up the phone. *That didn't go very well.* She returned the frozen dinner to the freezer and got a beer from the refrigerator. *Liquid dinner, maybe some popcorn later.* She wandered into the living room, sat on the couch, and picked up the remote. Looking for something interesting to watch, she flipped through the channels and eventually chose an old movie on cable. Putting her legs up on the coffee table, she threw a light blanket over them and settled in to enjoy the show.

An hour later, her stomach was rumbling. *Time for that popcorn, I guess.* She stood up just in time to see the headlights of a car turning into the driveway. *Who could that be?* Sam went to the window and looked out. It was a silver BMW.

She's here? I don't believe it! Sam backed away from the window and returned to the couch. She ran her fingers through her hair to straighten it. *Oh my gosh, she came back!* There was a light knock at the door. Sam went over and opened it.

Tina was standing there with a half grin on her face and a small paper bag in her hand. "Hi."

"Come in."

Tina did so and handed Sam the bag. "Special delivery."

"It certainly is!"

"Ahem. I meant what's in the bag."

Sam opened the sack. "This looks good." It was a hamburger from her favorite fast-food joint. She hugged Tina. "I'm so glad you're here."

"Well, I guess I missed you, too." *I sound like some lovesick kid. I'm definitely having some sort of midlife crisis.* "Are you going to eat that burger or not?"

"Are you kidding? Of course I am." Sam led the way into the

kitchen. "Would you like something to drink?"

"Yeah. A beer sounds good." *Maybe a six-pack.*

"I was just watching the end of a movie. Want to see it?"

"Sure."

They went into the living room and sat on the couch. Between bites of her hamburger, Sam, explained the entire plot and who each character was as they watched the last fifteen minutes of the movie. Tina was amused at the animated way in which Sam told the story. Her whole face would light up as she'd say, "And *then...*" before launching into the next bit of her description. *She is so full of life, and somehow — when I'm with her — I feel more alive, too.*

The show ended and Sam passed the remote to her guest. "Is there something you'd like to watch? Um, are you staying?"

Tina reached in her pocket and pulled out her keys. She handed them to Sam.

"Why are you giving me these?" Sam glanced down and saw her key on the ring with the others. "Oh." She clutched the keys to her chest and looked at Tina. *I love you.* Afraid she might say it out loud if she sat there a second longer, she stood up. "I usually take a shower before bed. You can watch TV..."

Tina pressed a button on the remote and shut the TV off. "Or...um..." Sam was getting warm from the way Tina was looking at her. *How does she do that?* She could feel the sexual tension in the air.

"I could use a shower, too." Tina got up, pulled the fair-haired woman close, and murmured in her ear, "Maybe it's *my* turn to help *you.*" She took Sam's hand and escorted her to the bathroom.

The BMW was parked in the driveway every night that week.

Chapter 13

Sam woke up and looked at the clock on the bedside table. *Nine o'clock?* She turned over and hugged the pillow next to her, breathing in Tina's scent. She missed getting to see Tina in the mornings, but the restless woman woke up very early anyway, so they had agreed that she might as well go home and get ready for work. Much to Sam's delight, she found short notes left for her on the coffee table each day.

"Have a good day. See you tonight." Or: "Good morning! I'll bring dinner around 7." Or, her favorite: "It was hard to leave this morning. See you later."

Sam saved each one, tucking them away in a manila envelope in her desk. *I wonder what she wrote today?* The sound of children playing outside broke into her thoughts. *Children? Oh, it's Saturday. Tina might still be here.* She hopped out of bed, pulled on her pajama shirt, and hurried into the bathroom to freshen up.

A few minutes later, Sam entered the living room and found Tina sitting on the couch, reading. "Good morning."

"Hi."

Sam joined Tina on the sofa and immediately cuddled against her. "It's nice to have you here in the morning."

"Uh-huh." Tina resumed reading.

Sam looked at *Tropical Storm* in Tina's hands. "You're already almost finished with that?"

"Yeah. I've been reading a little every day before I leave."

"You know what?"

Tina closed the book, unable to concentrate with the talkative woman beside her. "What?"

Sam pointed at the novel. "They remind me of us."

"Really?" Tina pondered that. "Maybe, but they're younger."

"Yeah," Sam agreed. "And richer."

"And perfect looking." Tina tossed the book onto the coffee table. "I mean — do real people actually look like that?"

Sam put a hand on Tina's shoulder and pulled herself up to a kneeling position. She straddled Tina's hips and sat on her lap, gazing into her face. "Oh, I'm sure there are a few who fall into that category." *Like you, for instance.*

Tina reached up to take off her glasses. "Samantha—"

"Wait, let me." Sam carefully removed the glasses and laid them on the end table next to the couch. "Has anyone ever told you how absolutely sexy you look in these?"

"Samantha—"

"Words can not express..." Sam ran a finger along the side of Tina's face and under her chin, "...how beautiful I think you are." Sensing that Tina might interrupt again, she continued quickly, "In my eyes, there's *nobody* better looking than you, in real life *or* in fiction."

Tina felt the heat rise in her cheeks. *I cannot be blushing. Since when has flattery had any effect on me?* She put an arm around Sam and pulled her close. *Since I met this one, that's when.*

Sam nuzzled Tina's neck. After a few moments, she moved so she was lying on the couch with her head resting on a strong thigh.

Tina looked down at the small woman. *I'm in trouble here. She means too much to me already. Whatever happened to clear-cut, uncomplicated sex?* "How come you're not in a relationship?"

Sam was caught off guard by the question. Tina had never asked anything about her past before, nor had she told Sam anything about her own. In addition to that, Sam was trying to wrap her mind around the concept that Tina didn't consider what they had to be a relationship. *I guess we haven't made as much progress as I thought.* "What do you mean?"

"I mean — you're wonderful, caring, giving...and adorable. I would have thought someone would have snapped you up by now."

"I...I guess I never found the right person to settle down with." *Until you.* Sam deliberated for several moments before continuing. "I kind of thought my last girlfriend was what I'd always wanted, but I was wrong."

"How so?"

Sam sighed. *I didn't think I'd end up talking about this today.* "Um, Kimberly was...is...a friend of Lisa's. At some point, the two of them were talking and the subject of gay people came up. Lisa said she had no problem with it and mentioned that I was gay. Seeing that Lisa was open-minded about it, Kim told her that *she* was gay. Well, Lisa thought Kimberly would be perfect for me, so she introduced us. We dated for a while and hit it off. Kimberly was everything I always believed I wanted in a girlfriend. She was attractive, fun, stable, domestic, had a good sense of humor...and she loved me very much. We were together for about three years."

"What happened?"

"I...broke up with her."

"Why?"

Sam considered the same question that Kimberly had asked her over and over. *Why?* "I...something was missing. I wasn't sure what it was, but it just didn't feel...right." Sam's voice was tinged with sadness. "I wanted it to work. I tried to convince myself that I should be happy. Then, last Valentine's Day, she gave me a ring. I should've been thrilled that this terrific person wanted to spend her life with me, but in all honesty, I couldn't accept it." Sam wiped a tear from her eye. "I never doubted that she loved me..." She found it as difficult to explain it to Tina as it had been with Kimberly. Except now, Sam had the missing piece of the puzzle. *She wasn't you.*

The women were quiet for a while, each one deep in thought. Sam, feeling that turnabout was fair play, finally mustered the courage to ask, "What about you?"

"Me?"

"Yes, you. A beautiful woman like you probably had suitors lined up waiting for a chance to claim you. No one has ever captured your heart?"

"No."

Sam waited. *I know you can tell me more than that. C'mon, open up a little bit.*

"I was engaged once."

Sam waited a while longer.

"I guess I was doing what I thought I was supposed to do. You know — go to college, get a good job, get married, have kids." Tina shrugged.

Sam nodded, completely understanding those expectations.

"But it didn't feel...right. Kind of like what you said. So, I put the marriage plans off several times, and then the accident happened."

Sam took one of Tina's hands in her own. She kissed it and held it against her chest.

"I fell apart for a while after that and he eventually got tired of waiting for me to pull my life back together. It was all my fault, really."

Pile on a little more guilt, eh? Sam was just about to ask another question when a loud clap of thunder boomed. She shrieked as she grabbed onto Tina.

Tina laughed. "It's just thunder." There was more rumbling as rain began pouring down.

Sam relaxed as the thunder receded. "I'm sorry. Sometimes storms scare me a little."

"It's okay." *I like protecting you.*

The rain persisted and the pair remained on the couch, listening to the drops tapping on the windows and roof.

"Tina?"

"Hmm?"

"I'm really glad you came to the reunion."

"Me, too."

Sam sat up so she could look into Tina's eyes. "I've come to think of it as *our* reunion."

"Our reunion?"

"Yes. I mean — all those years ago, I watched you at track practice. Who would've ever thought we'd meet again and end up..." *Be careful* "...like this?"

"Yeah. You sitting at the top of the bleachers, pretending to study, and—"

"What?" Sam pointed her finger accusingly. "Are you saying you remember me from high school?"

Uh-oh. "Um, yes."

"Oh, you." Sam pounced on Tina and started tickling her.

Tina was trying to fight off the onslaught so she could retaliate. Soon, both of them were laughing and wrestling with each other all over the couch. Tina started to get the upper hand and she tickled Sam relentlessly. The blonde wriggled free and ran. Tina chased her into the bedroom, tackling her just as she reached the bed. "Gotcha."

"Yes." Sam was breathing heavily from the exertion of the wrestling match. "You most certainly do."

Tina looked into the sparkling eyes of the woman lying beneath her, and she smiled.

There it is — that real smile that lights up her whole face...just like at track practice. "Tina?"

"Yes?"

"In high school, at practice, sometimes your brother would talk to you. I always wondered what he said to make you smile."

Tina rolled onto her back and stared at the ceiling.

Sam snuggled next to her. *I hope I didn't go too far by mentioning Steven.*

A few minutes passed before Tina answered. "He would tease me."

The words were spoken so softly that Sam barely heard them. "Tease you? About what?"

"Um, mostly, you."

Sam propped herself up on an elbow so she could look at Tina. "Me?"

"Yes. He would say I was showing off because you were watching." *And he was right.*

"I...that is...unbelievable. I didn't even think you knew I existed."

"He called you my number one fan."

"Well, he was right about that." Sam kissed Tina's cheek before lying back down. She was stunned by the information she had just heard.

"He thought you were cute."

"Really? G'wan. Now you're teasing *me*."

Tina positioned herself over the blonde again. "No. It's true." She brushed Sam's bangs out of her eyes. "And I agree. You were cute, and you've turned into a beautiful woman."

Sam was astonished. *I cannot believe this. I am never going to forget this day.*

"I think he would approve of...us." *He'd want me to be happy, and you make me happy.*

Tina's eyes were full of emotion, and Sam had a glimpse into the heart and soul of the woman she loved. She reached up and stroked the side of Tina's face. "You know I want to be the one to capture your heart."

"Yes, I know." Tina lightly ran her fingers up Sam's thigh.

"Are you going to let me?"

Tina kissed Sam's neck. "I..." At that moment, grumbling sounds emanated from Tina's midsection. They both looked down at the offending stomach.

"I'm sorry. I've usually had breakfast by now."

"Oh. I don't have anything here. Do you want to go to brunch? We can go to—" Sam's next words were smothered by a kiss.

"Maybe later," Tina said before kissing her again. *Much later.*

~ * ~ * ~ * ~ * ~

Sam sat on Tina's lap and put her arms around the dark-haired woman's neck. "See? I told you this was going to be fun."

Tina nibbled on Sam's ear. "Mmm-hmm."

"You'd better stop that." Sam grinned. "We have a job to do here."

Undeterred, Tina continued nibbling.

The doorbell rang and Sam leapt to her feet. "C'mon." She pulled Tina up from the couch. "You have to earn that brunch I bought you."

"I think it turned out to be a late lunch," Tina corrected.

Sam opened the door and a chorus of discordant voices shouted, "Trick or treat!" Sam distributed the treats and complimented the children on their costumes. She smiled at Tina as the tall woman closed the door. "You're having fun, aren't you?" Sam had talked her into helping to pass out Halloween candy while Lisa and Mike took the boys trick-or-treating around the neighborhood. In between visitors, the women had spent their time cuddling on the couch.

Tina wrinkled her brow as she pretended to give the question considerable thought. "Hmm. Yes." Tina leaned down and kissed Sam while her hands roamed over the blonde's body. "I must say it's been quite enjoyable."

"Oh, you are so—" The doorbell rang and Sam picked up the bowl of candy as Tina opened the door.

"Trick or treat!"

The couple looked down at a small girl who appeared to be four or five years old. She was dressed in a brown costume with a plastic sword strapped to her back. She held out her bag expectantly.

"And who are you?" Sam asked.

The girl straightened her shoulders and attempted to look fierce. "I'm the Warrior Princess. Yi, Yi, Yi, Yi, Yi!" her little voice warbled. The girl's father, standing behind her, rolled his eyes.

Tina looked at Sam and said in her most serious tone, "I think you'd better give her the candy."

Sam complied and they watched as the girl and her father walked to the sidewalk. Tina closed the door and both women burst out laughing.

"Gosh, was she ever cute," Sam exclaimed.

"Good thing you gave her that candy or we would've been in big trouble."

"I think you're right."

The door opened. "We're home," Mike called out. Lisa and the boys followed him in with Beethoven.

"Look what *we* got!" Aaron opened his bag and Sam looked inside.

Joshua went over to Tina and opened his bag for her to see. She knelt down on one knee and inspected its contents with interest. "You sure have a lot of candy here. Do you think you can eat it all?"

"Oh, yes! But you can have some if you want."

Tina chuckled. "That's all right." She spotted one of her favorite candy bars. "Well, maybe that little Milky Way there."

Joshua gave the woman the requested candy. His eyes were sparkling. "Just for you, Tina."

She gave him a hug. "Thanks, Josh."

Sam was observing the exchange with amusement. *She's so good with him. And Joshua is crazy about her. Heck, so am I.*

"So, how did things go here?" Lisa asked.

"Fine. We had a steady stream of kids the whole time you were gone."

The doorbell rang and Beethoven barked.

"I'll take the dog upstairs with me," Mike said. "Come on, Batman and Robin. Time to get out of those costumes."

"All right," Aaron said. "Then can we eat some candy?"

"We'll see. Maybe one or two pieces after Mom and I check everything over."

The boys followed their dad up the stairs, chattering with excitement about the evening.

Lisa passed out candy to the children who had rung the bell. After closing the door, she turned off the porch light. "Whew, that's enough for me."

Sam laughed. "You love it and you know it."

"Yeah, yeah." Lisa led the way into the kitchen. "You two want a cup of coffee or something?"

"No, thanks," Sam answered. "We're going to watch a video."

"Well, I appreciate the help tonight. It's nice when both Mike and I can go with the boys."

"No problem, sis." Sam took hold of Tina's hand. "Ready to go?"

"Yes."

The women exchanged good-byes and Lisa watched as her sister walked across the yard, never releasing Tina's hand. *She's happy, and Tina seems to adore her. Maybe this is going to work out after all.*

~ * ~ * ~ * ~ * ~

After they entered the garage apartment, Sam closed and locked the door. "Want me to make some popcorn?"

"Okay." Tina followed her into the kitchen.

Sam put the popcorn in the microwave and got two beers from the refrigerator.

Tina leaned against the counter. "I can't believe you've never seen the movie *Halloween*."

"I like Jamie Lee Curtis, but I don't usually watch horror movies." Sam shrugged. "Sometimes I get scared."

"We don't have to watch it. I just figured it being Halloween and all..."

"With you here, I think I'll be okay."

The microwave beeped and Sam poured the popcorn into a large bowl. The couple went into the living room and got comfortable on the couch. Sam nestled against Tina as the video began. It wasn't long before she had her arms tightly gripped around Tina's waist and her face buried against a strong shoulder. She remained like that for the majority of the show.

Tina loved every minute of it. "It's over now."

Sam peeked toward the television set. The credits were scrolling on the screen. "Is he really dead?"

"Well, there are several sequels, so I don't think so."

"Oh."

"It's only a movie, Samantha."

"I know," she replied uncertainly.

"Ready for bed?"

"Almost. But first I have something for you." Sam jumped up and dashed out of the room. A few seconds later, she returned with a purple gift bag.

Tina took the present offered to her. "I wasn't aware that Halloween was a gift-giving occasion."

"Well, it's not. But I wanted to get you this." Sam put her hands on her hips. "Just open it, okay?"

"Okay." Tina moved the tissue paper aside and pulled out a large white tee shirt with Mickey Mouse on the front. She looked at the shirt and then at Sam. "Why are you giving me a—"

"There's more."

Tina reached into the bag again and felt something made of very smooth material. She removed the article and laughed when she saw it was a pair of silk, Mickey Mouse boxer shorts. "Boxer shorts? For me?"

"They're for pajamas. You don't have anything here and I just thought..." Sam was suddenly unsure of her decision to give Tina the gift. "So, um, do you like them?"

"Yes, I think so." Tina stood up. "How about I go try them on?"

"Yes!"

Tina headed toward the bedroom.

Sam turned off the television and took the remnants of the snacks into the kitchen. *Whew. She seems to like the pajamas. All the time she spends in this apartment and she doesn't have a single personal item here. Maybe this will make her feel like something, some part of her, is here all the time. I hope she likes that idea, because I sure do.* Sam switched off the kitchen light and went into the bedroom. Tina was in the bathroom, so she sat on the edge of the bed and waited.

After a few minutes, the door opened and Tina stepped out. *I can't believe I'm wearing this.* She spread her arms wide and looked down at her outfit. "What do you think?"

Sam was unable to suppress a wide smile at the sight. "You look—"

"Ridiculous?"

"No." Sam got up and hugged Tina. "Cute."

"Samantha." Tina sighed. "Sometimes I wonder about you."

"Only sometimes?" Sam stood on her tiptoes to kiss the taller woman.

"Hmm." *What was I saying?*

"I'm going to get ready for bed." Sam yawned as she went into the bathroom.

Tina got under the covers. *I can't believe she bought me pajamas. And of all things, Mickey Mouse pajamas. Guess I never was a Victoria's Secret kind of gal.*

Sam came out of the bathroom, turned out the lights, and crawled into bed. She pressed her body against Tina's and ran her hands over the new clothing. "This feels nice."

"Yeah. I like them. Thanks."

"You're welcome." Sam rested her head on Tina's shoulder and threw an arm and leg across her body. "You know what?"

"What."

"I really like you being here."

"I think I already knew that." *But for some reason, it feels good hearing it.*

Sam yawned again. "I just really...like...you."

Tina kissed the top of the drowsy woman's head and stroked her hair. She listened as Sam's breathing became deeper. In moments, the blonde was asleep. Tina looked up at the ceiling. *What a week this has been. Has it really only been that long since she sang to me at the Beach Bar and I brought her home? I haven't been able to stay away either, driving here every night.*

Sam turned to lie on her side and Tina curled up behind her. It was their usual sleeping position and soon both of them were slumbering.

"T."

Steven?

"Ti..."

Stevie? Tina opened her eyes.

"Ti..." Sam tossed and turned in obvious distress.

"Shh, it's all right," Tina murmured. "I'm here." She watched as Sam appeared to calm down. *No more scary movies for you. I should have known better.*

Sam woke up with a gasp. "Tina!"

Tina grabbed the frightened woman and held her tight. "It's okay; I'm right here."

Sam was shaking. "I'm sorry. I had a bad dream."

"There's nothing to be sorry about. I never should have suggested you see that movie in the first place."

"I'm *so* glad you're here."

"Me, too."

"Tina?"

"Hmm?"

"I need to stay awake for a few minutes. Sometimes, if I go right back to sleep, I go directly into the nightmare again."

"Okay." Tina propped herself up on an elbow and looked at Sam. "What were you dreaming about?"

"Someone was chasing me, and I was trying to get away, but it was like I was moving in slow motion. Has that ever happened to you?"

"No."

"I tried to yell for help, but no sound was coming out."

"I heard you." Tina trailed her fingers along the side of Sam's face. "You called me."

"I did?"

"Yes, really. I heard you." She leaned forward and kissed Sam gently before lying down next to her.

"Tina?"

"Hmm?"

"Do you ever have nightmares?"

"Yes."

It was Sam's turn to prop herself up so she could see her companion. "You do?"

"Yes." *Please don't ask me.*

"What are they about?"

Tina looked into the interested eyes above her. *Tell her; you can tell her.* "About...the accident."

Sam picked up one of Tina's hands and linked their fingers together. "Do you want to tell me?"

Tina shook her head. *I should, but I don't want to.*

"Okay." Sam lay down and rested her head on the silent woman's shoulder. *I won't push you.* She was just about to doze off again when Tina spoke.

"It was...Labor Day."

Afraid that Tina might not continue, Sam didn't move; she barely breathed.

The words came haltingly. "I...I wanted to go running at the track. I called Steven to ask him if he'd go with me. He didn't want to. He was supposed to attend a cookout with his girlfriend later that day. I told him I'd get him back on time, talked him into it. Everything was fine...we worked out and were on our way home. It started to rain — one of those sudden summer downpours." Tina paused.

Sam squeezed their still-linked hands. *You can do it. Tell me what happened. I love you.*

"I should have pulled over. It was raining so hard I could hardly see...but I had promised to get him home. We were on Fruitville Road. We were laughing because I was teasing him about his girlfriend...he was worried he was going to get in trouble if he was late. Then a car coming from the other direction swerved into our lane. I tried to pull out of the way...and we started skidding on the slick road. ..."

Tina's voice shook with emotion and Sam's eyes filled with tears as the distraught woman struggled to keep going.

"I...I couldn't get control of the car. It all happened so fast. We spun around in a circle before crashing into the culvert on the side of the road."

There was a prolonged silence as Tina gathered her strength to finish the story.

Sam was trying desperately not to cry. *She needs me to be strong right now. Crying is not going to help.* She kissed their entwined fingers.

"We were both wearing our seat belts, but we had been thrown sideways when we went into the ditch. I guess that's how I hurt my back. But...Steven," Tina's voice cracked as she said her brother's name. "He...he had hit his head against the passenger window. I could only see that he was unconscious. I didn't know...I didn't know how injured he really was. I couldn't move, my back...hurt so badly. Someone must have called 911 right away because the next thing I knew I was being pulled out of the car. They put us in the same ambulance to take us to the hospital. I kept calling to Steven, trying to wake him up. He...he didn't wake up. He...never...woke...up." Tina couldn't contain her grief any longer and she began to cry.

Sam put her arms around the weeping woman and pulled her into an embrace. She tucked Tina's head under her chin and whispered words of comfort as she caressed her. It was several minutes before Tina's breathing evened out and she relaxed in Sam's arms.

Sam looked at the tear-streaked face resting on her chest. *I don't imagine you've told that story to many people. Vivian was right. You'll open up if I give you enough time. And for you, Tina Mellekas, I'll make all the time in the world.*

Chapter 14

Sam opened her eyes and squinted in reaction to the brightness in the room. The French doors were ajar and she could feel the gentle breeze that accompanied the light pouring through. *I wonder where Tina is?* She pushed the covers back and sat up. Hearing voices outside, she listened for a moment. *That's Aaron and Josh; they must be playing. Wait a minute.* Sam cocked an ear toward the sounds drifting in from below. *Is that Tina?*

Curious to see what was going on, she hurried to the balcony and looked down into Lisa's yard. Her nephews were trying to dribble a soccer ball past Tina to score a goal. The lanky woman was running back and forth as the boys kicked it to each other. Suddenly, Joshua feinted and went around Tina. He passed the ball to Aaron, who scored. The boys jumped up and down, shouting with excitement.

Tina slapped high fives with them. "Okay. It's my turn." She positioned herself at the area designated as midfield and started dribbling. Aaron and Joshua ran to her and tried to steal the ball. Amid much giggling, pushing, and shoving, the boys got it and kicked another goal. They cheered again. Tina laughed heartily.

Sam smiled. *She's like a big kid sometimes. And it's so nice to hear her laugh. She doesn't do that often enough.* After quickly dressing, Sam jogged down the stairs. She waved to her nephews and their soccer buddy. "Hi, guys."

"Hi, Auntie Sam," Aaron and Joshua chorused.

"Hi." Tina grinned at the new arrival. "Wanna play?"

"Are you sure there's room in this game for one more?"

"Yes!" the boys exclaimed.

"How about Josh and I take on you two?" Tina suggested.

"We can beat them, Auntie Sam," Aaron said with assurance.

Sam crossed her arms and scrutinized the opposition. "I'm not as confident as you are about that, but we'll give it our best try, okay?"

"Okay."

A rousing game ensued. Finally, with the score tied, Tina made a break for the goal. Sam, unable to steal the ball from her, grabbed her around the waist. Aaron got hold of one leg. Tina fell to the ground and Sam started tickling her. Joshua jumped onto the pile and joined in. All of them were laughing and attempting to tickle each other when a voice of authority spoke.

"*Samantha!*"

Everyone instantly stopped. They looked up to see an older version of Sam standing there, glaring at them.

"Mother." Sam scrambled to her feet.

"What in the world are you doing?"

"We...we were playing soccer," Sam replied, nervously running her fingers through her hair.

The rest of the group stood up.

"Hi, Grandma." Aaron ran and hugged his grandmother.

Joshua wrapped his arms around Tina's thigh and leaned against her.

"Mom." Sam could not, would not, hide the pride in her introduction. "This is Tina."

Neither of the women offered a hand or said anything. An uncomfortable few seconds passed.

"Aaron, Joshua," Mrs. Whitwell said sternly, "go in the house."

Aaron started toward the patio. Joshua didn't move.

Mrs. Whitwell pinned the smaller boy with a look of displeasure. "I said, go inside."

Tina felt the arms around her leg tighten. She bent down and spoke softly to the youngster. "Josh, I need to have breakfast. How about I come and get you after that and we'll take Beethoven for a walk? Just you and me."

"Promise?"

"Yes, I promise. Now, go on in the house, okay?"

"Okay." Joshua slowly let go of Tina's leg and did as he was told.

Lisa came rushing outside. "Mom, how are you?"

"I dropped by to discuss our plans for Thanksgiving and I find—"

"Well, come on in." Lisa took her mother's arm and began leading her to the back door. "Would you like some coffee?"

"Yes. That would be nice." Mrs. Whitwell glanced back at Sam. "I'd like to talk to you, too."

"I'll be right there," Sam said dejectedly. As her mother and Lisa disappeared into the house, she sighed and turned to Tina. "I dread the holidays. Every year it's a fight."

"Is there anything I can do?"

"No. I have to deal with it. But having you here makes it easier."

"I was leaving to get some stuff to make breakfast when I saw the boys playing. I'll go now if you want. How does bacon and eggs sound?"

Sam gave Tina a quick hug. "It sounds wonderful."

"I'll be back in a little while." Tina removed her car keys from her pocket. "Good luck with your mom."

"I'll need it." Sam took a deep breath and went into the house.

~ * ~ * ~ * ~ * ~

Tina pulled into the driveway. *Well, the car is gone; Grandma must have left.* She gathered the plastic grocery bags, climbed the stairs, and entered the apartment. Seeing no immediate sign of Sam, she went into the kitchen and put the food away before wandering into the bedroom. *Ah, there she is.*

Sam was sitting in one of the lounge chairs on the balcony.

"Hi." Tina relaxed into the unoccupied chair. "You okay?"

Without a word, Sam got up and moved over to sit on Tina's lap. She laid her head on the taller woman's shoulder.

Tina put her arms around the uncharacteristically quiet blonde. *Geez, her mother certainly knows how to push her buttons.*

They sat in silence for a bit, Sam apparently needing the closeness and Tina glad she was there to provide it.

Tina's stomach grumbled loudly.

"I'm sorry." Sam started to get up. "You're hungry."

Tina gently pulled the woman back down. "It's all right. I can wait."

"No, really, I'm fine." Sam looked into eyes that radiated anger. "Are you mad at me?"

"No, not at all."

"It's just that you look...kind of mad."

"I'm angry that your mother upsets you like this."

"I won't be speaking to her for quite some time, so that shouldn't be a problem."

"Oh." *Whatever happened, it didn't go well.*

"Now, moving on to a more pressing topic." Sam lightly brushed her lips against Tina's. "Didn't I hear you say you were going to cook breakfast this morning?"

She doesn't want to tell me about it. "Yes."

"Okay." Sam tried to get up again, but found herself held securely in place.

"Wait." Tina gazed deeply into sad green eyes, allowing Sam to see how much she cared. Then she kissed her, ever so tenderly, much differently from the passionate kisses the younger woman was used to.

"Sometimes," Sam murmured, "you know just the right thing to do."

"Not often enough, Samantha." *Definitely not often enough.*

"You're doing fine." The blonde grinned as Tina's stomach growled again. "And it seems that making breakfast right now would be an excellent thing to do."

The women enjoyed a leisurely meal, sharing the Sunday paper and reading aloud when they saw something interesting.

"Look at this." Sam turned the page toward Tina. It was an advertisement for a musical.

"Yeah?"

"This is where I'm working next weekend. The orchestra is playing the music."

"At the Tampa Bay Performing Arts Center?" *Near my place.*

"Yes." Sam folded the paper and laid it down. "It makes for a long weekend, though. The play is performed Friday night, twice on Saturday, and for a matinee on Sunday. I won't be home all that much, but you have the key. If you want to come over—"

The ringing of the phone interrupted and Sam answered. "Hello?" Her face broke into a smile as she listened to the caller. "Let me have you talk to her." She handed the phone to Tina.

"Hello?"

"Hi. This is Lisa. I have Joshua here. He's under the impression that you're coming to get him...to walk the dog?"

"Yes. I promised him I would. Is he ready?"

"You might say that. Hang on; here he is."

"Tina?"

"Yes?"

"Are we gonna take Beethoven for a walk?"

"Sure." She grinned at the sound of the boy's excited, high-pitched voice on the phone. "Do you want me to come over now?"

"Yes!"

"All right. I'll be there in a minute."

"Okay. Bye."

Tina hung up. "Well, I have a hot date with the young man next door."

Sam put her arms around Tina's neck and kissed her. "I guess it's okay, as long as you come back to me."

"You can count on it."

They heard Beethoven barking outside. "I need to go." Tina ducked her head for another kiss. "I'll be back soon."

Sam watched from the landing as Tina and Joshua walked down the driveway with Beethoven in front of them on the extendable leash. As they turned at the sidewalk, Joshua reached up to hold Tina's hand.

Sam's heart swelled at the sight. *Mom can disapprove of me all she wants, I'll never be ashamed of loving you.*

Back inside the apartment, Sam raised the windows to let in the cool, fall air. Then she went to the kitchen and washed the breakfast dishes. Next, she straightened the bedroom and made the bed. Returning to the living room, Sam heard someone talking outside. Peeking out the open window, she saw Tina and Joshua sitting on the bottom steps. Beethoven was lying on the ground, panting. Sam could clearly hear the conversation.

"Tina? It's good to like people, isn't it?"

"Yes, it is."

"I like you."

"I like you too, Josh."

"Aaron says you like Auntie Sam."

"Of course I do."

The boy thought for a moment before speaking again. "Grandma...she doesn't like you."

"I know."

"But...Mom always tells us to be nice to people." Joshua sounded confused.

"Your mom is very smart."

"Yup. And, I think...people who are nice...we should love them. Mom says love is important." He looked at Tina. "My mom and dad love me."

"I'm certain they do."

"Aaron says Auntie Sam loves you."

Sam's eyes widened in surprise. *Guess it's time to have that chat with the boys Lisa and I have talked about.*

Argh! Tina was completely flustered by the child's unexpected statement. *Aaron talks way too much.* She industriously tightened the laces on her sneakers while trying to come up with some sort of response. "Um...well...what do you think about that?"

"I think you're really nice."

Whew. "Thanks, Josh. That means a lot to me."

"Can I bring Beethoven in by myself?"

"Sure." Tina stood, ready to assist if needed.

"Bye, Tina." Joshua took the leash and started across the walkway. "C'mon, Beethoven."

The dog dutifully trotted after him.

"Bye, Josh." Tina watched as he and the dog got safely inside the house. She sat down on the steps with a thud. *What am I getting myself into? This woman has family...and these nephews. There's more to this than just the two of us. I don't think I'm ready.* The door above her opened.

"Hi." Sam sat next to Tina. "Did you have fun walking the dog?"

"Yeah. Joshua is a pretty neat kid."

"I think so, too. Though, as his aunt, I'm more than a little biased."

"I...I'm afraid he's getting attached to me."

"Why would you be afraid of that?"

"I don't want to hurt him. If...something...happens with us..."

"If at some point something happens and you aren't part of his life anymore, he would be sad. But he'd have happy memories of the time you spent together." Sam turned to face Tina and lowered her voice. "It's the same for me. I wouldn't trade the last few weeks for anything in the world. I'll never forget how I've felt, and how happy I've been. No matter what happens in the future, no one can take that away from me. It's in here." Sam placed a hand over her heart. "If later, things change, I'd feel lucky that I got to experience it for a little while, even though I'd be terribly hurt." *Devastated might be a better word.*

"How do you always make everything seem so...positive?"

"Life isn't perfect, but it helps to try to hold on to the good things and let the other things go."

"I...I have happy memories of Steven, but the accident..."

"Some things you might never be able to let go of, but you can learn to live with them."

Tina nodded. "You're helping me...learn."

Sam's face lit up. "I am?"

Tina nodded again and the women fell silent for several minutes.

Feeling that Tina had had as much personal discussion as she could handle in one sitting, Sam decided to change the subject. "It's almost time for the football game." She stood and reached for Tina's hand. "Don't you want to watch it?"

"Yes!"

"Come on, then." Sam led the way up the stairs and into the apartment.

As she walked through the doorway, Tina looked back at the spot where she'd last seen Joshua. *You're right, Josh: people who are nice...we should love them.*

Chapter 15

Vivian poked her head into Tina's office. "Good morning."

"Hi."

"I brought you some coffee." She placed a large cup on Tina's desk before settling into a chair.

"Thanks."

"You're welcome." Vivian watched her friend remove the plastic top from the coffee and take a sip. "How are you doing?"

"I'm fine."

"You seem tired. Are you still driving back and forth to Sarasota?"

"Yes."

"Tired but happy?"

"I...guess so."

"Tina," the older woman's voice had a no-nonsense tone, "it's all right to be happy."

"Maybe I'm just not used to it. It feels...strange."

Vivian chuckled. "You've denied yourself for too long. It's about time you allowed yourself to enjoy life again."

Tina leaned her elbows on the desk, looking at her boss with interest. "How did you do it?"

"Enjoy life again?"

"Yes."

"Well, when I lost Dominic, I tried to think of what he'd want me to do. And even though it was very difficult at first, I pushed through — one day at a time. I still think about him every single day, but I know in my heart he'd want me to go on living a full life." She paused. "It isn't easy, though."

"I can understand that."

"Most importantly, I had a wonderful friend who helped me through the worst of it." Vivian looked fondly at Tina. "That helped a lot."

"I didn't do anything."

"Ha! You don't fool me for one moment, Tina Mellekas. You never took another trip after Dominic died. You hovered around me like a mother hen, and Lord help anyone who upset me in any way."

"You exaggerate."

"I haven't even mentioned the half of it, and you know it."

There was a brief silence before Tina conceded, "All right. Maybe I helped a little."

Vivian smiled.

Tina cleared her throat. "You were telling me about Dominic?"

"Yes. What I want you to realize is — I was married for thirty-two years and I wouldn't trade in a minute of it. But I'm telling you, if I get a second chance I'm going to grab it. And he would approve." Vivian looked at Tina with solemn hazel eyes. "Chances like Samantha don't happen every day."

"I know."

"Okay." Vivian stood up. "I guess I've lectured you enough for now."

"Viv?"

"Yes?"

"Thanks."

Vivian waved her hand as she left the office. "Any time, dear."

Tina grabbed her backpack and rummaged through it until she found the piece of paper she wanted. She picked up the phone and dialed the number that was written in large print. *The writing is even big enough so I don't need my glasses. Samantha thinks of everything.*

"Hello?"

The familiar, sleepy voice made Tina smile. "Hi. Um, I found your phone number in my backpack. I figured you wouldn't have put it there unless it was okay to call."

Sam laughed. "It's okay. Yes." *I put that in there days ago. Wonder when she found it?*

"What are you doing?"

"I'm lying here hugging your pillow."

"Oh. I didn't mean to wake you."

"It's all right. I have a lot of things to do today before I leave for work."

"That's what I wanted to talk to you about." Tina played with a paper clip.

"About work?"

"Yeah." The paper clip had been unwound and now Tina was tapping the straightened piece of metal on her desk. "I...if you want to, you can stay at my place tonight. Well, tomorrow night, too. I only live about ten minutes from the Performing Arts Center. It would be much easier for you."

"Are you sure it's okay?" *You've waited until Friday to ask me. This must be something you've been thinking about all week.*

"Uh-huh." Tina picked up another paper clip and began unwinding it.

"Then I'll see you tonight."

"Okay."

"Tina?"

"Yes?"

"I..." *I wish I could tell you I love you without being afraid I'd scare you away.*

"Samantha?"

"Oh, um, I should be there sometime between ten and eleven. Is that all right?"

"I'll be looking forward to it." Tina's voice had become deeper.

Sam suddenly felt warm. "Me, too. Bye-bye."

"Bye." Tina hung up the phone and stared at it for a long time.

~ * ~ * ~ * ~ * ~

Tina held the condo door open. "Hi there."

"Hi. Ugh." Sam struggled to get through the doorway with her large duffel bag and the garment carrier she was holding.

"Do you think you have enough stuff?" Tina teased as she took the bag and shut the door.

"More than enough." Sam made a face. "It's a pain having to keep these work clothes on hangers."

"But," Tina grinned, "the end result is such an attractive outfit."

"Ha, ha." Sam looked down at her black tuxedo pants, white shirt, and black vest. "I suppose it could be worse. Thank heavens they don't make me wear a skirt."

"Let's put your things away."

They went into the bedroom and Tina opened the closet so Sam could hang up the garment carrier.

"I don't know where you want to put that stuff." Tina pointed at the duffel bag she had placed on the floor.

"Right there looks perfect." Sam ran her hand through her hair. "I really need a shower. Would that be all right?"

"Sure." Tina turned on the bathroom light. "I put some extra towels in here for you."

Sam walked into the large bathroom. "A walk-in shower!" She slid the door sideways and looked inside. "Cool."

"Let me know if you need anything."

"Besides you?" Sam hugged the tall woman.

Tina stiffened slightly at the contact. "Yes."

"Okay." *Uh-oh, she's tense. Better be careful.*

Sam took a shower and put on her pajamas. She went into the living room where Tina was watching the news on television and sat on the couch close to, but not touching, her. "So, how was work today?"

"Fine."

Okay, you don't want to talk. Sam didn't attempt any further conversation. After yawning a couple of times, she leaned her head on the armrest of the couch and, in no time at all, fell asleep.

Tina looked at the sleeping blonde. *You're so patient with me. Somehow you seem to know what I'm feeling, and you back off when I need it.* She reached over and swept a lock of still-damp hair off Sam's face. *And such a beautiful woman, with a pure heart. What is it you see in me?*

Tina turned off the television. She took the blanket that was draped over the back of the couch and placed it over the slumbering woman before carefully squeezing into the space behind her. *Sweet dreams, Samantha.* Listening to the musician's steady breathing, Tina felt herself beginning to relax. *This feels...right.* It was her last thought before drifting off to sleep

~ * ~ * ~ * ~ * ~

"Ow!"

"Hmm?"

Sam felt, as well as heard, the low sound from Tina, whose body was pressed closely against her back. "My neck," she mumbled groggily, "I slept on it funny."

"Hmm." Tina kissed the area in question. "Is that better?"

"Oh, yes."

More kisses to the affected region had Sam feeling *much* improved. She turned to face the woman she loved and caught one of those rare unguarded moments — when Tina's defenses were down and her eyes reflected her heart and soul.

They both held the eye contact, drinking in the emotions that were flowing between them.

"Let's go to bed," Sam suggested, still gazing into sky blue eyes.

"Good idea." Tina gave Sam a long, passionate kiss. "A very good idea."

They got up from the couch and Tina placed an arm around Sam's shoulders.

Sam leaned against Tina as they walked to the bedroom. Her heart was filled with joy. *She loves me. She may not be able to say it yet, but I saw it in her eyes. She loves me.*

~ * ~ * ~ * ~ * ~

Tina had been watching Sam for a while. Her view was unob-structed because the blonde had pushed the covers off during the night. Sam was lying on her back, with one arm bent over her head and the other one extended to the side. Her face was turned slightly toward Tina.

You are something else, Samantha Whitwell. You ingrained yourself into my life before I knew what hit me. And now, I can't imagine living without you. Do you have any idea how much that scares me?

Unable to restrain herself, Tina reached out to touch the peacefully sleeping woman. She lightly trailed her fingers along Sam's thigh, over the small rise of her stomach, and up between her breasts to the base of her throat. She retraced the path several times, delighting in the soft-ness of the skin she felt beneath her fingertips.

Sam stirred a little. "Mmm."

Tina pulled her hand back guiltily. *Don't wake her, T. You kept her up half the night; at least let her get some sleep.*

Sam felt warm. She lay in a half-awake state for a few moments, getting her bearings. *This is an extremely comfortable bed. And that warmth I feel — it must be heated, too.* Then, as she had become accustomed to doing each morning, she rolled over to reach for her bedmate's pillow. Bumping into a very solid object, she opened her eyes.

Tina was propped up on an elbow, smiling at her. "Good morning."

Sam blinked several times. "Hi."

"Sleep well?"

"Yes." Sam pushed Tina backward and sprawled across her. "I like you being here beside me in the morning."

"Me, too." *There I go agreeing with her again. I have never agreed with any-one so much in my entire life.*

Sam rested her head on the taller woman's chest, listening to the steady beat of the heart below her ear.

"How's your neck?" Tina asked. "I turned on the heater after you fell asleep. I thought it might help keep it from tightening up again."

"It's fine. Thank you." Sam patted the mattress with her hand. "This is a wonderful bed!"

"Yes, it is. I like it a lot."

"I like *you* a lot." Sam heard Tina's heartbeat rapidly increase and she was suddenly flipped onto her back. "Whoa!"

Tina looked down into surprised green eyes. *I'm going to agree with her again...What the hell.* "I like you a lot, too."

Sam was taken aback at the unexpected disclosure. *You said it out loud; you're really trying. Now, if I can break through those last few barricades of yours.*

Time to change the subject. "Samantha?"

"Yes?"

"When did you get this?" Tina touched the tiny rose design just inside the blonde's right hipbone.

Sam frowned and moved her hand to try to cover the tattoo.

Tina stopped her, taking the hand and bringing it to her lips so she could kiss it. "We don't have to talk about it if you don't want to."

I knew that sooner or later she was going to ask. "It was when I was in college. A bunch of us were partying one night and we all decided to do it. I don't know what the heck I was thinking." She shrugged. "It was one of those things that seemed like a great adventure at the time, but later..."

"You don't like having it?"

Sam thought about it. The tattoo had become such a part of her over the years, she couldn't envision not having it. "I...I don't know. My family wouldn't be happy if they knew."

Tina bent down and kissed the tattoo. "Is it okay if I really like it?"

"You do?"

"Yes." Tina ran her tongue along the outline of the rose before kissing it again. "I most definitely do."

"Why?" Sam felt her body immediately responding to the kisses. *You make me feel soooo good.*

Tina moved back up so she could look into Sam's eyes. "Well, first of all, it's part of you."

Sam smiled. *Mellekas, you* do *know what to say.*

"And secondly, it shows that maybe, just maybe, my all-American girl has a bit of a wild side."

"Am I?"

"What, wild?"

"No." Sam gently caressed the side of Tina's face. "Am I your girl?" It was only a couple of seconds before Tina answered, but it seemed like an eternity to Sam.

"I think so, yes." *Do relationships always take so much damn effort? No wonder I've avoided them.* "How about some breakfast? Then I thought we might go for a walk on Bayshore before you have to leave for work."

Sam was ecstatic. *She said I'm her girl! All right, don't overreact and scare her.* Trying to sound casual, she replied, "That would be nice."

They got out of bed. Sam picked her shorts up off the floor and started to look for her shirt. "You know, I can't seem to keep my clothes on when I'm around you."

"Ahem." Tina was standing at the foot of the bed, dangling the errant pajama top.

"Not that I *mind*." The naked woman walked over and reached for her shirt.

"Let me help." Tina turned the clothing right side out. Sam raised her arms like an obedient child and Tina put the shirt on her. "I'll go start breakfast."

"Okay." Sam headed toward the bathroom. *I could get used to this. Oh, yeah!*

~ * ~ * ~ * ~ * ~

"It's such a beautiful day," Sam commented as they walked along Bayshore Boulevard. Noticing that many of the people on the wide sidewalk acknowledged the couple as they passed, she asked, "Is everyone always so friendly?"

"Well, most of these people are out here every day. You start to recognize each other after a while."

"Do you run every day?"

"I try to, yes." Tina pointed to a bench tucked between a pair of palm trees. "Would you like to sit for a few minutes?"

"Sure."

The women sat close together and looked out at the calm water. Sam entwined her fingers with Tina's. "Thanks for breakfast."

"You're welcome."

"I think you're spoiling me. Normally, I only have coffee in the morning."

Tina shrugged. "It's not a big deal." *You should be spoiled a little.*

"I'm really glad you invited me to stay with you this weekend."

"Me, too." *I'm going to make myself run an extra mile every time I agree with her.*

"I'm going to miss you today. I wish I didn't have to work."

"Me..." *Oops. Close call there.* "I mean, what are you going to do for dinner?"

"We have about three hours in between performances. We usually go somewhere to eat and hang around downtown."

"You can come back here if you want. I can make something for dinner."

"I'd like that very much."

"How about chicken? Baked potato?"

"That sounds wonderful."

"All right then, let's finish our walk. You need to get ready for work." They started back toward the condo.

"Tina?"

"Yes?"

"You make me happy."

Tina looked at the blonde, who was practically skipping along beside her. *Hell, what's another mile?* "You make me happy, too." *If this keeps up, I'm going to be in the best shape of my life.*

~ * ~ * ~ * ~ * ~

I can't wait to see her again. Sam parked her Toyota and walked quickly to the elevator. She pressed the call button and waited impatiently. *C'mon, c'mon. I've got three hours and I don't want to waste a second of it.* She was just about to sprint for the stairs when the doors opened. *Finally.* Humming a tune as the car ascended, she sighed heavily when it stopped at the lobby.

Mrs. Burns stepped into the elevator. "Hello."

"Hi."

The elderly woman skimmed through the stack of mail in her hand before looking closely at Sam. "Aren't you Tina's friend?"

"Yes." Sam was watching the numbers light up as they passed each floor, willing the elevator to move faster.

"Are you going to be blaring that music over there again?"

"No, I don't think so." *I should have taken the stairs.*

Mrs. Burns tried to repress a grin as Sam nervously looked everywhere but at her.

The bell sounded as they reached their destination and Sam allowed the older woman to exit first. Then she rushed past her down the hallway to Tina's condo. As she raised her hand to knock on the door, it opened.

"Hi." Tina looked concerned. "Is everything all right? It's been a few minutes since you called for me to let you through the garage gate."

"The elevator took forever." Sam went in and waited for Tina to close the door. "But, yes." She reached up and put her arms around Tina's neck. "Everything is all right, now that I'm here."

Tina gazed into glimmering green eyes. *What is it that touches my heart so deeply when you look at me that way?* She bent down and kissed Sam. *Whatever it is, I don't want to lose it.* "C'mon. I need to check on dinner."

They walked to the kitchen and Tina peered into the oven. "It's going to be about another thirty minutes or so. Would you like something to drink?"

"Sure. How about a soda?"

Tina got a diet soda and a bottle of water from the refrigerator. "Want to go out on the balcony for a little while?"

"Okay."

They sat at the small metal patio table, sipping their drinks and watching the water. "Look at the boats." Sam pointed toward the horizon. "This is such a wonderful view."

"I like it."

"How long have you lived here?"

"About two years."

"And Vivian owns it?"

Tina shifted uneasily in her chair.

"I'm sorry. It's none of my business; I was just making conversation." *But I want to know everything about you.*

"It's all right." Tina took a sip of her drink before continuing. "Basically, I've refused to take any of the raises I've been offered over the years. As compensation, Vivian allowed me to travel quite a bit and picked up the tab for it. When I stopped taking trips, she practically forced me to get the car and this place. So, it was kind of a compromise."

"Sort of unusual — an accountant who doesn't care about money."

"I guess so."

"Then again," Sam flashed a big smile at the woman across from her, "you're anything *but* typical."

Tina rolled her eyes. "Let's go inside. I should get back to work on dinner."

"I'm going to change my clothes. Even if it's only for a couple of hours, I'd like to get out of this uniform."

Tina headed to the kitchen while Sam went to change.

"This is much better," Sam said a few minutes later as she walked through the living room and sat at the counter that overlooked the kitchen. She felt very comfortable in her gym shorts and the Florida State tee shirt she had found hanging on the hook on the back of the bathroom door.

Tina turned from the stove and whistled. "Awesome shirt."

"Is it okay if I wear it? I didn't think you'd mind."

"Yes. It's okay," Tina said as she approached Sam. "As a matter of fact, I find it very appealing." She traced the lettering on the front of the shirt. "Maybe not as appealing as the thought of me helping you take it off." She slid her hands under the fabric and lightly rubbed the soft skin she found there. *I can't seem to keep my hands off you. And the way you respond to my touch...*

Sam felt her body reacting to the words and physical contact. She lost herself in the intense blue eyes locked with her own. The kitchen timer dinged.

"Dinner is ready." Tina removed her hands from beneath the shirt. She smiled at the flushed face looking back at her. She couldn't resist leaning in for a lengthy kiss. "Why don't you put the radio on while I get the food?"

"Food?" Sam tried to focus. "Radio?"

Tina had already moved back into the kitchen. She grinned from the other side of the counter. "Uh-huh. It's time for dinner. Would you put on some music?"

"Oh, okay." Sam turned on the stereo, then adjusted the volume so that the music was audible but not loud enough to hinder conversation. *Plus, we don't want to offend Mrs. Burns, do we?* Returning to the kitchen, she took the dish Tina handed her. It was filled with strips of boneless chicken breast and a large baked potato. "This looks good."

"I have vegetables here. Would you like some?"

"Depends on what kind." Sam looked into the small pots on the stove. "Corn is all right. I could eat a little of that."

Tina added a tablespoon of corn to Sam's plate. "Well, it's a start."

As the women ate dinner, Sam talked about the play, describing the storyline as well as adding information about the various performers.

Tina was thoroughly entertained with the lively chatter.

At the conclusion of her report, Sam sat back in her chair and looked at her empty plate. "That was terrific. Thank you."

"No problem. I enjoyed cooking it."

"Let me help clean up." Sam picked up both plates and went into the kitchen.

They had rinsed the dishes and were putting them in the dishwasher when Tina heard the familiar bass line of one of her favorite songs.

"Bum, bumbum...bum, bumbum...bum, bumbum...bum, bumbum..."

"Do you hear that?" She grabbed Sam's hand and led her into the living room. She turned up the volume. High.

"It's too loud," Sam protested. "Your neighbor—"

Tina started singing along with the classic sixties tune. She pulled Sam close and they swayed to the music.

During the musical interlude, Tina twirled Sam under her arm and back again several times. As the final verse began, she pressed against the smaller woman from behind and wrapped her arms around her. She tilted her head down so she could sing along softly in Sam's ear every time the Temptations said, "My girl."

The music faded and the beginning of a commercial boomed through the speakers.

"I'd better turn that down." Sam reluctantly left her partner's embrace and lowered the volume. *Mrs. Burns is going to have a few choice words for me, I bet.* She turned back toward Tina and smiled. *But it's worth it.* "You're a good dancer."

Tina looked down at her feet. "Yeah...well, I thought...um...you might like that song."

"Oh, yes." Sam noticed the faint blush on Tina's cheeks. *You are so adorable.* "I like it very much. Even more now because we danced to it, and you sang to me."

Tina's hands found their way under the Florida State tee shirt again. "So, when do you need to be at work?"

"Seven."

"Mmm." Tina began nibbling on a tasty pink ear.

Sam felt her body temperature immediately start to rise. "The conductor is a real stickler for promptness. I can't be late."

"Hmm... Just enough time."

~ * ~ * ~ * ~ * ~

Mrs. Burns heard a door slam. *What on earth?* She opened her front door and looked out into the hallway just as two women went running by. One was tall and dark-haired, the other short and blonde. The smaller one was trying to put on her vest as she ran. They were noisily urging each other to hurry as they raced toward the elevator. When pressing the call button did not produce an instant outcome, they shouted in unison, "The stairs!" She heard another loud slam as the door was shoved open with such force that it hit the wall behind it. Footsteps thundered down the stairwell.

Mrs. Burns shook her head. *Well, that young woman seems to have worked a bit of magic on my reserved neighbor. And that music! She must have had her dancing over there again.* She smiled as she closed her door.

~ * ~ * ~ * ~ * ~

"Thanks." Sam took a deep swallow from the beer that Tina handed her. She groaned as she sat down on the couch and kicked off her shoes. "This has been a long day."

"Well, what happened? Did you get there on time?"

"Yes. I got to my seat just as the lights were dimming."

Tina was relieved. "Good." She lifted Sam's legs onto her lap and began to massage the exhausted woman's feet.

"Oh, that feels heavenly!"

After a few minutes, Sam appeared to be dozing off, so Tina removed the beer from her hands. "I think it's time for bed. Let's get you out of those clothes."

"That's what got me in trouble in the first place," came the mumbled reply.

Tina chuckled as she stood up. "Come on."

"Okay." Sam yawned, then slowly got to her feet. "You know what?" She put an arm around Tina's waist and they walked toward the bedroom.

"What?"

"I'm really going to need some help with my shower tonight."

"You think so, huh?"

"Yeah." Sam sat on the edge of the bed. She took off her vest and started fumbling with the buttons of her shirt.

Tina knelt down in front of the sleepy blonde. "Here, let me." Her large hands took over the job of undoing the buttons.

Sam's thoughts wandered. *That night at my apartment — taking a shower with me, letting me touch you. Granted, not as much as I wanted, but the most you have allowed...*

Tina looked up and was surprised to see a very sad face. "Are you all right?"

"I...maybe it's just that I'm tired." Sam felt tears spring to her eyes. *Don't cry.*

"What is it?"

"I...you..." A tear rolled down her cheek.

"Hey." Tina tenderly wiped the droplet away with her thumb. "Tell me what's wrong."

"Nothing. I'm tired, and a bit more emotional than usual. Coming up on that time of the month."

"I see." *More emotional than usual? As if you're not emotional enough on a daily basis.* "Tell me what's upsetting you."

"I...I need...you." Sam threw her arms around Tina's neck. "Tonight, I need to be close to you, touch you. I don't know why, but that's what I'm feeling."

"Um, okay." Tina's heart was pounding so loudly she was sure Sam could hear it. "Let's have that shower, then." She pulled back from the hug, got up, and began undressing.

Sensing the nervousness in the air, Sam sighed. "Don't worry. I mean closeness, not sex." She took off her shirt. "I'm way too tired for that anyway."

Tina went into the bathroom and turned on the shower. She got two large towels from the linen closet and placed them on the counter.

"I'm sorry." Sam stood in the doorway. "I'm sure I could've said what I meant better than I did." Receiving nothing more than a shrug in reply, she closed the distance between them. "I *know* I can express myself better than that." She rose up on her tiptoes and kissed Tina soundly.

Tina felt her entire body respond. *How is it that she can kiss me so gen-*

tly...so softly, and absolutely drive me wild? "If you keep that up, you won't be getting to sleep any time soon."

"You're probably right. And I really am too tired."

The pair stepped under the warm jets of water. Tina slid the door closed. Sam chose a bottle of bath gel from the assortment of soaps on the shelf. "Is this one okay for you?"

"You can pick whichever one you want."

"I like this one." Sam squeezed some gel onto her hands and began spreading it on Tina's shoulders. As she looked deeply into Tina's blue eyes, her delicate touch glided along prominent collarbones and full breasts. She leaned forward to place a kiss on Tina's heart. *I love you.*

When she felt the feather-light kiss, Tina closed her eyes. She fought to maintain control over the sensations pulsating through her body. *Relax. She needs this tonight, and maybe I do, too.*

Sam applied more gel to her hands and systematically washed the rest of the beautiful woman's body. She took great pleasure in touching the smooth skin and feeling the firm muscles lying just beneath the surface. *This is turning out better than I expected. She's more relaxed than last time, letting me do whatever I want.*

"All done." She rested against Tina, the warm water and physical exertion having made her even drowsier. "I'd do your hair for you, too, but I'm not tall enough."

Tina bent down for a quick kiss. "My turn." She picked up the bath gel that Sam always used. "I'm glad you brought this."

"You are?"

"Yes." Tina loved the golden-colored soap. It had a slight hint of perfume, which blended perfectly with the natural scent of Sam's body to create a wonderful aroma. "See the color?" She held the clear plastic bottle at arm's length. "It's like sunshine. That's what I think you smell like...I mean — if sunshine had a smell."

"That's so sweet." *That romantic side of yours seems to be sneaking out a lot more often lately.*

"Yeah, well." *I can't believe I told her that.* "Let's get you cleaned up." Tina used a generous amount of gel and washed Sam all over, occasionally kissing the soft skin she encountered along the way. She shampooed Sam's hair and her own. After rinsing them both thoroughly, she turned off the water.

Sam opened the shower door, grabbed a towel and used it to rub her hair before she wrapped it around her body. Tina took the other towel and did the same for herself. They combed their hair and brushed their teeth in companionable silence. Tina reached for her pajamas that were hanging on the door hook.

"Please, wait."

"Yes?"

"Tonight, I want my skin against yours...without clothes. Can we do that?"

"I don't like sleeping without something on."

"Just for tonight. And you can put your pajamas on after I fall asleep. Please?"

"Seeing as that should be in less than five minutes, I guess I can go along with that." Tina hung their towels on an empty hook.

"Good. Let's go then."

As soon as they settled into the bed, Sam sprawled on top of Tina. "Mmm, this is nice."

"Mmm-hmm."

"Tina?"

"Yes?"

"Thanks."

"You're welcome." Tina lightly ran her fingers up and down Sam's back. In a matter of moments, Sam was sound asleep.

Well, I don't think I can possibly get any clothes on with you draped all over me. Tina pulled the sheet up to partially cover them and stared at the ceiling. *What am I going to do? I have to talk to her, soon. I should've done it tonight, but she was so tired. Tomorrow. I'll have to do it then. And it isn't going to go well at all.*

It was a long time before sleep took her.

~ * ~ * ~ * ~ * ~

What a beautiful day. Tina sipped her coffee. *Better enjoy it while I can. All hell is going to break loose when I tell her about—*

"Good morning." Sam walked onto the balcony, placed her cup on the patio table, and sat down. "The coffee brewing smelled so good, I had to get up and have some." She looked out at the morning sun reflecting off Tampa Bay. "That's really pretty."

"Yeah."

They drank their coffee quietly, enjoying the view and each other's company. In need of a refill after a while, both women got up and headed into the kitchen.

"Tina, I really want to thank you again for last night. I don't know what got into me."

"It's all right."

Sam sat on a stool at the counter. "Can we talk for a minute?"

"Sure." *I need to talk to you, too.*

"I...it's important for me to tell you." She looked down at her hands in her lap. "I don't usually throw myself at women like I have with you."

"I know that, Samantha."

"But...I bet that happens to you all the time. You're so beautiful..." *And I want this to be different.*

Tina put a hand under Sam's chin and tilted her face up so she could make eye contact. "You're not like anyone I've ever met."

"That night in the bar at the...our...reunion. Did you want me?"

Tina paused before answering. *Tell the truth.* "Yes."

"But you didn't say...or do...anything."

"Because if I had, I would have taken you, used you, for no other reason than that I was bored." *Thank goodness, somehow, I knew you were too special for that.*

"Do you really think I would've slept with you that first night? What kind of woman do you think I am? I have *never*—"

Tina bent down and interrupted the indignant woman's speech with a passionate kiss.

"Well, " Sam felt the tingling caused by the kiss spread throughout her body, "it's unlikely. But even if that *had* happened, I believe we would still be here...together...today."

"Are you kidding? I would have taken what I wanted and been long gone."

Sam reached up to touch the side of Tina's face, feeling the warmth of the skin there. *Her body reacts just as much as mine does.* She slid her hand behind Tina's neck and pulled her down for a long, gentle kiss.

"Um, okay, maybe you're right."

They looked into each other's eyes, each of them smiling at the admission she'd extracted from the other. The moment was broken by someone knocking on the door.

"I'll be right back." Tina strode across the living room. *Who the heck could this be?* She opened the door and was greeted by several members of the condominium association. She stepped out into the hall to answer a few questions they had for a survey they were taking.

Sam went over to the coffeepot and refilled her cup. The phone rang, and while she considered whether she should go get Tina or not, the answering machine clicked on. She grinned as she heard Tina's voice telling the caller, in the briefest of terms, to leave a message. *Nope, she's definitely not one for chatting on the phone.* The machine beeped and a woman began speaking.

"Hi, Tina, it's me."

At the sound of the sultry voice, Sam put down her coffee. She walked toward the answering machine hesitantly, staring at it as if she could see the caller if she looked hard enough.

"Just reminding you about tonight."

Coming back inside the condo, Tina immediately froze.

"I really missed you last time, though I'm *sure* you'll be able to make it up to me tonight. See you soon."

The caller hung up. The answering machine reset. And the silence was deafening.

Chapter 16

Sam was mesmerized by the blinking red light on the answering machine.

Tina slowly walked across the room toward her.

"Don't." Sam put up a hand to stop Tina from getting any closer. "I need to go." She hurried into the bedroom and began throwing her belongings into her duffel bag. She got the last white shirt that was hanging in the closet, grabbed her tuxedo pants off the dresser, and went into the bathroom to get ready for work.

Tina waited for about twenty minutes, growing increasingly concerned with each passing second. "Samantha?"

The bathroom door was yanked open. "*What?*"

"I...I was worried. Are you all right?"

"No." Sam brushed by the tall woman. "I am *not* all right. Did you really think I would be?" She put her tee shirt and shorts into her luggage.

"Let me explain."

"I don't think there's anything you can say."

"Please, at least let me try."

Sam pulled a clean pair of socks from the duffel bag before zipping it closed. As she put on her vest, she looked around on the floor near the edge of the bed. "Where the hell are my shoes?"

"They're in the living room, remember? Last night—"

"Oh, yeah." Sam picked up her luggage, got the garment bag from the closet, and went into the living room. She laid her things next to the couch and sat down to put on her socks and shoes.

Tina trailed after her. "I...I'm just asking for a few minutes. You don't have to be at work for hours yet."

Sam finished with her footwear. Furious, she didn't answer, but she stayed seated on the couch.

Okay. I guess that means she'll listen, so...what do I say? Tina started pacing. "I...I have wanted to talk to you about this for a while, but I didn't know how. I've been very...confused. I've never been involved with anyone like I am with you." She glanced at Sam, who was sitting very still and looking intently at her hands.

Keep going, T. "Before I met you, I...um...dated...other people like me. People who didn't want a relationship — no strings, no emotional ties, that kind of thing."

"Sounds like an empty existence." Sam's voice was low but the underlying anger was palpable.

"I didn't know any better then. Now I realize that there can be so much more." *And apparently, just in time to lose it.*

"Were all of these 'people' women?"

"Not always, no."

"You're full of surprises today." Sam stood up. "Anything else I should know?"

"I'll talk to Andi tonight and explain to her..."

The sound of the woman's name was too much for the blonde to bear. "I need to leave." She reached for her bags.

"Wait, don't go yet."

For the first time since entering the living room, Sam looked directly at Tina. "I blame myself for this as much as, if not more than, you. I came into this knowing you couldn't make promises, but I misunderstood. I thought you meant you couldn't commit to a long-term relationship, not that you couldn't commit to one person." She shook her head sadly. "Chalk it up to the thought processes of a still naive thirty-nine-year-old. I never expected you'd cheat on me. Get tired of me, leave me — maybe. But to find out that I'm just one of your...your..." Tears trickled down Sam's cheeks and she wiped them away.

"I haven't cheated on you."

"You haven't slept with anyone else since our...the...reunion?"

"Not since the night I took you home from the Beach Bar."

"Well, three weeks! That must be some kind of record for you." Sam picked up her luggage. "A record that will evidently be broken tonight."

Tina sighed. *I'm not equipped to handle conversations like this. I say the wrong thing and only make it worse.*

Sam walked to the foyer and stared at the door. She stopped herself from launching the stinging, parting remark that was foremost in her mind. *Whatever I say now may be the last thing I ever get to tell her. Go with the truth rather than the cheap shot.* "It's been a good couple of months, especially the last few weeks."

Tina strained to hear Sam's softly spoken words.

"I truly believed — with all my heart — that we had something special. The mistake I made was thinking I could believe it enough for both of us."

"It *is* something special." Tina stepped up behind Sam but not so close as to invade her personal space. "And I want to believe in it like you do, if you'll give me the chance."

"I...don't know."

"Samantha, I'm sorry. I know I should have told you sooner. When you're ready, if you want any further explanations, I'll try. But for right now, I want you to understand that tonight I'm going to tell her that I can't see her anymore. I am *not* going to sleep with her."

"I...I'm not thinking too clearly at the moment. I'm upset, angry, and hurt." Sam opened the door. "I need to go."

Tina watched the small woman make her way down the hall. She closed the door and wandered through the condo, acutely aware of the quiet. *Samantha brings so much life to this place, and to me.* The bathroom light was on and she went to turn it off. Lying on the counter, neatly folded, was the Florida State shirt Sam had worn the day before. Tina touched the lettering, a sad half smile making its way to her face as she recalled the last time she'd done that. She picked up the shirt, brought it to her face, and inhaled Sam's scent. *My girl.*

Looking into the mirror, Tina studied her reflection until her eyes became shiny with tears.

And she cried.

~ * ~ * ~ * ~ * ~

The headlights of the silver BMW lit the driveway of the well-kept Hyde Park bungalow. Tina got out of the car and walked up the pathway to the house, trying to calm her frazzled nerves. *The odds against my having to take part in two conversations like this in the same day are astronomical. I'm sure this one won't go any better than the last. Samantha Whitwell, you have completely turned my world upside down.* As she approached the front door, it opened.

"Hi." Andi smiled and gestured for Tina to come in.

Andrea Donovan was almost the same height as Tina, but she had a slimmer, less athletic build. Wavy, dark brown hair that matched her eye color fell loosely to her shoulders. When she smiled, a large dimple materialized on each cheek. She was dressed in casual designer label clothes that accentuated her graceful curves.

"Would you like a beer?"

Tina nodded. She remained standing in the center of the living room while Andi went to get the drink. She looked around at the hardwood floors, antique furniture, artwork, and flourishing plants. *This is the last time I'll ever be here.*

Andrea settled on the couch and held the beer out. "Come and sit with me."

Tina took the drink and sat down.

"I'm glad you showed up tonight. I missed you last time."

Tina nodded, then gulped a sizable portion of her beer before beginning to fidget with the label on the bottle.

Andi watched her nervous guest. *Something's wrong. Most nights, we'd be on our way to the bedroom by now.* "What's going on?"

"I..." Tina continued to give her full attention to the drink in her hands. "Um, Andi?"

"Yes?" She reached over and gently turned Tina's face so she could look at her. "What is it?"

There was no answer, but Andi saw the truth in her eyes. "You're leaving me."

"Yes." Tina broke the eye contact and again focused on her beer. "I...met somebody."

"You 'meet' people all the time. That's never affected us before."

"This one is different." A smile tugged at the sides of Tina's mouth as she thought of Samantha.

Andi didn't miss the change in facial expression. "Amazing. Has someone really turned your head that much?"

Tina shrugged.

"Is it a woman?"

"Yes."

"I always thought if anyone could ever tame you, it would be a woman." Andi took one of Tina's hands in her own. "We've had this...arrangement for over a year. I think it's been working fine just the way it is. If you want to see this other person, too, it shouldn't change what we have."

"What we've had is the closest thing I've had to a relationship, until now." Tina shifted her position so she could look at Andi. "I don't know what's happening to me. Maybe I'm a fool for thinking I can do it, but I have to give it a try. And while I do, I can't continue...this, us."

"So, last time, when you cancelled, you were with her?"

"Yes."

"But you came back tonight."

"I thought I at least owed you a face-to-face explanation."

"Will you stay? Give me one more night?"

"I...I can't."

"Sure you can." Andi leaned forward. "You know you still want me, and I certainly still want you." She kissed Tina, hard.

After a brief moment of resistance, Tina fell into the demanding kiss. The familiarity of it felt good — two people fighting for control, and each one more interested in taking than giving. It ignited a passion within her that was hard to ignore. But Tina's considerable willpower overcame it and she broke the kiss. "I can't...we have to stop."

"Do you *want* to stop?"

Tina didn't reply right away. There was no doubt about their physical chemistry. And after the emotionally draining day she'd just had, the thought of an uncomplicated sexual encounter was more than enticing.

Andi moved forward for another kiss.

"No. Don't. Please." *I will not break my promise to Samantha.*

Tina's plaintive tone was so out of character that Andi immediately stopped.

"I'm sorry, Andi. I just...can't."

"She doesn't have to know about us."

"She already does."

"You told her?"

"It's a long story. The thing is — the reason I'm here is to tell you that, as much as I've enjoyed our time together, I can't see you any more if I want a real chance with her." Tina shrugged again. "I don't know what else to say."

Andi looked into eyes that were glistening with tears. *I've never seen her like this. If I didn't know her better, I'd swear she's in love.* "If it doesn't work out, I'll be here."

Tina stood up. "I hope that if I ever come back, you'll tell me you've found someone who has touched your heart and you don't want me anymore." She walked to the door and turned to look one last time at the woman still seated on the couch. "You deserve better than what we had here, Andi. Maybe we both do."

Too astounded to speak, Andi watched Tina — who had visited her faithfully twice a month for the last year — slip out the door and close it quietly. *I have found someone who has touched my heart, a woman that, given time, I'd hoped I could tame. And she just walked out of my life.*

Tina drove over the red cobblestone streets of Hyde Park toward Bayshore Boulevard and home. *Saying good-bye to Andi was harder than I thought it would be. I didn't want to hurt her. I guess I really do care about her, but it's completely different from the way I feel about Samantha. That green-eyed blonde has somehow taken hold of my heart, and it confuses the hell out of me. Like now, for instance. How do I go about convincing her to give me another chance?*

Tina parked the BMW and took the elevator up to her floor. Stepping into the dark condo, she put her keys on the table in the foyer. Without bothering to switch on any lights, she went into the kitchen and got a beer from the refrigerator. She opened the sliding glass door in the living room, moved out onto the balcony, and sat at the table. Sipping her drink, she looked at the stars. *It seems like forever since I sat here with Samantha having coffee, but it was only this morning. So much has hap-*

pened today, and not much of it was good.

Tina finished her beer, got another one, and went into the study. She turned on the computer and accessed her e-mail. Selecting the compose mail option, she typed in the address — SamIAm. Leaning back in her chair, she stared at the blank page on the screen. *Now, if I only knew what to write.*

~ * ~ * ~ * ~ * ~

Sam pulled into the driveway and breathed a sigh of relief. *The minivan is gone. They must be at dinner or a movie. Good, because I'm sure not up to any questions about my weekend.* She gathered her things from the back of the Toyota and trudged up the stairs.

She unlocked the door and smiled as she went inside. Home. The place she had fixed up with so much love and care always gave her a sense of peace. She dropped her luggage and went to the guitar that was resting in its stand next to the bookcase. With the amplifier on low, Sam strummed the instrument, occasionally humming a tune along with the chords. It was a ritual she had followed over the years — strumming her guitar when she was upset...finding that the rhythmic playing of the instrument had a way of comforting her.

It was almost an hour later when she heard voices in the driveway below her. She put down the guitar and looked out the window. Lisa, Mike, and the children were getting out of the van. The boys were talking excitedly about something or other. Mike put his arm around Lisa's waist as they all walked toward the house. Sam's vision became blurry with tears as she watched them. *As if I haven't cried enough today already.* She swiped at the tears with the back of her hand.

"Mom? Can I go say hi to Auntie Sam?" Joshua asked.

"All right, but just for a minute. You have school tomorrow."

"Okay." He dashed up the steps noisily.

When he reached the top, his aunt opened the door. "Hi there."

"Hi. We went to the movies! We got to see *Toy Story 2*."

"That's great." Sam ushered him inside. "Did you like it?"

"Yes. It was really good."

"I'm glad."

"Auntie Sam?" Joshua followed her as she took her luggage into the bedroom.

"Yes?" She began unpacking her duffel bag.

"Did you remember to tell Tina that I said hi?"

"Yes, I did. She says hi back."

The boy looked very pleased with his aunt's answer. He sat on the bottom of the bed. "Is she coming over tonight?"

Sam took the garment bag and hung it in her closet. She kept her back to Joshua as she struggled to get the words out. "No, I don't think so."

"Oh." He sounded disappointed. "I wanted to tell her something. If she does get here before my bedtime, will you ask her to call me?"

"Yes." *But I doubt she'll be showing up any time soon.* After taking a deep breath and trying to conjure up a smile, she turned and faced her nephew. "You'd better be getting home now, before your mom comes looking for you." *And I'm not ready to talk to her yet.*

"Okay." Joshua hopped down from the bed and hugged her. "Good night."

"Good night, Josh." She walked the boy to the door and watched him until he got inside the house.

Sam went into the bedroom and rummaged in her desk for a moment before she found what she was looking for. She sat in the middle of her bed, holding the manila envelope in her lap. *Where are you right now? Who is this Andi you're with?* She emptied the contents of the envelope on the bed. Her hands were shaking as she picked up each item and examined it: the business card on which Tina had written her e-mail address; the notes Tina had left for her each morning when she stayed over; the baggie of shells she had collected at Lido Beach. Sam couldn't see through the tears in her eyes. She lay down among the mementos and cried, until she cried herself to sleep.

It was hours later when Sam awoke and rubbed her eyes. *What time is it?* She sat up slowly and looked at the digital clock. *Almost midnight.* Stumbling out of bed, she switched on the light and went into the bathroom. A long, hot shower helped to relax the tension in her neck and shoulders. She finished getting ready for bed, returned to her room, and stood staring at the objects scattered about on the comforter. Sam picked up the items, put them back in the manila envelope, and placed the package in the drawer of her desk. She shut off the light and climbed under the covers. Out of habit, she grabbed Tina's pillow and pulled it close. Still able to faintly smell the woman's scent, she closed her eyes and drifted off to sleep.

Chapter 17

Tina took off her glasses and laid them on the desk. She glanced at her watch. *10:00 AM. Samantha might not even be up yet. She might not check her e-mail today. She might have deleted it before reading it. So, what am I going to do next?*

Vivian walked into Tina's office. "Good morning."

"Hi."

"I had my monthly brunch with the country club group today." Vivian sat down. "I talked up that New Zealand package you put together. We may get a few calls about it." She placed a cup of coffee on the desk. "I got this for you on the way back."

"Thanks."

"How was your weekend?"

"Fine."

Vivian recognized the stress in her friend's voice. "What's wrong?"

"Nothing." Tina fiddled with the plastic lid she had removed from the coffee.

The older woman waited patiently.

"I...I messed things up with Samantha. She may not want to see me any more."

Vivian was surprised. The budding relationship had appeared to be going quite smoothly. She reached over and closed the door to the office. "What happened?"

Tina fought to keep the tears back "She found out that I'm not worth having."

"What do you mean?" *She looks like she's going to cry. And what's this about not being worth having?* "Do you want to talk about it?"

"No, yes; I don't know."

"Did she say she didn't want to see you anymore?"

"She said she didn't know. She was angry...and hurt."

"About what?"

"Andrea Donovan."

Vivian was stunned at the mention of Andi's name. It had been about a year ago that the two women had met at one of her dinner parties. She had seen the mutual attraction between them, but had no idea that it had developed into a long-term relationship. "You've been seeing her?"

"Yes."

"What are you going to do?"

"I don't know."

"Tina," Vivian said gently, "what you need to do is look within yourself and decide what it is you really want."

"I want Samantha."

"She's different from the other people you've dated—"

"I know," Tina interrupted. "But if she'll give me the chance, I want to try."

"And what about Andrea?"

"I went over there last night and told her it was over."

"I see." *This must have been an interesting weekend, to say the least.* "So, you're going to try to work things out with Samantha?"

"Yes." There was a prolonged pause before Tina spoke again. "I...I never thought that I'd meet anyone like Samantha. She is...um...special. Just being with her makes me feel good, and...happy."

Vivian nodded, encouraging Tina to go on.

"Lately, I find myself thinking about the future, and all I see is Samantha. I can't imagine living without her. But I don't know how to talk to her, how to explain. She has me all confused. I find myself saying the stupidest things."

"Like what?"

"I...I'm constantly agreeing with her. Then I told her she was my girl." Tina propped her elbows on the desk and buried her face in her hands. "I even told her she smelled like sunshine."

Vivian smiled. *Sunshine? Sounds to me, my dear, like you've fallen in love.* "Those are wonderful things to say! Samantha is probably the kind of person who would appreciate words like that."

Tina felt the blush creep up her neck and into her face. "Yeah. I guess so."

"Do you want my opinion?"

Tina looked into sincere hazel eyes. If there was anyone's opinion she valued, it was Vivian's. After a decade of working together and being friends, she also knew she'd hear the truth. "Yes."

Vivian collected her thoughts for a few moments before she began speaking. "I've known you for a long time. Over the years, I have learned that you show people you love them by doing very thoughtful, meaningful things. You've demonstrated this to me on countless occasions and I know that you love me, even though you've never said so in those exact words. I love you, too. You have been like a daughter to me, the daughter I never had. And I want you to know that if I *had* been fortunate enough to give birth to a daughter, I wouldn't change a thing. I'd want her to be just like you."

Both women had tears in their eyes.

"Now, what does all that have to do with the current situation?" Vivian went around the desk and leaned against it. She looked down at Tina and rested a hand on her shoulder. "I think you knew right from the beginning — that weekend at the reunion — that there was something special between the two of you. But you were afraid to let go of your past. You made a mistake continuing with Andi after you met Samantha. So, you're going to have to talk to Samantha. Reassure her that you know what you want and you are prepared to do whatever it takes to make it work. And you're going to have to find the words to do it, because that's what she'll understand."

"Okay."

Vivian smiled at the typically brief response. "I've always hoped that you'd find some happiness in your life, and I think you have an opportunity for that with Samantha. However, a relationship takes effort, commitment, and you have to be willing to give one hundred percent of yourself. Do you think you're ready to do that?"

"For Samantha, yes."

"Then you'd better start thinking about what you're going to say." Vivian walked to the door. "Meanwhile," she turned and winked at Tina, "flowers are usually a nice touch."

Flowers? Why didn't I think of that? Tina jumped up, grabbed her backpack and followed her boss out of the office "I'll be back in a little while." She strode quickly toward the front of the travel agency.

Vivian smiled as she watched the love-struck woman leave. *I've never known you to fail at anything you've set your mind to. Let's hope this time will be no exception.*

~ * ~ * ~ * ~ * ~

It was midmorning when Sam awoke again. She made herself a cup of instant coffee, sat at the kitchen table, and thought about the day ahead. *Thank goodness I don't have to work today. I'm not feeling up to that.* Running a hand through her hair, she sighed. *Guess I might as well try to get a few things done around here.*

At the opposite end of the small kitchen, she opened a set of bifold doors, exposing a stackable washer and dryer. She turned on the washer so it would start to fill, went back to her bedroom and got her laundry, then sorted the clothes into two piles. After putting in the first load, she dusted and vacuumed the apartment, glad to have something to do to keep her busy. *I know I'm in trouble when I enjoy doing housework.*

Sam filled her large mug with water and put it in the microwave to heat for another cup of coffee. As she leaned against the counter, she glanced at the memo board on the side of the refrigerator. Tina's handwriting caught her eye and she reached out to touch the name written there. *I was so thrilled when I found your number here. I should have known I wasn't the only one you gave it to.*

The beeping of the microwave jarred her from her reflections. She prepared her coffee before moving the clean clothes into the dryer and putting the second load in the washer.

Taking her drink, Sam walked through the living room, picked up her keys, and went outside. After locking her door, she strolled over to Lisa's house. Everyone was either at work or school, so Sam used her key to get in. She received an enthusiastic welcome from Beethoven, and he trotted after her as she went into the study. The dog plopped down next to her when she sat at the desk and turned on the computer. She connected to the Internet and then clicked on her e-mail. *Three messages. Oh!* Sam gasped. The third message was from T1Run. *Tina.*

Sam read and answered the first two messages — one from a coworker in the orchestra who was worried after seeing her visibly upset the day before, and the other from a good friend who wanted to get together sometime over the weekend. The third note remained unopened for several minutes while Sam decided whether or not she should read it. Taking a deep breath, she opened the e-mail. The first thing she noticed was that the note was extremely short. *No surprise there.*

> *Samantha,*
> *I miss you already. I guess I just wanted you to know that.*
> *Tina*

She has a fantastic memory. Sam couldn't help but smile. The words on the monitor were the exact ones she had used when she had called Tina the very first time. Unsure of how to convey her sense of emptiness at the absence of the tall, dark-haired woman, Sam had simply ended up saying she missed her.

Tina knew these words would make me understand what she's feeling. Oh, you are good, Mellekas. You can come up with the right sentiment when you really want to. She closed the mail program and shut down the computer. *I'm not ready to talk to you yet. I have no idea what to say.*

Sam picked up her coffee cup and went into the family room. Beethoven followed her, wagging his tail. Sitting at the piano, she depressed the keys with one finger.

Plink, plink, plink...plink, plink, plink, plink, plink, plink...plink, plink, plink.

Memories. That's the problem, isn't it? That amazing memory of hers makes it hard for her to let go of the past. It never fades for her. Sam dropped her hand from the keyboard and petted Beethoven's head resting in her lap. *However, if that's true, then she remembers the good things, too: us playing "Heart and Soul" on the piano; the sunset at the beach; me singing to her; her calling me "my girl;" all of it.*

She stood up and wandered out to the kitchen. *Well, there's one thing I'll never forget — looking into her eyes and seeing love. I know it's there. She knows it, too. But if she isn't ready to commit to one person, a hell of a lot of good it's going to do me.*

Sam said good-bye to the dog and went back to her apartment. *I'll have to talk to Lisa today. If there ever was a time I didn't want to hear "I told you so," this is it.* She folded her laundry, ran some errands, and stopped by a fast-food drive-through on her way home to grab a late lunch. After eating, she put on her bathing suit and sat in Lisa's yard to take advantage of the beautiful fall afternoon.

~ * ~ * ~ * ~ * ~

"Hi there."

"Huh?" Sam's eyes popped open and she quickly raised one of her hands to block out the blinding sunlight.

Lisa grinned at her younger sibling. "It seems you dozed off out here. Want to come in for some ice cream? The boys are at soccer practice."

"Okay." Sam put on the oversized tee shirt she had brought along and followed her sister into the house.

"So, how was your weekend at the luxurious condo in Tampa?" Lisa opened the freezer door and got the ice cream.

"It was...okay." *I knew I'd fall apart as soon as she asked me about this.*

Lisa put the ice cream on the counter and turned to look at Sam. *Uh-oh. She's upset.* "What happened?"

Sam couldn't speak. She threw her arms around her sister and cried.

Lisa rubbed Sam's back and let her cry. *Whatever this is, 10 to 1 Tina Mellekas is responsible.*

"I...I'm sorry."

"It's all right. That's what family is for, isn't it? To be here for each other." Lisa brought a box of tissues with her to the kitchen table. "Let's sit down and talk about it." She waited quietly while Sam got seated and collected herself.

"It's really nothing." *Yeah, right.* "We had our first...um...argument."

"Do you want to tell me what it was about?"

Sam shook her head.

"Okay." *That means it's something major.* "Is there anything I can do?"

"No, but thanks for asking."

Lisa got up and busied herself scooping ice cream into two bowls and adding chocolate sauce. She placed one in front of Sam before sitting across from her again.

Both women ate in silence.

Lisa was done first and put her bowl in the sink. "Are you coming over for the game on Saturday? I had thought you might watch it at Tina's, but if things have changed..." She looked at Sam questioningly.

"Game? Oh, yeah." It was the biggest college football game of the year in Florida: the University of Florida Gators versus the Florida State Seminoles. It seemed as if everyone in the state had an allegiance to one of the teams. Pregame coverage dominated the news all week and Mike, a graduate of U of F, hosted a party each year on game day.

"You're always welcome here."

"I...I just don't know right now."

"That's okay." Lisa picked up Sam's empty bowl. "You never have to give advance notice to come over here. We'll be delighted if you join us."

"Thanks, sis."

"No problem." Lisa took the leash off a hook near the door. "I need to take Beethoven for his afternoon jaunt." The dog began rubbing against his owner, excited at the prospect of going out. It took a moment for her to attach the clasp to the collar of the active animal.

"I should be going anyway." Sam stood and put her used tissues in the trash.

"If you want to talk later, I'm here for you."

"I know. Thanks."

They walked outside just as a white van was turning into the driveway. The lettering on the side of the vehicle said Hyde Park Florist. An older gentleman got out of the van, clipboard in hand. Beethoven barked and Lisa attempted to shush him. The man, keeping his distance from the rambunctious dog, looked at his clipboard and then at the two women. "Samantha Whitwell?"

"Yes? That's me."

"I have a delivery for you." The man put his clipboard on the dashboard, then went to the far side of the van to open the sliding door.

Lisa looked at Sam. "Flowers?"

Sam shrugged.

The deliveryman came back holding a clear glass vase that contained a single rose. The flower was just blooming and the outermost petals had started to open. There was a small card attached to the sea green ribbon wrapped around the vase. He handed it to Sam.

"It's just like my..." Catching herself, Sam stopped abruptly.

"Just like what?" Lisa asked.

"Oh, nothing." Sam read the card. *I saw this and it reminded me of you. T.* She looked at the deliveryman. "Give me a second, I'll go get you a tip."

"No need for that, miss. The customer already took care of it. She insisted that you not be allowed to tip." He climbed into the van and backed out of the driveway.

"Hyde Park? That's an awfully long way to go for a delivery," Lisa commented. "Don't they usually call a local affiliate?"

"I guess so."

"Well, whatever happened with Tina, it sure looks like she wants to make up."

Sam touched the bit of greenery that surrounded the stem. "Hmm, maybe." *But on her terms or mine?*

Having waited as long as his energy level permitted, Beethoven started pulling on the leash. "Want to come for a walk with us?" Lisa asked as she started down the driveway.

"Not today, sis." Sam went into the backyard and got her towel and book from the lounge chair. She went up the stairs to her apartment, where she positioned the vase in the center of the coffee table. She had just finished changing into a tee shirt and shorts when the phone rang. "Hello?"

"Um...hi, Samantha. It's Tina."

Sam's heartbeat increased rapidly. *As if you had to say who it was. That deep voice...and the way you say my name...*

"Are you there?"

"Yes," Sam finally managed to answer.

"I..." *What the hell do I say?* "I..."

Sam could picture Tina, phone in hand, restlessly pacing back and forth. *If I could see you...read your body language...look into those blue eyes, I'd probably know whatever it is you're trying to say.* "Thank you for the rose."

"Oh, you got it? You're welcome. I...um...it's nice to hear your voice. I...I miss you." There was no response, so Tina plunged forward. "I'd like to talk to you, if you'll let me. Not on the phone, though. Can I see you?"

Sam considered the request. *We have to work this out, one way or the other. May as well get it over with.* "Okay."

"When?"

I'm not ready for this today. "Tomorrow."

"I can bring dinner if you want."

"No." That kind of experience was still too fresh...back when things were oh, so different.

"All right. I'll see you tomorrow night, then."

"Okay."

"Good night, Samantha."

"Bye." Sam hung up the phone, went to her guitar, and began strumming. She played well into the night.

~ * ~ * ~ * ~ * ~

Tina turned the engine off and sat for a moment, gathering her courage. *Just tell the truth and hope for the best.* Taking her backpack and a small box from the passenger seat, she got out of the car.

One of Sam's nephews came running across the yard. "Hi!"

"Hi, Joshua."

"You know what?"

"What?" Tina sat on a step and the boy joined her.

"Daddy's football team is playing your team this weekend."

"Oh, yes." *I haven't even been paying attention to the hype about the game. That isn't like me at all.*

"I wanted to tell you," the boy said excitedly, "I think your team is gonna win. I saw them on TV. They have this really cool cheer and they have a guy who has a horse. He rides on the field and throws a spear and everything!"

"Yes, they do." Tina smiled at his enthusiasm. "I think they're going to win, too, but maybe we should keep that between us. We wouldn't want to hurt your dad's feelings, now, would we?"

"I guess not."

Sam had seen the BMW pull in the driveway. When her guest didn't show up after a minute or two, she opened the door and saw Tina sitting with her nephew down near the bottom of the stairs. *Oh, good. He wanted to talk to her. I'd forgotten about that.*

"Will you teach me the cheer? It's *so* cool."

"I don't know if your dad would like that."

"Please?"

There's too much of Samantha in this kid. "Okay. It goes like this..."

Sam covered her mouth to keep from laughing as she watched the unlikely duo wave their arms in the tomahawk chop and perform the FSU chant.

"Thanks, Tina!"

"You're welcome."

Joshua ran back to his house. As Tina turned to go up the stairs, she saw Sam standing in the doorway.

"That was quite a performance. I didn't know you gave lessons."

A faint blush colored Tina's face when she realized that Sam had overheard. "Only for Joshua." She reached the top of the stairs and they went inside.

Sam closed the door behind them. "You mean I can't have a lesson if I want one?"

"You can have anything...everything, just ask."

That's a heck of an opening line for the evening. "How about if we start with something small?" Sam pointed at the gold-colored box. "Maybe that?"

Tina handed over the gift. "I remember you said these were your favorites when we were at the Godiva Store in Hyde Park."

"I feel like I'm being courted."

"Is that a good thing?"

"Maybe."

They went into the living room. Sam put the box of candy on the table next to the rose as she sat down on the couch. Feeling that a certain amount of distance was appropriate under the circumstances, Tina chose the large chair. It was dreadfully silent for several minutes.

Sam was debating whether she should speak first. She'd spent a great deal of time thinking about everything that had happened and, even though she was still hurt, she realized that communication lapses by both of them had played a part in their current predicament.

Apprehensive, Tina was having difficulty staying seated. *C'mon, T, you're here to talk, so talk.* She studied her feet as she began to speak in a soft, emotionally tinged voice. "I'm sorry I hurt you. If there's only one thing I say tonight that you believe, I want it to be that." She took a deep breath to calm her nerves. *Start at the beginning.* "Um...I...I've been kind of confused ever since I met you. I haven't had many close friends in my life and I really enjoyed the time we were spending together. I...I knew I was physically attracted to you, but I tried to keep that...contained. I thought sex would only mess up the special friendship we had."

"I guess it didn't help that I was constantly throwing myself at you," Sam said, ashamed. *And ignoring all the warnings you gave me, because I wanted you so much.*

Tina shook her head. "You've done nothing wrong, nothing...to deserve...this." Unable to stay seated any longer, she got up and paced back and forth. *Now, if I can just get past this next part.* "For about a year before I met you, I'd been seeing Andi. She was...um...a person like me — not looking for anything more than a tumble in the sheets a couple of times a month." Tina's voice became laced with self-loathing. "People like that...like me...have no business getting tangled up in the lives of people like you." She wiped her eyes with the back of her hand.

"Tina—"

"No. Please, let me finish. After you and I slept together, I knew I had to break up with Andi, but I wasn't sure how to do it. And then there was you. I was afraid to tell you about her. I knew it was going to hurt you, that you'd be disappointed in me." She stopped pacing and forced herself to look at the woman who had come to mean so much to her. "I'm sorry I didn't tell you. It was...I was...wrong."

"Tina, both of us made mistakes. Having thought about it, and hearing what you've said here tonight, I can see that I pushed you into something you weren't ready for. I never asked what *you* wanted."

"I should have told you about Andi."

"I should have asked." *It seems so obvious in hindsight.* "I think back now about how you always tried to stop me, but I pushed and pushed. I wanted you and that was all that mattered."

Emotionally drained, Tina dropped down into the large chair. *Well, she hasn't tossed me out yet. That's a positive sign.* She clasped her hands together in her lap to try to stop them from trembling. *One more thing to say, then it's up to her.* "Samantha?"

"Yes?"

"I...um...there have only been a few times in my life when I've felt a profound sense of loss. The first was when I was a little girl and my father left. My whole world changed in the blink of an eye and I didn't really understand why." *I guess I never did.* "The second was when Steven died." She cleared her throat and tried to maintain her composure. "The last time was when you walked out of my place on Sunday morning. I...I wasn't able to do anything about the first two. But maybe, if you'll give me a chance, this time can be different." Her next words were barely audible. "I don't want to lose you."

"I don't want to lose you, either," Sam said sadly. "But I can't be in a relationship with someone unless she is committed to me...and *only* me."

"I know."

"Are you still seeing...her?"

"No! Absolutely not. And even if you don't want me anymore, you've taught me there's so much more to life than what I'd been experiencing. I don't ever want to go back to the way things were, the way I was."

"Do you really think you're ready for...capable of...a serious, committed relationship?"

"Yes. I want to be with you, *only* you, and I hope you'll give me the opportunity to prove it."

"I want to be with you, too, but this whole thing has shaken me up. We have a lot to talk about. I have so many questions. I want to know...everything."

Tina sighed. *I only wish you'd like what you're going to hear.*

Sam realized that the taciturn woman was way beyond her quota of talking for one day. *She looks totally exhausted. We need to take a break.* "I think we've talked enough for now, don't you?"

Tina looked relieved. "We have?"

"Well, we've established that we're going to work this out, right?"

"Yes."

"And we're going to start over — in a committed relationship that's going to last for a long, long time." *Like forever.* "Right?" *Please say yes.*

"Yes."

Good answer. And she didn't hesitate. "We'll talk as much as we need to...because that's important in a relationship."

"Yes."

"We've accomplished a lot, wouldn't you say?"

"Yes." *I like this part where I can say yes or no. This is much better.*

"So, we don't have to discuss our entire lives in one evening." Sam smiled. *At our ages, that would be impossible anyway.*

Tina was aware that she was purposely being giving a respite and she was very thankful for it. *It's so nice to see her smile again.* "I...I suppose I should be going, then." She stood up.

"Do you want to go?"

"No, not really."

"Then why are you leaving?"

"I don't know." Tina looked puzzled. "I guess I still have a lot to learn about this relationship thing."

"I have a feeling you'll be a quick study." Sam went over and hugged her. "We're okay for now. We need to spend time together, get close again."

Tina returned the hug. "I like the sound of that."

"What do you say to watching a little TV?"

"Okay."

They sat on the couch and Sam picked up the remote from the coffee table. "Let's see what's on." She started flipping through the channels. "An Indiana Jones movie; how's that?"

"Fine with me."

"Why don't you lie down? I'll be your pillow."

Tina stretched out and rested her head on Sam's lap. While they watched the movie, Sam stroked Tina's jet-black hair and lightly trailed her fingers along any bare skin within reach.

The movie ended and Tina rolled onto her back so she could look up at Sam. "I...I like this."

"Me, too."

Now she's agreeing with me. Maybe I can subtract a mile when that happens. "Well, I have to work tomorrow. I really do need to get going." They both stood and Tina picked up her backpack from next to the chair. "May I use the bathroom?"

"Of course."

"Thanks." She went into Sam's room, then stopped and listened to make sure she wasn't being followed. Quickly, she opened her backpack and carefully removed an item. Lifting the edge of the comforter, Tina slipped the item underneath, placing it on the pillow. Grinning, she started tiptoeing toward the bathroom.

"Everything all right?"

Tina just about jumped out of her skin. She spun around and almost crashed into Sam.

"I'm sorry. I didn't mean to scare you."

"I'm sure you didn't. It's okay."

"You were going back in?" The blonde pointed toward the bathroom.

"Oh...um...I decided maybe I should go back and splash some water on my face. I got a little sleepy watching TV."

"Okay." Sam sat on the bed to wait.

"I'm fully awake now, thanks to you." Tina smirked as she took Sam's hand and pulled her off the bed. "So I don't need the water." She took long strides out of the room and the shorter woman had to jog to keep up.

They arrived at the door and Tina, unable to think of what to say, put her arms around Sam and hugged her.

"This really is like starting over, isn't it?" Sam murmured.

"Yes."

"Are you coming over tomorrow night?"

"If you want me to, yes."

"I want you to."

"Then I'll be here." Tina gave her a reassuring squeeze before breaking the embrace. "Good night, Samantha."

"Good night."

Sam watched Tina go down the stairs, then closed and locked the door. She paused before turning off the lights, looking at the rose and box of candy on the coffee table. *You certainly get an A for effort, Mellekas.*

She took her shower and got ready for bed. When she pulled back the comforter to get under the covers, she saw something on the pillow. *What's this?* A big smile spread across Sam's face as she recognized the Florida State shirt she had worn while she was at Tina's. She picked it up and a note fluttered out. She read the beautiful script:

I thought maybe wearing this would bring back some good memories.

T.

Let's change that A to an A plus. Sam put on the shirt and glanced at the bedside clock. *She won't be home yet.* She lay awake in bed, thinking about Tina. Finally, she picked up the phone and dialed.

"Hello?"

"Hi, it's Sam."

"Hi, Samantha."

"I found the shirt. I'm wearing it."

"I was hoping you would."

The women listened to each other breathe.

"I miss you already."

"Me, too." *So much for subtracting that mile. I may as well sign up for a marathon.*

For a moment or two, there was only the sound of breathing.

"We're still not very good on the phone, are we?"

Tina laughed. "I guess not."

It's nice to hear you laugh again. "Well, good night."

"Good night, Samantha."

Across the miles, each of them lay in bed thinking about the other. Sam fell asleep first, a smile on her face and pillow clutched tight. Tina was more restless, replaying in her mind what had been said that evening...and what had not. She also pulled a pillow close, inhaling the fragrance of the woman she missed holding in the night. And so they slept.

Chapter 18

Hmm. Tina examined the information on her computer screen. *That looks perfect.* She printed out the page and put it in her backpack. *The Internet is a wonderful thing.* Her intercom buzzed and she picked up the phone. "Yes?"

"Samantha Whitwell for you on line one."

"Thanks, Brenda." Quickly pressing the appropriate button, Tina took off her glasses and leaned back in her chair. "Hello."

"Hi, Tina."

"Hi, Samantha."

"I was wondering what time you were going to come over tonight. I thought if you could get here a little early, we could walk on the beach while we talk."

"That's a great idea."

"Around five o'clock?"

"I'll be there."

"Do you want to meet at my house first, or at the beach?"

"At the beach. I can cut right across from the interstate and miss some of the rush-hour traffic."

"All right. I'll see you later, then."

"Bye, Samantha."

"Bye."

Tina knew she was grinning from ear to ear, but she couldn't help it. A soothing warmth had spread through her body when she'd heard Sam's voice on the phone. *She has an effect on me like no one else.*

"How about some lunch?"

"Huh?" Tina hadn't noticed her boss standing in the doorway.

Vivian laughed. "You seemed lost in thought there, but it must have been a very nice thought."

"Oh, um...yeah."

"Would you care to join me for lunch?"

"Sure."

They went to the Cactus Club and Vivian was able to obtain a concise summary of the previous night's discussion from her friend. She was happy to hear that the two women were working things out.

"But we still have a lot to talk about." Tina tinkered with her utensils. "I was going to leave a little early today, if that's okay."

"Since when do you need to ask?" Vivian joked. "You virtually run the place now."

"I do not."

"You know darn well I'm telling the truth. You took my little hole-in-the-wall travel agency and transformed it into a thriving, prosperous business. Then, you invested my profits so now I have more money than I know what to do with. And all the while, you continued to make the wages of an office clerk, refusing any efforts of mine to give you a raise."

Embarrassed by the compliments, Tina traced the patterns on the tablecloth. "I have the car and the condo, what else do I need?"

"Samantha...that's what else you need. Although you seem to have finally figured that out on your own." Vivian reached across the table and rested her hand on Tina's arm. "Don't think for one minute I'm unaware that your substantial talents have been wasted on my small business. When I think of the money you could be making at some big—"

"I like working for you. It's where I belong." *And Samantha was right. Everyone needs to belong somewhere.*

"I'm awfully lucky that you feel that way."

"No. I've been the lucky one."

The women smiled at each other, affection evident on their faces.

"So," Tina asked again, "is it okay if I leave a little early?"

Vivian rolled her eyes heavenward. "Yes, dear. You can leave early."

~ * ~ * ~ * ~ * ~

Tina drove around St. Armand's Circle and made a left onto the nearly deserted street that ran alongside the beach. She immediately spotted Sam's Toyota and pulled into the vacant space behind it.

Taking a sweatshirt with her, she walked to the beach access and broke into a jog as she started over the wooden footbridge. She paused at the top when she saw Sam at the shoreline, looking out at the water. Leaning against the railing, Tina watched her. *I never thought I could feel this way about someone. I think I belong with her. It just seems so...right.*

Sam checked her wristwatch. *Almost five o'clock. She should be here soon.* She turned and was surprised to see Tina standing on the footbridge. She waved and began making her way across the sand. Tina met her halfway and they stood in uncomfortable silence for a few seconds.

"Let's walk a little, okay?" Sam suggested.

Tina nodded.

They went down near the water's edge and began strolling in a southerly direction. The women walked for a while, not speaking, both of them feeling nervous.

Sam decided to get the most pressing issue out of the way first. *Even if I'm not sure I'm ready to hear this...we have to talk about it.* "Tell me about Andi."

"Um...around a year ago, Vivian had one of her occasional dinner parties. I usually don't go to those things, but somehow or other, she talked me into it that night. Andi happened to be there and we...we were attracted to each other. We flirted throughout the evening, and when I was getting ready to leave she asked me if I wanted to go over to her place for a drink. I hadn't done anything like that in a while, but I went...and I stayed." Tina peeked at the blonde, whose eyes were fixed on the ground. "Um...I saw her again after that. Then she asked me if we could have a couple of set days a month that we could...meet. I'd never done that before, but I don't know, I was tired of the way things had been. It seemed like a step in the right direction, so I agreed."

Tina had to consciously slow her pace so she didn't move too far ahead of Sam. "I'm not sure what else you want to know."

"You were tired of the way things had been? What does that mean?"

"I'm not sure. Several things happened at once. I turned forty and it...I...I wondered where my life had gone, what I was doing, where I was going. Right around then, Vivian's husband died. She was overcome with grief and I...well...I understood. I stopped traveling and ran the business full-time while she was dealing with that. I was so busy between the agency and keeping an eye on Vivian, I didn't really think about dating. I went a long time without being with anybody."

"Then you met Andi?"

"Yes. I guess I was...lonely, and having some major angst about being old."

"Did you see anyone else while you were with her?"

"No, but she assumed I was seeing other people the whole time. I never told her any different."

"You didn't want her to know you were faithful?"

Tina shrugged. "I...I didn't want her to think it meant...something."

"Well, didn't it?"

"I don't know."

They walked quietly for a few minutes.

"I'm not sure what I expected, but I didn't think you'd say you've only been with one person in the last couple of years. I had visions of you telling me you've conquered most of the known world." *And you're gorgeous enough to do it.*

"Well, um..." Tina looked contrite. "We haven't talked about what happened *before* I turned forty."

"Let's deal with the more recent past first."

"Okay."

"You said that having this relationship with Andi was a step in the right direction. How so?"

"I felt like I should settle down. I'd been running from everything and everyone since Steven died and I was tired of it."

"And it was going well?"

"For what it was, yes. But we...we never went anywhere together...or watched a sunset...or danced. We never did anything like that. It wasn't really a relationship, but it was the closest I'd been to it in a long time."

Sam tried to ask the question that had been on her mind for days. "Did you...did she...I mean — you wouldn't let me..." *C'mon, spit it out.* "Did you let her make love to you?"

Tina looked down at her feet, trying to formulate a response that would make sense to someone like Samantha. She realized there wasn't one.

The nonanswer confirmed Sam's fears. Unable to restrain her tears, she wandered away from the shoreline.

I have to explain. But how? Tina followed the weeping blonde. "Please don't cry."

Sam headed for one of the benches that were sprinkled along the beach and sat down.

Tina sat next to her. "Samantha, what Andi and I had was just...sex. I know that sounds terrible, but it's the truth. What you want from me is so much more. It...it scares me. I've been overwhelmed by this whole thing. I don't even know how to explain it." Tina considered what else she should say. *Tell her everything.* "Ever since I met you, I've wondered what it is you see in me. Sometimes you look at me with such...I don't know. I knew it was only a matter of time before you'd discover I didn't deserve that look." Her voice shook with emotion. "I...I wished at the fountain that I could be whatever it was you thought you were seeing, but not all wishes come true."

"You *are* everything I see," Sam sniffled. "Maybe someday you'll let yourself see it, too." She slid over and leaned against Tina.

"I can't change my past. Lord knows, if there was any way—"

"I'm not judging you, Tina. Everyone does what he or she has to do to get through life. You had some rough times and you did what you needed to do to cope. But I can't help it if some of it is hard to hear."

"I'm sorry."

"I don't want you to be sorry for who you are. Whatever we've had to go through in our lives, it's brought us here. And being together now, that's the most important thing, isn't it?"

"There's that positive thinking again." *Making things sound better than they really are. Making me sound better than I really am.*

"I...I have to tell you something."

Tina tensed. *Uh-oh.*

"It's nothing bad. At least I hope you don't think so." Sam looked deeply into blue eyes. "All my life, I've wondered if there was someone special, someone meant just for me, to share my life with. When I saw you at the reunion," she reached up and lightly trailed her fingers down the side of Tina's face, "and looked into your eyes, I knew you were the one."

"I felt something, too." *And it scared me. Hell, I'm still scared.*

"Do you believe in love?"

Tina put her arms around Sam and pulled her close. "I guess so. But I always believed it was for other people, not me."

"Why?"

"I don't know. Just thought that's the way it was."

"Have you changed your mind?"

"You've changed my life, Samantha. If anybody can make me believe in love, it's you."

"I'll take that as a yes."

Tina kissed the top of the blonde head tucked beneath her chin before adding, in a voice so soft it was almost lost in the sounds of the surf, "Yes."

Sam smiled as she listened to the rapid beating of the heart beneath her ear. *Well, that's quite a lot of progress for one day.* "Look." She pointed toward the horizon. "The sun will be setting soon."

They watched the beautiful view in silence as they snuggled together on the bench.

"You ready to go?" Tina could feel Sam starting to shiver as the temperature quickly dropped. "Here." She held out the maroon FSU sweatshirt she had brought along. "Put this on."

"Thanks." Sam donned the heavy top.

"Would you like to go get some dinner?"

"That sounds good."

As they walked back toward the footbridge, Tina saw that the beach was almost empty on the cool November evening. She reached over and held Sam's hand. *I hope this is okay.* She looked at her companion and got a big smile in return. *Yeah, it's okay.*

They walked along, hand in hand. "This is nice, isn't it?" Sam asked.

"Yes. I like this place."

"Really?"

"Yes." Tina stopped at the base of the footbridge. She brought their joined hands up to her lips and kissed their entwined fingers. "I like *you*."

"I like you, too." Sam grinned, waiting as the tall woman shuffled her feet in the sand, obviously trying to find the words to say something.

"Have you noticed that we agree a lot?" Tina asked.

"We do?"

"I think so, yes."

"That's good, isn't it?"

"Um, yes." Tina sounded a bit perplexed. "But I...I'm not used to it."

"Well, you'd better get used to it, because I have lots of things I want you to agree to."

"You do?"

"Oh yes!" Sam stood on her tiptoes and kissed Tina.

As they started over the bridge, Tina said, "What do you think about me training for a marathon?"

"A marathon?"

"They're having one in Tampa this spring."

The women's voices faded into the night.

~ * ~ * ~ * ~ * ~

Sam pulled into the driveway. *What in the world is that?* A large blue flag hung from a pole attached to the garage. She got out of her car and looked up at the cloth fluttering in the wind. It was a University of Florida banner with a big gator on it. She marched to her sister's house and entered the kitchen. "Hello?"

Lisa was unloading the dishwasher. "Hi, Sam. What's up?"

"Where did that flag come from?"

"Mike got it on the way home from work. You should've seen him putting the flagpole up." Lisa chuckled. "Mr. Handyman, he's not."

"Couldn't you have put it on the front of your house?"

"I told him it was the garage or nowhere. I'm not having that thing hanging on my house."

"Well...it's awfully...big."

"Speaking of big," Lisa regarded the oversized FSU sweatshirt her sister was wearing, "I see you're still a Seminoles fan."

"Yes."

"How's it going with Tina?"

Sam sat at the kitchen table. "We have some stuff to work out, but it's going to be okay."

"Are you sure you're all right? If she did anything…"

"I'm fine. Really. I'm the one who caused the problem, not Tina."

"You? What do you mean?"

"I pushed her too hard. I got us into a physical relationship before she was emotionally ready. She tried to tell me any number of times, but I didn't listen."

"So, what's going to happen now?"

"We're kind of starting over." Sam smiled. "It's just a matter of slowing down a little bit and talking a lot more. She wants to be with me, Lisa, in a serious relationship. I can hardly believe it."

"Of *course* she wants to be with you. Do you think she actually stood a chance against the Whitwell charm?" They both laughed.

Mike came into the kitchen. "Sam, did you see the flag?"

"It's pretty hard to miss."

"Isn't it great?"

"Yeah, it's…great." Sam sounded less than enthused.

Mike rolled his eyes as he noticed the FSU sweatshirt. "Wait a minute, you're not going to cheer for the Seminoles this year, are you?"

"Well…"

"You can't! Not after all the years you've been a Gator fan with me."

"I'm sorry." Sam could see the disappointment on her brother-in-law's face. "I didn't go to either school, so it doesn't matter to me who wins. I was happy to cheer with you before, but now I think I should stand by Tina and support her team."

"It won't be the same without you."

Sam got up and hugged the downcast man. "I don't think things will ever be the same again, but in a good way. I've found the person I'm going to spend the rest of my life with."

Mike looked over at his wife, who smiled at him and nodded her head. "Then I guess you can be a Seminoles fan," he grumbled, "but I don't have to *like* it."

"I even promise not to tease you after the Gators lose."

"*What?*" Mike picked up the small woman and slung her over his shoulder.

"Hey, put me down!"

"Which team is the best?"

"Florida State."

"Wrong answer." He jostled her up and down.

"They're *both* good."

He spun around in a circle. "Which team is *best?*"

"Ugh. I...just...ate."

"Michael," Lisa admonished, "put her down. Honest to goodness, this is precisely why I went to a college that didn't have a football team."

He gently returned Sam to her feet. "We were just kidding around." He gave his wife a kiss on the cheek before grabbing the leash from the hook on the wall. "I'd better take Beethoven for his walk." The dog came charging into the kitchen when he heard his name and Mike attached the leash to the animal's collar. "I'll be back in a few minutes."

"Sorry, Lisa." Sam sat back down. "I know you hate football."

"I find it amazing that grown people can get so crazy about a game. Every year this rivalry gets all blown out of proportion."

"That's part of the fun of it."

"So it would seem. I take it this means you won't be at Mike's party?"

"Tina and I haven't talked about it yet, but I doubt it."

"You're going to leave me alone with all those maniac Gator fans?" Lisa sighed. "At least in the past you were here to help me keep my sanity."

"It'll be so different — not being with you guys for the game."

"But a good kind of different, right?"

"Yes." Sam's face lit up. "*Very* good."

"I'm glad to hear it's working out." Lisa opened the refrigerator and removed a large pan covered with aluminum foil. "I made extra lasagna tonight."

"For me?"

"Yes. No mushrooms, no vegetables — just meat and cheese."

"Thanks." Sam took the pan from her sister. "I can invite Tina to dinner tomorrow night."

"You're welcome."

They walked to the door together and exchanged good-byes. Lisa watched as Sam crossed the walkway to her apartment. *I hope you're right that it's what both of you want. Maybe I should have a chat with Tina myself and find out.*

~ * ~ * ~ * ~ * ~

"Argh." Sam put her pillow over her head. The doorbell rang again. Throwing back the covers, she got out of bed. *9:05 Who could this be so early in the morning?* She shuffled to the door and looked out the window. A deliverywoman was standing there holding a cardboard box. Opening the door a crack, Sam asked, "Yes?"

"Samantha Whitwell?"

"Yes."

"Hyde Park Courier Service. I have a delivery." The messenger held out an electronic signature pad. "You'll have to sign for it."

Sam blinked in the bright sunlight and tried to see where she was supposed to sign.

The courier pointed to a blank gray area on the pad. "Right here, ma'am."

Ma'am? That's a first. Sam signed on the spot indicated and traded the pad for the box. "Thanks."

"You're welcome. Have a good day."

Sam closed the door and looked at the return address on the box. *Exclusive Travel. It's from Tina.* She went into the kitchen and put a mug of water in the microwave for coffee. She got a knife, cut through the tape on the box, and looked inside. *A portable CD player?* There was a note, and she smiled as she read the script.

> *A good friend once told me that a song can say something better than plain words. As usual, she was right. Track three is from me to you. T.*

She put on the headphones and pressed track three. *I wonder what this is going to be?* The first few notes of the top-forty love song filled her ears. *Oh, I know this.* She turned up the volume.

Sam held the CD player to her chest and swayed to the music. She sang along with the chorus as it repeated several times before the song ended. Sam pressed track three again. After the fifth repetition, she finally turned off the CD player and removed the headphones. *If I didn't have to go to work, I'd drive to Tampa right now and hug her, kiss her, look into her eyes.*

Sam reheated the mug of water in the microwave for a minute before preparing her coffee. She picked up the phone and dialed the number for Exclusive Travel. Brenda answered the phone and Sam waited to be connected to Tina's office.

"Hello, Samantha."

"Hi. Guess what?"

"What?"

"I got a package this morning."

"You did?" Tina glanced at the clock. *I hope they waited 'til after nine like I requested.*

"Yes. I was wondering — are you the jealous type?"

"What?"

"It seems that I have an admirer."

Tina gripped the phone tightly. "Really?"

"Yes. Some person named T. First, I got flowers and now...a lovely song."

"Oh." Tina relaxed. "Yeah, that's me." *I signed it T? I wasn't even thinking.*

"Is that shorthand? Or a nickname?"

"How about I explain it next time I see you?"

"Okay. I have lasagna here. Would you like to come over for dinner?"

"Yes."

Sam smiled at the tone of the one word answer. A response so brief, yet filled with emotion. *I'm starting to get the hang of this.* "I was going to stop and pick up some Italian bread on the way home from work. Do you want salad?"

"I can get the salad on the way. I might as well get the bread, too, while I'm there. Anything else?"

"Just you."

There was a pause before Tina responded in a soft voice, "For as long as you want me."

"That's going to be a *long* time."

"I think I like the sound of that."

"Me, too."

"I'll see you tonight, then."

"Okay. Bye."

"Bye, Samantha."

Sam hung up the phone, then listened to the song three more times before rushing to get ready for work.

Chapter 19

Tina walked up the driveway with a plastic grocery bag in each hand. She frowned at the Gator flag hanging from the garage.

"Stop it!"

"Ow!"

The shouting drew her attention to Lisa's yard, where she saw Aaron and Joshua fighting.

"Hey!" Tina put the bags on the steps to Sam's apartment and ran to the boys. She pulled them apart.

Lisa came out of the house. "What's going on here?"

Joshua was crying. "He...he...hit me."

"Aaron, we've talked about this," Lisa scolded her older son.

"I *told* him to stop that stupid tomahawk chant. He likes the Seminoles, Mom. We're supposed to cheer for the Gators. He's never even been interested in football before, and now he wants *them* to win!"

Lisa crossed her arms and looked at Tina, who was standing there guiltily in her FSU tee shirt. "Any bright ideas, Ms. Florida State?"

"Um..." *Where is Samantha?* "I'm sure we can get this straightened out. How about if I talk to Joshua?"

"All right." Lisa took Aaron by the arm. "You come with me." They went into the house.

Tina looked down at Joshua, who was still sniffling. "Let's go sit on the steps, okay?"

The boy nodded and followed Tina. She moved the grocery bags out of the way and they sat down.

"What happened?"

"We were just playing around and then Aaron...he started saying, 'Gators rule! Gators rule!' I said the Seminoles were gonna win and did the FSU chant. He got mad and he hit me."

"Hmm..." *What do people tell children in situations like this?*

"Tina? You want the Seminoles to win, right?"

"Absolutely."

"Then it should be okay for me to want them to win, too."

"It's perfectly all right for you to cheer for any team you choose."

"Aaron doesn't think so."

"Joshua, during your life, you're going to meet people who want you to think the same way they do. They get an idea into their heads and believe they are so right that they try to make everyone else think the same thing." She looked at the confused expression on the boy's face. *I'm not doing very well here.*

"I don't care what Aaron thinks. I want the Seminoles to win."

"That's good, Josh. You should stick to what you believe in. But—"

The door opened above them and Sam poked her head out. " I thought I heard someone talking out here. Mind if I join you?"

"Not at all." *Thank goodness. Help has arrived.*

Sam sat on the step behind Tina. "What's up?"

"The boys got into an argument. We're trying to sort things out. I'm glad you're here."

"Aaron hit me!" Joshua piped in.

Tina sighed. "What we need to discuss is how to handle it when you disagree with someone. Fighting is not the solution."

"Aaron started it."

"Well, let's look at that. Your brother was expressing his feelings about the game. You kind of challenged him by doing the FSU chant. He took that to mean you didn't respect his opinion."

"He doesn't respect my opinion."

"Well, that's something you have to learn to deal with. What happens is...when you tell people what you think, sometimes they'll respect your opinion and sometimes they won't."

"Aaron won't."

Tina glanced over her shoulder. "Feel free to jump in here any time." *Please.*

"Joshua," Sam looked affectionately at her nephew, "your mom and I used to argue a lot when we were kids. Now, as adults, we're the best of friends. That'll probably happen with you and Aaron, too. But for the time being, you should try to get along with him as much as you can. Let the little things go, rather than arguing with him, and if you think it's something important, you may want to wait until your mom or dad are around to talk about it. They can help you two work out your disagreements without fighting."

"Auntie Sam, he picks on me because I'm younger. He does stuff on purpose to make me mad."

"Your mom did the same thing to me. I guess it goes with being the oldest."

"That's true," Tina agreed. "And I should know because I had a younger brother."

Joshua was immediately interested. "Did you tease him?"

"Yes. But he found a way to get me back."

"What did he do?"

"Well, sometimes he would ignore me and keep doing whatever he was doing. But the thing that *really* got me was when he would just smile — like whatever I was saying didn't bother him at all, or like he knew something I didn't."

Joshua giggled. "I could try that."

"Well, it certainly worked for my brother. I usually gave up and stomped off. It was no fun annoying him when he didn't get upset."

"Are you friends with him now that you're grown up?"

"He...he...died a while ago. I miss him very much."

Joshua threw his arms around her. "I'm sorry."

"It's all right." Tina spoke softly. "What you need to remember is that Aaron loves you, even though he may tease you and make you miserable sometimes. Having a brother is a special thing." She pulled back from the embrace so she could look in his eyes. "Can you remember that?"

The child nodded solemnly.

"You feel a little better now?"

"Yeah. Thanks."

"Joshua!" Lisa called from the patio. "Time to come in!"

"I have to go. Bye." The boy ran across the yard and into the house.

Sam moved down a step and sat next to Tina. "You were very good with him."

"I was sweating bullets. If you hadn't shown up..."

"You were doing fine." Sam looked out at the driveway. "Where's your car?"

"It's on the street in front of the house. There was no way I was going to park it under that flag."

Sam shook her head. "You're as bad as my nephews."

"I promise not to get into a fistfight with Mike."

"I'm happy to hear that."

Tina's face brightened and she smiled. "The Seminoles are going to win," she said confidently.

"You think so?"

"Yes."

"I *love* the Seminoles," Sam said enthusiastically.

"You do?"

"Oh, yes." The blonde leaned in close. "Because they make you smile like that." She gave Tina a quick kiss before standing and picking up the grocery bags. "C'mon, let's get dinner started."

Pleasant chatter filled the kitchen as they began preparing their meal. Tina talked about the New Zealand trip she had organized for Vivian's clients, and Sam discussed the busy holiday schedule the orchestra had coming up. Once the salad was made and the lasagna was in the oven, they went to sit on the balcony.

"We missed the sunset," Sam said with disappointment as she sat in her chair. "I like it much better during daylight savings time when the sun sets later."

Tina stretched out on the other lounger. "Yeah, but look at all the stars. It's a beautiful sky tonight. See the constellations?"

"Yes." *I never figured you for a stargazer. There's so much more to you than you let people see.*

They relaxed quietly for a while, until Sam's curiosity about their earlier phone call prompted her to speak. "Tina?"

"Hmm?"

"Will you tell me how you got your nickname?"

"Oh, sure. Why don't you come over here?" She patted the space next to her on the chair. *I'll need you near me for this.*

Sam happily fulfilled the request. She lay half in the empty space and half on Tina, resting her head on a strong shoulder. They snuggled for several minutes, both of them enjoying the physical closeness. Strengthened by the presence of the small woman, Tina began.

"My given name is Christina, though for as long as I can remember, people have called me Tina. My brother...um...as soon as he was able to make sounds, he would try to talk to me. You know...babbling, like babies do. Then, when he started to walk, he toddled after me everywhere I went, jabbering away."

She paused, suddenly aware of the lump in her throat. *After all these years, why is it still so hard to talk about him?* She kissed the top of the blonde head tucked against her. *She makes it easier, though.* "He followed me around, calling me 'T.' He couldn't say my whole name, but he sure had the T part down. As we grew up, it just kind of stuck. It was a special thing between us. He was the only one who ever called me T."

Sam lifted her head and looked into eyes that revealed pain, sorrow, and the vulnerability that was usually kept well hidden. "That's a wonderful story, and such a nice memory for you to have. I'm so glad you told me."

Tina lightly brushed the back of her hand against Sam's cheek. "I was thinking. If you want to, you could call me T."

"I...I..." Overcome with emotion and unable to string any words together, Sam used a tender kiss to convey the depth of her feelings.

Tina tried to catch her breath after the kiss. *Wow!* "I assume that means yes?"

"Y...yes." The barely audible response was accompanied by an emphatic nod.

"I've missed this." Tina pushed a few stray hairs behind Sam's ear and let her fingers linger along the side of the younger woman's face. *I need this.*

"Me, too."

Hearing the words of agreement that had become a frequent part of her life lately, Tina smiled. "Is there some name other than Samantha that you prefer?"

"No!"

"Okay. I was just asking."

"I love the way you say my name."

Not half as much as I love saying it. "Really?"

Sam laid her head down and nuzzled Tina's neck. "Mmm-hmm."

When the oven timer buzzed, they reluctantly got up from their comfortable place on the lounge chair. In the kitchen, they fixed their plates and took their dinner into the living room. They watched a popular new game show on TV while they ate, having fun trying to pick the correct answer out of the four choices given for each question. Both of them did well in certain categories, like current events, old TV shows, and pop culture from the sixties to the present. Tina knew all the math answers and anything to do with world or ancient history. Naturally, Sam was a whiz at anything related to music, and she was also quite knowledgeable about movies. Between the two of them, they got most of the questions right.

"If they allowed team competition, we'd win a million dollars!" Sam exclaimed as the women went into the kitchen and put their empty plates in the sink.

"I doubt that."

Sam got the tin foil from the cabinet and began covering the left-over food. "Can you imagine what it would feel like to win that much money?"

Tina came up behind the blonde and wrapped her arms around her. She murmured into the shorter woman's ear. "I think it would feel like...when I'm with you."

Sam dropped the foil on the counter, leaned back against Tina, and placed her hands over the larger ones that were holding her. She closed her eyes, allowing herself a quiet moment to absorb the words. "Do you remember the first time you held me like this?"

"When I caught up with you at the beach."

"Yeah. You run pretty fast, I had a big head start." Sam tried to turn and long arms loosened their grip so she could. She looked at Tina's grinning face. "And then, when we stood like this, I wanted...hoped...you might kiss me."

"Would you like me to do that now? You know what they say —
better late than never."

"I guess I can give you a second chance."

Tina slowly bent down to give Sam a gentle kiss. However, once
she started, she found it difficult to restrain her feelings. It became
lengthy, and passionate.

It took Sam a minute to recover enough to speak coherently. "If
you had kissed me like that on the beach, I probably would've fainted."
In fact, I'm feeling a little weak in the knees right now.

"I'm sorry. I didn't mean to get so carried away."

"I'm not complaining. Let's just make sure that this time we're *both*
ready before we take it any further. Does that sound okay to you?"

"Um...okay."

Sam turned toward the counter to finish covering the food and put
it in the refrigerator. "Would you like to come back tomorrow night and
help me polish off these leftovers?"

"Wild horses couldn't keep me away."

"You are full of it tonight!"

"What can I say? You bring it out in me."

"Yeah?" Sam moved to the sink. "Well, how about bringing yourself over here and helping with the dishes?"

Tina willingly assisted with the kitchen duties. When they were
done, the women cuddled on the couch and watched TV until the news
came on.

"I should get going." Tina got up and stretched.

Sam walked her to the door. "I'll see you tomorrow night."

"I'll be here."

They shared a hug and a kiss before Tina left. Sam closed and
locked the door, then she went to the phone and dialed a number she
knew by heart.

~ * ~ * ~ * ~ * ~

Tina sang along with the car radio all the way home. As she let herself into her condo, the blinking light on the answering machine caught
her attention. *Who could that be?* She thought about the last time there
had been a message and the disastrous results when Sam heard it. She
walked over, reached out a shaking hand, and pressed the button.

"Hi..."

Tina smiled. *Samantha.*

"It's Sam. I just wanted to tell you I miss you already. Also, I
thought maybe I'd give this nickname of yours a try. So, good night, T.
Bye."

She replayed the message and saved it. Seemingly unable to remove the smile from her face, she prepared for bed. Shortly after pulling the covers up under her chin, Tina was sound asleep. She was still smiling.

~ * ~ * ~ * ~ * ~

Sam closed her book. It was getting dark and difficult to see the print. *Tina should have been here by now. I hope nothing's wrong.* Hearing the chirp of the BMW's alarm, she smiled. *She's here! She must have parked in front of the house again.*

As anticipated, Tina appeared, walking up the driveway slowly, backpack hanging off one shoulder. She saw Sam sitting on the steps to the apartment, waiting for her. *I've been looking forward to seeing that smile all day.* "Hi."

"Hi. I was getting worried."

"Traffic was terrible."

Sam heard the weariness in Tina's voice. "Are you okay?"

"Yeah. Just tired."

They went upstairs. Tina headed straight to the couch and dropped down on it with a heavy sigh.

Concerned, Sam sat next to her. "Are you sure you're all right?"

Tina pulled her into a hug. "It's been a long week. We've been swamped at work. It seems like every one of Vivian's clients has decided to travel somewhere for Thanksgiving. Then, rush hour was a mess."

Sam realized that a large part of Tina's fatigue was probably due to the emotional turmoil that she had been through since Sunday. *And she's driven to Sarasota and back every night after work.* "T?"

"Hmm?"

"Would you like to rest for a little while? I'll let you know when dinner's ready."

"No. Really, I'm fine." It was an unconvincing, halfhearted protest.

"A short nap and you'll feel much better." Sam got up and took Tina's hands, helping her from the couch.

"Well, maybe just for a few minutes."

"Uh-huh." Sam walked her to the bedroom, where Tina went directly to the bed, slipped off her sneakers, and lay down. Sam closed the drapes, then sat on the edge of the mattress. "Do you want a blanket?" Tina's eyes were already shut as she shook her head.

Sam watched the drowsy woman as her breathing deepened and she drifted into a peaceful slumber. *You are totally exhausted, but you drove here anyway. Yet another example of you showing me how hard you're trying, how much you want this.* She lightly brushed the dark bangs from Tina's forehead and placed a kiss there. *I love you.* Carefully, she eased off the bed and left the room, closing the door quietly behind her.

Sam tiptoed around the kitchen making the dinner preparations. First, the lasagna went into the oven to heat. *I'd better turn the temperature on low; I don't know how long she'll sleep.* She buttered the Italian bread and put it on a cookie sheet, ready to be warmed up just prior to mealtime, and transferred some of the leftover salad into a small bowl for Tina before returning it to the refrigerator to remain cool.

Sam looked at the dinette set in the corner. *Hmm, maybe a quiet, relaxing dinner is in order. No eating in front of the TV tonight.* After ten minutes of searching, she found the white tablecloth that was seldom pressed into service. She gathered several candles and set them in the center of the table, then arranged the plates, utensils, and condiments neatly around them. Standing with her arms crossed, she proudly surveyed her efforts. *I hope Tina likes it.* As she wandered into the living room, she was drawn to her guitar. She turned the amplifier on its lowest level and played, sometimes singing along softly.

Tina woke and glanced at the clock on the nightstand. *Damn. I've been asleep for almost two hours.* She hurried into the bathroom to freshen up before opening the bedroom door and peeking out. *Where's Samantha? I'm going to get her for letting me sleep that long.* The kitchen was dark, so she stepped toward the living room, stopping suddenly when she saw Sam playing the guitar. Leaning against the wall, Tina smiled as she watched and listened. *I love to hear her sing.*

Sam was surprised to see the tall woman in the doorway. "You're awake." She put the instrument in its stand and went over to give Tina a hug. "Are you ready for dinner?"

"It's late. You should have woken me." Tina tried to sound angry but the warm body pressed against her made it impossible. Her voice softened. "You must be starving." *So much for being mad at her.*

"Well," Sam released Tina from the hug and led the way into the kitchen, "I had a couple of Ring Dings to tide me over." She turned on the light and pointed toward the table. "What do you think?"

Tina looked at the nicely decorated area. "It's perfect." She leaned down and kissed Sam. "Mmm-hmm. Perfect."

"I think so, too."

They busied themselves getting the meal served, then sat at the table. Sam lit the candles. "Oh, wait." She quickly went and flipped the wall switch, turning off the overhead illumination. Returning to her seat, she smiled across the flickering candlelight at her dinner companion. "That's more like it."

Extremely hungry because of the late hour, both women ate heartily. They didn't talk much, preferring to gaze at each other instead.

"This was a nice idea." Tina commented as she stood and collected the empty plates.

"Thanks." *This was a fantastic idea — candlelight reflecting off those beautiful blue eyes.*

"Seeing as you did all the cooking, I'll take dishwashing detail."

"I don't know if reheating lasagna is actually cooking, but the dishes are all yours." Sam chuckled as she headed into the living room. Sitting on the floor in front of one of the bookcases, she rummaged through the bottom shelves and selected several photo albums. She put the books on the coffee table and then turned on the stereo, finding a radio station that played soft rock. She went back into the kitchen to check on the progress of the dishwashing. "How's it going in here?"

"Almost done."

Sam opened the refrigerator and took out two beers. "Would you like a drink?"

"I'd better not. It's late and I have to drive back."

"You don't *have* to go."

Tina wiped her hands on the dishtowel and hung it over the handle of the stove. "I don't think—"

"What I'm saying is," Sam put the beers on the counter and wrapped her arms around Tina, "you could stay. Just to sleep. I miss you holding me at night."

"I miss it, too."

"Then will you stay?"

As if I could say no to you. "Okay."

"Great!" Sam grabbed the drinks. "C'mon, I want to show you something."

"That sounds like an offer I can't refuse."

"Ha ha, very funny."

They sat together on the sofa and Sam picked up one of the large photo albums. "I thought maybe it was time I shared a little of *my* history."

Tina put her feet up on the coffee table, getting comfortable. "I'd like that."

They looked at baby pictures, with Sam supplying explanations and funny stories about some of the shots. Many of the photos included other family members, so Tina got an introduction to the extended Whitwell clan. They went through a couple of the albums, with school events and family gatherings illustrated on the pages, ending with pictures of the senior prom. They laughed when they saw the teenagers dressed in the style of the day.

"I can't believe the clothes, and look at my hair!"

"That blue ruffled shirt your boyfriend wore with the tux — very hip."

"Oh, yeah?" Sam poked Tina in the ribs. "Wait until I get to see your prom pictures."

"You can't, because I didn't go."

"Why not?"

Tina shrugged. "Too busy with other stuff. I never dated in high school. But," she pointed to the handsome boy in the photo, "who is this hunk you were dating?"

"That's Bobby Jacobs. He was in the band with me."

"So, you dated boys in high school. You weren't gay then?"

"Well, back in those days, I wasn't even aware there was such a thing as gay people. Nobody ever talked about it. All I knew was — something wasn't right. All my friends were swooning over boys...talking about how they felt when they kissed them. I thought there was something wrong with me because I didn't feel like that. I really had no clue until I went to college and fell head over heels in love with one of my female classmates. It was all very confusing. It took me a while to come to terms with the whole thing." Sam closed the book and put it on the table. "What about you?"

"Me? Um, I don't know."

"You said that you were with men, too. I thought maybe you were implying you were bisexual."

"Truthfully, I've never felt like I fit into any group. I didn't have time to hang out with a gang of friends because I had school, track, work, and Steven." She paused, not sure she had made any sense at all. *Try to explain it, T. She wants to understand.*

"What I mean is — in high school, I concentrated on my classes and track because I needed a scholarship to go to college. I was also holding down a part-time job, putting away money for books and expenses. So, my attention was not on boys, or parties, or proms. Then, in college, the pressure was enormous. I carried a heavy academic load and I had to do well in track to retain my scholarship. The athletic talent at that level is phenomenal. It was very hard work just keeping my spot on the team. I was completely focused on school and track, and I didn't have the time or inclination for socializing and dating."

"You must have had offers."

"Every now and then, someone would ask me out. But the other things were more important. My family was counting on me to do well."

"So much responsibility for one young girl," Sam said sadly. *You never did have a childhood.*

"Nothing I couldn't handle. Anyhow, it wasn't until after college that I started dating and met the guy I got engaged to."

"Did you love him?"

Tina pondered the question for a minute before answering. "I liked him a lot. We got along well." A wisp of a smile crossed her features. "He made me laugh."

"He sounds wonderful."

"He was a good guy. I...I guess I thought I loved him, but I had no frame of reference. He was my first serious relationship. Then...then the accident happened and well, everything changed after that."

At the mention of the accident, Sam reached for Tina's hand, entwining the longer fingers with her own. "And at some point, you started seeing women."

"Do you really want to know about that?"

Sam nodded into the shoulder she was leaning against.

"Let's see, after I had worked for Vivian for a while and my back had healed sufficiently, I started traveling. I would scout out new places for vacation packages and unique ways to sell the typical big-ticket tourist locations. During that time, I went through something of a wild period. I...I drank too much. And I discovered that, when I was in the mood for it, I could lure people into my bed without too much effort. I began going after more and more challenging men. It didn't matter if they were single, engaged, or married..." *This sounds awful. It is awful.*

"When you were in the mood for it? How often was that?" Sam didn't realize she was holding her breath while she waited for the answer.

"I was still grieving. There was so much...pain. I...I pretty much kept to myself. But on those trips when I was so far away, sometimes I'd feel..." Tina's voice trailed off.

"Horny?" Sam supplied helpfully, "Lonely?"

"Yeah." Tina sighed and was quiet for several moments.

"It's okay," the blonde said with compassion. "Keep going; tell me everything."

"One night, a woman caught my eye. I felt a very strong physical attraction to her, which surprised me. It was something I hadn't considered before. But I talked to her and I was...intrigued. I slept with her."

"Then what happened?"

"I...I liked it. And I found a whole new territory to conquer."

"Did you still sleep with men?"

"At first, yes. But as time went along, I found I...I liked being with women. So, now that I think about it, I guess I'd fall into the gay category."

"I'm not asking you to put a label on yourself. I was just wondering, that's all."

"Hey." Tina tilted Sam's face up so she could look into her eyes. "If wanting to be with you means I'm gay, then I'm gay. I don't care what label people put on it. Though maybe you don't want to be with me anymore after listening to that part of my history."

"Of course I still want you."

"How can you, after hearing...that?"

"What I heard about was a woman who felt lost. She latched onto something she had control over and she used it. It gave her some semblance of power over her life. She traveled all over the world searching for something — not knowing what it was until she found it. And it was right here at home all the time." Sam's eyes radiated love. "*I was right here all the time.*"

Tina shook her head. "I was a b—"

"Was. That's the operative word. That's not who you are now. At some point, you have to quit beating yourself up about the past and start living in the present."

"I...I know."

"I'm sorry. I wanted to talk about me tonight, give you a break. And here we are, dredging up painful memories of yours."

"I needed you to know all of it, but I've been afraid of what you'd think of me."

Sam traced the curve of Tina's cheek with her fingertips. "Those things happened a long time ago. I have things in my past I wish I'd done differently, too. Everybody does. But I have no regrets for a single minute I've spent with you." She slid her hand behind Tina's neck and pulled her into a kiss.

They came up for air with faces flushed and pulses quickened.

Tina fought back tears as the emotion of the moment overwhelmed her. *I've told her the worst of it and she still wants me.* "Samantha?"

"Hmm?"

"You called Kimberly your girlfriend."

Sam was busy kissing Tina's neck. "Mmm-hmm." *This is no time to be talking about my ex.*

"What other terminology do couples in gay relationships use? I mean, I'm kind of old to be somebody's girlfriend."

"You're not old." *She's saying we're in a relationship, a couple!* "There are a number of expressions — girlfriend, lover, partner—"

"Partner? I like that. Two people together, partners in life."

Sam's head snapped up and she looked into serious blue eyes. "Really?"

"Yeah. Would that be okay with you?"

The answer was a kiss that left no doubt as to how the younger woman felt. It left both of them breathing heavily.

"So," Sam smiled at the look of lust on Tina's face, "I'd say it's time for dessert."

"Yes."

"I hear the ice cream calling to us."

"Ice cream?"

"Yes." Sam laughed. "Nice, cold ice cream. It's gotten a little warm in here, wouldn't you say?" She gave Tina one more kiss before getting up to go in the kitchen. *That look of desire on her face...I bet she needs this ice cream as much as I do. One thing is certain — she wants this relationship, even though she's still scared. She trusted me enough to tell me about her history. Slowly but surely, she's letting me past those walls she's built around her heart.*

Tina picked up the *TV Guide* from the coffee table and fanned herself with it. *A little warm? She's got to be kidding.* She hastily dropped the magazine when Sam came around the corner of the living room carrying a large bowl of chocolate chip ice cream with chocolate syrup on it.

Tina's eyes grew wide when she saw the amount in the bowl. "That's not for me, is it?"

"No. It's for both of us. You don't mind sharing, do you?"

"Sharing?" *That sounds...interesting.*

"Yes." Sam sat sideways on Tina's lap and rested her back against the arm of the couch. She took a spoonful of the dessert and fed it to her partner.

"Mmm, that's good."

Sam had the next spoonful. "Yum. It sure is." She continued her serving duty, thoroughly enjoying her task. When the ice cream was almost gone, she announced, "Last spoonful. And it's always special to get the last one." She acted as if she was going to eat it herself before giving it to Tina and then swiftly leaning in to taste the sweet dessert on her lips. After the kiss, she pulled back slightly, so she could see Tina's face. She was pleased at the open look of love in her partner's eyes. "I take it you liked the ice cream?"

"Yes, and the server, too."

Sam put the bowl on the table so she had both arms free to hug Tina. They sat like that for a few minutes until Sam yawned.

"Oh, it's late. Let's get you to bed."

"You'll stay? You said you would."

"Yes. I'll stay."

Sam turned off the stereo and made sure the door was locked. Tina took the empty dessert bowl into the kitchen and rinsed it out.

The blonde yawned again as they went into the bedroom. "I'll shower in the morning. I'm too tired to do it tonight." She handed Tina her neatly folded pajamas. "All washed and ready for you."

"Thanks."

Feeling somewhat awkward, they silently changed and took turns in the bathroom.

Sam climbed into bed first. "C'mon." She held open the covers to encourage the nervously pacing woman to join her.

"Are you sure this is all right?" Tina asked as she laid down on the farthest edge of the bed.

"Yes." Sam immediately sprawled across Tina's body. "We belong together. Don't you know that yet?" She rested her head on her partner's chest and the sound of the steady heartbeat beneath her ear lulled her to sleep.

A feeling of contentment settled over Tina as she gently caressed the woman dozing in her arms. *I've missed this so much. She's right; we belong together. And the way she makes me feel...is this what love is? It must be. I must be...in love.* Once again, she fell asleep smiling.

Chapter 20

Tina closed the newspaper, took off her glasses, and placed both items on the coffee table. She'd been awake for quite some time and had already made a trip to the neighborhood convenience store. She had bought eggs and bacon so she could make breakfast when Sam got up. She'd also purchased the all-important paper, which had a detailed analysis of the Seminole/Gator game to be played that evening. Walking over to the front window, she stood for several minutes, looking out at the college flag flapping in the breeze.

Smiling, she went into the bedroom to check on her partner. Lying down next to the sleeping woman, Tina propped herself up on one elbow, watching as Sam slowly wakened and pale lashes fluttered open. "Good morning."

"Mmm." Sam snuggled against Tina. "I'm glad you're here."

"Me, too."

"Mmm."

Tina rolled onto her back, pulling Sam with her. They lay quietly, their breathing matched in a slow, steady rhythm until a commotion outside disturbed them.

"What's that?" Sam raised her head and listened. "It's Mike. Something's wrong!" She jumped out of bed and headed for the door.

Tina followed Sam through the house and down the steps to the driveway. Mike was screaming and yelling and waving his arms at no one in particular. Lisa and the boys came running from the house.

"What is it, Mike?" Lisa asked as she got to the driveway.

He pointed at the flag hanging from the garage. "Look at that!"

The assembled group obediently looked up. Sam gasped. Tina smiled.

"Oh my!" Lisa exclaimed.

"Yes!" Joshua yelled.

"How did *that* happen?" Aaron asked.

Suspended from the flagpole was a gigantic Florida State Seminoles flag.

The furious Gator fan resumed his ranting. *"Do you believe this?*

What the hell is going on here? I am going to—"

"Michael!" Lisa hastily moved closer and began whispering to her husband.

As he listened to his wife, Mike's eyes shifted to his two sons, who were watching him curiously. He took a deep breath and tried to calm down. "Well...heh, it looks like someone has played a prank on me."

"What's a prank?" Joshua asked.

Tina bent down on one knee to answer the child. "It's like a joke, a way to tease someone."

"Someone is teasing Daddy?"

"Yes, it certainly seems that way."

Mike turned his attention to Tina. "*You* wouldn't know anything about this, would you?"

"Me?"

Sam burst out laughing at the attempted look of innocence on Tina's face.

"It's a pretty red flag," Joshua commented.

"It's not red, it's maroon," Aaron said haughtily.

"Actually, it's garnet. Garnet and gold are the FSU colors. It is pretty, isn't it?" Tina gave Joshua a quick hug and spoke into his ear before standing up.

The boy smiled and went to retrieve a plastic bag from beneath the steps to Sam's apartment. "Look, Daddy, here's your flag." He ran back and handed the package to his father.

"I've got people coming over here today." Mike opened the garage door. "If they ever saw that..." He scowled at the object in question before going inside.

Sam looked at Tina, who was grinning from ear to ear. "You sure started this day off with a bang. How did you put that up there without a ladder?"

"See how close the flagpole is to your window?"

"It's not that close." Sam tried not to think about Tina precariously extending her body from the window to the flagpole in the middle of the night.

"I have long arms."

"Uh-huh."

Mike came out of the garage lugging a wooden ladder.

This is definitely a scene for the family album. "I've got to go get my camera." Sam dashed up the steps.

"Let me help you." Tina held the ladder steady while Mike climbed to the top.

Sam snapped pictures as the Seminole flag was removed and replaced by the Gator one. Mike put the ladder back in the garage and closed the door. "Come on, boys, I want you to help me decorate for the party."

"Cool!" The children scampered after their father.

Lisa sighed. "Well, I'd better get moving. I've got a ton of stuff to get done before the guests arrive."

"Wait." Sam handed the camera to her sister. "Will you take a picture of us first?"

"Sure."

The couple hugged and Lisa took the picture.

"Thanks, sis," Sam said before looking up at Tina.

Lisa snapped once more, catching the two of them gazing into each other's eyes. "One for good measure." She smiled as she handed back the camera and the women said their good-byes.

"What's this about a party?" Tina asked as they returned to the apartment.

"Oh." Sam went to the kitchen, filled two coffee mugs with water and put them in the microwave to heat. "Every year Mike invites a bunch of his friends to the house to watch the game." She opened the refrigerator to get the creamer and saw the bacon and eggs. "You got stuff for breakfast."

"Yeah, but if you have people coming over, maybe I should get going."

"I don't have anyone coming over. It's Mike's party, and it doesn't even start until this afternoon." She put the breakfast things on the counter. "Don't you dare try to leave so soon." She grabbed Tina around the waist and held her tight.

"I'll stay for a little while, but I'd rather not be here when those Gator fans show up, okay?"

"Okay."

The microwave beeped. Sam ignored it, enjoying the embrace for a few more moments before letting go to prepare the coffee.

They had their breakfast, with Tina excitedly discussing the upcoming game. Sam smiled as she listened to her go on and on about the Seminoles.

As she finished her meal, Tina realized that she had monopolized the conversation. She looked across the table. "What are you smiling about?"

"You."

"Me? What about me?"

"You're happy." Sam went over and sat on Tina's lap. She put her arms around the dark-haired woman's neck and looked into her eyes. "I like seeing you happy."

"You. You're what makes me happy."

"Hmm." Sam couldn't resist leaning in for a quick kiss. "I think that Seminole football team of yours might have a bit more to do with your disposition today than I do."

"No. It's you." Tina paused, trying to calm the emotions that seemed to surface so readily when she was with Sam. "I never thought I could feel like this. You...I..." The words escaped her and she was unable to continue. She pulled Sam close and stroked her soft, blonde hair.

The phone rang, startling both of them. Sam went into the living room to answer it while Tina cleared the table and began washing the dishes.

Sam returned to the kitchen and picked up the dishtowel. "That was my friend Kathy. She e-mailed me last weekend asking if I could get together with her tomorrow for lunch. It's a good thing she called to remind me or I would have forgotten all about it." She dried the dishes as they were placed in the drainer, and then put them away. "She was teasing me, saying I must have met someone, because I've disappeared recently."

"I'm sorry. I've been keeping you from your friends."

Sam laughed. "You're not 'keeping' me from anybody."

"You have friends. You should be spending time with them. I've—"

"Listen to me for a minute. Please." Sam took Tina's hands from the dishwater and dried them with the towel before kissing them softly. "There's nowhere else I'd rather be, no one else I'd rather be with than you."

"But—"

"When people first start going out, it's kind of all-consuming. My friends know that because they've been through it themselves. That's why Kathy was teasing me. She knows I must be seeing someone." Sam studied the large, strong hands she held in her own. "My friends are going to want to meet you sometime, especially after I tell Kathy how wonderful you are at lunch tomorrow." *And word will travel fast. I wonder if Lisa told Kimberly I'm dating someone.*

"I...I don't think I'm ready for that yet."

"I know, but there's no hurry, right? We have the rest of our lives."

The rest of our lives? Tina removed one of her hands from Sam's grasp so she could reach under the smaller woman's chin and tilt her face upward. Eyes full of love looked back at her.

Realizing what she had said, Sam tried to backtrack. "I mean..."

"It's okay." Tina took a deep breath, willing her voice not to shake. "I...not too long ago, hearing words like that from someone would have sent me running in the opposite direction as fast as I could go. But now, with you, it just sounds right." Tina bent down to kiss her very surprised, very happy partner.

Someone knocked on the door. Sam, who had been about to throw caution to the wind and kiss Tina for everything she was worth, groaned. "I'd better go see who that is." She went to the door and opened it to find Joshua standing there, hands full of orange and blue crepe paper.

"Hi, Auntie Sam. Daddy gave me a job. I have to put this on your railing. Can Tina help me?"

"Let's ask her." Sam turned and called into the apartment, "T, someone is here to see you."

Tina came to the door and smiled when she saw Joshua. "What's up?"

"Will you help me?"

Tina stared at the brightly colored paper. *He wants me to decorate for the Gators?* "Um...I don't know." *How can I get out of this?* "I was doing the dishes..." She looked to Sam for corroboration.

"That's all right." The blonde grinned. "I'll finish the dishes."

"Cool!" Joshua beamed. "Thanks, Auntie Sam."

"Yeah. Thanks, Auntie Sam," Tina said sardonically.

"No problem." Sam playfully nudged the woman out on the landing. "Have fun." She chuckled as she shut the door.

Tina looked down at a delighted Joshua, who promptly gave her the decorations. She grimaced at the offending collegiate colors in her hands. *When was it that I totally lost control of my life?*

"Ready?"

"Yes." Resigned to the fact that she now had a job as an assistant decorator, Tina managed a half grin. "So, boss, what's the plan?"

The two worked together, winding the streamers around the railing and fashioning them into a big blue and orange bow at the bottom. They stood out in the driveway admiring their work.

"It looks awesome, Tina. Thanks for helping me."

"You're welcome."

"You're not going to be here for the party, are you?"

"No."

"I didn't think so," he said disappointedly. "Neither is Auntie Sam."

"She's not?"

"Nope. I heard them talking. She told Daddy she wants to cheer for the Seminoles."

Mike and Aaron came from the backyard and joined them in the driveway. "Hey, that looks great, Josh!" Mike ruffled his son's hair. "You do good work."

"I had help, Daddy."

"So I see."

The two adults eyed each other for a moment. Tina held out her hand. "Truce?"

Mike shook the offered hand. "Truce. Good luck tonight."

"You, too."

"All right, boys," Mike took the car keys from his pocket and jingled them, "time to go get the balloons."

"Yay!" The children ran to the minivan, where they immediately got into an argument over who was going to sit in the front seat. Mike settled the dispute by announcing that Joshua would ride in front on the way to the store, and Aaron would on the way back.

Tina waved good-bye and ascended the stairs. *I remember having the exact same argument with Steven when we were kids. I guess some things never change.* Inside the apartment, she heard singing. Following the sound, she went to the doorway of the bedroom and saw that Sam was finishing making up the bed.

"Hi."

"Hi there. All done decorating?"

"Yes. Thanks so much for volunteering me."

"You're welcome." Sam laughed at the expression on Tina's face. "You're not pouting, are you?"

Tina shrugged.

"Aw." Sam went over and hugged the sulking woman. "You poor thing — forced to put up decorations for a Gator party." Suddenly, strong arms grabbed her and propelled her backward. "Hey!"

They fell onto the bed and Tina began tickling Sam. She continued until the blonde begged for her to stop.

"I feel much better now," Tina said smugly.

"Oh you—" Sam's words were cut off by a searing kiss from her partner. *My goodness, what was I saying?*

"I was wondering." Tina smiled at the somewhat dazed look on Sam's face. "I usually just watch the game alone at my place, but would you like to come over?"

I thought you'd never ask. "I'd really like that."

"Maybe you could bring Josh along, too? He's going to have a rough time of it if he stays here with all those Gator fans."

"I think that's a terrific idea. I'll ask Lisa and Mike if it's okay."

"I need to get going, then." Tina stood and helped Sam off the bed. "I'll stop by the store and get hot dogs and chips."

"I was going to go to Lisa's for a while and help her. How about I come over later this afternoon?"

"All right."

They hugged and kissed good-bye. When Sam walked Tina outside, she pointed to the railing. "Nice job with the Gator orange and blue."

Tina reached toward her, wiggling her fingers as if she were going to tickle her.

Sam ran away. "Okay. No more talk about the decorations, I promise."

"You know I can always catch you," Tina bantered.

"Oh, I'm counting on it."

Tina laughed as she got into her car. As she drove away, she looked in the rearview mirror and saw Sam there, waving. *I love you, Samantha Whitwell.*

Chapter 21

"Are we almost there yet?"

"Yes." It was at least the fifth time Joshua had asked the question, and Sam was relieved that she could finally answer in the affirmative.

The boy had been positively beside himself with excitement ever since his parents had given him permission to go to Tina's with Sam. He hugged the Seminole flag he'd been holding in his lap. "She'll be glad to get this back."

"I think you're right. It was nice of you to ask your dad for it." *And Mike was thrilled to get rid of the thing before anyone arrived for the party.* She turned the car into the driveway at Bayshore Palms. At the call box, she pressed the code on the keypad and Tina answered.

"Hello?"

"Hi! We're here!" Joshua shouted across Sam and out her window.

A low chuckle rumbled from the speaker. "Come on up, you two." The gate opened, allowing them to pull into the garage and park.

"Wow! She has an elevator!" Joshua ran ahead of his aunt. "Can I press the button?"

"Yes."

The elevator came and they got in. "What floor, Auntie Sam?"

"Four."

He pushed the appropriate number and then danced around happily in the confined space until the doors opened.

Tina was standing there waiting for them.

"Hi." Joshua handed her the flag. "Look what I brought for you."

"Thanks." She bent down and hugged him. "You ready for the big game?"

"Yes!"

"Good." She straightened up and smiled as she reached for Sam's hand. "Hi."

"Hi."

Joshua took Tina's other hand and they walked down the hallway to the condo. "This is cool!" he exclaimed when they got inside.

"Glad you like it."

"Can I use the bathroom? It was a long ride here."

"Yes." She showed her small guest the way through the kitchen to the bathroom. Striding back to the living area, she almost bumped into Sam, who was slowly making her way around the edge of the room, eyeing the answering machine warily.

Tina wrapped her arms around the distracted woman. "Whoa!"

"Oh! I...I'm sorry." Sam sniffled as she leaned into the embrace. "It's hard seeing that and remembering the last time I was here."

"It's...we're...going to be all right," Tina murmured in her ear. "I promise."

"Tina?" Joshua yelled from the bathroom. "Is it okay to use the towel that's here? My mom says sometimes towels are only to look at."

"Yes, you can use it," she answered him.

Sam wiped her eyes with the back of her hand. "You'd think at my age I'd have a better grip on my emotions. I just need a minute." She hurried out onto the balcony.

The boy returned and Tina quickly tried to think of something to occupy him. "Would you do me a favor, Josh?"

"Sure."

"I don't have many pictures around my place. Do you think you could draw something for me?" She moved the large chart she had been working on from the dining room table and put it on the kitchen counter. "You can sit right here." She patted a chair that faced away from the balcony.

"I can make you something nice!" He smiled as he sat down.

"Thanks, I'd like that." She collected the markers and paper that were strewn about the table and placed them closer to him. "Meanwhile, I need to talk to your aunt for a few minutes, okay?"

He had already started on his artwork. "Okay."

Satisfied that Joshua was engrossed in his project, she stepped outside and stood near Sam, who was resting her arms on the railing and looking out at the water. They both were quiet for several minutes.

It was Tina who eventually broke the silence. "I want you to know — she was never here."

"W-what?"

"C'mere." Tina gently guided her partner to the inner corner of the balcony, away from view of the street. "I'm saying that Andi...has never been here. No one has ever slept in that bed but me...and you."

It took Sam a moment to find her voice. "Why didn't you tell me? Were you afraid I'd think it meant something?"

"No. I wanted you to know it did...does...mean something. I just didn't get a chance."

"Oh, Tina." Sam hugged her. *No wonder you waited so long to ask me to stay over. It was a huge step for you. And then, I stormed out of here in a huff. Now I see that I wasn't the only one who got terribly hurt that day.* "I will never, ever leave angry again. No matter what happens, we'll resolve it together. Does that sound good?"

"Yes." Tina glanced through the patio door and saw that Joshua was still busily working. She bent down for a kiss. "I...I love...it...when you're here."

They gazed into each other's eyes, oblivious to everything around them until a high-pitched voice rang out from the condo.

"I'm done!"

"Whose bright idea was it to bring that child with me today?" Sam teased.

"Well, it seemed like a good idea at the time," Tina whispered as she followed her partner into the dining room.

Joshua waved a colorful paper at them. "Look at what I made!"

"Let me see." Tina took the artwork and held it at arm's length. "This is very nice." It was a drawing of the three of them standing under a big yellow sun. Tina was in the middle with Joshua and Sam on either side of her. They were all smiling and holding hands. It was a picture brimming with happiness. "I like it a lot. Thank you."

"Are you going to hang it up?"

"Of course."

Sam watched with amusement as Tina held the paper in various locations throughout the condo and Joshua offered his opinion on whether it was the perfect place to put it. In the end, they decided to hang it from the fireplace mantel.

"It's almost game time." Tina turned the TV on and they all piled onto the couch. The FSU graduate hung on every word as the announcers discussed both teams at length. Sam was paying attention to the Gator band in the background, performing the pregame show on the field. It didn't take long for Joshua to start asking questions.

"How can they play football in a swamp?"

"It's not *a* swamp, it's *the* Swamp. That's the name of the Gators' football stadium," Tina explained. "It's much harder to beat a team when you're at their home field."

"That's a big band. What instrument do you like best, Tina?"

"Hmm." She paused so she could finish hearing what the broadcaster was saying about the quarterback rotation the Gators would be using. "I think I like the drums best."

"What does he mean, the Seminoles are top ranked?"

Sam interrupted the inquisition. "Josh, she's trying to listen to the TV. Don't ask so many questions." *She likes the drums?*

"It's okay." Tina smiled. "I don't mind." And, true to her word, she patiently answered every question Joshua asked. When the first quarter started, she described the basic concepts simply enough that he quickly gained an understanding of the flow of the game. In no time at all, the two of them were hooting and hollering at the action on the screen.

Sam was enjoying their unbridled enthusiasm much more than the game itself. *I love seeing her happy.*

"It's good!" Tina yelled as a field goal attempt sailed between the uprights. She quizzed Joshua to see if he remembered what she'd told him. "How many points is that worth?"

"Three."

"Right!" They slapped hands in a high-five.

And so it went throughout the first half, as they watched the teams move up and down the field. At halftime, FSU was ahead, 13-6.

"We ready for some hot dogs?" Tina took a long drink of beer to soothe her throat, which was hoarse from all the cheering she'd been doing.

"Yes!" Joshua answered. He got up and looked out the large sliding doors. "Can I go on the balcony for a while?"

"Sure." Tina headed into the kitchen as the boy scurried outside. "Samantha?"

Sam went to see what she wanted. "You called?"

"Uh-huh." Tina pulled the surprised woman into the laundry room and kissed her. "I've been wanting to do that during the whole first half."

Sam laughed. "You were so involved in the game, I didn't think you were even aware I was here."

Tina's voice became deeper. "I always know when you're around. You make me feel..." She ducked her head down again for a long, lingering kiss.

"My goodness!" Sam felt her body tingling from head to toe. "What's gotten into you today?"

"I...um...I'm trying to tell you more...stuff."

"So I see, and you're succeeding wonderfully." Sam ran a shaky hand through her hair. "We'd better get back in there before Josh comes looking for us." Or *before I barricade the door and attack you right now.*

"Okay. I need to hurry up and cook those hot dogs." Tina led the way into the kitchen and began getting the food ready.

Sam saw the large chart lying on the counter. It had horizontal and vertical lines, with dates in some of the columns. "What's this?"

"I'm making a training schedule."

"For what?"

"The marathon."

"You're serious about doing a marathon?"

"I thought it would be kind of a challenge, test my abilities."

"Should you push yourself that much with your back condition?"

Tina turned from the stove where the hot dogs were sizzling in the frying pan and faced Sam. "I think I can do it. I want to try."

"But why?"

"Well, after graduating from college, I didn't run for over a year. There had been so much pressure on me to get, and keep, that scholarship, I was totally burnt out. Then one day, Steven talked me into going to the track with him. I actually had fun, running for no other reason than my own enjoyment. I'd almost forgotten what that was like." Tina turned around to resume her cooking duties. "I never ran competitively again, though."

"Does it have to be a marathon?" Sam walked over to Tina and looked up at her. "It's so punishing on the body. I'm worried about you getting hurt."

"I'm pretty tough for an old lady." Tina stacked the hot dogs on a plate and filled a large bowl with chips.

"You are not old." *Hmm, some of this evidently has to do with that age thing.* "And if you want to do this, I'll support you one hundred percent." *Even though I have reservations about it.*

"Thanks. That means a lot to me." Tina gave Sam a quick kiss before handing her the bowl of chips.

They arranged the food on the coffee table, refilled their drinks, called Joshua from the balcony, and settled in for the second half. Tina almost choked on a potato chip when the Gators intercepted a pass and ran for a touchdown in the third quarter. Consequently, she didn't snack for the rest of the game. The teams battled on and with three and a half minutes remaining, the Gators scored to make it 30-23 with the Seminoles still in the lead. But FSU couldn't move the ball on their next drive, which gave the Gators a final attempt to score. Tina was pacing the room and directing all sorts of advice at the television, as if the coaches and players could hear her. The orange and blue team moved the ball down the field until there was only enough time left for one more play.

"It's going to be a Hail Mary," Tina mumbled, still pacing back and forth.

"They're gonna say a prayer?" Joshua asked.

Sam grabbed the boy and pulled him closer to her. "Shh. Now is *not* the time to ask questions."

The three of them watched the ball leave the quarterback's hand and arc very high in the air. It came down in the end zone and a crowd of players from both teams jumped up to try and catch it. It bounced off the fingers of a Gator player before falling to the ground. The game was over. The stadium erupted into pandemonium as Seminole players shouted, "We're number one!" and stomped all over the Gator logo painted on the grass at midfield. The FSU band played the music for the tomahawk chant and the contingent of Seminole fans that was in the stands cheered wildly.

After a little jumping around and yelling herself, Tina joined her guests on the couch. "Pretty exciting game, huh?"

Sam and Joshua wholeheartedly agreed.

"We're still undefeated. Next we'll play for the national championship." She looked at Joshua and explained, "That's like the Super Bowl for college teams."

"Cool!"

"Yeah, it's way cool." Tina stretched her legs out and put her feet up on the table. "Let's see what the coach has to say."

As Joshua and Tina watched the postgame interviews, Sam took the dishes into the kitchen and washed them. She put away the leftovers and wiped off the counters. Before leaving the room, she took a moment to examine the marathon training schedule more closely. There were already numbers in some of the spaces indicating how many miles had been run on those days. *What are you trying to prove? Whatever it is, it must be important or you wouldn't be doing this.* She looked at the dates that extended well into spring and sighed. *There's still plenty of time for her to change her mind, not that I think she will.*

The football program ended and Tina shut off the TV. She leaned her head back and closed her eyes. *I had more beers than I should have. I'll pay for that in the morning when I have to get up and run.*

Sam returned to the living room to find one adult and one small boy practically asleep on the couch. "Joshua," she called softly, "it's time to go."

"Mmm-hmm." He yawned. "I need to use the bathroom first." He got up and groggily walked past her.

Sam sat down next to Tina. "Are you okay?"

"Very okay." Blue eyes opened and regarded her. "When you're here."

Sam took a large hand in her own and kissed it. "I need to get Joshua home." She entwined her fingers with Tina's.

"I wish you could stay."

"Me, too."

"I'd drive to your place, but...I've had a few beers."

"Yes, you certainly did." Sam smiled at the slightly drunk woman. "I'll call you after I have lunch with Kathy tomorrow. Maybe you can come over then?"

"I'd like that."

The women shared a few quiet moments holding hands and sneaking kisses while they waited for Joshua.

"I'm ready." The boy was standing at the door, smiling.

"How long has he been there?" Sam whispered.

"I don't know."

Tina escorted her guests to their car. In between yawns, Joshua expressed his thanks for being invited over and for the football lesson.

"He'll be asleep before we get to the interstate," Sam commented.

The tall woman chuckled. "You're probably right."

Tina watched them get in the car and drive away before she headed for the elevators.

The next morning, the former track star forced herself to go running even though she felt sluggish from her beer drinking the night before. *No more overindulging until after the marathon, T.* She did some housework and a load of laundry before having a light lunch. Glancing at the clock for the umpteenth time, she decided to sit on the balcony and read a book until Sam called. When the phone finally rang, she quickly jogged inside to answer it. "Hello?"

"Hi, Tina?"

"Yes?"

"This is Lisa...Sam's sister."

Tina heard the stress in the woman's voice. "What...what is it?"

"Today Sam went to lunch with a friend of hers."

"Yes, I know." Tina felt her stomach twist into a knot. "What happened?"

"I'm at Sarasota Memorial Hospital; she's been in a car accident."

Chapter 22

No...not again. Please, not again. Tina moved unsteadily to the couch before her legs gave out completely. *Car accident...no...no...no.* She collapsed onto the soft surface as everything became dark and white dots danced in front of her eyes. After she blinked a few times, the room slowly started to come back into focus and she became aware of a far-away voice calling her name. It took a moment for her to realize it was coming from the telephone that had dropped into her lap. She picked it up with a trembling hand.

"Tina...Tina...Tina!" Lisa was shouting into the phone.

"Y-yes?"

"She's all right! The doctor ordered some X-rays to be sure, but he doesn't think there are any major injuries."

Tina began sobbing uncontrollably.

Lisa was surprised by the emotional outburst from the normally cool, calm, and collected woman. *I guess this answers any questions I had about how much she cares for Sam.*

Tina fought to regain her composure so she could speak. "I...I'll be there as soon as I can."

"I think I should warn you. My mother is here."

Uh-oh. "Maybe I shouldn't...I mean...what does Samantha want?"

"She's been quite adamant about that." Lisa chuckled. "She wants you."

"Then I'm on my way."

"Okay. I'll tell her."

"Lisa?"

"Yeah?"

"Thanks for calling me."

"You're welcome."

Tina hung up the phone and made her way to the bathroom. She splashed some cold water on her face and looked in the mirror. *C'mon, T, don't fall apart; Samantha needs you.* She pushed aside her own feelings as she concentrated on the important matter at hand: *Samantha needs me.* Energized by that single-minded sense of purpose, she went into the living room, grabbed her backpack, and ran out of the condo. She didn't bother to wait for the elevator, instead choosing to gallop down the stairs at breakneck speed. She jumped into her car and zipped through the streets of downtown Tampa, relieved that it was Sunday and traffic was light.

Once on the interstate, Tina had to use a substantial amount of restraint not to press the accelerator to the floor. Not that the car couldn't handle it. The BMW could go well over 100 miles per hour with ease. She was more concerned about being pulled over for a ticket, which would delay her reaching Sam. Given what had happened in her past, Tina was a careful driver who rarely speeded or took unnecessary chances. She decided to set her cruise control to fifteen miles per hour over the posted limit and hoped she didn't get caught.

Thirty minutes later, Tina arrived at Sarasota Memorial. After parking in the visitor's garage, she raced to the hospital entrance, stopping abruptly when she got there. She stared at the automatic doors. *I swore I would never set foot in this place again.* An ambulance siren wailed in the distance. Memories of the day ten years ago when she and Steven were brought there flashed through her mind. She took several deep breaths to calm her thundering heart. *I can do this...for Samantha.*

Hesitantly, she stepped into the busy lobby. People were coming and going, brushing past her as she tried to get her bearings. Tina rubbed her temples to try to alleviate the pounding in her head. *Aspirin. I need aspirin.* Spotting a water fountain, she went over and leaned against the wall next to it. She unzipped her backpack and pulled out the bottle of extra-strength aspirin she always carried with her in case her back pain flared up. *This should help.*

She took a sip of water to wash down two of the tablets before glancing around for a sign indicating the way to the emergency room. A flash of blue in her peripheral vision caught her attention. *What's that?* Tina peered through the large glass window of the gift shop and smiled at the cute teddy bear sitting on one of the shelves. She went inside the store to examine it more closely. The stuffed toy was approximately a foot tall, and somewhat unusual because it had dark black fur rather than any of the more typical shades of brown. A sky blue ribbon was tied in a bow around its neck. *I bet Samantha would like this a lot.* She lifted the bear off the shelf and took it to the cashier.

"Will that be all?" the clerk asked.

"Yes." Tina paid for her purchase and borrowed a pen to sign the heart-shaped tag dangling from the toy's ear.

Armed with the bear and directions to the ER from the cashier, she walked out into the lobby with a bit more confidence. She went past the elevators and turned right, following the hallway until it ended at the emergency room.

The place was full and very noisy, with the TV blaring, babies crying, and people talking. A nurse's station was positioned near a door that apparently led to the treatment area. Tina approached the counter and waited impatiently for the sole employee manning the station to acknowledge her.

"May I help you?"

"I'm here to see Samantha Whitwell."

The nurse picked up a clipboard and looked at the top page. "Yes, she's here."

"I know that. Can I see her?"

"Are you a relative?"

"Um...no."

"According to this," the woman tapped the clipboard with her finger, "Ms. Whitwell already has two family members with her. You'll have to wait out here until she is released. It shouldn't be long now." The phone rang and she reached for the receiver.

"Wait a minute!" Frustrated, Tina attempted to bang her fist on the counter. However, she forgot she was holding the teddy bear and only succeeded in plunking the adorable animal right in front of the employee. "I need to see her!" Lowering her voice considerably, she continued, "She's my...um...partner."

The nurse paused, her hand resting on the still-ringing phone. She smiled at the bear before raising her eyes to the person it very much resembled.

"Tina!"

Both heads turned toward the doorway to the patient area, where Lisa was gesturing for her sister's visitor to come in.

"Go on." The nurse waved Tina away before grabbing the phone. "Sarasota Memorial, emergency room. May I help you?"

Tina nodded her thanks and hurried over to Lisa. "How is she?"

"She came back from getting X-rays a few minutes ago. We're waiting to hear the results."

"The...the accident, what happened?"

"Kathy was driving Sam home after lunch." Lisa led the way through the bustling hallway. "They were waiting at a stoplight and when it turned green, they started into the intersection. Some guy going the other way ran the red light and hit them. Thank goodness he wasn't going very fast, but he hit the passenger side of the car. Kathy wasn't hurt, but she's pretty shaken up. I took her home a little while ago."

They arrived at the last curtained cubicle in the row and Tina peeked around the cloth. Sam was lying on a semi-inclined hospital gurney, eyes closed and face turned away from her mother, who was sitting in the only chair available in the cramped space. Mrs. Whitwell rose from the seat as soon as she saw Tina, and the two women exchanged reciprocally unfriendly looks.

Lisa quickly slipped between them. She gently took hold of her mother's arm. "Let's go get a cup of coffee." She ushered Mrs. Whitwell away, continuing to talk in order to quash any protest that might be forthcoming. "I think there's a beverage machine in the lobby. Maybe by the time we get back they'll have the information about the X-rays."

Tina sighed as she watched the mother and daughter leave. *I owe you one, Lisa.* She turned to check on Sam and was pleased to see she was awakening.

Sam rubbed her eyes. "Am I dreaming, or are you really here?"

"I'm really here." Tina sat on the edge of the bed. "How are you feeling?"

"I'm okay. The diagnosis at this point is just some bad bruising to my right side. If the tests come back showing no internal injuries, I can go home."

"I'm so glad you're all right. This...it...scared me."

"Hey," Sam said softly, "I'm fine."

"You could've been..." Tina didn't dare say it out loud. *Killed.*

"You listen to me, Ms. Mellekas. I may be small, but I'm tough!" Sam flexed her left arm and made a muscle. "See?"

Tina nodded, not sure that she could speak without bursting into tears.

Sam observed the silent woman, who was fidgeting with a stuffed animal. *We're going to have to talk about this, but not now. She's barely keeping herself together.* "T?"

"Hmm?"

"Is that for me?"

"Oh...um...yeah." Tina handed the teddy bear over. "I thought you might like it."

Sam grabbed the tall woman's arm and pulled her close. "I love...it."

Only inches apart, blue eyes met green, communicating better than words ever could.

The doctor strode in, skidding to a halt when he saw the couple. He shuffled the papers he was holding. "Ahem."

Tina sprang off the bed.

"Hi, Doc." Sam grinned at the blushing resident. "This is my partner, Tina."

The doctor shook hands with the equally blushing visitor before addressing his patient. "The X-rays show no damage to any internal organs. There are no broken bones, though you do have some deep bruising. You're going to be sore for the next few days, but otherwise you'll be fine."

"So, I can go home now?"

"Yes. I'm going to write you a prescription for medication for tonight and tomorrow. By Tuesday you should be able to use an over-the-counter pain reliever as needed. The nurse will be back with release papers for you to sign, and then you're free go."

"Thanks, Doc."

"You're welcome." The resident left, pulling the curtain closed behind him.

Sam grinned at Tina. "See? Just a few bruises. Nothing to worry about." She tried to sit up and the grin quickly vanished. "Ugh!"

"Samantha!" Tina gently pressed the woman back against the pillows. "What are you doing?"

"I need my clothes. I think they're under the bed."

"I'll get them." Tina found the plastic bag of clothes on the shelf beneath the gurney and helped the blonde get dressed.

Sam groaned in pain several times during the exceedingly slow, difficult process. Exhausted from the effort, she had to gather her strength to speak. "Tina?"

"Yes?"

"Thanks. I've been so worried today, being in this flimsy hospital gown. I was sure my mom or Lisa was going to see my tattoo."

Tina finished tying the laces on Sam's sneakers. "Any time." She moved to the head of the bed. "Though I much prefer taking your clothes off to putting them on," she whispered as she bent down for a tender kiss.

"I feel better already."

"Good." *Me, too.* Tina straightened up. "They'll be back soon."

Sam sighed. *I am not ready for that.*

"You okay?"

"My mom...we kind of argued earlier."

"Here at the hospital?"

"Yeah. She wants me to go to her house so she can take care of me. I told her no, but she wasn't listening."

"What do you want to do?"

"I'd like for you to drive me home."

"Then that's what we'll do."

"Hello?" Lisa alerted the women before pulling open the curtain. "Any news yet?"

"Yes," Sam answered. "The doctor was just here. No broken bones, no internal injuries. I'm waiting to sign some papers and then I can leave."

"Great! I'll call Mike and let him know."

"Lisa." Mrs. Whitwell's voice stopped her daughter in midstride. "After you call, go get the car. We'll meet you outside after Samantha signs—"

"Mom," Sam interrupted, "Tina is taking me to my house."

"We already had this conversation."

"Excuse me, Mrs. Whitwell," Tina said, "but it's Samantha's decision to make."

"You, of all people, shouldn't be telling *me* what's best for my daughter!"

"Mom, please don't," Sam implored.

"This is neither the time nor the place for this discussion," Tina reasoned. "Anything you have to say to me can wait until after I get Samantha home."

There was an uncomfortable silence as the women glared at each other.

"Hello." A nurse breezed in with a clipboard. She looked at the patient. "Are you ready to go home?"

"Ab-so-lute-ly."

"These are the doctor's orders." The nurse tilted the clipboard so Sam could read along. "No work for three days; get plenty of bed rest; medication for tonight and tomorrow. Any questions?"

"Nope."

"I need you to sign here."

Trying to keep her arm as still as possible, Sam clumsily wrote her name.

"Here is your prescription and your copy of the doctor's orders." The nurse gave the papers to Sam. "I have a wheelchair for you. Is someone going to bring a car to the door?"

Tina spoke first. "I am." She reached for Sam's hand and squeezed it. "I'll see you in a few minutes."

"Okay."

Tina went through the ER waiting room and outside. There was a circular drive where patient drop-off and pick-up was allowed. She jogged along the sidewalk, past the main entrance of the hospital and to the parking garage. By the time she got back to the emergency room, the group was already outside. She got out of the car to open the passenger door while Lisa helped Sam up from the wheelchair. After adjusting the leather seat so it reclined a little and the injured woman assured her she was comfortable, Tina fastened the seat belt. She closed the door and turned to face Lisa and her mother.

They stood quietly for a moment, no one sure of what to say. Once again, Lisa came to the rescue. "We'll go get the prescription filled and meet you at Sam's."

"All right." Tina walked around to the driver's side of the car and got in. She looked at her partner. "Ready?"

"Yes." The normally cheerful woman was definitely out of sorts and it was evident in her tone. Her side was throbbing painfully and her head ached from the emotional stress. She hugged the teddy bear in her arms. "I just want to go home."

"You got it." Tina put the car in gear. *I don't know what's going to happen when we all get there, but I doubt it will be good.*

It was nightfall when she backed the BMW into the driveway, parking with the passenger side of the car closest to the steps of the garage apartment. It had been a quiet ride from the hospital, with the dark-haired woman sneaking frequent glances at Sam, making sure she was all right. "We're here," Tina said softly as she turned off the engine.

"Hmm?"

"We're home." Despite the somberness of the occasion, a half grin momentarily graced Tina's features. *I like the sound of that.* Her expression changed to one of profound affection as she reached over and lovingly straightened Sam's hair with her fingers. *Home.*

Mike and the boys had been sitting on the steps waiting for them to arrive. They rushed to the vehicle.

"Tina!" He pulled open her door. "Lisa called and told us you were on the way." Mike's eyes swept toward Sam. "How's she feeling?"

"She hasn't had any pain medication yet," Tina answered as she got out of the car. "She's feeling pretty sore."

"When Lisa phoned, she said they were at the drug store. They're getting the prescription filled now."

Aaron and Joshua were staring at their aunt through the passenger window. Sam managed a weak smile and a wave at her nephews.

Mike looked at the boys and sighed. "They've been terribly worried; we all have." He went over to his sons. "Now that you've seen she's okay, I want you two to go in the house. I'll be right there."

The boys dragged their feet as they left, grumbling that they always got sent away whenever anything interesting was going on.

Mike opened the door and squatted so he was at eye level with Sam. "Let's get you upstairs. I think you'll feel a lot better once you're tucked into your own bed." He unfastened the seat belt and scooped her into his arms.

"I can walk!"

"I'm following orders from Lisa." He stood slowly, making sure he had a secure hold of his precious cargo. "You don't want me to get in trouble with my wife, do you?"

Sam shook her head. The aching in her side had intensified when she was lifted and she gripped her teddy bear tightly, trying not to cry.

Tina pushed the car door shut before bounding up the stairs ahead of them and using her key to unlock the apartment. She turned on the lights as Mike carried his sister-in-law into the bedroom and carefully laid her down.

"Oww! Laying flat, not good. Oww."

Tina quickly propped several pillows behind Sam. "Is that better?"

The worst of the throbbing pain started to recede and Sam nodded.

"I'm going to get back to the boys." Mike started out of the room. "If you need anything, let me know."

"We will. Thanks." Tina was already removing Sam's shoes and socks. After dropping the footwear on the floor, she lightly massaged her partner's feet.

"Mmm, you're very good at that."

"You think so?"

"Mmm-hmm."

Tina smiled, glad that she was able to take Sam's mind off her injury for a few minutes.

"T?"

"Yes?"

"My mom will be here soon."

Tina tried to keep the irritation out of her voice. "I know."

"I'm sorry she was rude to you. Don't take it personally. It's me she's angry at."

"I'm fine. You just concentrate on getting well."

"I already feel better. Being with you, it makes me feel...stronger."

"Shh. You should be resting."

"C'mere, please?"

Tina complied, cautiously sitting on the edge of the bed.

Sam took Tina's right hand in her left. She studied their joined hands as she began to speak.

"In the past, I was willing to give up part of myself if that was what it took to have a relationship with my mother. She demanded that I come to family functions on the holidays but wouldn't allow me to bring my...anyone...with me. I went along with it because I hoped that, in time, things would improve." Sam sighed. "It hasn't, and I refuse to do it any more. When my mom came over here — that day we were playing soccer with the boys, I told her I wasn't going to her house for the holidays this year." *Not without you.* "She didn't take it very well."

"Maybe you should reconsider—"

"No." Sam promptly dismissed the suggestion. "Maybe it's because I'm almost forty." She shifted her attention from their clasped hands and looked at Tina with adoration. "Maybe it's because I want to be brave like you. Maybe it's a little of both."

"Brave? I'm not brave."

"Yes, you are," Sam disagreed. "You had so much responsibility heaped on you...and then the tragedy with your brother. But you started over...all alone. Always so strong, so brave. And you know what I think is the most courageous thing of all?"

"Um...no."

"You've risked your heart — for me."

"You," Tina gazed deeply into misty green eyes, "are very much worth the risk."

That got Sam smiling. "You know what else?"

"What?"

"I think those doctor's orders said something about lots of kisses helping to promote a more speedy recovery."

Any further words were smothered by a gentle kiss...and another... and another.

There was a knock at the front door. "Hello?" Lisa called out as she entered the apartment.

Tina sat back and grinned at the flushed face of her partner. "Was the doctor's advice right?"

"Totally. I see a Nobel Prize in that man's future."

"I see my future right here," Tina murmured as she leaned in once more for a kiss. "And it's way better than any Nobel Prize."

"Hello?" Lisa came into the bedroom. "Oh! Maybe I should come by later."

"It's okay, Lisa." Tina let go of Sam's hand and stood up. "Now that you're here to keep an eye on our patient, I'm going to take the opportunity to go get my backpack." She went outside, pausing on the top landing as the early evening breeze cooled her heated skin. *I may have to send that doctor a thank-you note.* As she descended the stairs, she saw Mrs. Whitwell coming across the walkway from Lisa's house. *Uh-oh, round two.*

The women met at the bottom of the steps. Again, they traded icy glares.

"Well? Are you going to let me pass?" Sam's mother didn't make an effort to contain her hostility. "Or are you attempting to keep me from seeing my daughter?"

"There's no need for us to be adversaries—"

"You have influenced my daughter to turn against her family. I have every right to be upset!"

Tina thought of all the things she'd like to say, probably would have said in her younger, more impetuous years when her temper frequently got the best of her. But working with Vivian had taught her plenty, not the least of which was how to control her anger. She swallowed the harsh comments she wanted to make and spoke from her heart, for Samantha. "Mrs. Whitwell, you have a wonderful daughter who loves you very much. She's told me how...disappointed...she is that your relationship with her is strained."

"Well, you certainly aren't helping in that regard—"

"Let me finish," Tina interrupted. "I haven't tried to influence Samantha. She's a grown woman who is perfectly capable of making her own decisions. It would make her extremely happy if you would accept her for who she is, but it seems to me that you just aren't willing to do that."

"She's confused. She doesn't really know what she wants."

"Oh yes, she does," Tina retorted. "And, somehow or another, I'm fortunate enough to be it."

"We'll see about that." Mrs. Whitwell stepped forward, eliminating any personal space between them.

Tina didn't move. "I'm warning you — if you push Samantha into choosing, you're going to lose her." Her eyes flashed with anger. "And you'll have no one to blame but yourself."

Lisa came outside and saw the women locked in a standoff. "Mother?" She hurried down the stairs. "I gave Sam her medicine. Do you want to see her before she falls asleep?"

"It's been a long day," Mrs. Whitwell remarked wearily. "She needs to rest. I'll visit her tomorrow."

Without a word, Tina turned and went back up to the apartment.

"It has been a long day." Lisa pulled her car keys from her pocket. "But the most important thing is Sam's all right." *What the heck happened out here? I can't believe she isn't going in to see her.* "Ready for me to take you home, then?"

"Yes."

Tina closed the door and leaned against it. *That probably didn't help any, but at least I gave it a shot.* She went to the bedroom to check on Sam. She was resting comfortably, teddy bear firmly tucked under her arm. *I don't think she's let go of that thing since I gave it to her.*

As if she sensed the presence of her partner, Sam opened her eyes halfway and mumbled something unintelligible.

In two long strides, Tina was there, kneeling next to the bed. "Go to sleep. I'll be right here. I promise."

"I...I...lo...ve..." Sam's eyelids became heavy and she succumbed to the effects of the medication.

Tina stayed for a few minutes, watching her sleep. *I'd do anything to take away the hurt you're feeling. I guess I can't protect you from everything...but that won't stop me from always trying.*

Reaching for the plastic bottle of pills on the bedside table, Tina looked to see how often the medicine had to be taken. *Damn!* Unable to read the small print, she realized her glasses were still out in the car in her backpack.

She heard several popping sounds as she slowly stood. "Ugh." *You're getting old, T.* She looked down at Sam. *That thought doesn't seem so horrible anymore, though. Not when I have you to grow old with.*

Tina took the blanket from the end of the bed and spread it over the sleeping woman. She reverently touched Sam's cheek, almost as if to convince herself that she was real. *I love you, too.*

~ * ~ * ~ * ~ * ~

Tina called Vivian to apprise her of the situation and let her know she wouldn't be at work in the morning. Then, after retrieving her backpack from the car, she attempted to relax on the couch by reading a book. Finding it impossible to concentrate on the words, she gave up and tried the TV instead. She idly flipped through the channels before turning it off and sighing. *Might as well go in there, T, 'cause that's all you really want to do.*

She went into the bedroom and moved the rocking chair around to the left side of the bed, where she would have a clear view of Sam. A sense of peacefulness descended over Tina as she sat in the darkened room. *This is more like it. This is where I belong.*

It was three in the morning when she heard the first sound of distress. Tina was out of the chair and next to the bed in an instant. Her eyes were accustomed to the dark and she had no trouble seeing the pained expression on Sam's face. "Are you all right?"

"I'm sliding off these pillows. My side hurts."

Tina carefully helped her into a more inclined position. "Is that better?"

"Yeah. Thanks."

"Time for another pain pill?"

Sam nodded.

Tina got a fresh glass of water and handed it to Sam, who quickly took her medicine. "Please stay with me?"

"I haven't left. I've been sitting right here—"

"No. I mean in the bed."

"I'm afraid I'll bump into you. I...I don't want to hurt you." *Never again.*

"Please?"

Unable to refuse the heartfelt plea, Tina relented and climbed onto the bed. She lay alongside Sam and carefully draped her arm across the smaller woman's body. "Is this okay?"

"Mmm-hmm."

Exhausted, Tina closed her eyes.

Sam heard her partner's breathing immediately deepen. She placed her hand over the larger one resting on her stomach. *I know you won't hurt me.* Smiling, she watched the beautiful woman slumbering beside her until she couldn't keep her eyes open any longer.

Chapter 23

Lisa kissed Mike good-bye. "Have a good day." She waved to her children and husband as the minivan backed out of the driveway. Climbing the steps to the garage apartment, she hoped her sister or Tina was awake.

She tapped lightly on the door. When there was no answer, she used her key to get in. The morning light poured through the windows of an empty living room. *They must still be sleeping.* Lisa tiptoed to the bedroom and peeked in. *Well, isn't this a sight?* Sam looked the same as when she had last seen her, propped against the pillows and holding the teddy bear. But now Tina was curled up beside her with a protective arm wrapped around her waist. They were sound asleep.

They'll be hungry when they wake up. I'd better go get their breakfast ready. Lisa jotted a short message on a pad of paper that was lying on the desk. She put the note under the bottle of pills on the nightstand before quietly slipping out of the apartment.

About an hour later, Lisa's phone rang.

"Hello?"

"Hi, sis."

"Good morning. How are you feeling?"

"A little better, thanks," Sam said.

"I made some breakfast. Are you hungry?"

"Yes!"

"Would you ask Tina to come over and give me a hand carrying it?"

"Sure."

"All right. I'll see you in a few minutes." Lisa hung up the phone. She pushed the switch on the coffeemaker and a fresh pot began to brew while she got busy preparing a breakfast tray. Shortly thereafter, there was a knock on the slightly ajar kitchen door.

"Lisa?"

"C'mon in, Tina."

"Samantha said you needed help?"

"Yeah. I just have a few more things to do and we'll be ready to go."

Tina leaned against the counter and watched as Lisa buttered some toast. "This is very nice of you. Thanks."

"You're welcome."

"I also want to thank you for yesterday...with your mom."

Lisa turned and faced her former teammate. "It isn't often that I get a chance to intervene on my sister's behalf. Has she told you what's been going on?"

"She said your mother doesn't accept that she's gay, and...um, she's not going over there for the holidays."

"There's a bit more to it. Would you like some coffee?"

"Yeah."

Lisa poured each of them a cup. "Let's sit down for a minute, okay?"

"Okay."

They sat at the table.

"When Sam came out to Mom, they had a huge argument. My sister made me promise not to get involved. She felt it was her battle to fight and didn't want anyone else getting caught in the crossfire." Lisa sighed. "It hasn't been easy."

Tina nodded in understanding.

"Has she told you our parents are divorced?"

"No."

Lisa took a sip of her drink. She seemed to be having difficulty deciding what to say next.

"Look," Tina started to get up, "this is really none of my business..."

Might as well take the direct approach. "Do you love my sister?"

Tina sank back into her chair. "Wh-what?"

"Are you in love with Sam?"

After fidgeting for a few moments, Tina stared into her coffee and softly answered, "I...um...yes."

"Then it *is* your business. You're part of the family now." Lisa paused, waiting for Tina to look at her, before adding sincerely, "And I'm glad."

They drank their coffee in silence until Lisa continued in a voice shaded with sadness. "The divorce was arduous for everyone. I'll let Sam tell you the details when she's ready, but what I want you to know is our mother never really recovered from it. She's become terribly embittered these last few years. She hasn't always been like this."

"I figured as much. Anyone who raised two of the nicest people I've ever met can't be all bad."

"Thanks."

Tina shrugged. "I know when your life suddenly changes, it can be hard to...adjust."

"Yes, that's true." *I'll bet you're an expert on the subject.* "Sam had a very tough time dealing with the divorce. On top of that, she's been determined to work things out with Mom on her own, and she's ended up carrying the burden all by herself."

"Not anymore."

"You're right." Lisa smiled. "I was surprised when she asked me to call you from the hospital. I didn't think she'd do that with our mother there. And then, even more surprising, was when you arrived, Mom stayed."

"Yeah. Then things rapidly went from bad to worse."

"Well, to put it in perspective, you're the only one of Sam's girlfriends Mom has ever met. Whenever my sister would visit, she went alone and there was no discussion about her being gay. You are the first flesh-and-blood personification of Sam's lifestyle she's ever seen. And, I'm sorry to say, you've had to bear the brunt of the years of animosity she's fostered about it."

"I can handle it. I don't care if she hates me, but Samantha...she doesn't deserve to be treated like that."

"Well, whatever transpired between Mom and you has definitely started something."

"I'm sorry. I never intended—"

"No. I mean in a good way. She asked me about you when I drove her home last night. The fact that she would show any interest whatsoever in who you are is a big step. It was the first time in ages we've talked about Sam. So, I should be thanking you."

"I don't want Samantha to miss the holidays with her family." *I know what that's like.*

"I can tell you, from years of experience, you have a snowball's chance in Hell of changing Sam's mind when she makes a decision."

"She certainly can be obstinate."

"But it some cases," Lisa grinned and looked pointedly at the woman across from her, "that's a good trait, wouldn't you agree?"

Tina felt a blush start to creep up her neck to her face. *How much has Samantha told her about us?* The phone rang, saving her from having to respond to the question.

"Hello?" Lisa listened to the caller and rolled her eyes. "Yes, Sam, we're on our way." She hung up and chuckled. "It seems we have a hungry patient waiting for us." She used a pot holder to take a shallow metal pan from the oven. Pulling back the tin foil, she transferred scrambled eggs and bacon onto two plates. After placing the dishes and silverware on the tray, she covered the whole thing with a clean dishtowel.

Tina rose from her seat. "What do you need me to do?"

"Would you carry the pot of coffee? And grab that trivet so we have something to put it on when we get over there."

Tina picked up the items. She led the way, handling the door duties because the other woman had her hands full with the tray.

"Room service!" Lisa placed the breakfast tray across her sister's lap and removed the towel.

"Thanks, I'm starving!"

"You're feeling better, then."

Tina put the trivet on the desk and placed the coffeepot on it.

"Coffee." Sam's eyes lit up. "It smells good."

"I'll go get the cups." Tina headed for the kitchen.

Lisa looked down at her sister. "I think you're right."

"About what?"

"She's a keeper."

Sam grinned. "I'm very happy you think so."

Tina returned with the coffee cups and poured for everyone. She sat in the rocking chair and balanced her dish on her lap. Lisa stayed and kept them company while they ate, telling funny stories about her sons' latest antics. The hungry women cleaned their plates.

"That was great, sis. Thanks."

"Yes, it was." Tina put her empty dish on the tray with Sam's.

"Well, as much as I've enjoyed chatting, I need to get to work. I told them I'd be in by eleven." Lisa got up from the end of the bed where she had been sitting. "Mom called this morning. She said she'd be over to see you around noon."

"Okay."

"Tina," Lisa lifted up the tray, "if you'll bring the coffeepot and open the doors for me again, I'd appreciate it."

"Sure."

They took the things back to the house and loaded the dishwasher.

"I need to get going." Lisa collected her briefcase and purse from the counter. "Thanks for the help."

"Any time." Tina followed the woman outside. "I was wondering...I want to cook something special for Samantha. Does she have a favorite food?"

"That's easy." Lisa laughed. "If you really want to score points" — *not that you need any* — "make homemade chocolate chip cookies."

"I was thinking of something a bit more...nutritional."

"She loves the typical Thanksgiving fare." Lisa smiled as she got into the car. "And I believe she's available for dinner on that day."

"Thanks, for everything." Tina jogged up the stairs. *Hmm, Thanksgiving dinner...*

Having had several cups of coffee, Sam was alert, even though she had taken a pain pill earlier. Tina helped her wash up and put on fresh clothes before shepherding her directly back to bed.

Tina settled into the rocking chair again. "Samantha?"

"Yes?"

"What do you think about going to my place? My bed...I can incline it so you can sleep comfortably. Then, if you want, on Thursday, I could make a Thanksgiving meal."

"That sounds great! Let's go."

"Hold it." Tina held her hand out like a stop sign. "Your mother is coming to visit you. Remember?"

"Oh. Yeah. But will you pack some things for me while we're waiting? There's a duffel bag in the closet."

"Okay." Tina got the bag and filled it according to Sam's instructions.

"I'd like to take my guitar, too."

"Your guitar?"

"I'll have to have something to do when you're at work, right?"

"I wasn't planning on going to work."

"You said it's been very busy," Sam said logically. "Vivian probably needs you there." *And you'd go stir-crazy sitting around baby-sitting me all day.*

"I guess so."

"I'll more than likely spend most of the time sleeping. I'll be fine."

"Do you promise to call me at the office if you need anything?"

"I promise."

"All right." Tina took the luggage and strode toward the living room. "I'll go put your stuff in the car."

Sam called after her, "The case for the guitar is in the corner. I'll need the little practice amp, too."

She does not know the meaning of traveling light. Tina slung the jam-packed bag over her shoulder and held the guitar case in one hand, the amplifier in the other. She lumbered down the stairs and put the things in her trunk. As she closed the lid, a car pulled into the driveway.

Sam's mother got out of the vehicle and walked toward the steps to the apartment.

"Mrs. Whitwell..."

The woman stopped, but continued to face away from Tina. "Yes?"

"I'm sorry if I was out of line yesterday. I meant no disrespect."

Mrs. Whitwell turned around. She knew the apology was genuine; she had a feeling this was a person who wouldn't say anything she didn't mean. "The whole situation has been...difficult. I wasn't very pleasant, either."

Tina nodded, acknowledging the return apology, such as it was.

"I'd like to ask you something, if you don't mind."

"Okay." *Today certainly is a day for questions. If she asks me if I'm in love with her daughter...*

"What does your mother think about...you...and Samantha?"

"My mother and I haven't spoken in a long time."

"Does she know you're...gay?"

"No."

"I see. But you feel qualified to tell me how I should handle this?"

"Mrs. Whitwell, I don't have any idea what it's like to be a mother. However, I do know what it's like to be a daughter who hasn't fulfilled her mother's expectations. It's hard to live your life cognizant of the fact, each and every day, that you're not what your mother may have hoped or dreamed. Nonetheless, you keep on going, striving to do the best you can under the circumstances. It never seems to be enough, though." Tina looked at her feet. "But a daughter...still needs to feel love and acceptance for who she is. Without it, she carries a hurt deep in her heart. It's not something Samantha should have to endure. She's good, and kind, and...um...she loves you very much."

"I appreciate your honesty."

Tina raised her eyes and the women regarded each other with a newfound, mutual measure of respect.

Mrs. Whitwell turned and began ascending the stairs.

Tina ran her hand through her hair. *Whew. Round three has concluded.* She sat on the steps to wait. *This family thing is way too stressful. How in the world do people deal with it all the time?*

After a short visit, Sam's mother left, giving Tina a perfunctory nod as she passed.

The tall woman immediately went back into the apartment. *I hope they didn't argue again.* As she entered the bedroom, she saw her partner wiping her eyes with her shirtsleeve. *Oh, no.* "Are you all right?" She got the box of tissues from the bathroom and handed it to Sam.

"Yeah."

"Why are you crying?"

"My...mom..." Sam sniffled.

"What about her?" *I never should have gotten involved. I've only made things worse.*

"She...she told me she loves me."

Relief flooded through Tina as she sat on the edge of the bed. "Of course she loves you." *Thank you, Mrs. Whitwell.*

"She said she needs some time to process the whole thing, but she doesn't want to become estranged from me."

"Well, that's good news, isn't it?"

"Yes." Sam took hold of Tina's hand. "She said you talked to her."

"Um, yeah. A little bit."

"What did you say?"

"I don't know. I kind of rambled on about mothers and daughters. I'm not sure I made a whole lot of sense."

"I don't think anyone would ever accuse you of rambling." Sam smiled. "Whatever you said, it reached her. This is the first real progress we've made since I told her I was gay."

"So, are you going over there for Thanksgiving?"

"No. I said I wouldn't go without you. She's not quite ready for that yet."

"I'm sorry."

"It's all right. I like the idea of us having our first Thanksgiving together alone, don't you?"

"Truthfully? Yeah. That whole family thing can be a little over-whelming."

"Then it's working out perfectly, isn't it?"

"Yes, I think it is." She leaned forward and kissed Sam. "Are you ready to head over to my place?"

"Mmm-hmm. Maybe one more kiss before we go?"

Just before they left her apartment, Sam insisted on grabbing a video. "It's my turn to provide the holiday movie," she explained. When Tina tried to see the title, Sam tucked it away out of sight. "We have to watch it on Thanksgiving Day, and that's all you need to know for now."

"Okay." Tina helped her down to the car and buckled her seat belt. "Comfortable?"

"Yes." Sam hugged the teddy bear she had refused to leave behind.

Tina pulled the BMW out of the driveway. Sam was resting with her eyes closed, and by the time they merged onto the highway, she appeared to be asleep. Tina reached for the knob to turn the radio down and was surprised when her hand was caught in midair by her partner. She drove the rest the way to Tampa with one hand on the steering wheel, the other entwined with Sam's.

Chapter 24

"Mmm." Sam slowly awakened to the sensation of light kisses along her neck.

"Happy Thanksgiving," Tina murmured into the sleepy woman's ear.

The blonde turned over and hugged her partner. "Our first Thanksgiving." *And I love the way it's beginning.*

"How are you feeling?"

Sam snuggled a little closer. "Wonderful."

"I meant your side." Tina couldn't keep the concern from her voice. After Sam's accident they had been reclining the bed a little at a time, and the previous evening the rapidly recovering woman had declared she was ready to sleep lying flat again. "Are you sure it was okay last night?"

"Yes, I'm sure." Sam breathed in the fresh scent of Tina's soap and shampoo. "You took your shower already."

"I ran, showered, set the table, and put the turkey in the oven. I'm all yours for the rest of the day."

A wide smile appeared on Sam's face. "I like the sound of that." She had missed Tina terribly during the last few days. As she had begun to feel better, she had watched TV, read a book, and played the guitar. But mostly, she'd kept her eye on the clock, eagerly waiting for her partner to get home from work.

"Didn't you say you wanted to see the parade this morning?"

"Mmm-hmm."

"It's going to start in a few minutes."

Sam's head popped up. "It is?"

"Yes."

"We have to watch that. It's a Thanksgiving tradition!"

"I'll go turn on the TV while you take your aspirin."

"Thanks." Sam gave Tina a quick kiss before getting out of the bed and hurrying toward the bathroom. "I'll be right there."

They sat on the couch, drinking coffee and enjoying the Macy's Thanksgiving Day Parade. Tina periodically went to the kitchen to check on the turkey. As noon approached and the parade was winding down, she prepared the side dishes.

"Hurry! It's Santa!"

Smiling at Sam's enthusiasm, Tina hustled into the living room in time to see Santa waving to children and adults alike from his sleigh. "So, are you ready for some turkey now?"

"Yes!" Upon hearing that the Thanksgiving meal would be ready around twelve, Sam had declined a late breakfast. More than ready to sample the food she had smelled cooking all morning, she followed Tina into the kitchen.

The women filled their plates and carried them into the dining room. They took their seats at the table, which had been decorated with a colorful cloth and a vase full of beautiful flowers. Tina lit the candles she had purchased for the occasion, thinking Sam would like them.

Sparkling green eyes surveyed the festive setting before coming to rest on her dinner companion. "This is really nice."

Tina took hold of Sam's hand. "I haven't had a lot to be thankful for in a long time. But I want you to know I'm very thankful to have you in my life."

"It's appropriate that we're spending this particular day together, then," Sam lifted their joined hands and kissed them, "because I feel truly blessed to have found you."

"I..." A trace of guilt crept into Tina's voice. "I'm sorry you're missing being with your family, though."

"I *am* with my family." Sam pulled Tina close so she could give her a long, sweet kiss. She released Tina's hand and picked up her utensils. "We'd better get started on this fabulous meal before it gets cold." *Or before I forget about Thanksgiving dinner entirely and drag you into the—*

"Gravy?"

"What?"

"I was asking," Tina held the gravy boat near Sam's plate, "would you like some of this?"

Yes! "Oh, yes."

They ate their meal, spending much of the time holding hands, sharing kisses and exchanging smoldering looks.

"That was fantastic!" Sam helped clear the table. "You weren't fooling when you said you were a good cook."

"I'm glad you enjoyed it."

They worked together, rinsing the dishes and loading the dishwasher.

"Time for the movie." Sam led the way into the living room. She picked up a black plastic videotape case from the end table.

Tina sat on the couch. "I finally get to find out what it is?"

"Well, this is my *favorite* movie."

"*Pilgrim's Progress?*"

"Noooo."

"What is it?"

"*Miracle on 34th Street* — the original black-and-white version with Maureen O'Hara and Natalie Wood. Have you ever seen it?"

"If I did, it was a long time ago. Something about a man who says he's the real Santa Claus?"

"Yes." Sam put the tape into the VCR. She went back to the couch and cuddled next to Tina. "But there's *much* more to it than that."

"There is?"

"You'll see."

The movie began, and it didn't take Tina long to see why it was Sam's favorite. Underlying the amusing tale of a man who proclaimed he was Santa and the lawyer who took on the task of proving it, was a love story.

Tina immediately became engrossed in the plot, watching as a disillusioned woman's world was suddenly turned upside down when her life became entangled with those of the lawyer and Kris Kringle. The two men joined together to help the lady and her similarly cynical young daughter learn to trust, have faith in people, and believe that wishes could come true. In typical Hollywood fashion, it had a happy ending.

"Isn't that a wonderful movie?" Sam used the remote to turn off the VCR and TV.

"Yes." *I can see why you wanted me to watch it.*

Hearing the emotion in the single-word response, Sam glanced up at Tina and was surprised to see traces of tears in her eyes. She pretended not to notice. "You know what?" she asked cheerfully.

"What?"

"We're going to live happily ever after. Just like the movie."

"Real life isn't a fairy tale, Samantha," Tina said sadly.

"Life is what you make it," Sam replied with certainty. "And I want to make *my* life...with you."

"I...I can't promise you things will be...perfect."

"Living happily ever after doesn't mean things are always perfect." Sam adjusted her position so she could look directly at Tina. "It means you meet the person you know you belong with, the one who makes you feel a love so strong that sometimes you think your heart might burst at the intensity of it." *The way you make me feel.* "You commit yourself to living your life with that person, knowing that together, you're better than you ever were apart. And when there are hard times, it's a little easier to bear because you help each other through them. And the good times...well, the good times are even more joyful, because you have someone special to share them with."

"You." Tina affectionately tucked some loose hairs behind the blonde's ear. "You're special."

"You are, too." Sam tilted her head to the side and asked hopefully, "So, do you think you can believe in a happily ever after like that?"

You are utterly adorable. "I...I think...maybe...I can." The bright smile she received for her answer gave Tina courage. "I...um...I have something for you."

Sam was instantly curious. "A present?"

"Kind of."

"I wasn't aware that Thanksgiving was a gift-giving occasion," she joked, remembering Tina saying the same thing to her on Halloween.

"Well, if you don't want it," Tina teased.

"Yes! I want it!"

Tina reached into the pocket of her shorts and removed a silver key. "I thought you should have this."

Sam stared at the shiny piece of metal. *It's the key to her condo.* She looked up into loving eyes. *It's the key to her heart.* "Oh, Tina." Sam hugged her partner tightly. "Where's my key ring? Did we bring it?"

"No. I locked your door when we left."

"Then let me put it right here, so I won't forget it." Sam took the key and set it next to the video case on the end table. *Not that there's a chance in Hell I'd ever forget it.* "I have something for you, too." She got up, removed her guitar from the case, and turned on the amplifier. Sitting on the couch again, she strummed the instrument a few times to steady her nerves. "I've been working on a new song."

"Something you're going to sing with the band?"

Sam shook her head and looked down at her guitar. "This song is intended for an audience of one." *If I can get my hands to stop shaking, maybe I can play it.* She took a deep breath, played the chord progression, and began singing with a trembling voice.

"Heart living in the shadows, you've been so all alone
Moving through life within yourself, behind those walls of stone
It doesn't have to be that way, that's not how life should be
There's nothing to fear, it's just you and me here

And it's love, it's only love
It's plain to see, yes it's clear to me
That it's love, it's only love
You and me — it's love"

Tina was astounded. *It's a song about me...about us.* She sat as still as a statue, enthralled by the words and music.

"Step out from beneath that big oak tree
Stand in the sunlight, stand with me
Don't be afraid, don't run away
I'm here beside you, you'll be okay
'Cause it's love, it's only love
There's nothing to fear, it's just you and me here

And it's love, it's only love
It's plain to see, yes it's clear to me
That it's love, it's only love
You and me — it's love

I wanna be the only one
The searching is over, let history be done
You've got a chance to make a new start
I wanna be the one to capture your heart

'Cause it's love, it's only love
There's nothing to fear, it's just you and me here
And it's love, it's only love
It's plain to see, yes it's clear to me
That it's love, it's only love
You and me — it's love"

Sam played the series of chords leading to the last verse. She didn't dare glance up to see what reaction her song might be causing, afraid that, once again, she'd overstepped Tina's emotional boundaries. *Too late to turn back now.*

"Heart living in the shadows, you've been so all alone
Moving through life within yourself, behind those walls of stone
It doesn't have to be that way, that's not how life should be
There's nothing to fear, it's just you and me here

And it's love, love
It's plain to see, yes it's clear to me
That it's love, love
I need you to be, forever with me
'Cause it's love, love
Can't you see, it's our destiny
And it's love, love

You and me — it's only love"

Sam continued to stare down at her guitar after the last note had dissipated into the air. "I'm not much of a songwriter. I'm more on the performance end of the spectrum than composition. I know it still needs work..."

"No. Please, don't change a thing."

"You...you liked it?" Sam finally raised her eyes. "I've never written a song for someone—"

"You *have* captured my heart. I'm not sure when...or how, but it's yours to do with what you will."

It was the closest Tina had come to an outright declaration of love and Sam savored the words as they gazed at each other, drowning in the waves of emotion passing between them.

Tina took the guitar and laid it on the coffee table. She leaned forward and kissed Sam with a fervor that left both of them breathless.

"We...we have to st...stop," Sam managed to stammer as Tina began nibbling on her ear.

"Hmm?"

"We agreed to...to wait...until you were ready."

"I'm ready."

The words growled so close to her ear made Sam's body tingle all over. "You...you're sure?"

"If my back would allow it, I'd sweep you into my arms and carry you into the bedroom..."

"Oh no, you don't." Sam scrambled to her feet. "We're not going to take any chance of you hurting your back right now." She smiled as she reached for Tina's hand. "Although I do appreciate the sentiment."

They walked to the bedroom in silence. Stopping next to the bed, Sam pressed down gently on Tina's shoulders, guiding her to sit on the edge of the mattress. She moved in close, standing between her partner's legs and looking deeply into her eyes. "Are you sure?"

"Yes. I want you. I want...this."

Sam grasped the bottom of Tina's tee shirt and slowly lifted it over the compliant woman's head. She dropped it on the floor and leaned in for a kiss, reaching around and unclasping Tina's bra at the same time. She slid the straps off broad shoulders and down lengthy arms. The bra quickly joined the shirt on the floor.

"I've wanted you for so long," Sam said softly. *How many times have I fantasized about this? Too many to count, probably. And now that we're here and it's really happening, I'm suddenly feeling nervous.*

Hesitantly, Tina slipped her hands under the blonde's shirt, needing to feel the smooth skin she knew she'd find there.

Sam's eyes closed at the contact, her body instantly responding to the familiar touch. She was snapped from her reverie as Tina grabbed her by the waist and pulled her onto the bed. They both groaned as the abrupt movement caused a sharp twinge in Sam's side and a protest from Tina's back.

Pushing herself up to her hands and knees, Sam grinned. "Let's see if we can get through this without a major injury, okay?" They both laughed, breaking the tension for the moment.

Straddling Tina's hips, Sam tugged off her tee shirt. The cool air in the room felt good on her exposed skin. She smiled at the beautiful woman beneath her. "Ohh...I *like* it up here."

Tina tried to calm her racing heart as she looked at her partner. A light sheen of sweat made Sam's skin shine, and her chest rose and fell in a rhythm suggesting her heart rate had increased significantly as well. Tina's eyes moved to still-conspicuous bruises. "Your side, is it hurting?"

"Well," Sam bent down and gently kissed a path from Tina's belly to her neck, "I'm feeling a lot of things right now, but believe me, *none* of it hurts." She raised her head so Tina could see the truth in her eyes. "I've wanted to tell you for the longest time — I...I love you. I think I have right from the beginning, when I met you at the reunion."

"*Our* reunion."

"Yes." Sam smiled. *You don't forget anything.* "And when we made a wish at the fountain, I wished that you'd let me love you...not just physically, but for everything that you are." She placed her hand over Tina's heart. "Completely."

Tina rested her hand over the smaller one. "I guess some wishes do come true."

With renewed confidence, Sam resumed her tender kisses and caresses, pleased that Tina seemed to be responding to her attentions. *So far, so good.* As she continued, however, she sensed a tension in the quiet woman that she was unable to dispel. *What's going on in that head of yours?* At a loss as to what else to do, Sam began singing softly, "There's nothing to fear...it's just you and me here..." She hummed the next section of the song, lightly trailing her fingers up and down Tina's body as she did so. In a matter of seconds, she felt a distinct change under her fingertips. *You like my voice; I should have known. I've been so busy concentrating on how things are going, I wasn't talking to you.*

"I love you, Tina." Sam kissed the woman's neck. "I need you." She started moving the feather-light kisses upward. "I want...to kiss you...to touch you..." she arrived at Tina's ear and whispered, "to taste you."

Tina moaned.

Sam smiled. *I think this is going to work out just fine.*

Chapter 25

Tina cut the turkey sandwiches and put them on a large plate. She smiled when she heard the water running in the bathroom. *Samantha's awake. Good thing I made enough for two.* After grabbing a couple of drinks from the refrigerator, she took the snack into the living room and set it on the coffee table.

Sam came out of the bedroom, wearing one of Tina's Florida State tee shirts. As she walked in front of the large patio windows, the fading afternoon light behind her made the white cloth translucent. It was obvious she wore nothing else. "Hi."

"Hi." Tina looked at her approvingly. "Nice outfit."

"You like it?"

"Yes." Tina put her arms around the blonde. "Very much so."

"This is elegant." Sam ran her hands over the smooth, navy-colored material of the silk robe Tina had on. The light blue piping around the edges of the long-sleeved, knee-length garment matched her eyes.

"Vivian gave it to me one Christmas. I've never worn it before." *Never had a reason to.*

"It's beautiful." Sam untied the belt and slid her hands inside the robe, happy to discover only bare skin underneath. "But nowhere near as beautiful as the woman wearing it."

Tina reacted to the soft touch with a sharp intake of breath.

Sam smiled and looked up at her partner. "Have I told you lately that I love you?"

"Um...yeah...I think so."

"I hope I didn't get too carried away for you. It's just that I waited forever to say it, and once I did I couldn't seem to say it enough."

"It's okay." Tina inclined her head to give Sam a kiss. "I couldn't seem to hear it enough, either."

"Really?"

"Yes. I..." Tina paused when her stomach rumbled loudly. "I made some sandwiches." She pointed at the snack. "Are you hungry?"

"I'm starving!"

They sat on the couch, devouring the sandwiches and grinning at each other whenever they made eye contact. Sam noticed that it was beginning to get dark outside and glanced at the clock on the VCR. "I guess I slept for quite a while."

"Yes, you did." A playful twinkle appeared in Tina's eyes. "Though, I must say, your timing wasn't the best."

"What?"

"Well, as I recall, I had just taken off the remainder of your clothes and was about to—"

"Oh!" Sam felt a blush rise to her face as she realized what had happened. "I'm sorry—"

"It's all right." Tina took the soda the blonde was holding, put it on the table, and pulled her into a hug. "I think maybe you overexerted yourself." She chuckled. "You have to take it easy. You're still recuperating from your injury."

"I don't want to take it easy." Sam kissed the hollow of Tina's throat. "Now that I've had my nap and sandwich, I'm feeling...um..."

"Revitalized?"

"That's one word you could use." Small hands made their way beneath the silky material again. "This has certainly been a memorable Thanksgiving, hasn't it?"

"And it's not even over yet."

"Excellent point. What do you say we go back to bed?"

"Good idea." Tina pulled Sam up with her as she stood. "Let's go."

They quickly retired to the bedroom. Sam slid the robe off Tina's shoulders and trailed her fingers along warm skin. "I love touching you."

Tina responded with a passionate kiss before lifting the tee shirt over Sam's head. They lay on the bed with Tina propped up on one elbow so she could look at her partner.

Several moments passed and Sam smiled at Tina's expression. It was a mixture of love and vulnerability, with a dash of childlike wonder. *I'm the only one she allows to see this side of her. I'm the one she's let into her heart. I'm the one she loves, even though she still doesn't seem ready to say it.* "T?"

"Hmm?"

"What are you thinking about?"

"Um...how beautiful you are...how you stir up so many feelings inside me...how I wish I could put it all into words for you." Tina's voice dropped to a whisper. "How I know you need to hear it."

"That's a pretty good start."

"It is?"

"Yeah." Sam moved her arms up over her head. "It'll do for now."

Tina shook her head at the woman's position. "Y-you don't have to do that."

"It's my choice. I want you to know that body, heart, soul, every-thing — I'm yours."

"I...I..."

"Shh. I know." Sam looked into eyes that were full of love. "Show me."

~ * ~ * ~ * ~ * ~

Mrs. Whitwell scrutinized the group of relatives seated at the large dining-room table. Everything was going according to plan. She'd fielded all the questions concerning Sam's absence, and everyone seemed satisfied with her explanation that her daughter was not quite up to the hustle and bustle of a holiday party so soon after a car acci-dent.

Mike kissed his wife's cheek. "You okay?"

"Yeah. I'm just missing Sam."

"Me, too."

Lisa watched as her mother buzzed about the room. *She loves this kind of thing: playing the hostess, a house full of people...except for my sister...*

"Mom?" Aaron's voice interrupted her train of thought.

"Yes?"

"May I have another glass of milk?"

"Sure."

"I'll get it." Mrs. Whitwell put a hand on Lisa's shoulder before she could move. "I'm already up." She took Aaron's glass to the kitchen.

"Where's Sam today? She never misses these family gatherings."

Lisa looked down the table at her cousin Frankie. He had arrived just as dinner was being served and evidently hadn't heard the story her mother had told the other guests.

"She was in a car accident, but thank goodness, she's all right," Aunt Mary said.

"She's in the hospital?"

"She's at Tina's." Joshua smiled, happy to mention his special friend.

All eyes shifted to the young boy who had volunteered this new piece of information.

"Joshua!" Lisa hissed across the table, trying to stop her son from saying anything further.

"Who's Tina?" Frankie asked.

Mrs. Whitwell stopped in the doorway, glass of milk in her hand. *Did someone say Tina?*

Joshua, thrilled to suddenly be the center of attention, continued, "She's Auntie Sam's girlfriend."

There was a split second of silence before the glass slipped from Mrs. Whitwell's hand and shattered on the ceramic tile floor. Mike leapt from his chair to catch the pale woman as she fainted. Then everyone seemed to start talking at once.

~ * ~ * ~ * ~ * ~

Less than a mile to go. Tina picked up the pace as she ran toward home. *I've only been gone for an hour, but I can't wait to get back to Samantha.* She shook her head in disbelief. *I'm turning into such a wuss.* A silly half grin cracked her normally serious running expression. *And lovin' every minute of it.*

Long legs continued to move in a steady rhythm, and she began silently singing along to the beat of her sneakers hitting the sidewalk. *It's plain to see, yes, it's clear to me, that it's love, love. I need you to be forever with me 'cause it's love, love. Can't you see, it's our destiny.* She approached Bayshore Palms and was surprised to see a lone figure standing out on one of the balconies on such a chilly, overcast November morning. *My balcony.* A smile sprang to her face and she waved. *My girl.*

Although Sam was cold, she stayed outside, watching until Tina crossed the street and entered the building through the front lobby. *Brr. How can she enjoy running in this weather?* The blonde hurried inside and closed the patio door tightly. She went to the kitchen and got a bottle of water from the refrigerator, thinking it would be the first thing the runner would want.

Tina strode into the condo, her energy filling the room. "Hi!"

"Hi." Sam held out the drink. "I thought you'd want this—"

Tina put her arms around the smaller woman. "You were right." She kissed Sam soundly.

Okay, water was the second thing. Sam returned the kiss enthusiastically. *I like this being first much better.*

"Now, what was that about a drink?"

Sam handed over the plastic bottle that had been momentarily forgotten. With pleasure she observed the expanse of bare skin that was visible beyond the nylon shorts and sleeveless tee shirt. "Weren't you cold?"

Tina took a large gulp of water. "Nah." She stepped into the living room, sat on the floor, and began her postworkout stretches. "This is the best time of year to run. It's toughest in the summer when it's hot and humid."

"If you say so." Sam settled on the couch. "I don't know much about running." *Except that you make it look like an art form.*

"All those afternoons you spent at track practice and you never wanted to try it?"

"I specifically remember, during my freshman year, being required to run a mile in gym class. I quickly discovered it wasn't something I'd ever do on a voluntary basis."

"Why not?"

"The major reason is I'm inherently lazy," Sam admitted with a chuckle.

"Running isn't for everybody." Tina joined Sam on the couch. "In my case, it seems very natural to me; it's a big part of who I am. Kind of like music is for you."

"I understand." Sam snuggled against Tina, nuzzling her neck and kissing the still-damp skin that tasted slightly salty. "Mmm...I love you."

Tina laughed. "You might love me more after I have a shower."

"I don't think," Sam murmured into her partner's ear, "anything could make me love you more than I already do."

Tina turned her head and gazed into eyes that were so open, honest, and loving that her vision became blurry with tears. It took several seconds for her to find her voice. "I...um...feel like that, too."

Sam was delighted by the emotional response. "You're really getting the hang of this." She slid her hand behind Tina's neck and gently pulled her in for a kiss.

The phone rang and, without breaking the embrace, Tina reached over to the end table and fumbled for the receiver. *Whoever this is, it better be important.* She reluctantly pulled her lips away from Sam's and spoke curtly into the phone. "Hello?"

Lisa paused for a moment, not sure she had dialed the correct number. "Tina?"

"Yes?"

"This is Lisa."

Tina adjusted her tone to a more hospitable one. "Hi. Samantha's right here; hold on." She gave the phone to Sam, stealing a quick kiss in the process.

"Hello?"

"Hi, sis. Are you all right?"

"Of course I am." Sam tried to concentrate on the conversation while swatting at the large hands that were trying to sneak under her shirt. "Why wouldn't I be?"

Lisa breathed a sigh of relief. Sam had been calling every day to chat and discuss how her recovery was progressing. Yesterday, she hadn't called to say happy Thanksgiving and when there was no word from her again that morning, Lisa had become worried. "I'm just making sure you're okay. I didn't hear from you yesterday."

"I'm sorry. We got caught up in...um...things around here and it totally slipped my mind."

"I see. So you had a nice holiday?"

"It was the best Thanksgiving ever."

Lisa heard the absolute bliss in her sister's voice. *Sounds like things are more than okay.* "Well, I'd better let you go. I didn't mean to interrupt anything, but I wanted to remind you about rehearsal tonight."

"Thanks. I had forgotten all about it. I'll be there."

"Okay. See you later."

"Bye." Sam hung up the phone.

"Is something wrong?"

"Not really. I forgot I have band practice."

"You do? Where?"

"At my house, in the garage. We have two gigs in December and we need to go over our Christmas songs."

"I guess we should get you packed, then." Tina started to get up.

Sam grabbed Tina's arm to stop her. "Not yet, please? It's been so special here, I don't know if I'm ready to let anything or anybody from beyond these walls interfere with how happy I am right now."

"I...I'm happy, too."

"Then can we stay a little longer? I don't have to be home until six."

"We can stay as long as you want." Tina relaxed against the cushions, smiling when Sam promptly cuddled next to her again.

They sat holding each other for a while, both of them savoring the quiet time together, knowing that their intimate holiday would soon be over.

"T?"

"Hmm?"

"Does that fireplace work?"

"The realtor said it does."

"You've never used it?"

"No."

"I was thinking — since Thanksgiving turned out so well, maybe we could spend Christmas here, too? We could have a fire...and a tree...and lights...and—"

"Yes," Tina answered before Sam could suggest a sleigh-and-reindeer display on the roof. She kissed the top of the fair-haired head that was tucked snugly against her shoulder. "That's a wonderful plan." *A real Christmas...it's been a long time.* Tina felt tears in her eyes. *How come, if I'm so happy...I keep crying? I ought to ask Vivian.* She brushed the tears away and cleared her throat. "How about helping me polish off the rest of the leftovers for lunch?"

Sam wasn't fooled by the less than subtle change of topic. "Sure!

Are there any more of those mashed potatoes? The gravy was really good, too. Oh, and the cranberry sauce..."

"Now you're making *me* hungry." Tina led the way into the kitchen. She heated up the food and they shared a second Thanksgiving feast. Afterward, Sam insisted on doing the dishes in return for the fabulous meal.

Having been shooed out of the kitchen, Tina decided it was as good a time as any to take a shower. A short while later, she stepped out of the bathroom, drying her hair with a towel. She smiled with amusement at Sam, who was wrestling with the duffel bag, trying to get a final few items inside the already overstuffed space. "Need some help?"

"Yes!" The exasperated blonde turned and held out an article of clothing in each hand. "How did you get all these things in there?"

Tina walked to the bag and saw the haphazard manner in which it was packed. She took the shorts and tee shirt from Sam. "We can fix this one of two ways. I can take everything out and start over, or...um..."

"Or what?"

"Or, maybe you could leave some of it here. I have room in the dresser—Oof!" Small arms were thrown around Tina with such force that she was knocked backward onto the bed. The towel, tee shirt, and shorts she'd been holding flew in every direction.

Sam landed squarely on top of the surprised woman. "That's a *great* idea!"

Tina looked at her partner's happy face. *I said something right again.* "Okay. I'll show you where—"

"Mmm." Sam's hands began roaming beneath the silk robe. "I think I already know where the important places are."

Tina felt her body react to the soft touches. She reached for the front of Sam's shirt and tugged on the material, bringing her forward for a passionate kiss.

The next thing Sam knew, she was flipped onto her back and Tina was looking down at her with a sexy smile. "I know where the important places are, too."

They were both right.

Chapter 26

There was quite a bit of traffic on the trip to Sarasota, particularly in the vicinity of the large outlet mall in Ellenton. People were out in droves getting a start on their holiday shopping, and the cars slowed to a crawl for several miles. Tina became concerned that the traffic jam might cause them to be late. Glancing at the clock on the dashboard as they exited the interstate, she was relieved to see they still had plenty of time.

Sam cuddled the stuffed animal she was holding on her lap. "I really like my teddy bear."

"I've noticed that."

"Know what my favorite thing about it is?"

"It reminds you of me?"

"It certainly does." Sam held the bear out and examined it. "It's almost as cute as you." *But that's not my favorite thing.* "You know what else?"

"What?"

"The card."

"Oh?"

"Yes." For what must have been the hundredth time, the blonde looked at the heart-shaped tag dangling from the bear's ear. *Love, T.*

"I...um...I'm glad you like it."

Sam grinned at the slight blush that accompanied the answer, amazed that, with just a few words, she could elicit such a response in a woman most people found intimidating. *And I love that I'm able to do it.*

A horn honked as they turned the final corner. "It's Mike!" Sam waved at the minivan passing in the opposite direction. "He usually takes Josh and Aaron somewhere when we have band practice. A 'boys night out' kind of thing."

Tina pulled into the driveway. The garage door was open and she could see Lisa inside setting up her keyboard.

"Park behind me." Sam pointed at the Toyota that was sheltered under a carport extending from the side of the building. "The guys will need enough space to back the truck in."

Once Tina moved the BMW to the designated spot they began unloading the trunk. Tina slung her backpack over her shoulder before grabbing the guitar and amplifier. "You want these in the garage?"

"Yeah." Sam lifted the duffel bag, which was substantially lighter now, with approximately half of its former contents in one of the dresser drawers at the condo.

"Nice to have you home," Lisa called out as she hurried across the driveway to give her sister a hug. "How about some coffee? I can put on a pot of decaf."

"We'll be right there after we put my stuff away."

"Great. I'll get it started." Lisa headed into the house.

After putting the musical equipment in the garage, the couple went upstairs. Tina unlocked the door and pushed it open.

Sam stepped inside and suddenly stopped short, gawking at the living room. "Lisa is a sweetheart!" The area had been vacuumed and dusted, and there was a hint of lemon furniture polish in the crisp fall air that came in through the partially open windows. She rushed over to peek into the bedroom. "It's all straightened up in here, too!" she exclaimed, going in and depositing her duffel bag and teddy bear on the neatly made bed.

Tina followed, chuckling at her partner's excitement. "Are you ready to go have some coffee and tell her how wonderful she is?"

"Not yet." Sam crooked an index finger and beckoned for Tina to come closer. "We have something very important to do first."

"We do?" *I don't think we have time for this. Lisa's waiting...*

The enticing smile Tina received in reply made it impossible to resist the invitation. She set her backpack on the desk and eagerly complied.

Rising up on tiptoes, Sam put her arms around Tina's neck and kissed her.

It was one of those tender kisses that always set Tina's heart racing. She immediately forgot about coffee, sisters, and anything other than the pleasurable sensations she was feeling.

Sam broke the embrace, anxious to explain what the important thing was. Blue eyes that had darkened a shade gazed back at her. *Uh-oh...*

Tina leaned in for another kiss. "Mooore."

"Wait!" Sam planted her hands between them and moved backward a step. "I have a...request."

Tina raised an eyebrow. *Well, this is interesting.* With a rakish grin, she perused Sam's body from head to toe and back again, before saying in a deep, sensuous voice, "Name it."

Goodness, now I know what it means to have someone undress you with their eyes. "It's not *that* kind of request." Sam laughed and reached into her pocket for the silver key she had recently acquired. "I wanted to know if you'd put this on my key ring for me."

"Will I get another one of those kisses as a reward?"

"Yes."

Tina quickly plucked the shiny piece of metal from Sam's hand. "You've got a deal."

They found the key ring on the table near the door. Tina added the condo key, positioning it next to the brass one for the apartment. She displayed the completed project with a flourish.

"Together," Sam indicated the location of the keys on the ring, "just like us."

"Yes." Tina pulled Sam close. "I seem to recall hearing something about a reward..."

Lisa looked out the kitchen window, wondering if her sister had changed her mind about the coffee. Just then, Sam and Tina came outside and descended the stairs. Holding hands as they started across the walkway, both women looked euphoric.

Ah, new love...there's nothing like it. Lisa opened the door for them. "Come on in."

"Sis." Sam hugged Lisa. "Thanks for cleaning my place!"

"You're welcome. I know how devoted you are to your housework, but I thought that under the circumstances, you wouldn't mind if I helped a little."

"Yeah, right." Sam good-naturedly accepted the teasing about her domestic habits. "Like there are circumstances when I *wouldn't* want somebody to clean my house?"

The women prepared their cups of coffee and sat down, sipping their drinks as Lisa recounted the events of Thanksgiving dinner with the Whitwell family. "...and then Joshua said, 'She's Auntie Sam's girl-friend.'"

Tina almost spewed her mouthful of coffee all over the table. Sam was momentarily speechless.

Lisa continued the story, knowing it was necessary for her sister to be aware of what had occurred, even if it was upsetting to hear. "Mom dropped the glass and fainted—"

"Fainted?" Sam asked, finding it hard to believe that her mother was capable of such a thing.

"Yes, but just for a few seconds. We got her to the couch, gave her some water, and she was fine."

"Oh my God!" *Mom will be furious with me; my absence ruined her holiday gathering.*

"There was a lot of confusion, some people were hovering over

Mother, others were cleaning up the broken glass, and the boys got into a fight." Lisa sighed. "Evidently, Aaron had told Josh about you two and sworn him to secrecy."

"I'm sorry," Sam said sadly. " I never—"

"Don't apologize," Lisa interrupted. "You haven't done anything wrong. And now that everybody knows, maybe we can finally move past this and get back to being a family again."

"Do you really think so?"

"Well, Mom's worst fear was that the relatives would find out. She probably figured sooner or later you'd come to your senses, meet a nice guy, and no one would have to know about this 'phase' you went through. Thanks to Joshua, that's no longer an issue." Lisa looked at Tina. "I'd appreciate it if you'd talk to him. He's terribly worried that you'll be mad when you find out what happened."

"Mad? At him?"

"He doesn't really understand what all the fuss is about," Lisa explained. "But he knows how angry Aaron is. And Mom...he thought he'd caused her to have a heart attack or something. It took us a while to convince him that she wasn't seriously injured."

"Maybe not physically," Sam commented quietly, "but emotionally..."

Tina reached for her hand. "She's a strong woman. She'll get over it."

"Yeah." Sam managed a small grin. "I just hope it's during my lifetime."

"Don't we all!" Grateful for a chance to change the subject, Lisa went to the counter and picked up one of the CDs stacked next to a boom box. "I have a new song for you to sing." She laid the plastic case on the table in front of her sister.

Sam looked at the cover and recognized the artist from a music channel on television. "*Country?*"

"It's not *country* country," Lisa clarified. *You're going to love it.*

"Which song?"

"Track seven."

Sam turned the case over and read the title. "I guess I can give it a try."

Lisa smiled. "Why don't you take the CD with you and listen to it before practice? We can run through the song tonight."

"Okay. We should get going, then."

The couple expressed their gratitude for the coffee and returned to the apartment. They sat on the couch, snuggling together in silence. Tina lightly stroked Sam's hair. *She's way too quiet.* "Are you all right?"

"Honestly? No."

"You know what I think?" *Not that I have any idea what to do in a situation like this.*

"What?"

"Give your mom some time to sort things out. She'll come to the realization that the world didn't end when people found out her daughter is gay. Then, call her to say hi — don't even mention Thanksgiving — and see how it goes."

"I suppose I can do that. As long as you're with me when I call her."

"I promise."

"I feel better already." Sam smiled, her mood much improved now that she had a course of action.

"Good." Tina felt immensely pleased with herself for lifting her partner's spirits.

"It's almost time for practice. I need to listen to that CD my sister gave me."

"Let's hear it."

Sam went over and put the disc in the stereo. "Country music isn't really my thing," she remarked while advancing the player to the seventh track, "but Lisa has a fondness for it and keeps trying to convert me." Just as she was about to press the play button, the phone rang. She picked up the receiver. "Hello? "

"Hi, Sammie."

"Hi, Dad!"

Not wanting to eavesdrop on the conversation, Tina wandered into the kitchen. *We're going to need something for dinner.* A quick inventory revealed a nearly empty refrigerator, a freezer containing ice cream and frozen dinners, and cabinets bountifully stocked with microwave popcorn and Ring Dings. *I bet there's not a single vitamin lurking among the so-called food items in this house. A trip to the grocery store is in order.*

She ambled into the bedroom and got her backpack. Feeling the weight of it, she remembered slipping some clothing into the bag when Sam had been in the bathroom at the condo. Tina pulled open the top drawer of the dresser and shook her head at the disorderly jumble of garments. She tried each drawer, eventually finding enough space in one of them to place her tidily folded things in the left-hand corner. *Well, this is another first.* Closing the drawer, she studied her reflection in the mirror above the dresser. *I may look the same on the outside, but everything's changed since the day I met her.* A smile edged onto her face as she thought about the vivacious blonde flirting with her at the reunion. *Though I've learned that change can definitely be a good thing.*

"She's wonderful, Dad. I can't wait for you to meet her." Sam grinned as the subject of their discussion came into view. "Okay. Yeah,

I'll call you soon. Bye-bye." She hung up the phone and swiftly crossed the room to hug her partner. "My dad is coming to visit after New Year's!"

"That's nice." Tina groaned inwardly. *More family to contend with?*

"Yeah. I've missed him a lot since he moved to Atlanta."

Atlanta? "Does he visit often?"

"A couple of times a year, sometimes more when his schedule allows it. He plays in a popular jazz band and they have very steady work. They're booked solid for the holidays, but they have some time off coming up in January." Her eyes were sparkling. "I told him all about you."

"You did?" *Let's hope he doesn't own a gun.*

"Yes." Sam laughed. "He's a great dad. You'll like him." She looked questioningly at the backpack Tina was holding. "Are you going somewhere?"

"I thought I'd go to the grocery store and get something for dinner." *And breakfast...and lunch...*

"Oh! I'm sorry. I usually don't have much here."

"That's all right; I don't mind. I just figured I should leave before the guys bring the truck and block me in."

"Okay. But will you come downstairs later and let me introduce you to them?"

"I guess so."

"They're cool. Don't worry."

"I'll try."

Knowing that meeting new people wasn't easy for the aloof woman, Sam didn't press her further. "Well, I'd better listen to that song Lisa gave me."

"I'll be back in a little while." Tina bent down for a quick kiss. "Bye."

"Bye." Sam went to the window and watched until the BMW had backed out of the driveway before pressing the play button on the stereo. The song began with a twanging guitar and she rolled her eyes as she opened the lyrics sheet from inside the CD cover.

~ * ~ * ~ * ~ * ~

Tina took her time, strolling up and down the aisles of the supermarket, filling the cart with a variety of foods that would keep both women well fed for at least a week. Realizing she was going to have to carry the ample supplies up the stairs when she got home, she instructed the employee at the check-out counter to put as much as possible in each bag. *Home.* Tina smiled. *I finally have a home. Though I never suspected it would be a person rather than a place.*

"Ma'am?"

"Oh, thanks." Tina took the receipt the clerk had been attempting to hand her and pushed the cart out to the car. She loaded the groceries into the trunk, mentally deciding which bags she would carry together when she got back to the apartment. She planned well and it only took three trips to unload the car, which she had to park on the street in front of Lisa's house because the driveway was full. Uncapping a bottle of water, she drank a good portion of it before beginning to put away the provisions. Clearly able to hear the band playing in the garage beneath her, she hummed along to the mixture of holiday tunes and top-forty songs they were practicing.

It was over an hour later when Tina was finished in the kitchen. Dinner was ready to be heated up and two dozen homemade chocolate chip cookies sat on a large platter, waiting to be discovered. Meanwhile, the band had begun working on some new songs and there was much starting, stopping, and repeating of the music. The current selection had a catchy melody that sounded a bit country-ish and Tina assumed it was the song Lisa had suggested. *Yes, that's Samantha singing, but she's not using the mike.* Tina strained to hear the words. *I may as well go down there. I need to meet these people anyway.* She strode to the door.

"I think we've got it," Lisa addressed the group. "Let's run through the whole thing."

Sam picked up the microphone and held it in one hand, the lyrics to the love song in the other. The band played the introduction and she began to sing.

After completing the first verse, Sam glanced up and was so surprised to see Tina standing in the entryway of the garage that she missed the next line. She quickly returned her attention to the paper in her hand.

Tina took a seat on the large black equipment box just inside the doorway.

Sam sang the second verse, then, as the chorus started, she laid the lyrics sheet on her amplifier and slowly walked toward Tina. Still crooning words of love into the microphone, she moved in close and lightly brushed her fingers along the side of Tina's face.

Lisa, Robbie, and Bryan joined in for a repeat of the chorus. Sam, who was supposed to be singing several phrases over their lines, sang nothing. Everything faded into the background as she lost herself in the beautiful blue eyes staring back at her. All sense of time and place vanished as she kissed the woman she loved.

At some point, Sam became conscious of the fact that there was no music playing. She pulled back from the kiss and looked in the direction of the band. The members of the group were fanning themselves with CD cases and grinning from ear to ear. They began to applaud, cheer, and whistle at the pair, whose faces reddened in embarrassment.

Sam put her hands on her hips and smirked at the musicians. "All right, I'll admit it. I'm developing an...appreciation...for country music. Is everyone happy now?"

"Yes," Kyle replied. "But apparently, not as happy as you."

The rest of the band heartily agreed.

"Well, after that passionate...rendition, I think we could all use a cold drink." Lisa led the assemblage over to the patio, where there was a cooler filled with ice-cold beverages. Everyone relaxed on cushioned deck chairs and Sam introduced Tina to Robbie, Kyle, and Bryan before turning the conversation to details about their next gig. Tina sat back and listened as the group chatted for a while, the comfortable dialogue and friendly banter plainly showing the affection they had for one another.

"Hi, everyone." Mike opened the screen door and the boys dashed inside.

Joshua ran directly to Tina. "Hi!"

"Hi, Josh." She ruffled his hair. "I've missed you."

"I missed you, too."

The noise level rose as Mike talked with the band members and Aaron animatedly told his mother about their excursion. Tina bent forward and spoke softly in Joshua's ear. "Been having a rough time lately?"

The boy nodded.

"Want to talk about it?"

Big brown eyes became wet with tears and he gave her another nod.

"Okay."

"Dad said we had to get ready for bed as soon as we got home. Will you come up and tuck me in?"

"Sure. I'll be there in a few minutes."

"You won't forget, will you?"

"No, I won't forget." Tina watched him go inside. *What the heck am I going to say to him?*

"He's adorable, isn't he?" Sam asked.

"Yes." *He takes after his aunt.*

"Sam, Tina." Mike smiled at the women. "Glad to see you again."

"Thanks." Sam took hold of Tina's hand. "It's nice to be back. How was your evening with the boys?"

"The miniature golf was okay, but I thought I'd never get them out of that arcade."

"Uh-huh. And how many games of air hockey did *you* play?"

"Well, there was this teenager in there that thought he was a hot-shot. *Somebody* had to teach him a lesson, right?"

"Right." Sam grinned as she stood up, tugging her partner along with her. "If you'll excuse us, Mr. Air-Hockey Champion of the World, I'm going to show Tina where Joshua's room is. She needs to talk to him before he falls asleep."

Mike nodded in understanding. "Good luck."

The women went through the kitchen and hallway to the staircase. Sam gestured to the second floor. "It's the first door on the left."

"What do I say to him?"

"You'll think of something. I trust you."

Reluctantly, Tina climbed the stairs. She poked her head into Joshua's room and looked around. She saw posters of superheroes covering large sections of the walls, action figures arranged on shelves over a student-sized desk, and a wooden bookcase overflowing with books and toys.

Joshua came out of the bathroom. "Hi." He flipped the light switch off, leaving only a small lamp on the nightstand casting a dim glow near the bed.

"Hi." Tina stepped into the room.

"I'm glad you didn't forget." He got under the covers.

"I wouldn't forget you, would I?"

"I dunno. I thought you might be mad."

Tina sat on the edge of the bed. "I'm not angry with you."

"But...Grandma fell down...and Aaron said he's never gonna tell me anything important again."

"What did you do that was so wrong?"

"I...I said you were Auntie Sam's girlfriend."

"You're absolutely correct. I *am* your aunt's girlfriend." Tina paused, trying to decide how much more she should say. "Do you know what that means?"

"You kiss and do mushy stuff like Mom and Dad."

Yup, he knows. "Are you okay with that?"

"Sure." Joshua smiled at Tina. "Auntie Sam always tells me how special love is."

"Indeed it is."

"Then why did everyone get upset?"

"Well..." Tina racked her brains for a tactful explanation. "Remember when we talked about how some people won't agree with your opinions?"

"Yes."

"Well, there are people who don't like that your aunt and I

are...together."

"Grandma doesn't like it. That's why Aaron told me to keep it a secret. But on Thanksgiving, I forgot."

"It's all right, Joshua. You should never be ashamed of telling the truth."

"So, you're really not mad?"

"Nope."

"Cool."

"I guess I ought to let you get to sleep."

"Will you tell me a story first?"

"A story?"

"Yeah."

Tina looked over at the bookcase. "Which is your favorite book?"

"I'd rather have a made-up story, like Auntie Sam does."

"Made-up?"

"She tells the *best* stories. There's usually someone in trouble and a hero comes and saves the day."

Tina smiled, picturing Samantha telling the boy a lively tale that would hold him spellbound. "I'm not sure I could invent one like that."

Joshua tilted his head to the side and asked hopefully, "Please?"

Sighing in defeat, Tina collected her thoughts and began. "Once upon a time..."

Chapter 27

Samantha is going to be so *surprised.* Smiling, Tina clicked the Web site closed and leaned back in her chair. *I'm worse than a kid, the way I'm getting all excited about Christmas. But instead of it being just another day, this year it's going to be special.* She shut her eyes for a moment, thinking about what tasks needed to be completed before she could go home. *Home...Samantha...*

"Hi."

Tina was jolted awake by the sound of her boss's voice. "W-what?"

"It appears you were dozing." Vivian chuckled as she entered the office and sat down. "Strenuous weekend?"

Tina pulled her glasses off and rubbed her eyes. "I...um...we..." She unsuccessfully tried to keep a blush from rising to her face.

"It's all right, dear," Vivian waved off Tina's attempt at an explanation and winked at her. "So, it's safe to assume Samantha has recovered from her injuries?"

"Yes." *If the enthusiastic response to finding those chocolate chip cookies is any indication, she's in tip-top shape.*

"And I take it you had a nice Thanksgiving?"

"We had dinner at my place and then we went to Samantha's for the weekend." Tina started fiddling with a credit card that was lying on the desk. "She's brought such joy into my life, Viv. I never imagined that I could be this happy."

"It feels good, doesn't it?"

"Yeah," Tina admitted. *It feels so damn good it's scary.* "How was your trip?"

"Typical Thanksgiving at my sister's. I just got back and wanted to stop by to see how you were doing before I went home."

"Everything's going really well." Tina tapped out a rhythm with the plastic card on the desk's surface. "But...um..."

"But what?"

"There's something I don't understand. If I'm so happy, how come I keep getting all teary-eyed lately? I mean, is that normal?"

"Love is a strong emotion. It's bound to bring a lot of different feelings to the surface." Vivian spoke gently. "I'd expect this to be an emotional time for you."

"I guess that makes sense."

Seeing the beginnings of dark circles under her friend's eyes, Vivian suspected there was more to Tina's tiredness than evenings filled with passion. "Are you having nightmares again?"

"I wasn't for a while, but after Samantha got in that car accident..." Tina shrugged.

"Have you told her?"

"No."

"One of the benefits of being in a relationship is having someone to share things with. Especially the difficult things."

"She'll worry. I don't want to upset her."

"She's going to worry about you whether you want her to or not." Vivian smiled. "She loves you."

Tina looked down, suddenly seeming to have a great interest in the credit card she was holding. "It's hard to believe, isn't it?"

"It's not hard to believe at all." Vivian moved around the desk, placed a hand under Tina's chin, and tenderly tilted her face upward. "She can see into your heart...just like I can."

Tina's eyes filled with tears and she threw her arms around Vivian's waist, hugging her tightly.

Almost pulled off balance by the sudden embrace, Vivian leaned into the hug and stroked the sniffling woman's hair, comforting her. "You love her very much, don't you?"

It was more a statement of fact than a question, and Tina nodded in agreement.

"Then everything's going to turn out fine, dear. You just need to give yourself time to accept all the changes you're experiencing."

Tina let go of Vivian and wiped her eyes with her shirtsleeve. "See what I mean? Crying *again*!"

"It's good for you." Vivian patted Tina's cheek fondly. "Cleanses the soul."

"I suppose that couldn't hurt me any."

Both women laughed.

Vivian looked at the credit card and checkbook lying on the desk. "Are you taking Samantha on a trip somewhere?"

"No." Tina's expression brightened noticeably. "I ordered her Christmas present on the Internet. I needed to use the corporate card." She opened her checkbook and tore out the check she had already written. "I'll save this for when the statement comes in."

Vivian raised her eyebrows. *It must be something very expensive.* "Do you mind if I ask what it is?"

"Oh!" Tina grabbed a paper from next to her computer keyboard and, grinning from ear to ear, handed it over.

Vivian opened the tattered-looking document that had obviously been folded and unfolded many times. "My goodness, that's quite a gift. Are you sure that's what she wants?"

"Yes, I think so. I'm going to have it delivered here. I don't want Samantha to know anything about it until Christmas."

"While we're on the subject of Christmas, please tell me that, for once, you won't insist on working during the holidays."

"I'm going to try to have everything done early. I already have the Y2K stuff taken care of and most of the information for the taxes for this year and—"

"I'm positive you have things covered, Tina," Vivian interrupted, well aware of her employee's conscientiousness. "I'm not the least bit concerned about that."

"I was thinking maybe I'd take the week after Christmas off and spend time with Samantha."

"That's a splendid idea!" *A week off? If Samantha only knew how much she's influenced this stubborn friend of mine. I haven't been able to get her to take any kind of vacation since Dominic passed away.* "Would you like to go somewhere for New Year's? It's awfully late to make arrangements, being the Millennium and all, but I'm sure I could pull a few strings. You just name the place and I'll take care of it."

"Thanks, Viv. I'll ask Samantha and see what she says."

"You're welcome." Vivian handed the paper back to Tina. "I'm going to go home and unpack. I'll see you in the morning."

"Bye." Tina put on her glasses and studied the printout of the present she had chosen for her partner. *It's going to be a special Christmas, all right. And the Millennium New Year's celebration to boot. Wonder where Samantha would like to go?*

~ * ~ * ~ * ~ * ~

Sam went flying into the kitchen with an envelope in her hand. "Hi, sis! I got the pictures developed."

"What pictures?" Lisa slid a tray of chicken into the oven, closed the door, and set the timer.

Sam sat at the table and took out the photos. "The ones from when Tina put up the FSU flag."

Lisa laughed as she sat next to Sam. "That's a day Mike will never forget."

"There are some from Joshua's birthday party, too. I'd forgotten they were on this roll of film." Sam passed each picture to her sister as she went through the stack. "He loved getting that bike, didn't he?"

"He sure did," Lisa agreed, smiling at the snapshot of her youngest son sitting on the mountain bike he'd wanted ever since he was able to ride without training wheels. "He's so proud to have a big-boy bike now."

"Here we go." Sam giggled as she gave the next few photos to Lisa. "Mike is taking the flag down. Look at the expression on his face!"

"He's not a happy guy there."

"Nope."

"This is my favorite." Sam held out the print of herself and Tina smiling at the camera.

"Nice-looking couple."

"I think so, too." Sam continued to gaze at the picture.

"Ahem. Are there any more?"

"Oh! Just one. It's another really good shot of Tina and me." Sam gave the photo to her sister.

"I remember this. I snapped an extra one." *And what a picture it is.*

"Lisa?"

"Hmm?"

"I wanted to talk to you about Christmas."

Uh-oh. Lisa put the photo down. "You talked to Mom?"

"No." Sam shook her head. "I'm going to wait a while before I do that. I think she's still in shock from Thanksgiving."

"That's probably true."

"You know I always come over here Christmas morning and we exchange gifts before going to Mom's for the family brunch."

"Yes." *Though I have a feeling that's about to change.*

"Tina and I will be spending our first Christmas together at her place. I don't want to miss sharing the holiday with you guys, though, so I thought maybe we could visit with you on Christmas Eve. We can sing carols and open our presents." Sam looked at Lisa anxiously. "What do you think?"

"Sounds workable to me."

"Thanks, sis! You're the best!"

"But what about Mom? Now that the relatives know you're gay, she might invite you and Tina to the brunch."

"Even if she does, we're not going this year," Sam said determinedly. "We've already made plans."

Lisa grinned at her sister. "It appears that some of your partner's assertiveness is rubbing off on you." *It's wonderful to see.*

"Mom!" Aaron ran into the room. "Joshua's bothering me!"

The smaller boy arrived just behind his brother. "I am *not!*"

"Well, this seems to be the perfect time for me to leave." Sam put the pictures back in the envelope and started toward the door. "Tina will be here soon."

"Tina's coming?" Joshua's face lit up. "Will you ask her to tuck me in tonight?"

Sam glanced at Lisa, who nodded her approval. "Sure I will, Josh."

"Cool!"

"You're such a baby," Aaron taunted. "Still getting tucked in."

"I am *not!*"

"Yes, you *are!*"

"Aaron, that's enough," Lisa warned her son sternly. "Now, I want both of you to bring me your homework so I can check it before dinner."

The boys groaned as they turned and left the kitchen.

Lisa sighed. "Were we ever that annoying to each other?"

"Yes! You teased me incessantly."

"The way I remember it, you bothered me all the time."

The sisters laughed at their contradictory childhood memories.

"I just hope that when Aaron and Josh grow up, they end up as close as we are." Sam hugged Lisa.

"I hope so, too."

"I'll talk to you later, okay?"

"Okay." Lisa watched from the doorway as Sam walked across to the garage apartment. *My little sister is finally coming into her own.* She smiled as she closed the door and leaned against it. *Who would've ever thought I'd have Tina Mellekas to thank for it? It's going to be an interesting Christmas.*

~ * ~ * ~ * ~ * ~

Sam looked at the two photos she had attached to the refrigerator with magnets. *Tina's going to like these.* Hearing the front door close, she rushed into the living room and greeted her partner with a big smile and a kiss on the cheek. "I'm glad you're home."

"Hi." Tina returned the smile. *Home.*

"What's that?" Sam asked, noticing a red piece of paper in Tina's hand.

"It was on my windshield. It's an announcement about the tree lighting ceremony at Hyde Park Village. I thought you might want to go."

"Christmas tree lighting?" Sam took the flyer and skimmed over the information. *Wednesday night. Ohh, music and carolers...*

"Yeah." Tina put down her backpack and sat on the couch. "They have it every year."

"Do you usually go?"

"No, but I've seen bits and pieces of it. You know — walking to the parking garage after work."

Cuddling next to Tina, Sam imagined how lonely she must have felt passing by the Christmas celebration year after year. "I'd love to go."

"Okay. Why don't you meet me at the office and we'll have dinner at the Cactus Club? And, if you want, we can stay at the condo that night."

Sam peeked up and saw that Tina had her head resting against the back of the couch with her eyes closed. *One less time for you to be driving back and forth to Sarasota, too. You look exhausted.* "It's a date."

"Good."

"T? Let's make it an early evening. I can order a pizza—"

"Uh-uh. I promised I'd cook spaghetti."

"We can have that tomorrow." Sam straddled Tina's legs and sat on her lap. "Please?"

Dark lashes fluttered open. "I'm all right, just a little tired."

"We'll have pizza, and then Joshua wanted to know if you'd tuck him in. After that, directly to bed for you and a good night's sleep."

"How about a compromise?"

"Like what?"

"I'll make the spaghetti, tuck Josh in, and we can go to bed early."

We? Very sneaky, T. "I think I can live with that compromise." Sam leaned forward and gave Tina a tender kiss.

"Mmm. Keep that up and we won't be getting much sleep at all."

Sam chuckled at the empty threat. *I do appreciate the thought, however.* "Guess what?"

"What?"

"I have something to show you."

"Oh?" Tina raised an eyebrow. "Is it in the bedroom?"

"Nooo."

"Is it under here?" Tina slipped a hand beneath Sam's tee shirt.

"Nooo." Sam playfully slapped the roaming hand away. "It's in the kitchen." She climbed off Tina's long legs and darted out of the room. "C'mon!"

Tina dragged herself from the couch and followed. *She's right. I need more sleep than I've been getting. Those damn nightmares...*

"I saw your note and put the sauce on low about an hour ago."

"Is that what—" Spotting the pictures on the refrigerator, Tina abruptly stopped speaking and stared at them for several moments. The first one was nice, showing the couple posing for the camera and smiling, but it was the second snapshot, a candid of them looking at each other, that Tina focused on. She observed the grin tugging at the corners of her mouth, the arm protectively wrapped around the smaller woman's waist, and the love in her eyes as she looked at Samantha.

Sam came over to hug her pensive partner. "Do you like them?"

"Very much."

"So do I."

"May I have this one?" Tina pointed to her favorite.

"If you want it, it's yours."

"I definitely want it, and I definitely want you."

"That's good to hear." Sam smiled at Tina. "Because I'm hopelessly in love with you."

"I...I look at that picture, and I know you see...it...in my eyes."

"Yes. I've known for a long time."

"I...um...you've been more than patient with me."

Sam laughed. "Patience is not one of my stronger qualities." *But pushing you into things led to near disaster before. I won't make that mistake again.* "For you, I'm making an exception."

Tina slowly lowered her head and kissed Sam.

It was a gentle kiss, meant to convey love rather than passion, and Sam understood. Her eyes were moist with tears as she laid her head against Tina's chest and listened to the rapidly pounding heart. *She's trying so hard. Whatever it is that's holding her back, ultimately, she'll tell me. I may use up my lifetime ration of patience while I wait, though.* "Hey, how about that spaghetti? You ready to cook now?"

"Yeah." The single word was choked with emotion.

"Great, because I'm hungry!" Sam busied herself setting the table and getting their drinks, allowing Tina a chance to gain her composure.

Having something physical to do always helped calm Tina, and she gladly went about the business of preparing the meal.

While her partner cooked, Sam chattered away about how kind the orchestra members had been when she'd arrived at work that morning. They'd given her a big card signed by everyone, and Sam went to get it from the entertainment center in the living room. She smiled at the assortment of cards there, touched at the volume of get-well wishes from friends and family. Lisa had brought over the huge pile of mail that had collected while Sam was recuperating at Tina's.

She showed the card to Tina and then continued to do most of the talking. Tina occasionally nodded or said, "uh-huh," to signify she was listening. After describing the orchestra's busy schedule for December, Sam voiced her discontent at how little time they would have to spend together before Christmas. "But the good news is," she said cheerfully, "I have from Christmas Eve to New Year's off."

"So do I."

"You do?"

"Yeah." Tina finished filling the plates with food and put them on the table. "I asked Vivian and she okayed it."

"It's going to be a *wonderful* week!"

"I think you're right."

They sat down to eat and Sam explained the plans she'd made with Lisa for Christmas Eve, elated when her partner liked the idea.

As they were discussing the holidays, Tina decided to bring up the trip Vivian had mentioned. "What about New Year's Eve?"

"The band usually has a gig, but because of the Millennium, we all decided to take this year off and celebrate with our families." Sam reached across the table and took Tina's hand. "In my case, that would be you."

"Well, Viv offered to send us anywhere we want to go."

"You've got to be kidding."

"Nope. Anywhere in the whole wide world. You name the place and she'll arrange it."

"Tina, we can't accept a gift like that."

"She's already made up her mind. Besides, she'd enjoy doing this for us."

"I don't know what to say."

"Why don't you think it over for a day or two? We can't wait beyond that to give Vivian the location, because she needs to make reservations as soon as possible. And, if it's out of the country, we'll have to get you a passport."

"You should pick. You're the one who's traveled and knows the best places."

"I don't care where we go," Tina lifted their still-linked hands and kissed them, "as long as I'm with you."

Sam's heart was bursting with happiness. "I feel the same way."

They didn't talk much after that, both of them eating heartily and smiling at each other between bites.

"You go watch TV." Sam started clearing the table. "I'll take care of this."

"I'll help."

She shook her head and gave Tina a slight push toward the doorway. "Out."

Too tired to argue and sure she wouldn't win anyway, Tina went into the living room. After collapsing on the couch, she used the remote control to cruise through the stations, catching a portion of the nightly news before leaving the channel set on an innocuous game show.

Sam rinsed the dishes and put them in the compact dishwasher. When she had renovated the garage apartment, she'd seen no need for the appliance, but her sister had correctly foreseen that someone else might actually cook and the convenience would be worth the added expense. Sighing, Sam wondered, not for the first time, why anyone would want to cook when it involved so much work. *A hamburger from the drive-through is much simpler.* She put the leftovers in plastic containers, washed the pots, and started the dishwasher.

"All done!" she declared as she plopped down next to Tina on the couch. "I should tell you, I can't guarantee I'll be quite that willing to do the dishes on a regular basis. It's part of my aversion to cooking, having to clean up afterward."

"Really?"

"I mean it's fine for special occasions and stuff, but I wouldn't want to do it every night. Maybe we can order take-out food a couple of evenings a week..."

"It's not a problem. I'll handle the dishwashing duties."

"But if you make dinner, you shouldn't have to—"

"I want to cook for you. I...it gives me the feeling I'm contributing something to...us. How about you being in charge of setting the table and keeping me company while I cook? I'll do the dishes. Does that sound reasonable?"

"Is this another one of your compromises?"

"I guess it is."

"It seems to me that I'm getting the better end of these deals."

"No." Tina looked at her partner in total seriousness. "I am."

There were a few seconds of silence as Sam absorbed the words. "You know what?"

"What?"

"You're getting very good at this relationship thing."

"You think so?"

"Yeah." *Absolutely...positively...yeah.*

They nestled together watching TV until the phone rang.

"I bet I know who that is." Sam went to answer it. "Hello?"

"Hi, Auntie Sam."

"Hi, Josh."

"I have to go to bed now. Is Tina gonna tuck me in?"

"She'll be right over."

"Cool! Bye."

"Bye."

Tina stood, stretched, and ran a hand through her hair. "I'll be back soon."

"I hope so." Sam gave her a lingering good-bye kiss.

"I'll hurry."

As Tina strode out the door, Sam grinned. *I need to hurry, too.* She got the boom box from the closet and set it up on the desk in the bedroom. Looking through her extensive selection of CD's, she chose an instrumental, setting the volume so that it was just loud enough to be heard. Humming to the music, she turned down the bed and lit the candles that were situated around the room.

Sam got out a clean towel and laid it on the counter in the bathroom. A check of the shower confirmed that there was a sufficient supply of soap and shampoo. Rummaging under the sink, she found the bottle of body oil she was searching for and put it on the bedside table. She brushed her teeth, combed her hair, and sat on the end of the bed.

~ * ~ * ~ * ~ * ~

Tina trudged up the stairs. *Damn, I'm tired.* Entering the apartment, she was surprised to find the living area dark. "Samantha?" She locked the door before heading toward the light flickering from the bedroom.

Sam smiled when Tina appeared in the doorway. "Hi." She waved an arm at their candlelit surroundings. "What do you think?"

Blue eyes never strayed from the blonde. "Beautiful."

I love when she looks at me like that. "I thought this would be the perfect night for a relaxing massage." Sam went over, took Tina by the hand, and led her to the bathroom. "First, I want you to take a nice, hot shower."

"Together?"

"No. Just you."

Tina put on her best pouting face.

"That's not going to work, Ms. Mellekas. We're getting you to sleep early and that's all there is to it," Sam said, as much to convince herself as Tina.

"Okay."

Sam knew that Tina agreeing so easily was a telling sign of how fatigued she really was. "See you in a little bit." She closed the door behind her and sat on the bed to wait.

It wasn't long before Tina came out. Her wet hair was combed straight back, accentuating the classic bone structure of her face. She was also completely naked. "Do you want me to lie down now?"

Sam was having difficulty articulating any kind of response as she gazed at the statuesque woman standing in the candlelight.

I love when she looks at me like that. "Samantha?"

"Oh...yes." Sam patted the mattress. "Right here."

Tina lay on her stomach and Sam knelt above her. She picked up the bottle of oil, unscrewed the cap, and let a few drops fall onto Tina's back.

"What's that?"

"Body oil...by the same company that makes my soap. Do you like it?"

"Yes."

Alternately kneading tight muscles and trailing her fingertips lightly over soft skin, Sam tried to concentrate on something...anything...other than attacking the tantalizing woman under her. Tina's periodic moans of contentment were not helping in the least. *Let's see. New Year's. That's something to think about. It's like a fairy godmother granted us a wish to go anywhere. Paris...London...Where did T say she liked? New Zealand. Maybe we could go to Australia for their big celebration and then visit New Zealand.*

The combination of the massage, soothing music, and mildly scented oil soon had Tina on the edge of sleep.

Sam moved to lie beside her and pulled the sheet over them. "How was that?"

"Mmm."

"I'll take that as a vote of approval."

"Mmm-hmm."

Propped up on an elbow, Sam watched as Tina fell asleep. She stayed for a time, assuring herself that her partner was slumbering soundly before she rose to turn off the music and blow out the candles.

I know where I want to go for New Year's.

~ * ~ * ~ * ~ * ~

Tina woke gradually. The first thing she was aware of was Sam's deep, steady breathing in the otherwise quiet room. The air still held the faint scent of candles and body oil. She realized she was on her stomach, in the same position she had fallen asleep. *I was so tired I didn't budge all night.* Opening her eyes, she studied the woman resting peacefully next to her. *How does she always know what I need?* Raising her head to look at the clock on the nightstand, Tina was astonished to see that it was almost five a.m. *Over seven hours of sleep? And no nightmares.* She rolled onto her back and stretched, relishing the feeling of relaxed muscles. *That massage was worth a month of cooking dinners.*

She got up and moved about stealthily, even though it was unlikely any noise she might make would wake Sam. Retrieving clean underwear from the dresser drawer, she smiled, remembering how excited the blonde had been when she'd found the small stash of clothing Tina had put there. *It wasn't long before she had me all excited, too.*

After washing up in the bathroom, she dressed quickly and returned to the bedroom. As had become her routine, she stood beside the bed for a minute, saying a silent prayer to anyone who might be listening, asking that Samantha be watched over and kept safe. She placed a feather-light kiss on the sleeping woman's forehead. *I love you.*

It was the beginning of what would be another lengthy day, but that didn't bother Tina. Knowing she would see Samantha that evening was more than enough to carry her through the intervening hours. Stopping in the kitchen, she left a note and took the picture she liked so much from the refrigerator. She put a banana, a multigrain bar, and a bottle of water in her backpack and exited the apartment, locking the door behind her.

The road was nearly empty as Tina traveled north on Interstate 75. She listened to the radio, ate her breakfast, and thought about what she wanted to accomplish at work. Daylight was breaking by the time the BMW pulled into the parking garage at Bayshore Palms. Tina took the stairs to the lobby and checked her mailbox, happy to find the extra gate remote-control mechanism she had ordered from the condominium association. She rode the elevator to the fourth floor, let herself into the condo, and prepared for her morning workout. Examining the training chart that now hung on the wall in the study, she evaluated her progress thus far. She had recently increased her distance and it was going well. She made a mental note to bump up the mileage again after the holidays.

She ran, showered, and drove to work. As usual, Tina was the first one there, but the others soon arrived and the office was bustling with activity. Brenda and Vivian were busy going through the list of their clients' holiday reservations, confirming with the hotels and airlines that everything was in order. That type of attention to detail had earned Exclusive Travel its reputation as the agency to book your travel with for a carefree trip. Tina had end-of-the-year paperwork to contend with, in addition to the mountain of payments in and out, due to the large number of clients traveling at year's end. At lunchtime, Brenda brought her a sandwich, which she ate at her desk while she continued working.

Around four o'clock, Vivian knocked on Tina's door. "How's it going?"

"Good." Tina took off her glasses and leaned back in her chair.

"We'll start printing out the finalized itineraries tomorrow." Vivian went in and sat down. "The envelope-stuffing party will probably be Friday."

"Okay." Tina enjoyed the tradition Vivian had of closing the agency for an afternoon, pulling the blinds, and turning up the music. The women would kick off their shoes and get comfortable in the front office area. Then, they would match all the itineraries with the corresponding tickets, related brochures, maps, and any other information the clients could possibly need. Three sets of eyes made sure everything was as it should be before the prelabeled envelopes were sealed and the mound of mail went into a big cardboard box. Tina and Brenda flipped a coin each year to see who would lug the carton to the post office to get the envelopes weighed and mailed.

They would conclude with a drink, toasting to their clients' safe travels. From that point on, Brenda and Vivian's workloads would be considerably reduced. There would be a few calls from people with questions about their itineraries, or one or two last-minute arrangements to be made, but the bulk of the holiday rush was over for them. Tina's days would still be very full, with all the accounting responsibilities that had yet to be completed.

"By the way," Vivian smiled, "I just had a call from Samantha. She wanted to thank me personally for the New Year's trip."

At the mention of Sam's name, Tina glanced at the snapshot that was taped to the computer monitor. "I talked with her about it last night."

"She told me where she'd like to go."

"Really?" Tina bent forward expectantly. "Where?"

"I'm not saying. She wants to be the one to tell you."

"Will she need a passport?"

"You'll not get any hints from me, so don't even try."

"Humph!" Tina crossed her arms and sighed.

"Well, I'm going to go home." Grinning at her sulking friend, Vivian stood. "Why don't you walk out with me?"

"I have reports to finish..."

"Samantha also said to tell you she hoped you'd be there soon. She's waiting for you."

"Oh? Um...yeah. Maybe I should escort you to your car."

Within an hour, Tina strolled into Sam's apartment.

"You're home!" Sam turned off the television show she'd been watching and went to hug her partner. "You're early tonight."

"I heard you were waiting for me." Tina dropped her backpack and ducked her head for a passionate kiss.

Oh my! Sam tried to catch her breath. "Yes. I talked to Vivian today..."

"Mmm-hmm." Still in the embrace, Tina started moving toward the bedroom.

Sam found herself being skillfully propelled backward. "Where are we going?"

"I thought that's what you were going to tell me."

"I...um..." Sam felt the bed behind her legs and sat down.

Tina knelt in front of her. "Where are we going for New Year's?"

"You said it could be anyplace I wanted, right?"

"Yes." Large hands slipped under Sam's shirt.

"I was thinking — this will be our first New Year's together, so it should be very special."

"I agree."

Sam was getting warm and her thoughts were beginning to wander almost as much as Tina's hands, which had somehow already unclasped her bra.

"Are you going to tell me?"

"Yes. I want to stay at your condo."

"Why?" Tina's hands stilled and she pulled back enough to give Sam a questioning look. "Of all the places you could choose..."

"I want to be with you. Only you. Maybe curled up in front of a fire watching TV when the ball drops at Times Square. Having a glass of champagne and toasting to our future together. We can make love all night until the sun comes up. And then, I want to greet the new millennium by seeing the first sunrise of my life from your balcony...with you." Sam paused, trying to gauge Tina's reaction, which seemed to be a mixture of bewilderment and surprise. "If you prefer something else..."

"No. It's just that you're passing up the opportunity to go anywhere in the world..."

"*You're* my world."

Understanding began to emerge in Tina's eyes. *She's telling me I'm more important than the trip...than anything.*

"So," Sam smiled at the loving look she was now receiving, "does that plan sound okay to you?"

"Yes." Tina's voice deepened. "Especially the all-night part." She stood, simultaneously removing the blonde's tee shirt and bra. "But we're not teenagers..."

"My partner is in training for a marathon." Sam lay back on the bed. "I *know* she has the stamina."

"Well, one has to train appropriately for specific events." Tina reached for the bottle on the bedside table. "I really like this body oil." She twisted off the cap and poured a small amount between Sam's breasts. Gentle fingers spread the liquid before soft lips followed the same trail.

"That...oh...feels...ohh...gooood."

"Mmm. It tastes good on you, too." Tina picked up the bottle again. "I think this requires further exploration."

Sam closed her eyes as some of the cool oil was applied to her belly. *I made the right choice. It's going to be a New Year's we'll never forget.*

It was quite a while later that they sat down at the kitchen table for dinner. Sam dug into the chicken parmesan Tina had made to have with the leftover spaghetti from the night before. "This is fabulous!"

"Glad you think so." Tina ate her meal at a slower pace, getting more pleasure from watching Sam's gusto than from the food on her own plate. "How did you persuade Vivian to go along with your New Year's idea?"

"Well, I did have to consent to her springing for a meal somewhere nice, and she's going to have champagne delivered to us."

Tina shook her head in amazement. *Two women I can't say no to, and they get along like gangbusters. I'm in deep trouble.*

The phone rang and Sam went to answer it. Bringing the portable receiver back to the kitchen, she gave it to Tina. "Lisa wants to talk to you."

"Hello?"

Curious as to why her sister was calling, Sam listened with interest, gleaning not a single shred of information from Tina's series of one-word answers to whatever Lisa was saying.

"Okay. Bye." Tina turned the phone off and laid it on the table.

Sam immediately asked, "What did she want?"

"Hmm?" Tina resumed eating her meal.

"Lisa. Why did she call?"

Taking her time chewing a mouthful of chicken, Tina enjoyed the look of impatience on her inquisitive partner's face as she waited for a response. "One shouldn't ask too many questions around the holidays. There are lots of secrets—"

"T!"

"Hmm?"

"Please?"

"Joshua and I made a pact. Whenever I'm here at his bedtime, I'll go over and tuck him in. He told Lisa about it and she was verifying his story."

"That's very sweet of you."

"He's a good kid."

"He loves you." Sam hesitated, deliberating whether or not to ask something she had often wondered about. "Does he remind you of Steven?"

Tina thought for a moment before answering. "I guess in some ways he does. Being around him brings back happy memories about Steven when he was little. But mostly, Joshua reminds me of you."

"Me?"

"Yeah. He's a lot like you." Blue eyes met green across the table. "So, how could I not...love...him?"

Sam smiled and said nothing, choosing instead to savor the word she knew was intended for her.

"Um...speaking of the holidays, would you like an early present?"

"Yes!"

Tina chuckled as she went to get her backpack. She returned to the table and instructed Sam to close her eyes and put out her hand. "No peeking."

"No peeking, I promise." The blonde felt an object placed on her palm and she closed her fingers over it. Her face scrunched in concentration as she tried to figure out what it was. "Can I look now?"

"Yes."

Sam looked down at the remote control. "Um...thanks." She inspected the device more closely. *A garage door opener?*

Seeing that Sam had no clue as to what it was, Tina explained, "It's for the gate at the condo. You won't have to use the call box—"

"Oh! It's a wonderful present!" Sam sat on Tina's lap. "Thank you." A tender kiss further expressed her gratitude.

"You're welcome."

They cuddled for a few minutes, basking in the love that surrounded them like a comfortable cloak.

"I still have room for dessert." Sam murmured, placing light kisses near Tina's ear.

"Mmm. Ring Dings?"

"Nope, something better."

"I didn't think there was anything better than Ring Dings."

Sam stood up. "Oh yes, *much* better." She took Tina's hand and pulled her toward the bedroom.

Chapter 28

Sam walked along the festively decorated streets of Hyde Park Village. She was looking forward to attending the tree-lighting ceremony with Tina and there was a pronounced spring to her step. Arriving at Exclusive Travel, she opened the door and went inside. Brenda was busy talking on the phone, but she greeted Sam with a smile and waved her toward the back of the agency.

Treading quietly, Sam made her way to Tina's office. Her partner was examining data on the computer monitor and she was able to watch undetected for a few moments. *Just looking at her still takes my breath away. My dream come true, and it's more than I ever imagined it would be.*

Tina finished proofreading the report she'd been working on and clicked the print icon. *Glad I got that done. Samantha should be here soon.* She rolled her shoulders, trying to alleviate the stiffness that had come from sitting and typing for so long.

"Mind if I help?" Sam moved into the room and went behind the desk. Placing her hands on Tina's shoulders, she gently massaged the tense muscles.

"That feels wonderful."

"Good." *You deserve to feel wonderful.*

Tina swiveled the chair around and pulled Sam onto her lap. "Hi."

"Hi." Sam tugged playfully on Tina's denim button-down collar. *My favorite shirt!* She took notice of the khaki slacks and brown hiking boots that completed the outfit. "No jeans today?"

"Well, I thought I'd put on something different for this hot date I have tonight."

Sam grinned, enjoying the close-up view of the eyes twinkling from behind the glasses she wished Tina would wear more often. "Hot date, huh?"

"*Very* hot." The claim was substantiated with a kiss.

"I see what you mean. I'm beginning to feel warm already."

They kissed again until a knock at the door interrupted them.

Sam almost fell off Tina's lap at the unexpected sound, but strong arms held her securely as Tina rotated the chair to face her boss. "Hi,

Viv."

"Hello." Vivian smiled at the sight of the women nestled together. "Nice to see you again, Samantha."

"It's nice to see you again, too." Blushing in embarrassment at the circumstances in which she'd been caught, Sam wriggled out of Tina's grip and stood up. "We were just about to go to the Cactus Club. Would you like to join us?"

"Thank you, but no. I've got a little more work to do here and then I'm meeting a friend for dinner. Perhaps another time."

"I'd like that."

Tina shut down the computer and put her glasses in her backpack. Vivian accompanied the couple to the door, where they exchanged good-byes.

As they walked to the restaurant, Sam commented excitedly on the large Christmas tree in the middle of the park and a stage with risers that she was sure would be for some sort of choral group. "This is going to be so cool, don't you think?"

"Yes." *Because I get to share it with you.*

The Cactus Club was packed, and the women had a drink at the bar before being shown to a table. Sam looked at the menu and quickly decided to get the cheeseburger platter, as she'd done the last time. "Can we bring my dad here when he visits? He'd like this place."

"Sure."

"He's really going to like you."

"I don't know about that. I certainly hope he does."

"He's always told me he just wants me to be happy." Sam reassured Tina. "And you make me very happy."

"He..." Tina stopped speaking as the waiter approached to take their orders. She waited until he left to continue. "Your dad totally accepts that you're gay?"

"Yes. It was one of the things my parents disagreed about." Sam looked down at the table. "I think it might have been the final straw."

"We don't have to talk about it."

"It's okay. I should have told you. It's been...hard, knowing that I was partially responsible."

"They're adults. They made their own decisions."

"True, but I can understand why my mom is terribly upset with me. First she finds out her daughter is gay, then her husband sides with the kid." Sam sighed heavily. "It's been a big mess."

"We'll get through it." Tina reached across the table and laid her hand over Sam's. "Together."

Misty green eyes rose to meet pale blue. "I love you."

"You're trying to butter me up so I'll buy you ice cream later."

Sam smiled, appreciative of the attempt to lighten the mood. "Maybe you want to buy the ice cream to butter *me* up, so you can have your way with me when we get home."

"I think that's an exceptional strategy." Tina raised an eyebrow. "Will it work?"

"Absolutely."

They laughed and went on to chat about less serious subjects. By the time they stepped outside, it was dark. There were sparkling white lights in the shop windows, along the walkways, and in the oak trees around the park. Holiday music played over speakers located throughout the area. A large crowd had congregated, waiting for the program to begin.

Tina guided Sam to one of the trees on the periphery. She positioned the smaller woman in front of her where they both would have an excellent view of the proceedings.

"This is a great spot."

"Glad you like it." Tina grinned. She had spent the better part of her lunch break checking out the site, trying to determine the best place to stand.

It wasn't too long before several dignitaries and a choir dressed in silky red robes assembled on the stage. The music was turned off and an older gentleman approached the microphone. He welcomed everyone and introduced a local minister who would be leading the group in an invocation. A hush fell over the gathering as the minister said, "Let us pray."

Tina bent her head down slightly and watched Sam, who had her head bowed and hands folded. At the conclusion of the prayer, the blonde joined the large group of people who said, "Amen."

There were a few short speeches as sponsors of the event were recognized and thanked. The president of the Hyde Park Business Association had the honor of lighting the tree, and did so with much fanfare. The spectators responded with thunderous applause.

Sam glanced over her shoulder at Tina. "Isn't it beautiful?"

"Indeed it is."

The choir began singing carols and Sam chimed in. She leaned back against Tina and was pleasantly surprised when a long arm curled around her waist and stayed there.

Tina surveyed their immediate surroundings, relieved that everyone was focusing on the stage and paying no attention to the two of them standing closely together. She didn't sing, preferring to listen to Sam's voice mingle with those of the choir and audience.

The program ended and the crowd began to disperse. Sam turned and looked up at Tina. "Are we going shopping now?"

"Shopping?" *In this mob?*

"Yeah! We're here, the stores are open, and Christmas is coming. Shopping seems like a good idea."

N. O. Two little letters. Put them together and you get..."Okay."

They wandered through the stores. Sam bought some gifts, explaining to Tina why each was perfect for the recipient she had in mind. In the hardware store that was reminiscent of an old general mercantile, Sam had a field day looking at the wide variety of items on display. "Look at this!" She worked one of the metal clasps on a bright yellow raincoat. "Remember these? I had one with matching galoshes."

"So did I. I hated the hat that went with it, but my mother made me wear it anyway."

"I'd like to see a picture of that." Sam laughed. "Oh! Isn't this cute?" She picked up a tiny flashlight from a bin. The top rotated 360 degrees and was designed to fit into tight spaces. "Mike could use one of these." She struggled with it, twisting the handle and top, trying to find the on/off mechanism. "How the heck do you turn it on?"

Tina took the flashlight and promptly twisted the bottommost section of the handle. The light popped on and off. "There you go." She smirked and gave it back.

"Show off." Sam tossed the flashlight back in the bin. "Let's go to the Sharper Image."

They crossed the street and went into the store. Tina began playing with gadgets while Sam browsed around. The younger woman was absorbed in her shopping when an object hit her neck. She picked up a sponge disk approximately the size of a quarter that had landed on the counter next to her. *What's this?* Looking to her left and right, she could see nothing out of the ordinary.

Tina chuckled from the end of the aisle. She loaded more disks into the shooter that was shaped like a starship from a popular television series. Creeping closer to her target, she took careful aim.

"Aha!" Sam whirled and faced her would-be assailant. "Caught ya!"

"W-what?" Tina hid the toy behind her back.

"I know what you're up to."

"Me?"

"Yes, you." Sam reached behind Tina and grabbed the weapon. "Now it's *my* turn."

Tina dashed away with the blonde in hot pursuit. Several shots hit their mark before the couple dissolved into laughter near the door. An employee eyed them warily and Sam laid the toy on the counter. "We'd better leave before we get into trouble."

Hurrying outside onto the sidewalk full of shoppers, they became part of the flow walking in the general direction of the ice cream shop.

"So, it's about time we got some ice—" Sam was stopped in her tracks when Tina's arm suddenly extended in front of her. The people behind them crashed into their backs. "Ugh!" She looked up at her partner. "What are you doing?"

Tina was standing completely still, staring at something in the distance. She didn't answer.

"T?" Sam balanced on her tiptoes in an unsuccessful effort to see above people's heads. "What is it?"

"Samantha...I'm sorry."

Something's wrong. "What is it?"

Tina slowly turned and looked into her partner's concerned eyes. "It's Andi."

There was a gap in the stream of people, allowing Sam to see a stylishly dressed, strikingly beautiful woman walking toward them. Her dark, wavy hair bounced in time with her long, graceful strides. Sam couldn't help but be impressed. *She looks like she just stepped off the cover of a fashion magazine.* She squared her shoulders and sucked in her gut. *This ought to be interesting.*

"Tina!" Andi smiled. "What a surprise. I didn't think this was your kind of event."

Tina shrugged. "Things change."

"So I see." Her eyes shifted to Sam. "Hello. I'm Andi."

"Hi." Steadfastly meeting the gaze, the blonde moved closer to Tina and wrapped a hand around her bicep. "I'm Sam." *And she's mine.*

There was a moment of uncomfortable silence before Andi nodded, acknowledging both the greeting and the possessive stance. "You're a lucky woman."

"I know," Tina and Sam replied in unison, then looked at each other and grinned at their like-mindedness.

"Honey," Sam explained, "I think she was talking to me."

"Oh." Tina blushed and shuffled her feet. *Honey?*

Andi watched her ex-lover. *Amazing, she's blushing! Evidently, keeping my feelings to myself wasn't the best plan. I was afraid she wasn't ready and I'd scare her away, but I ended up losing her anyhow.* "Well, I'll let you get back to your shopping. I'm glad I got a chance to see you and say merry Christmas." She stepped forward, kissed Tina on the cheek, and whispered something to her. Then, taking off rapidly in the opposite direction, she was gone.

Without a word, Tina suddenly sprang into motion, heading for the parking garage.

"Wait." Sam hurried to catch up.

Clearly rattled by the encounter, Tina implored, "Let's go home. Please."

"Home it is."

They walked to the garage and rode the elevator to the third level where they had prearranged to park.

"I'm over here." Sam pointed to the left. "I'll follow you." After quickly throwing her shopping bag in the rear of the SUV, she got behind the wheel and trailed Tina's car the short distance to Bayshore Palms. She used her new remote at the gate, impatiently having to wait for it to close after the BMW before being able to open it again. When she pulled into the empty space next to the silver car, Tina was already pacing in front of the elevator.

Sam jogged over and they went up to the condo. As soon as they got inside, Sam put her arms around Tina. "It's all right."

Tina reciprocated the hug. "I'm sorry."

"There's no reason for you to be sorry. How about we sit on the couch and talk a little bit?"

"Okay."

"I could use a beer. Would you like one?"

"Yeah."

Neither of them moved.

"Um, T? You're going to have to let go of me so I can get it for you."

"I don't ever want to let you go." Tina loosened her grasp just enough to duck her head for a kiss. "Ever."

"I like it when you think that way." *Especially when you tell me.* Sam smiled and backed out of the embrace before they could kiss again, knowing where that would lead. *Right now, more than anything, we need to talk.* She turned on the lamp by the couch. "Why don't you take off your shoes and relax while I get the beer?"

Tina took the advice and was sitting with her feet propped on the coffee table when Sam returned to join her. They were quiet for a few minutes, sorting through their thoughts while they sipped their drinks.

Sam spoke first. "She's very beautiful."

"I guess so. I...it never occurred to me that we'd run into her."

"It's a small world. I'm sure you'll meet an ex or two of mine somewhere along the line."

"I don't think I'll like that."

"It can be an awkward situation, but, if all else fails, you can always give them that glare of yours."

"Uh-huh."

"Besides, I don't have anyone from my past quite as...stunning...for you to meet."

"I never loved her."

"I know." Sam gently brushed the trace of lipstick from Tina's cheek. *She's in love with you, though.*

"She told me she's glad I'm happy and...um...she misses me."

"Of course she does." Sam had been extremely curious as to what Andi had whispered and was pleased that Tina had shared the information without being asked. "Do you miss her?"

"I...care about her. I'd like for her to be happy, too."

She'll have to get over you first. "Everybody has to find their own way, in their own time."

Tina put her drink on the end table. "C'mere." She gathered Sam into her arms. "It may have taken me a while, but I found what I want."

"Are you sure?" Insecurity crept into Sam's voice. "I mean — you're so gorgeous, it's a given that people...beautiful people...will flirt with you, want you. I don't know how to compete with that."

"I'm very sure. And there is nobody for you to compete against. With one look...one word...one touch, you're in here," Tina tapped her chest, "hugging my heart."

An enormous smile lit Sam's face. "Really?"

"Really." Tina smiled back, delighted her words had helped ease Sam's doubts. *I need to tell her stuff like this more often.* She pulled the bottom of the polo shirt out of the waistband of Sam's jeans, then slid a hand underneath. "It doesn't hurt that you have a sexy little body, too. Soft...with curves." Her hand cupped a full breast. "For me, you're just right."

The combination of compliments and gentle caresses turned Sam a rosy shade of pink. "You certainly know how to flatter a girl."

"Only you."

"I'm going to hold you to that."

"Good. I like it when you hold me."

"So do I."

Several minutes of contented snuggling passed.

"T?"

"Hmm?"

"I'm sorry if I've been acting jealous. It's not the most endearing of traits. The problem is, anything involving you seems to send my emotions into overdrive."

"I understand the feeling. The thought of losing you..."

"There's no chance of that."

"I get a pain in my stomach just thinking about it."

"I'll never leave you." Sam kissed Tina tenderly. "I promise."

Tina's eyes filled with tears. "What if something...bad...happens?"

"We can find a way to get through anything."

"I...um...guess I should tell you I've been having nightmares again."

Sam was immediately worried. "About the accident?"

"Kind of." Tina took and released a shaky deep breath. "But it's not Steven. It...I...lose...you."

"That *won't* happen. Not if I have anything to say about it."

"Steven and I said we'd always stick together. I told him I...loved...him."

I bet you've never told anybody that since then. Sam carefully considered how to respond. She decided that, as difficult as it might be, she had to be realistic. "We can't anticipate everything life has in store for us. If, as unlikely as it is, something happened, I'd fight until the end to stay with you. And, no matter what, even if I was physically...gone, I'd be in your heart forever."

"I...need...you. I don't know what I'd do..."

"Promise me you wouldn't run away again and close yourself off from everyone."

"I can't promise that."

"What about Joshua?"

"Josh?"

"Yes. If something happened to me, he'd need you to help him deal with it." *Almost as much as you'd need him.*

"I don't think I'd be much help."

"Just being there for him would be enough." Sam used her thumb to wipe the tear trickling down Tina's cheek. "Not that we have to be bothered with such thoughts, because we're going to grow very old together."

"I hope so."

"For now, our main objective should be to get you a dream catcher."

"The Native American thing?"

"Yeah. You hang it by the bed. It filters out bad dreams and lets the good ones through."

"Does it really work?"

"It's worth giving it a shot, don't you think?"

"Okay."

"I'll pick one up tomorrow. But for tonight, I think I'll hold you and see if I can keep all the bad dreams away."

"I like that idea."

"Well, it will take both of us to make it work."

"What do I have to do?"

"You have to believe that I love you, that I'll protect you, and I'll never leave you. Can you do that?"

Tina looked into Sam's eyes, seeing only love and devotion shining back at her. *How can I not believe it?* "Yes."

That night Tina slept peacefully, wrapped securely in Sam's arms. The next morning, she told the blonde not to buy her a dream catcher. She already had one.

Chapter 29

The next few weeks passed in a whirlwind of activity. Between working longer hours and taking care of their holiday shopping, the pair didn't have a great deal of time together. When Sam learned she would be getting off work early one afternoon, she convinced Tina to do likewise and meet her at the condo for some much needed rest and relaxation.

She's going to be surprised. Sam put her hands on her hips and looked around the cheerfully decorated room with satisfaction. Tiny white lights twinkled from a garland spread across the mantel, where two stockings were hung. Blankets and large pillows were strewn about the floor in front of the fireplace. A three-foot tree was centered on the coffee table, waiting to be trimmed with the ornaments lying next to it. Through the sliding glass doors, multicolored lights blinked merrily from the balcony railing. *She should be here soon.* Humming to the Christmas song playing softly in the background, Sam went to the kitchen and stirred the cider that was warming on the stove.

Tina unlocked the door and stepped inside. She stood quietly for a moment as she took in the sight of her transformed living quarters. "Samantha?"

"Hi!" Sam ran to the foyer and gave her an enthusiastic hug. "Seeing as we're going to be here for Christmas, I thought we should have the proper atmosphere. Do you like it?"

"Yeah, a lot."

She tugged Tina toward the kitchen. "Here's the best part." She stopped in the entryway and pointed up. A red ribbon dangled from the ceiling with a sprig of greenery fastened to the end.

"Mistletoe?"

"Mmm-hmm." Sam put her arms around Tina's neck and pulled her down for a kiss. "Good thinking, huh?"

"Excellent, as usual."

"I've got apple cider for you. Lisa gave me cinnamon sticks to put in it."

"It smells nice."

"Want some?"

"Yes." Tina leaned in for another kiss.

"I meant the cider!"

"I'll have some of that, too."

"Come on, then." Sam chuckled and led the way to the stove. "I'll pour us each a cup and we can decorate the tree."

"Okay."

As they brought their drinks into the living room, Tina walked to the fireplace and touched the stocking with the Florida State emblem on it. "Where'd you ever find this?"

"At a sports store in the mall. I thought it would make it easy for Santa to figure out which one is yours."

And you knew I'd love it. "I got the fireplace working. Do you want me to turn it on?"

"Can we wait 'til Christmas Eve? It'll make it extra special."

"Sure."

"Let's decorate the tree." Sam picked up the string of lights and started to randomly drape it on the branches.

"Wait a minute." Tina grabbed the end. "The plug needs to be down at the bottom. We should do this in a logical manner."

Tina took charge, giving precise directions that resulted in a perfectly symmetrical lighting design. Next, they alternated turns hanging the ornaments. Sam would quickly pick any open space in which to put hers. Tina studied the tree at length before carefully choosing a spot.

Thank goodness it's not a six-footer; it would take a week to decorate. Sam picked up the tinsel. "I bet you're going to put this on one strand at a time, aren't you?"

"Um, yes."

Sam laughed and gave half the contents of the box to her partner. "I believe in 'the more tinsel the better' theory." She started tossing the stuff at the tree by the handful. In less than thirty seconds, she was done.

Tina hung single strands on the scant number of bare branches that were left. When she finished, the women sat cozily on the couch.

"Samantha, thanks for doing this. The place looks wonderful."

"You're welcome. Would you prefer that we stay here this weekend? You do too much driving."

Tina shook her head. "I don't want to miss tucking Josh in."

"He told me you're quite the storyteller."

"Actually, it's only been one story so far. He always asks for the same thing."

Sam was very familiar with Joshua's penchant for listening to a tale over and over. "Maybe I can hear it sometime?"

"Maybe."

Maybe almost always means yes. Sam smiled and cuddled closer.

They sat silently for a bit, each one lost in her own thoughts.

"T?"

"Yes?"

"I think I'd like to call my mom."

"Are you sure?" Tina picked up the phone from its base on the end table.

Sam nodded, taking the receiver and holding it against her chest while she gathered her emotional strength. Finally, she took a deep breath and dialed, then waited nervously as it rang twice before she heard her mother say hello. "Hi, Mom; it's Sam."

Tina listened alertly to the younger woman's side of the conversation, prepared to intervene if necessary.

"How are you? ... Yes, I'm completely healed. Even the bruises are all gone. ... Yes. ... No. ... Um, Tina and I are going to be spending Christmas in Tampa, so I was wondering if we could stop by to see you on Christmas Eve? ... Probably late afternoon. ... Okay. Bye, Mom." Sam pressed the off button, dropped the phone on the cushion next to her, and hugged Tina. "She said yes!"

There might be hope for you after all, Mrs. Whitwell. "Guess it's a good thing I got her a present."

"You did?"

"Yup."

"Why didn't you tell me?"

"I didn't want you to feel any pressure about calling her. I had Lisa help me pick out something just in case."

"I love you." Sam nuzzled Tina's neck and nibbled on her ear. "What is it?"

"That? I'd say it's my ear."

"You're impossible, Tina Mellekas!"

"But that's one of the reasons you love me, right?"

"One of many, many, many reasons, yes."

Tina gently reclined the blonde down onto the couch and gave her a searing kiss.

Wow. Sam suddenly felt extremely warm. "You wouldn't be trying to avoid discussing that present, would you?"

"Present?" Tina asked as her hands began to roam. "What present?"

~ * ~ * ~ * ~ * ~

The BMW moved slowly along a street lined with middle-class

homes.

"There it is." Sam indicated a peach colored, two-story house with white trim.

Tina parked in the driveway. She looked at her passenger, who had been unable to conceal her increasing anxiety as the time had come for their visit to her mother. "Are you okay?"

"I...I've hoped for this for years." Sam idly picked at the ribbon tied to the gift on her lap. "But..." She shrugged. "I think I'd better apologize in advance. If this should turn into a fiasco..."

"Don't worry. It's going to be fine," Tina said matter-of-factly, even though she was feeling as apprehensive as her partner. "Remember what you told me? We can get through anything together."

"You're right." The assertive words calmed Sam's nerves a little. "Plus, I may never find out what that present is if we don't go in there."

Tina reached into the rear seat for the gift she had gotten Mrs. Whitwell. "Want to shake it and see if you can guess?"

"Yes!"

"You'll have to catch me first." Tina bolted out of the car and dashed up the walkway.

Sam quickly followed, catching the runner by the back of her shirt just outside the front door. "Give me that present!"

"Nope." Tina grinned and held the brightly wrapped package high above her head.

"But I caught you!"

"Indeed you have. And it's the best thing that's ever happened to me."

"Don't even try to change the subject—"

Suddenly, the door was pulled open. "I thought I heard someone..." Mrs. Whitwell looked at the startled couple. *Did I interrupt something?* Her eyes traveled up the length of Tina's arm to the still-elevated present.

"Um...hi, Mom, I was about to ring the bell."

"Really?" Mrs. Whitwell said skeptically, glancing at the neighboring houses to see if anyone was observing them. "Come on in." She directed the guests to the living room. "Would you like a cup of coffee? Or a soft drink?"

Sam and Tina politely declined and sat down on the couch. Mrs. Whitwell took a seat in the chair across from them.

After a few seconds of tense silence, Sam spoke. "Thanks for having us over. I know this isn't easy for you."

"I can't say I understand the lifestyle choice you've made, nor do I approve of it."

"Mom, please—"

"I wasn't finished."

"Sorry."

Mrs. Whitwell looked at her younger daughter fondly and softened her tone, "I love you, Samantha. To be honest, I don't know how successful I'll be at accepting this whole thing, but I'm willing to try."

"Would it help if I told you I'm incredibly happy?"

"Yes." Mrs. Whitwell's tone was resigned. "I suppose that helps."

Sam jumped off the couch to hug her. "I love you!"

Tina felt her stress level subsiding. *We might survive this yet.*

"I got you something." Sam sat on the arm of the chair and handed her mother the gift. "Merry Christmas."

Mrs. Whitwell unwrapped the box and removed the top. "It's beautiful, Samantha." She picked up the cloth-covered journal. "Thank you."

"Look inside."

"There's more?" Doing as her daughter asked, she saw the inscription.

> *Dear Mom, This is for all the happy memories you've given me, and my wish for many more ahead.*
> *Love, Samantha*
> *Christmas 1999*

She flipped through page after page of writing. *Memories...all happy memories.* "This is so thoughtful of you. I like it very much."

"And here, Mom." Sam showed her the blank sheets toward the end. "This is where you can put new entries...if you want to."

"It's a unique gift and I'll cherish it always."

Smiling, Sam returned to her seat next to her partner. "Oh, Tina got you something, too." *I can't wait to find out what it is.*

"You shouldn't have..."

Tina passed her the present without further ado. "Merry Christmas."

Sam watched with interest as her mother tore the wrapping from the package, pushed the tissue paper aside and burst out laughing. Taking the set of crystal drinking glasses from the box, she gave Tina a wry smile. "They match exactly! Thank you."

"Well, I felt it was appropriate. It's partly my fault you have an incomplete set."

"Only partly?"

It was Tina's turn to laugh.

Mrs. Whitwell went over to the Christmas tree in the corner of the room, selected a gift, and brought it to her daughter.

"To Samantha and Tina. Love, Mom." Sam read the tag, carefully peeled it off the paper and gave it to Tina. "I want to keep that." She swiftly ripped off the decorative wrap and opened the box, then gasped when she saw the silver-bordered photo album inside. The cover had an oval-shaped cutout in the center for a picture and the words Our Life Together in script underneath. Sam had admired the album when her mother purchased it for Lisa and Mike as an engagement present. "Mom? How did you..."

"I got an additional one after you told me how much you liked it. I've been saving it, thinking that someday..." There was an uncomfortable pause. "Anyhow, Lisa explained to me that it would be fitting for your...status."

Sam wiped at the tears in her eyes.

"Thank you," Tina said sincerely. "It means a lot to us."

"Now, don't be getting the notion that I approve of...this. I just couldn't see any reason to let the thing sit and gather dust any longer than it already has. Might as well get some use out of it."

"We understand." Sam ran her fingers lightly over the words on the album before putting the top back on the box. "You've made another happy memory for me today, Mom."

"I won't be forgetting it any time soon, either," Mrs. Whitwell quipped.

They all laughed at the indisputably true remark.

Sam looked at her watch. "We should get going. Lisa is cooking dinner."

"And I have baking to do for the brunch tomorrow." Mrs. Whitwell rose and walked them out.

They traded holiday wishes and Sam gave her mother a heartfelt hug.

Mrs. Whitwell shut the door and rested against it. *That was...different.* She went to the living room to clean up, but found she was drawn to the journal her daughter had given her. She took the book to the study, sat at her desk and thumbed through it, stopping to read passages here and there. Coming to a blank page, she looked at it contemplatively for a long time. Then she raised her pen and began to write.

~ * ~ * ~ * ~ * ~

"They're here!" Joshua ran into the kitchen. "Can we eat now?"

Lisa closed her eyes. *One...two...three.* The anticipation of Christmas the next day and exchanging gifts with Sam and Tina that evening had caused the boys to be hyperactive all day, testing the limits of their mother's patience. "Shouldn't we at least let them get in the house?"

"I'll carry the presents!" He sprinted off.

"Slow down!"

"Hey there, pretty lady." Mike came into the room and put his arms around his wife. "How's it going?"

"Do you really want to know?"

Mike rubbed Lisa's back soothingly. "Maybe after the kids go to bed, I'll pour us some wine and we can sit by the fire—"

"We still have to bring the boys' gifts in from the garage and get the basketball hoop assembled."

"I'll take care of that."

"I get to drink wine and supervise while you play Santa?"

"Mmm-hmm." Mike kissed Lisa's neck and whispered in her ear. "You can even have the cookies this year."

"Ahem." Sam stood in the doorway with Tina. "Should we come back later?"

"No!" Joshua was struggling with a large plastic bag full of packages. "Don't leave. We have to eat and open the presents!"

"Come in." Lisa laughed, letting go of her husband. "Dinner is almost ready."

"That's my cue," Mike said, getting out the carving knife. "Time for me to slice the ham."

"Josh?" Tina grabbed one side of the bag before the child dropped it. "Let's put this in the family room, okay?"

"Okay."

Sam smiled, enchanted by the scene of the twosome heading down the hallway with the sack between them.

Lisa was setting bowls of food on the table. "How'd it go at Mom's?"

"It went way better than I expected! She told me you talked with her. I can't thank you enough."

"It was nice to have a rational discussion on the subject. It's obviously a foreign concept to her, so I tried to emphasize the similarities, not the differences. She didn't say much, but she seemed to be listening."

"She was. I can hardly believe it."

"I'm glad it's finally working out." Lisa poured the boys' milk.

"Me, too," the blonde said happily. "Want me to round up the troops?"

"Sure."

Sam went to get Tina and her nephews. Shortly thereafter, they all sat down and enjoyed the good food and lighthearted conversation.

"Tina?" Joshua swallowed the last bite of his pumpkin pie. "Did Grandma like her present?"

"Yes, I think she did."

"What?" Sam glowered at the group. "Everybody knew about that but me?"

The adults mumbled noncommittal responses, hastily scooping forkfuls of dessert into their mouths to avoid the necessity of saying anything more. Joshua and Aaron giggled, nodding yes.

"Ohh..." Sam pinned Tina with a look. "I am *so* going to get you for this."

Tina chewed her food with an aura of total innocence that triggered gales of laughter from the rest of the people at the table.

Lisa stood and collected the plates. "Would anyone like coffee?"

"Mom!" Aaron pleaded. "Can't you do that later?"

"You and Josh have to do the dishes."

"Mom," the boys whined.

"The sooner it's done, the sooner we can open the presents."

Aaron got the step stool and climbed on it to rinse the dishes in the sink. He then handed the items to Joshua, who stacked them in the dishwasher.

"No coffee for me," Mike said. "I'll go get the fire started."

Lisa served the drinks and the women had a chance to relax and chat while the children did their chores. Sam filled her sister in on the details of the visit at their mother's. They all agreed that, although progress still needed to be made, it had far exceeded what any of them would have predicted.

When the dishes were done, everyone retired to the family room. Mike was in the overstuffed chair near the crackling fire with Beethoven at his feet. The dog trotted toward the newcomers and received plenty of petting before everyone got seated.

Lisa took her place at the piano, tinkling the keys to limber her fingers. Then they sang Christmas carols, one after another, with each person suggesting their favorites.

Tina didn't know what to make of it. *I thought this kind of thing only occurred in greeting-card commercials.* She felt Sam pressed tightly against her on the couch. *Okay, maybe an alternative greeting-card commercial.*

"What about you, Tina?" Lisa asked. "Do you have a request?"

"Um...no."

"You must have a favorite," Sam prodded.

"Well, I kind of like 'The Christmas Song'."

Lisa played the introduction and they all sang.

During the final chorus, Tina pulled Sam into her lap. Caught up in the moment, she followed the last word with a kiss.

"Eww!" Aaron made a face. "Mushy stuff!"

Mike grasped Lisa's hand and brought her into an embrace. "That seems like a fine idea." He kissed his wife.

"Eww! More mushy stuff!" Joshua covered his eyes.

The adults looked at the boys and laughed.

"Okay," Lisa announced. "Time for the presents!"

The boys excitedly searched under the tree for packages bearing their names. Sam went over as they unwrapped the toys she had given them. Squeals of joy confirmed that she had chosen well. The boys insisted she open her gift right then and there, and she thanked them for the much-needed guitar strings.

Tina took the opportunity to put a large, rectangular gift in Lisa's hands. "Merry Christmas."

Lisa stripped the paper off a picture frame that displayed a collage of newspaper articles about the track team. In the center was a photo of Tina and Lisa in their uniforms, holding trophies. The caption in dark print stated: Mellekas and Whitwell to represent Sarasota at State Competition. "Where on earth did you get these?"

"From my scrapbook. I scanned them on my computer."

"You have a scrapbook?" Sam went to investigate what they were looking at. She had badgered Tina to no avail and remained in the dark as to what gifts her partner had chosen. "Oh my gosh! You're so skinny!"

Two pairs of eyes stared at her frostily.

"Um...I..."

Tina shook her head. "It would be wise to quit before you dig yourself any deeper."

Joshua squeezed in front his mother to see. "Is that you?"

"Yes, with Tina. We were on the track team together in high school."

Mike was peeking over Sam's shoulder. "We can hang that in here. It'll go with our sports theme."

Lisa propped the picture frame on the piano and smiled at her former teammate. "Thanks."

"You're welcome." Tina picked up a present and gave it to Mike. "I felt like a traitor getting this, but here's something for your mantel."

The man ripped the wrapping off and looked at the collegiate football encased in Plexiglas, then at Tina, dumbfounded. "This is *unbelievable!*" He put the box on the table, grabbed Tina, and swung her around. "Thank you!"

"What's so special about a football?" Aaron asked his mother.

"I don't know."

"It's personalized!" Mike had everyone view the writing next to the Gator logo on the ball: *To Mike, Class of '77.* Underneath was the coach's signature. "You met him in person, Tina?"

"No. My boss has tons of connections. She got it signed for me."

"Yeah, Vivian is terrific." Sam held out an envelope. "She helped me with my present for you and Mike, too."

"I'll take that," Lisa said, "because I don't think he's going to let go of that football." She read the information in the packet and her jaw dropped. "Are you serious?"

"Yes." Sam smiled. "And my baby-sitting services are included."

"Baby-sitting?" Mike inquired. "What's this about?"

"It's a weekend getaway...some fancy resort on Siesta Beach." Lisa hugged her sister. "What a wonderful present!"

While Sam talked about the vacation with Lisa and Mike, Tina motioned for the boys to come closer. "I think I have something here." She produced two packages and tossed them to Aaron and Joshua.

The children decimated the wrapping in a flash and yanked the gifts from the boxes.

"It's just like yours!" Joshua pulled the Florida State shirt, identical to the one Tina was wearing, over his head.

Aaron examined the silky material of his professional soccer jersey. "Awesome!"

"Very nice!" Lisa admired the new apparel. "Boys, did you say thank you?"

"Thanks, Tina!" they choroused.

Mike carefully laid the football on the mantel and got a present from under the tree. "Sam, Tina, this is for both of you." He put an arm around his wife's waist and grinned. "From us."

"You unwrap it, T," Sam urged. "I opened the one at Mom's."

"Okay." Tina took the gift and meticulously detached the wrapping at the edges, then extricated the object without causing a single tear in the paper.

Sam had to fight the impulse to seize the thing and open it more speedily.

Joshua was on his tiptoes trying to get a look. "What is it?"

Tina didn't answer. Her focus was on the pencil sketch matted in dark gray and bordered with a high-gloss black frame. The drawing was of herself and Sam, modeled after the photo Lisa had taken of them.

"So that's why you borrowed those negatives," Sam accused her sister. "You said you wanted to make copies of the pictures of Josh on his bike."

"I wanted those, too. But, yes, I had an ulterior motive."

"Did you draw that, Daddy?" Joshua asked.

"Yes, and Mom got it framed."

"It's superbly done," Tina said quietly. "Thank you."

Lisa smiled at the reaction. *She loves it!*

"Joshua!" Aaron tussled with his brother. "I wanna give it to her!"

"I wanna do it!" Josh wailed. "Mom, he won't let go of Tina's present!"

Tina gave the sketch to Sam and rushed to the children before the quarrel escalated. "What do you have there?"

"It's for you," Aaron answered, "but he won't let go of it."

"For me?" Tina sat in the chair and extended her hand.

Neither child wanted to relinquish his grip on the gift, so they cooperatively set it in her palm.

"Thank you." Tina looked at the package, covered with an abundance of tape and a bow that was askew.

"We wrapped it ourselves," Joshua informed her.

"Really?" Tina explored every angle, looking for a possible point of entry. Finding none, she wrestled with it until she could wrench the tape free and open the box. *Oh no....*Lying on cotton bedding was a long silver chain with rubber loops at each end.

Seeing the unreadable look on Tina's face, Aaron clarified, "It's for your glasses!"

"Yes, I know."

"Auntie Sam helped us pick it out," Joshua added.

"Did she? I'll have to thank her personally later."

Mike and Lisa laughed, but Sam sensed the hint of hurt in her partner's retort. Before she could ask about it, Tina continued speaking.

"The best part is," she said as she closed the box, "I'll think of you boys every time I wear it." *When I turn sixty.*

"Joshua? Aaron?" Lisa held a large garbage bag. "It's getting late. Let's throw the trash away."

The children tidied the room, put cookies and milk on the table for Santa, and hugged everyone good night.

"You're gonna tuck me in, aren't you?" Joshua asked Tina.

"Of course."

"Cool!" The boy stampeded up the steps behind his brother.

Tina's long arms enveloped Sam. She kissed the top of the blonde's head and said softly, "Would you like to come hear the story?"

"Yes!"

"C'mon." Tina took hold of Sam's hand and they ascended the stairs.

When they got to Joshua's room, Sam stood against the wall near the door, not wanting to interfere with the ritual. She watched as Tina pulled the covers neatly over the boy and sat on the side of the bed.

There were some preliminary questions about hand washing and teeth brushing before Tina seemed satisfied that Joshua was ready for the story. Acutely aware of her partner's presence in the room, she cleared her throat and began.

"Once upon a time, there was a very special little girl. She had hair the color of sunshine and eyes as green as the grass after a spring rain. She was a happy child, who was kind and gentle and good. She had an older sister and they squabbled, as children sometimes do, but eventually they turned out to be the best of friends.

"The little girl had hopes and dreams, like everybody does, and she often thought about what her life would be like when she grew up. Mostly, she dreamed of love. Not just any love, mind you. I mean the kind you hear about in fairy tales — where two people meet and find that they're destined to be together...forever.

"Well, time passed, and the girl became a beautiful woman. She was still as kind and gentle and good as she'd been as a child. She was full of life, with a sparkle in her eyes and a smile that shone so brightly it could light up a room. Or the darkest of hearts.

"She had friends and family who loved her and she loved them in return. So, all in all, things were going pretty well. But deep down inside, she felt as if something was missing. And as the years continued to go by, she wondered if she'd ever discover what it was.

"Now around this same time, there was a dark-haired woman who was moody and sad. She'd suffered a great loss and was having trouble finding her way in the world. She was...lonely.

"As fate would have it, one night, the two women met. And when they looked into each other's eyes, they both felt something. It was almost...magical. Immediately, the blonde woman knew the other one needed her. How she knew it, I'm not sure. But she was right.

"The dark-haired one...well, she wasn't sure *what* she felt. Except whatever it was, it scared her a lot. So, she pretended like she didn't feel anything. She was very good at that.

"However, the blonde was not the type to give up easily. She worked hard to make friends, demonstrating by example how it was okay to be happy, to have someone to confide in...and to trust.

"Now, don't be thinking that this all went smoothly, because there were bumps in the road and mistakes were made. But the fair-haired woman never wavered from her belief that they were meant to be together. She'd had to believe it for the two of them for a long time, but not anymore. Because they both believe it now.

"So, you see, the hero saved the day. And she didn't need guns or any kind of violence to do it. She used the most powerful force in the universe as her weapon.

"She saved the day with love."

Tina hesitated, as she usually did at this juncture, knowing that Joshua would remind her there was more.

The boy smiled. "Don't forget the end, Tina. Tell what happened to them after that!"

"Oh, um...they lived happily ever after."

Tina ruffled the child's hair, kissed him on the forehead, and turned off the bedside lamp. "Sweet dreams, Josh."

"You too, Tina."

Sam stepped out into the hallway, wiping her eyes with her shirtsleeve. She flung her arms around her partner the instant she appeared. "I love you."

Tina responded with a prolonged kiss. "Is it time to go to my place?"

"Yeah." With a look of unadulterated lust, Sam grabbed the waistband of Tina's jeans and pulled her toward the stairs. "Let's go."

Tina raised an eyebrow, grinned, and followed willingly.

Chapter 30

Tina unlocked the condo door and pushed it open. Sam zipped past her, carrying the two-handled shopping bag her sister had given the couple when they said their good-byes. It contained the gifts they had received as well as a few wrapped ones that Lisa said were from Santa and not to be opened until the following day. Sam went directly to the tree, turned on its lights, and added the presents to the pile already stacked on the coffee table.

Tina plugged in the strings of lights for the balcony and mantel. She looked at Sam, whose face was softly illuminated by the tree's twinkling bulbs. "With the Christmas lights and the fireplace on, we may not need any of the lamps. What do you think?"

"I think," Sam got up and hugged Tina, "I'm the happiest person on the planet tonight."

"You can't be, 'cause I am."

"Did I mention that the story you told is the best present I've ever gotten?"

"Yes, I believe you did." *At least three times, but who's counting?* "Perhaps I should return the other gifts I have for you. They may pale in comparison."

"Not on your life!" Sam threatened. She smiled at the low chuckle she heard where her ear was pressed against Tina's chest. "Though, as much as I love getting presents, I already have everything I really need right here in my arms."

Tina tilted Sam's chin up and looked into loving eyes. "I feel the same way."

"I like it when you agree with me." Sam stood on her tiptoes to give her partner a kiss. "Let's change into our sleep clothes so we can be comfortable while we enjoy the fire."

"Okay."

Sam handed Tina a gift from under the tree. "Here's something you might want to wear."

Tina pulled the paper off and unfolded the silk Florida State University boxer shorts. "These are great!"

"I know you like the Mickey ones at my place, so I thought you might want a pair for here."

"I have something for you to put on, too." Tina chose a package from the table and handed it over.

Sam ripped through the wrapping, uncovering a tee shirt that had a large *S* inside an inverted triangle embossed on the front. "I...I've never thought of myself as anybody's hero."

"Real heroes never do," Tina said softly. "Thanks for being mine."

"There's one thing you've definitely got right — I'm yours."

"That's the best gift I could ever have."

"So," Sam smirked, "I can return your other presents?"

Tina clutched the silk shorts to her chest. "Not on your life!"

They both laughed.

"I'm going to get changed." Sam gave her partner another kiss. "Don't go away."

"No chance of that happening." Tina watched the blonde saunter toward the bedroom. *I've got it bad. She has me wrapped around her little finger.* Tina went to the fireplace and switched it on. *And I love it.* She stared into the flames for a few moments. *I love her.*

Sam added an extra sway to her steps, correctly guessing that Tina was observing her exit. After a record-breaking quick shower, she pulled on her superhero shirt. It reached to the top of her thighs and she decided no further clothing was necessary. She returned to the living area and saw that the blankets and pillows were already spread out and the fire was crackling. Her partner, however, was nowhere to be seen. "T?"

The laundry room door opened and Tina staggered through the kitchen, half carrying, half dragging a huge, colorfully wrapped rectangular box that was almost as tall as she was.

"What in heaven's name is that?"

Tina carefully laid the item on the floor. "One of your presents."

"You must be kidding."

"Nope." Tina traced the *S* on Sam's shirt. "This looks nice."

"Thanks." The blonde noticed Tina had changed into a button-up FSU baseball jersey and the new silk shorts. "How is it that you can make sportswear look so sexy?"

"It must have to do with whose company I'm in." Tina took Sam's hand and tugged her down onto the blankets next to the present. "G'wan, open it." Her eyes were sparkling with excitement.

"Okay." Sam stripped off what must have been several rolls of decorative wrap to reveal a plain cardboard shipping carton. She grappled with the top of the box, having to pull at one end and then the other before she could remove it. Inside, surrounded by packing material, was a hard-shell guitar case. The name of the manufacturer was prominently displayed on the exterior. "Oh...Tina...it can't be..."

"Let me help." Tina moved enough of the packing so Sam could undo the fasteners on the case. "There you go."

Sam's hands were shaking as she lifted the lid. She gasped when she saw the aged, but exceptionally well-maintained instrument. "My dream guitar."

"Test it out."

Sam cautiously took the guitar out of the case and gently twanged each string, adjusting the corresponding key on the neck to tune it. Then, with a grin at Tina, she strummed a chord.

Both women's eyes widened at the deep, rich sound.

Sam looked at the guitar in amazement. "Wow!"

"I hope it's what you wanted. If not, they said you can exchange it—"

"It's exactly like I imagined. Where'd you find it?"

"On the Internet. You commented that you liked old instruments, so I found a vintage guitar store—"

"Vintage?" Sam squeaked. "How old is it?"

"1968. I have the certificate of authenticity—"

"Oh my God. It must have cost a fortune!"

"It'll be worth every cent to hear you play it."

"Tina, I love it, but—"

"No buts. It makes me *very* happy to give it to you. You want me to be happy, don't you?"

"You know I do."

"So," Tina smiled broadly, "will you play something for me?"

"Of course I will." *Every day for the rest of our lives, if you want.* It didn't require a second's thought as to what the inaugural song would be. Sam played a familiar chord progression and began to sing.

"Heart living in the shadows, you've been so all alone
Moving though life within yourself, behind those walls of stone
It doesn't have to be that way, that's not how life should be
There's nothing to fear, it's just you and me here

And it's love, love
It's plain to see, yes it's clear to me
That it's love, love
I need you to be, forever with me
'Cause it's love, love
Can't you see, it's our destiny
It's love, love

You and me — it's only love."

The last chord hung in the air as the women gazed at each other.

Tina took the guitar from Sam's hands and put it in the case. "C'mere." She welcomed the blonde into her arms.

"You're making all my dreams come true." Sam snuggled against her partner's body. "And you call *me* the hero?"

They stayed like that for a while, content to just hold each other in silence.

"T?"

"Hmm?"

"I want to give you a present now." Sam stretched out an arm and took a gift from under the tree. "It's...um...not very big. But, as the saying goes, good things come in small packages."

"I can't argue with that." Tina carefully peeled off the paper. Inside was a velvet jewelry box with the initials of an established Sarasota jewelry shop imprinted in fancy lettering on the top. *Whatever this is, it's very high quality...and expensive.*

"Well, are you going to open it?"

Tina tossed the wrapping aside and opened the cover of the box. "It's beautiful." She lightly touched the silver *T* and gold *S* that were intertwined at the base of a silver and gold braided chain.

"I haven't seen you wear any jewelry, but I thought maybe..."

"I love it."

"You do?"

Tina nodded. She continued to look at the gift, even though her vision was somewhat blurred by her tears.

"May I put it on you?"

Tina nodded again.

Sam took the necklace from the box and leaned forward so she could reach behind Tina's neck to clasp the chain. When she finished, she sat back to see how it looked. Her breath caught at the sight of the silver and gold glinting against the tan skin beneath it. And, as she had hoped, the letters fell just below the hollow of her partner's throat. "It looks," Sam pounced on Tina, knocking her backward onto the pillows, "perfect."

"I'll never take it off, then."

"It might bother you when you're running, or—"

"Never!"

"Good, because I want people to know," Sam spoke between the kisses she was placing in a path alongside the chain, "that this gorgeous ... intelligent ... strong ... brave ... woman," she raised her head to look into Tina's eyes and her voice became husky, "is *my* woman." She followed the words with a demanding, passionate kiss.

It took Tina a moment to get her bearings under the unexpectedly intense onslaught. Resisting her own impulses, Tina tried to remain passive and give her partner free rein.

Sam continued the fervent kisses, simultaneously unbuttoning Tina's jersey and caressing the newly exposed skin. Her small hand crept downward, slipping under the waistband of the boxer shorts. The heat that met her probing fingers was in stark contrast to the cool, silky material above.

Tina was rapidly discovering that letting a highly aroused Samantha Whitwell completely have her way with her was an incredibly exciting thing. She groaned with displeasure when her partner stopped to catch her breath.

Sam was panting, trying to pull in some much needed air. "T?"

"Hmm?" Tina realized she was in a wonderful position to observe Sam's heaving chest.

"I...I don't know what's gotten into me. I'm not usually so... um...so..."

"Aggressive?"

"Yeah."

"Maybe it's the superhero shirt."

"Could be." Sam delicately stroked the side of Tina's face. "Or maybe I've just never been this much in love."

"There's a first time for everything." Tina slowly moved her arms up over her head.

"W-what are you doing?"

"I want you to know that body, heart, soul, everything — I'm yours." Tina paused before adding softly, "I...I love you, Samantha."

Sam smiled. *Finally!* Looking into the sea of blue that was her whole world at that instant, she saw no hint of fear or confusion, only love. She listened to the fire crackling, felt where her hands touched warm skin, and took in everything her senses could gather, trying to commit it all to memory.

"Samantha?"

"Yes?"

"I...um...I'm in kind of a vulnerable position here."

"So I see." Sam trailed her fingers along Tina's raised arms. "And I'm kind of liking it."

"Me, too." *If I keep agreeing with her like this, I'm going to have to run two marathons.*

"You know what?"

Yeah, I know what; there's entirely too much talking going on here. "What?"

"The story you told Joshua was right."

"It was?"

"Uh-huh." Sam nuzzled Tina's neck and murmured in her ear, "We're going to live happily ever after."

Two marathons it is. "I...I think so, too."

"I'm very glad to hear that." The blonde sat up and pulled off her tee shirt. "Think I can still be your superhero without this?" She dangled the cloth in front of Tina for a moment before tossing it to the side.

Tina's eyes darkened a shade as they lingered over her naked partner's body. "Absolutely."

Smiling at the response, Sam waited for the gaze to return to her face.

Tina blushed when she realized Sam had been waiting. "Oh...um..."

"It's okay. I love the way you look at me. And I know I've said it a lot lately, but I really love y—"

"Shh," Tina interrupted. She readjusted her arms over her head to a more comfortable position and looked deeply into Sam's eyes. "Show me."

And there, in the midst of the twinkling lights, brightly wrapped presents, and flickering firelight, they celebrated the greatest gift of all. They celebrated their love.